MAUREEN CHILD

Finding You

YOU'RE INVITED TO DINNER AT THE CANDELLANOS' HOME . . .

Mama Candellano's Lasagna

Mama's pasta sauce remains a closely guarded secret . . . so, feel free to use whichever sauce you prefer. (But if you use jar sauce, don't tell Mama.)

Grease a 13 x 9 x 2 glass baking dish and set aside.

1 lb. lasagna pasta
2 lbs. Ricotta cheese (part skim is good!)
½ cup Parmesan cheese
2 raw eggs
3 tbs. dried parsley flakes
shredded Mozzarella cheese

Cook the lasagna in boiling water until it's nearly done (al dente will make the lasagna easier to slice and serve later). Drain and cool the pasta by running cold water over it. In a separate bowl, mix Ricotta cheese, Parmesan, parsley flakes, and the eggs, stirring until well blended.

Make one layer of lasagna noodles in the greased baking dish, then add a layer of the cheese mixture, keeping it thick, but evenly spread. Ladle sauce on top, covering the cheese and noodles. Then repeat until you end with a layer of lasagna noodles. Ladle sauce over the top, then sprinkle with shredded Mozzarella.

Bake at 350° for 30 minutes or until the cheese is bubbling like crazy. Let the lasagna cool for ten minutes to make the slicing and serving a little easier!

Mangia!

FINDING YOU

MAUREEN CHILD

St. Martin's Paperbacks

FINDING YOU/KNOWING YOU

ISBN: 0-312-98920-2

Printed in the United States of America

St. Martin's Paperbacks edition / May 2003

St. Martin's Paperbacks are published by St. Martin's Press, 175 Fifth Avenue, New York, NY 10010.

10 9 8 7 6 5 4 3

For my Dad,
Edward A. Carberry, Sr.

May the road rise up to meet you,
May the wind be always at your back,
May the sun shine warm upon your face,
May the rain fall soft upon your fields,
And until we meet again,
May God hold you in the hollow of His hand.

An Irish Blessing
Anonymous

ACKNOWLEDGMENTS

THANK YOU TO JENNIFER ENDERLIN, and Matthew Shear of St. Martin's Press, for giving me the freedom and the encouragement to write the books I love to write. Your faith and support mean a lot to me.

A big thank you—in alphabetical order—to four friends I just couldn't do without: Cherry Adair, Amy J. Fetzer, Susan Mallery and Kelsey Roberts. Thanks for the plotting, for answering the phone when I'm in panic mode, and for the laughs.

To my friend Sandra Paul, for riding to my rescue and doing "emergency reads" at a moment's notice— no matter how many times I ask her to do it! Thanks, Sandy, for all your help.

My thanks to Geri Fegley at the San Francisco bus terminal, for answering all of my questions about the bus depot.

To Mary Ann Casaccio Child, my mother-in-law, who was the inspiration for Mama Candellano—thank you. You've been a great friend and a wonderful mom and Nana.

To my mom, who came through a very rough year with courage and grace.

And always, thank you to my kids for keeping my life interesting, and to my husband, Mark—for always being there and for making me laugh even while deep in Deadline Territory.

CHAPTER ONE

CARLA CANDELLANO WAS THE only reason her mother wasn't the mother of the bride.

"You're not getting any younger, you know," Mama said from the far side of the kitchen.

"I'm twenty-eight, not exactly applying for Social Security yet."

"I had four children at twenty-eight."

"Tough delivery," Carla murmured. She should have known her mother's hawklike ears would catch it.

"So smart. Mrs. Funny."

"Mrs.?" Carla perked right up and grinned. "Is there a Mr. Funny?"

"There should be."

"Here we go," Carla said, and watched her mother as the inquisition began anew. Every week, it was the same thing. One thing you had to give the Candellanos: they never gave up.

"So why don't you have a nice man?"

"Maybe I'm not looking for one."

"You don't want a man?"

"It's not that," Carla said. "I'm just not interested right now."

"Oh, so tomorrow would be a better time?"

Tomorrow, next week, next year. Just not now. A girl had to be in the mood for romance and Carla *so* wasn't in the mood.

"Mama, let it go, okay?"

"Hmmph." Angela Candellano sniffed dramatically and slapped her dish towel across her left shoulder. "You're a beautiful girl, Carla. There's no reason for you to be alone." Her expression shifted, changed as something brand-new occurred to her. "Unless . . . are you maybe looking for a nice *woman*?"

Carla gaped at her. She felt her mouth drop open and made a conscious effort to snap it shut. Never a dull moment around here, that's for sure.

"No, Mama, I'm *not* a lesbian." Carla lifted her gaze toward the ceiling and, when she got no sympathy from heaven, seriously considered banging her forehead on the kitchen table. But if she passed out, her mother would just lift her head and slide a plate of dinner under it, so what would be the point?

"Well," Mama said from the stove, "if you're sure."

"Trust me on this one." Granted, she was twenty-eight years old and there hadn't been a man in her life since God was a Boy. But celibate didn't mean gay.

"If you say so." Mama didn't sound convinced. "But I saw on *Oprah* how sometimes you don't realize these things until you're older, but then you see the signs were always there."

Signs? Mama wanted signs? How about signs of frustration? Signs of exasperation? Signs of incipient insanity? She should have thrown a brick through Mama's TV last week when she'd told Carla that according to the news, if you reached thirty and still weren't married, you might as well throw yourself in the river.

But then, her mother wouldn't stop until she had Carla married and pregnant. Good luck with that. Pickin's, as far as men went, were pretty slim in Chandler. Not that Carla was looking or anything. Nope. She had enough occupying her mind these days without trying to squeeze romance in. Besides, if Carla had a man, what would Mama complain about?

"You have got to stop watching *Oprah*."

Her mother gave her a look usually reserved for the kid who delivered pizza and always added his own tip into the price of the pie.

"It's not just *Oprah*. I read." Her mother opened the oven door, letting out a rush of hot air that carried the scent of the bubbling lasagna within. Which was, Carla reminded herself, the reason she was still sitting here, allowing herself to be tortured.

"Well, quit reading."

"This is how you talk to your mother?"

"You're trying to find out if I'm gay and *I'm* the rude one?"

"If your papa was still here"—she paused for a quick sign of the cross—"you wouldn't be talking to me like this."

If Papa was still here, Mama would be too busy hovering over him to spend so much time on her daughter's love life. *Coward,* Carla thought with another quick glance toward the still-silent heaven where her father, no doubt, was gleefully enjoying a little peace and quiet. Papa had spent most of his married life trying to sneak out and have a good time without Mama hunting him down and dragging him back. Two years ago, he'd finally managed to get where she couldn't reach him.

Of course, in doing that, he'd tossed his four children to the wolf—er . . . *Mama.*

Carla reached for the stack of paper napkins, the good kind, with the fold, and absently shredded the top one. It wasn't that she didn't love Mama. But for God's sake. She was twenty-eight. She didn't need her mother sticking her long but loving nose into *her* nonexistent love life.

"You were born in a barn, maybe?" Mama asked as she walked over and picked up the napkins, moving them out of reach.

"Hospital," Carla said, still shredding. "You remember. You were there."

"Oh, so now you make jokes."

Laugh or cry, she thought but didn't say.

"So, if you're not gay, then you should know Frank asked about you again today."

"*Frank?* Oh God." Okay, cry. Maybe if she slapped her forehead against the table hard enough, she'd pass out and wouldn't have to hear about Frank, of the shiny suits and white belts, again.

Her mother snapped the oven door closed and whirled around on her so fast, it brought back a flash of childhood, when one of Angela Candellano's dark looks could give Carla nightmares for a week. Instinctively she inched back on the green Naugahyde bench seat. As she did, memories raced through her mind. Of all the years she'd shared this breakfast booth with her three older brothers. Of the times she'd been kicked under the table. Of the times they'd offered to beat up some boy who'd made her cry.

A world of love was centered in this kitchen. It was the room everyone eventually ended up in. They'd talked while doing dishes, fought while setting the table, and forged bonds that still held fast today. That was something to be said for Mama and Papa both. They'd built a family together.

Here. In this room, where her mother was about to murder her.

"What?" Mama flung the dish towel from her shoulder to the counter, planted both hands on hips that had gone wide years ago, and scowled. Those fierce brown eyes of hers danced with impatience and the toe of her shoe tapped out a rhythm against the green-flecked linoleum. "You're too good for Frank Pezzini?"

"Yes." Heck, if Frank Pezzini was her only option, she'd *become* a lesbian. Her mother had to figure that Carla was desperate for a man to even suggest good ol' Frank.

"He's a nice boy."

"He's forty-six."

"He's got a good job."

"He works at his father's market," Carla pointed out, "*and* you're always complaining about his thumb being on the scale when he weighs the meat."

Facts rarely got in the way of Mama's arguments.

"He's thrifty."

"He's cheap."

"He's got a nice house."

"Ha!" Carla scooted out of the breakfast booth and stomped across the kitchen, knowing her mother hated it when she stomped. Which was why she'd paid for those ill-fated ballet lessons for three interminable years. "He lives over his parents' garage."

Angela frowned. "So he has money to spend."

Carla snatched up a raw carrot off the butcher block table and took a bite. Crunching, she still managed to say, "Spend? The last time Frank Pezzini opened his wallet willingly, the leather crumbled."

"He's Italian."

"Half the people around here are Italian," Carla countered. Heck, at the beginning of the century, Northern California had been a mecca of sorts for Italian immigrants. They'd come for the fishing industry, the canning factories in Monterey, and the vineyards. They'd made their culture and their joy in life a part of the local landscape. And with the passing generations, they'd slipped into the mainstream of California life and become integrated threads in the state's tapestry.

Her mother threw her hands wide, then let them slap down against her thighs. "Spoiled, that's what you are."

The back door opened. "I've been saying that for years," her brother Nick said as he walked into the room. "But does anyone listen to me?"

"Wipe your feet."

He rolled his eyes at their mother's back but wiped his feet before coming into the spotless kitchen. Carla'd never been so glad to see him as she was at that moment. She needed somebody else to divert Mama's attention. And if that meant tossing Nick into the flames, so be it. What were brothers for, anyway?

"So who's she trying to set you up with this time?" he asked, grabbing Carla's carrot and munching it before she could protest.

"Who else?"

"Ah. . . ." He nodded. "Fabulous Frank. Jesus, Mama, is Frank's mother offering a kickback if you can find him a wife?"

"At least he has a steady job. Not like you. Running around in tight pants playing catch."

Nick actually winced and Carla chuckled, delighted that the harassment ball had been handed off to her brother.

"Football, Mama. I play football."

And, because he played it so well, he was Chandler's pride and joy. The star of the high school team, Nick had attracted media attention in college and was snapped up by the pros the minute he graduated—a graduation Mama and Papa had insisted on.

"Play." She sniffed in mock dismissal. But she didn't fool anyone. Mama loved to remind people when Nick was going to be on *Monday Night Football.* "A grown man *plays* for a living."

Nick scooped his much smaller mother off her feet and gave her a twirl or two around the kitchen. When he plopped her back down again, he gave her a smacking kiss and wiggled his eyebrows at her. "Admit it. You love me."

She smacked him with the dish towel, but she was smiling. "Where's Paul?"

"We're just twins, Mama. Not Siamese." He reached

for a piece of sausage and had his hand slapped for his trouble. "I don't know where he is."

"Sunday dinner," Mama muttered. "One day a week is all I ask."

Carla choked on another carrot. One day a week. Mama would have them all still living at home if she could think of a way to handcuff them to the old Victorian. But she settled for Sunday dinner and it was a compulsory meal. No excuses accepted. If you were in a car accident, Mama expected you to heal and be hungry by Sunday night.

"What's all you ask?" The back door opened again and Tony, the oldest Candellano sibling, stepped through, a black-haired, brown-eyed toddler on his hip. His wife, Beth, right behind him, he handed his daughter off to Nick as he grabbed Mama in a quick, fierce hug.

"Let go; let go," she said, though she held on tightly and gave him an extra pat just for good measure. "I want to see my granddaughter." The baby grinned, drooled, and damn near leaped into her grandmother's arms. "Oh! She's changed so much."

Tony shook his head and grabbed a slice of fresh bread. "You just saw her two days ago."

"They change a lot at this age." Reaching out with one hand, Mama pulled Beth close for a kiss. "So, how's my Tony treating you?"

Beth's eyes narrowed on her husband, and when his jaw muscle twitched, Carla told herself this could be an interesting night. Which was good. Not that she wanted trouble in paradise, but if Mama's radar clicked onto Tony, then Carla was in the clear. At least for tonight.

"Mama was just telling me why Frank Pezzini is the right man for Carla," Nick tossed in, and Carla wondered if she could get away with murder. Probably not, she acknowledged, since Tony was standing right in front of her, still wearing his uniform. The downside to being related to the town sheriff.

"Oh, Mama, no," Beth said, and Carla wanted to kiss her for the support. "He's—for lack of a better word—*icky*."

"Summed up in one, Beth. Thank you."

She smiled, but it wasn't enough to erase the shadows in her eyes. A pang of sympathy darted through Carla and she made up her mind to get Beth alone soon for a little sister-to-sister chat.

"Frank Pezzini's not right for anybody," Paul said as he joined the weekly gathering. "Hell, even his mother keeps him in the garage."

"You're late," Mama said.

"I know." Paul checked his watch, shook his wrist for a minute, then held it to his ear. "I think it stopped again."

Big surprise. Something about his body chemistry killed every watch he'd ever owned. And yet Mr. Computer, the prototypical absentminded professor, always seemed to forget that little point. Despite being twins, Paul and Nick couldn't have been more different. Nick was always the athletic one and Paul the deep thinker. Of course, without his twin's help, Nick would probably still be sitting in Mr. Mondaca's biology class at

Chandler High. And thanks to Nick's interference, Paul didn't spend *all* of his time at the computer lab.

"This is how you treat your mother?" Mama demanded, hands on hips. "No kiss? No hello?"

Paul neatly avoided his niece's grubby hands as he bent in for a kiss. "Hello, gorgeous. Now can we eat?"

While the rest of them got down to the business of setting the table and hauling serving dishes to the dining room, Carla glanced out the kitchen window and stared at a single spot of light in the darkness beyond. Lamplight. In the Garvey house.

"What's so fascinating?" Nick asked as he came up behind her.

"Looks like the summer renters are here."

He took a quick look, and as they watched, more lights clicked on in the cottage on the point. Every year it was the same. New people. New faces. Around for three months, then disappear the way they'd come. Which wasn't altogether a bad thing. Since the rest of the year Carla had all the peace and quiet she could ask for. Still, she hoped this year's batch of temporary locals would be better than the last ones. She really didn't need another summer of heavy metal music pounding down on her all day and all night.

Nick dropped one arm around her neck, rested his chin on top of her head. "Look on the bright side, little sister. Maybe there's some poor lonely single guy over there. Then Mama's radar will slide off of Frank and onto fresh meat."

"Great. Just what I need." She pulled away and turned her back on the Garvey house.

"Maybe it is."

"Oh, not you, too."

"Well, hell, Carla. If you're gonna live like a nun, you might as well sign up and wear the outfit."

"I don't live like a nun. It only looks that way to Hugh Hefner."

"Hey—can I help it if I'm irresistible to the opposite sex?"

"Guess not. That humility of yours snags 'em every time, right?"

"It's a curse," Nick said, smiling.

"Try dating a woman with a brain for a change—instead of your usual pom-pom shakers—see what happens."

"Nothing wrong with a good set of pom-poms."

"You're unbelievable."

"Fine. Right. I'm a rutting pig and you're a delicate flower."

"Exactly." She smiled, picked up the basket of fresh bread, and handed it to him. "Here. Take this in and make yourself useful."

He studied her for a long minute. Ever since she'd come back home she'd had shadows in her big brown eyes that worried him. But it had been two years. Just how long was she going to punish herself? And how could he help if there was no one to beat up on?

"You okay?" he asked suddenly, knowing she wouldn't thank him for butting in, but what was family for, anyway?

"I'm fine."

"You don't look it."

"Gee, thanks."

"You know what I mean. Carla—"

"Nick, I love you. But butt out."

"That's plain enough, I guess." He headed for the dining room door. "You coming?"

"In a minute." When he was gone, she slapped her hands on the cool tile countertop and felt the chill seep through her. He meant well. Heck, the whole family meant well. But this wasn't something that was going to be "cured." It was just something she had to live with. And that would be a heck of a lot easier to do if everyone would quit worrying about her. Shaking her head, she opened the fridge and picked up the pitcher of iced tea. Then half-turning, she paused for another look at the lamplit cottage in the darkness before joining the family.

"You'll like it here," Jackson Wyatt told his daughter as they walked through the small house. He hit every light switch as they passed, showing Reese each room and hoping for a response he knew darn well wouldn't come.

Disappointment roared to life inside him, but he fought it down. Couldn't expect miracles—though a part of him had been expecting just that. But no. Not after a year. When the change came, it wouldn't be in one magical moment. It would come in fits and starts. Tiny steps. That's the way his little girl would come back to him.

And she *would* come back. He refused to think otherwise.

"It's a big kitchen, isn't it?" he asked as the light flashed on, revealing a long, narrow room. The walls were a startling white, with cool green-and-blue tile counters and a scarred wood floor. Glass-fronted cabinets with doily inserts completed the picture. A little too cutesy for his taste, he told himself. Sort of like fairy-tale land. But it was only temporary. Three months. A summer. The most important three months of his life, but hey. No pressure.

"It's nice, huh? Different from home, though," he said, and wondered if Reese was as tired of hearing him talk as he was. But he kept going. Because if he didn't talk, then the silence would be so oppressive, neither of them would survive it. "But different's good once in a while, too. Makes a nice change."

He glanced down at the child holding his hand. Six years old and beautiful, Reese Wyatt looked like the picture-perfect all-American girl. Long blond hair, pulled back into a crooked ponytail, because frankly, he was no better at doing her hair than he had been when the job had fallen to him a year ago. Her big blue eyes inspected the room with interest she wouldn't voice. But at least it was something. She was paying attention. Looking around.

One of his clients had suggested this tiny seaside tourist town as a getaway and Jackson had leaped at the idea. At that point, he'd been willing to try anything to reach Reese. He'd called a local realtor, rented the place sight unseen, and taken a chance. But the back of his mind had been filled with doubts up until this moment, when he saw a spark of interest in the child's eyes.

This *had* been a good idea, he told himself firmly. Getting away from Chicago. From the house that held too many memories. From the well-meaning people who clucked their tongues and shook their heads and offered vague attempts at help.

Reese turned her head and looked up at him with the same solemn expression that had become so much a part of her in the last year. His heart ached as he recalled a different child. One with enough enthusiasm for three healthy kids. In his mind, there was an indistinct memory of her voice. He couldn't quite recall the exact pitch or the sound of her laughter, but even in his dreams he could still hear her calling for him.

Grinding his back teeth into powder, he pushed that thought aside, forced a smile he didn't feel, and asked, "So, you hungry?"

She nodded.

He let go of her hand long enough to smooth the palm of his hand across her forehead, pushing her too-long bangs out of her eyes. "What do you say to a cheese sandwich?"

She nodded again, then held out both hands, mashing her palms together.

"Ah," he said. "You want it grilled and smashed."

Another nod, accompanied this time by half a smile, and Jackson felt like someone had just pinned a medal to his chest. If she could smile, she could speak. If she could speak, he'd be able to reach her again. He'd be able to find his daughter, locked somewhere inside the lost little girl in front of him.

All he needed was time.

Unfortunately, there wasn't much left.

"You got it, kiddo." Pointing at the kitchen table and chairs on the other side of the room, he said, "Take a seat and watch your father, the absolute world master of grilled cheese sandwiches, go to work."

He grabbed a pan from beneath the counter, then crossed to the refrigerator, where he'd already stored their so-far meager supplies. Have to find a store soon—at least before the frozen dinners ran out—he reminded himself as he snatched up the cheese, bread, and margarine.

Carrying it all back to the counter, he kept up a steady stream of conversation, more to fill the silence than because he thought Reese might respond.

"We'll go into town soon," he said. "Then maybe take a walk. Look around." His gaze lifted to the darkness beyond the window and landed on a two-story house not far off. Every light in the place was on, and even from this distance, Jackson saw shadows of people moving around.

But he looked away quickly enough. He wasn't interested in getting to know the neighbors. This summer was about Reese. About reaching her before she was lost to him forever.

CHAPTER TWO

IT WAS A PERFECT morning.

Carla plopped down onto one of the two forest green chairs on her front porch and propped her feet on the railing. Cradling her cup of coffee between her palms, she took a sip, sighed as the glorious liquid slid down her throat, and then leaned her head against the chair back.

"Nice, huh, Abbey?"

The golden retriever beside her stretched out on the cool cement porch and slapped her tail lazily.

"Yeah, I'm with you."

She loved her family, but a long evening with them was enough to convince Carla that living alone was just this side of heaven. And maybe that's part of the reason she wasn't interested in having a man around. Right now, there was nobody talking. Nobody making demands on her time. Nobody expecting anything from her.

Nobody to let down.

Okay, steer the brain away from that train of thought.

Reaching over to the table beside her, she picked up a biscuit for the dog and, saying, "Treat," tossed it. Abbey caught it on the fly, crunched it noisily, then laid her head back down as if exhausted from the effort. Smiling, Carla picked up an Oreo for herself and popped it into her mouth. Cookies and caffeine: the breakfast of champions.

Another sip and she felt herself starting to wake up. Slowly. Like it should be done. None of this leap out of bed, dress, hop in a car, and head for some office where you had to be nice to people you didn't like so you wouldn't lose the job you hated.

Of course it wasn't always like that. Sometimes you had a good job. She had. For five years, she'd worked it and made herself into one of the best in the business. But then it had all gone to hell one fine day and now she was here. Pretending to everyone, including herself, that she didn't miss it.

A pang in her chest eased away into a whisper of discomfort. She was all right. She was doing fine. She had her savings and the money she made from training search dogs. Everything was great. Right?

Carla frowned, ate another cookie, and had a coffee chaser. Thinking about it wouldn't change anything. It would only serve to remind her of the very thing she spent most of her time trying to forget. It was done. Over. At twenty-eight, she was starting fresh. And here in Chandler, she'd make it work.

Her bare feet crossed at the ankle, her denim shorts hitting just above her knee, she tugged at the fabric of her red T-shirt, then settled back again. Whatever the weather, she started her days with this morning ritual. Coffee, cookies, and a seat on the porch where she could watch the world go by. If the world actually passed this way. Which it didn't very often. Oh, there was the occasional car out on the road, fifty yards from the porch. But the street wasn't exactly Highway 101.

Chandler was a good mile to the east. Here on the outskirts, her closest neighbors were her mother—sometimes *too* close—on one side and, on the other, the Garvey cottage. Her gaze slid in that direction and she found herself wondering just who she'd be dealing with this year.

But then, dealing with a new batch of tourists every year was just part and parcel of living in Chandler. Most of the town's economy depended on a good summer, with people coming in from all over to stay in the B and Bs and cruise the art galleries and visit the local winery and the beach. By the end of summer, the fall crowd was trickling in, to watch the incredible show of color that Mother Nature put on every year. Winter was a time to relax and enjoy the quiet; then spring arrived and the first of the tourists began the whole cycle all over again.

But besides the tourist trade, there were the local commercial fishermen who ran a fresh fish market at the dock and the outlying ranches that fed the farmers' market every Thursday. They were within commuting distance of San Jose, and Monterey wasn't much farther. Of course, with one movie theater and no mall to speak of, the teenagers didn't have a lot to do, which led to plenty of mischief making. The clinic was too small for a growing town, and environmentalists held regular protests against the timber company. But other than that, Chandler was great.

Quiet.

Relaxing.

Damn near perfect.

Then the phone rang.

She scowled as Abbey lifted her head. "I know. It's an ungodly hour for anyone to call. Let's ignore it."

The dog flapped her tail against the porch again as the phone shrieked a second time, an irritating intrusion.

"Okay, fine. I'll answer it. But I won't be nice."

She stepped over the dog, crossed the porch, and went into the house. The phone was just inside the front door on a battered table that Carla liked to think of as "distressed." Sounded so much more trendy than "junk." Soft morning sunlight splintered through the oval stained-glass pane set above the picture window in the living room. The blue of the sea and the emerald green of the trees sent shafts of color dancing about what would otherwise be a plain but comfortable room.

And the morning quiet shattered again with the third insistent ring. Snatching up the receiver, she nearly snarled, "What?"

"Nice. Still your charming self in the morning, I see."

"Mike." At the familiar voice, Carla's hand tightened on the receiver. Strange. Even the sunlight seemed a little dimmer.

"Ah, she remembers."

"What's not to remember?" she said, hoping her voice sounded lighter than she felt at the moment. It was way too early to be talking to anyone. Let alone

Mike Shaner. She thought about going out to retrieve her coffee cup from the porch, then decided against it. She'd just get rid of him quickly—then try to reclaim her morning.

"Look," he said, and she heard the tone he would always use when he wanted her to go out on a job. For years he'd been laboring under the impression that he oozed charm. And maybe the people still working for Searchers had to go along with that. But she didn't work for him anymore, did she? "You been watching the news?"

"No." She never watched the news anymore. She'd sworn off. Too many disasters. Too many crises. Too many people needing help that she couldn't give. Nervously she walked around the room, straightening picture frames on the wall, kicking a throw pillow onto the sofa, then pausing long enough to write her name in the dust on the coffee table. Really had to get to that, she thought.

She picked up the postcard of an aqua blue sea rushing toward a pristine white beach and wished she'd gone with her best friend on that cruise. Then she wouldn't have been here to answer the phone.

Anything, she told herself. Think of anything but what Mike was calling about.

"Do you *get* the news out in that backwater you live in?"

Her eyes rolled. According to the gospel of Mike, any place outside of LA qualified as the boondocks.

"Not only do we have TV, but we may get a new thing called a refrigerator. The whole town is chipping in together. We're going to share it. It's *very* exciting."

"One cup of coffee or two so far?"

"One."

"God help me."

She sighed. "What do you want, Mike?"

"We have a situation."

"Not interested." Her stomach twisted, her palms began to sweat, and every bit of moisture in her mouth dried up. But despite the sick pool of dread swimming inside, she was also honest enough to admit, if only to herself, that her heartbeat quickened with a splash of the old adrenaline. "I told you that when I quit, Mike."

"It's been two years. Get over it."

She squeezed that receiver until it should have snapped. "Go to hell."

"Damn it, Carla." She could almost see him shoving one hand through his hair and then tugging at the knot in his ever-present tie. He probably had one cigarette burning in the ashtray and another one tucked into the corner of his mouth. The man was a walking ulcer waiting to happen. Of course, the six-pack of Mylanta he chugged almost daily would probably keep that threat at bay.

"I mean it, Mike. I meant it two years ago and nothing's changed." Just her life. Just her dreams. Just everything.

"It's a waste, that's what it is. You're the best, Carla, and you should be doing what you were born to do."

"I am."

"That's bullshit. You're hiding."

"If I'm hiding, how did you find me?"

"You know what I mean."

"Yeah, I do. And you know what I mean when I say no."

"Well, how about loaning me Abbey?"

Carla yanked the receiver away, glared at it, then slapped it back to her ear. "Abbey's *my* dog and you damn well know it. We're a team. Nobody else works her but me."

"Fine. Work her."

"We're retired."

"You can't retire; it's in your blood."

"I've had a transfusion." She could be just as stubborn as Mike. More so, with only one cup of coffee in her. "What about the dogs I sold you last year? They're excellent. Use them."

"They *are* excellent. You and Abbey are better."

She walked back toward the front door and stared out the screen. Fastening her gaze on the line of trees in the distance and drawing up an image of the ocean just beyond, she tried to center herself. Fought to remember that her life was here, now. Not in LA. Not in the middle of a disaster area. Not trooping through misery trying to keep a knot of hope alive.

She couldn't do it anymore. Couldn't be the one to look into tear-filled eyes and crush the last tiny flicker of optimism. If that made her a selfish bitch, then she'd just have to live with it.

"Listen, Carla. . . ."

Outside, Abbey stood up and walked across the porch, ears up, head tilted, obviously scenting something unusual. Carla took a step closer, watching her dog, not even listening to Mike anymore, though his voice rattled on, no more than a droning sound, a distraction. The dog stepped off the porch and headed around the side of the house, out of sight.

"Mike," Carla interrupted him. "I gotta go."

"No, damn it—"

"Bye." She hung up, and hit the front door. Crossing the porch in a couple of strides, she followed after Abbey, more curious than worried. Nothing ever happened in Chandler. It was one of the last bastions of small-town life in America. No one locked their doors. Neighbors watched out for one another. And no secret had a shelf life of longer than twenty-four hours.

She'd grown up here. Gone off to the big city to find herself, and when she didn't like what she found she'd come back home. It hadn't been easy to swallow her pride—admit she'd failed—but what was that old saying? "Home is the place that, when you have to go there, they have to take you in." Well, she was home again. To where she felt safe. And Abbey getting spooked wasn't going to spoil that feeling.

Jackson shoved his right hand through his hair and squeezed the telephone receiver in his left. "Damn it. Where could she have gone?" He paced back and forth in front of the wide lead-paned picture window gracing the house he'd rented for the summer. As he listened to the phone ringing on the other end of the line, his gaze scanned the grassy slope that led from the house down to the road. Nothing. No sign of her. His heart tightened in his chest. Less than twenty-four hours here and she was missing. For chrissakes, was this some kind of sign? Was somebody trying to tell him something?

Like maybe . . . *You're out of your depth, Wyatt.*

"Sheriff's office."

"Thank God."

"Is there a problem?"

Yeah, you could say that. Hell, you could say that about the last year. But that wasn't really the issue here, was it?

"Hell, yes, there's a problem!" Jackson nearly shouted. "My daughter's missing."

"Who is this?" Tony Candellano asked, swinging his feet down off the corner of his desk and rolling his chair closer. Reaching for a pen, he grabbed a pad of paper.

"Wyatt. Jackson Wyatt."

Instantly Tony's mind raced, going through every one of the names and faces of the people in and around Chandler. A man in his position got to know the people who elected him. And a town the size of Chandler couldn't hide a stranger for long. But the name Wyatt didn't ring any bells.

"Where are you located?"

"Sixteen-sixteen Robello Drive. You've got to send someone right out."

"Ah, the Garvey place." Okay now, that explained a few things. Summer renters. "I'll be there in a few minutes," he said in the practiced calming tone he'd discovered long ago cut right through incipient hysteria. "Now just stay put. Probably nothing to worry about. Chances are she's just wandering around taking a look at the place."

"She's *six*."

Shit. "Okay, Mr. Wyatt. Wait there. I'll be with you in a few minutes." But the man had already hung up. Apparently, his "calming" tone didn't work any better on Jackson Wyatt than it did on Beth. And, grumbling to himself, Tony headed for the door and the squad car parked right outside.

As she rounded the house, Carla's gaze swept the area. Trees, dozens of them, surrounded her lot. Pines, poplars, and even an oak that looked older than time tossed shade onto the grass and set the brass wind chimes hanging from the corner of the house to singing. A slider swing, painted a bright blue, sat empty beside a fountain that burbled noisily. The flower beds were just coming to life, tender green shoots spearing through the dark earth, and in a few weeks there would be splashes of color to brighten up the yard. The puppy enclosure took up the back half of the lot. Six golden retriever pups currently lived in the three large white doghouses set behind chain-link fencing—her house might be dusty, but the puppy pen was spotless.

Carla had never claimed to be Suzy Homemaker. Despite her mother's best efforts at taming her only daughter, Carla had always preferred being outside. Came from having three older brothers, she guessed. She'd played football and baseball and had been falling off her skateboard while other little girls were having tea parties with their dolls.

She pushed her hair back from her face and quickened her step. The still-damp grass felt cool against her feet, and a chill swept up her spine. From the direction of the puppies' enclosure came the sharp yips and barks that heralded the start of another day. But it was different this morning. Louder. More excited, somehow.

Carla headed for the chain-link fence and spotted

Abbey, sitting beside the fence, ignoring the puppies clamoring over one another on the other side. Of course, Abbey was a sucker for being petted. And the little girl rubbing the dog's head was clearly enjoying herself as much as the golden was.

"Hi."

The girl's head snapped up and wide blue eyes fastened on Carla as she approached. But an instant later, those eyes were shifting from one side to another as if the child was looking for a quick getaway.

"It's okay." Carla stopped and lifted both hands. "You're not in trouble or anything." The girl relaxed a fraction but still looked ready to bolt. Slowly Carla dropped her hands, then shoved them into her pockets. While Abbey whined and pushed her head beneath the child's hand, Carla studied the girl.

Young. No more than seven or eight. Blond hair messily pulled into pigtails on either side of her head. She looked too thin, as if she hadn't been eating enough, and her pink shorts and yellow-striped T-shirt were rumpled, not to mention mismatched. She wore neon green tennis shoes, with Scooby-Doo on the toes, and a wary expression on her face.

Her small hand continued to smooth over the top of Abbey's head, and knowing her dog, Carla realized the golden was about to melt into a puddle of affection. Where had the kid come from? Carla's first instinct was to take the girl inside and give her some milk while she called Tony at the station house. But a moment later, she realized that the kid probably belonged to the summer renters.

Oh, this is a good start to the summer, she thought

wryly. Not a house full of noisy teenagers this year—
but at least one small girl who obviously had a soft
spot for puppies.

But then, who didn't?

Carla looked past the girl at the puppies and smiled
to herself. "Cute, aren't they?"

The child didn't say anything, but her gaze shifted
to the puppies climbing over one another in an attempt
to get to her through the chain link. And a small smile
curved that little mouth.

"Yeah," Carla said, moving slowly as she walked
closer. "I think goldens are the cutest puppies ever.
They look like little white puffballs, don't they?" She
took a seat on the grass beside Abbey and carefully
kept her distance from the child. After all, Carla didn't
know what was going on here.

From the look of things, the girl was being ne-
glected. Angela Candellano would have *died* before letting one of her children go out looking like an orphan.
Orphan. Maybe she didn't have parents. Maybe she
wasn't from the Garvey house. Maybe she'd wandered
away from . . . *somewhere*. A campsite down by the
lake? On the beach? After all, it stood to reason that if
she was with the new summer rentals, wouldn't someone be out looking for her by now?

Carla watched the girl as she poked small fingers
through the gray chain link, letting the all-too-happy-
to-oblige puppies chew and suck at her fingertips.
There was a sweet but *lost* look to her, and Carla's
long-suppressed maternal instinct suddenly kicked
into high gear. Surprised the hell out of her.

"Are you lost?"

A quick shake of the head and one of those pigtails slipped another notch.

"Does your mom know where you are?"

Those big blue eyes fastened on her again and this time they were filled with sudden tears.

Oh, man.

"Reese!"

A man's voice, deep and scared, roared over the din of the puppies. The girl jumped, obviously nervous, and Carla came to her feet, waiting for whoever was coming. Abbey, too, went on alert, standing up and positioning herself in front of the girl.

He stomped around the side of the house. Long legs looked even longer in faded blue jeans. The black polo shirt he wore made his fair skin seem paler, and his light brown hair looked as though he'd shoved his hands through it repeatedly. His eyes were as blue as the girl's, and Carla watched as they scanned the yard frantically, finally coming to rest on the child beside her.

Relief rushed across his features, quickly followed by a carefully banked anger.

"Reese. You shouldn't have just left the house." He walked around Carla, not even acknowledging her presence. She didn't know whether to be impressed or insulted. He did, however, give a moment's pause to Abbey. But apparently not sensing any danger, the dog moved out of his way. Going down on one knee, he turned the child's face toward his and said, "Don't do that to me again. You scared me to death."

"Scared me a little, too," Carla said, not that anyone was listening. "I didn't know where she belonged."

Neither of them looked at her.

The child nodded, but he wasn't finished.

"You can't just wander off. It isn't safe. You could have been hit by a car when you crossed that road."

"It's not a busy road," Carla put in.

He ignored her.

"Now come on," he said, standing up and helping the girl to her feet. "We'll go home and I'll make you breakfast."

The little girl mimed putting her hand into a bag.

"Cookies?" the man asked. "No, you can't have cookies for breakfast."

Carla shrugged. Most people just didn't know how to live. "You know," she said, and waited until he was looking at her, finally, before she continued. "It's customary in some tribal communities to actually say *thank you* to someone who's helped you out."

"Thank you?"

"You're welcome."

He gave her a look that was decidedly ungrateful. "Look, Ms. . . ."

"Candellano. Carla."

He nodded. "I'm sorry my daughter and I disrupted your morning."

She smiled at the child before looking at him again. "*She* didn't disrupt me at all." She looked up into eyes the same color as the girl's and wondered what kind of man he was. He obviously wasn't paying enough attention to his daughter. The girl was running around alone, first thing in the morning, in a strange neighborhood—looking like an extra in *Annie*. "But you and her mother should keep a better eye on her."

Jackson glared at her, but she didn't back up an

inch. Any other time, he might have admired that. But this was now and, damn it, he'd already had enough trouble for one morning. His gaze swept her up and down, from the top of her black curly hair, to the tips of her bright pink toenail polish, to the tiny silver toe ring on her left foot. Her features were fine: a straight, even nose, full lips, and wide, expressive brown eyes that looked as though they could see through a man to his soul. Which was a little disconcerting when a man had a soul that no one should be looking at. She had a curvy body and a sassy attitude that was alluring and irritating all at once. An instinctive, purely male response blasted through him and was quickly shut down. One thing he didn't need at this stage of the game was a summer fling. The next three months were too important to blow on some brown-eyed free spirit with a smart but great-looking mouth.

"Her mother's dead."

Beside him, he felt Reese's withdrawal, and it was all he could do to keep his anger trapped inside. He shouldn't have blurted it out like that, but he wasn't going to stand here and be lectured by a woman he'd never seen before. And he'd figured that the blunt statement would shut her up so he could take Reese back to the house.

It didn't work.

"That's too bad."

She surprised him. Usually the first words someone said to him were, *I'm sorry.* As if they'd had something to do with Diane's accident. It was pointless pity. Good manners. Nothing more. And he appreciated the fact that she hadn't said it. For that alone he was almost ready to give her the thank-you she'd wanted earlier.

Almost.

"Yeah. Well, I've got to get back to the house. I called the police when I found Reese missing and I'd better go call and let them know she's been found."

"Oh," she said, waving one hand at him. "I'll do it."

"Why the hell would *you* do it?"

She cocked her head to one side and stared at him. "You're a real charmer, aren't you? Tony—the sheriff—is my brother."

"Perfect."

"Oh God, any more charm and I may swoon."

"Jesus, Carla," another voice piped up, and she half-turned to watch Tony stroll up, a solid, familiar figure in a buff beige uniform with a star pinned to his left breast pocket. "Cut the man a break." He narrowed his gaze on her. "One cup or two so far?"

"One."

"Perfect."

"Surrounded by crabby men." She paused and sighed dramatically. "A girl's dream come true."

"Sheriff?" Jackson Wyatt turned toward Tony like a man reaching for a life preserver in a stormy sea and held out one hand. "Thanks for coming."

He nodded, shook hands, and let his gaze cut to Reese. He smiled, but those sharp eyes of his were taking in the kid's appearance and Carla knew his cop's mind was churning. "Happy to help. Glad you found her."

"Reese came to visit the puppies," Carla said.

"It won't happen again."

The little girl's face fell as she shifted her disappointed gaze from her father, to Abbey, to the puppies as if she'd just been told Santa was dead and the Easter Bunny was rabid.

Carla idly stroked Abbey's head as the dog sat down beside her and leaned all of her ninety-five pounds against Carla's leg. Used to it, she simply locked her knee and leaned back in to the dog to keep her balance. Deliberately ignoring both men, she looked at the little girl and said, "She can come back anytime. It's okay with me."

The child's face lit up and her eyes shone as she turned and looked up at her father for permission just as he said, "It's not okay with me."

Carla wanted to kick him. Okay, he'd lost his wife. But he still had a daughter. A daughter who was obviously looking for something that he wasn't giving her.

"Now if you'll excuse us . . ." the man said, nodding to Tony and deliberately avoiding looking at Carla. "We'll be going home now."

She opened her mouth to say . . . well, she wasn't sure exactly what she would have said, but Tony's hand on her arm cut off the attempt anyway.

Once the Wyatts were out of sight, she looked at her brother. "Do you believe that guy?"

Tony sighed, bent down to rub the belly Abbey so thoughtfully provided by rolling over and losing every shred of her dignity. Glancing up at Carla, he said, "If you're gonna bitch at me, can you at least give me some coffee?"

CHAPTER THREE

"WHY DIDN'T YOU ASK him some questions?"

"Jesus, Carla. The man was a wreck, worried about his kid."

"Uh-huh," she said, and pulled the edge of the yellow-and-white curtain back so she could watch Mr. Charm and his daughter walk back to the Garvey cottage. The man matched his steps to the child's, and even from a distance Carla could tell that he was talking to her. Probably warning her away from the dangerous puppies—and any opportunity for fun.

"Poor kid," she muttered.

"She looked well fed and well dressed to me."

"Are you serious?" She dropped the curtain and turned around to glare at her brother. "Her hair looked like he took a weed whacker to it. And please. I mean, would Beth ever let little Tina out of the house in a mismatched outfit?"

Tony's gaze dropped to the surface of his coffee. He

began stirring it as though it required all of his concentration. "No. Beth's a great mother. . . ."

She frowned and watched him, suddenly noticing the body language she'd missed before. He sat hunched at her kitchen table, one hand gripping the stoneware mug, the other still using a spoon to churn the coffee hard enough (had it been milk) to make butter.

Carla loved all of her brothers, but that didn't make her blind to their flaws. And God knew, they all had plenty of them. But brooding had never been one of Tony's. Until today, apparently. Leaning back against the yellow-tiled counter, she crossed her arms over her chest.

"There's a 'but' hanging at the end of that sentence."

He glanced at her. "No, there isn't."

Hmm. Maybe she wasn't so far off the night before when she'd guessed that there was trouble in paradise. Tony and Beth had been high school sweethearts. Prom King and Queen. The captain of the football team and the head cheerleader. They were, in fact, every odious high school cliché ever written. And they'd managed to carry that right on through college. It would have been so easy to hate them both. Except for the fact that they'd been in love since the moment they met in freshman year.

They'd been the golden couple, and seeing them marry and have a baby and begin to live their happily-ever-after was . . . *comforting,* somehow. Especially to someone like Carla—whose legendary fiascoes in the romance department made Edgar Allan Poe's tales read like Harry Potter.

Like the time she decided to meet Jim Hennesey in Florida for the weekend. Hurricane Hilda swept through and ripped their little beach shack right down to its last palm frond. With them in it. Or the time she was sweet-talked into the backseat of Bob Bennet's Camaro. Just when things started to get interesting, the beam of a cop's flashlight landed on her naked behind and Bob shoved her away so fast, he swore later that he'd broken "it" and was now a eunuch. Then there was the blind date from hell. She arrived at the restaurant to find her "date" already there and buying drinks for the sock puppet he wore on his left hand. Of course, the sock insisted that Carla buy her own drinks. Which she had. Several of them, as she recalled. But she'd drawn the line at sharing her steak with the puppet.

She shivered at the memory. But it wasn't just her disastrous dating habits keeping her from diving into the singles pool. It was more that Carla just couldn't bring herself to care deeply about anyone right now. There was just too clear a chance for being hurt. And her heart was still a bit too bruised to take another hit at the moment.

Nope. Think I'll pass on romance, thanks.

But Tony and Beth were different.

Picking up the coffeepot, she carried it to the table, pulled out a chair, and sat down opposite her oldest brother. Refilling his cup and then hers, she asked, "So what's going on with you and Beth?"

His gaze shot to hers quickly. Actually *too* quickly. Good thing he was a cop rather than a criminal. His poker face stunk.

"Leave it alone, Carla."

"Hey, I didn't bring it up."

"Yes, you did."

"Okay, I did. But you can't really blame me. You're usually walking around with a huge irritating smile on your face and now—"

"Fine. I'll smile."

She blinked at the fierce expression on his face. "You're baring your teeth, not smiling."

"Whatever." He picked up his coffee, gulped it down despite how hot it was, then shoved back from the table. Standing up, he looked down at her. "I've gotta get back to work."

Carla glanced at the yellow-ducky wall clock hanging opposite her. Its battery-operated eyes rolled counterclockwise and its orange feet paddled back and forth as if swimming across the cream-colored wall. Shaking her head, she looked back at him. "Oh, yeah, it's nearly seven-thirty. Crime wave's about to start."

"Funny."

"Hey, it's early." She stood up, too. "Tony, if there's anything I can do to help—"

"I don't—*we* don't need help," he said, his voice cutting across hers like a whipcrack. She looked mad, but that was better than the glimmer of sympathetic concern he'd been reading in those brown eyes a minute ago.

Tony didn't need sympathy. He and Beth had been together for years and that wasn't going to change. Every married couple had arguments, he told himself, ignoring the cold, hard knot in his guts. They'd get past this. As soon as Beth stopped being so damn stubborn and started listening to reason again and . . . Carla was staring at him as if he'd lost his mind. And hell. Maybe he had.

"Tony."

"Carla, for the love of God, let it go." He headed for the kitchen door, eager to get back to work. He'd lose himself in paperwork. Chase down complaints. Anything. Hell, anything to keep from thinking about what he knew damn well was going to plague him all day. He grabbed the doorknob, twisted it, and paused long enough to look at his sister.

"Does Mama know what's going on?" she asked.

He actually paled. "God, I hope not."

Was a steak really worth this?

Carla groaned and rethought her decision to buy meat at the small local grocer/butcher shop. Next time, she swore silently, she'd drive into Monterey. Or San Jose. Go to a regular supermarket. It would be worth the forty-mile trip just to avoid Frank Pezzini.

She glanced up. Yep. Still watching her. As he weighed Mrs. Flannery's pork chops, he shot Carla what she guessed he thought was his sexy "hey-baby-wanna-get-lucky?" look. Oh, man. There just wasn't enough alcohol in the world for that.

Standing about five-foot-nine, Frank was only an inch taller than her, and his broad, once-muscular chest had slipped substantially closer to his waistline. The white belt he wore strained against the chore of encircling his belly and looked as if it were about to spring loose. If it did, it would probably whip around the room taking out half the housewives of Chandler.

Which would leave her and Frank alone to repopulate the town. What a hideous thought.

To avoid any more of same, she turned her attention to the gossip flying around her like bees in a garden.

"So, what've you heard?"

Carla glanced at Abigail Tupper. Ninety if she was a day, she wore two bright red spots of what she fondly referred to as "rouge" on her cheeks and a scarlet slash of lipstick bled into the deep wrinkles around her lips, but her nose fairly twitched with the urge to hear the latest news. Her still-sharp green eyes were fixed on her cohort, Virginia Baker. At seventy-five, Virginia wasn't quite as spry as her former baby-sitter, but she more than made up for the lack with the efficiency of her grapevine.

"Well." Virginia leaned in but didn't bother to lower her voice. "*I* hear he's on the lam."

Carla muffled a snort of laughter. The old lady'd been watching too many gangster movies on AMC again.

"*Really?*" Abigail was fascinated by the possibilities. "And with that sweet-faced little girl, too. Such a shame."

"No better than he should be is what I heard."

Another country heard from, Carla thought, and let her gaze slide sideways to watch Rachel Vickers, the mayor's wife, ooze up to join the conversation.

"What's that supposed to mean, Rachel?"

Good question, Abigail, Carla thought, still watching Rachel.

"Well, look at him. Hiding out there in the summer cottage. Hardly ever leaves the place. And he's been there a week." Rachel sniffed, clutched her pocketbook a little tighter to her impressive bosom, and looked down her nose at Abigail. "Not healthy, that's what I say. That poor child."

Carla shifted from foot to foot and felt just the

tiniest stab of sympathy for Jackson Wyatt. True, he wasn't the friendliest man on the planet. But she knew all too well what it was like to be the juicy piece of meat being chewed on by the local cats.

"I still say he's on the lam." Virginia nodded so firmly, one steel gray curl dislodged itself from her sprayed solid hairdo. "Probably selling drugs."

Carla eyed the woman, fascinated in spite of herself.

"Now, you don't know that, Virginia," Abigail said, dismissing that statement. "But perhaps the Ladies' League should pay a 'neighborly' call on the man. Let him know that the town ladies keep a watchful eye on the goings-on around here."

Oh, good God.

"Excellent idea. I'll make up my famous tuna-and-pineapple casserole." Rachel smiled and one dyed red eyebrow lifted into an arch that would have sent her husband running for the hills. "We'll take it over there this afternoon."

With their game plan set, the three women moved as one farther down the counter, ogling the meat. Carla was rooted to the spot. Okay, she could just butt out and let Mr. Charm suffer the pangs of not only the Ladies' League but also Rachel's tuna surprise. Or she could do the neighborly thing—hell, the *humane* thing—and warn the man that he was about to be invaded.

All right. She'd do it. Not for his sake, of course. But the image of that poor little girl trying to choke down tuna, mayonnaise, and pineapple was enough to tear her heart out.

"Carla," Frank said, and his voice was loud enough to carry all the way back to Produce. "You're next." He wiggled bushy eyebrows at her, gave her a "come-hither" leer, and offered, "My chops are good today. What'dya say?"

What *could* she say?

"Ooooh. . . ." Abigail primped her thin thatch of snow-white hair and practically purred. "I do believe someone here is sweet on someone."

Somebody shoot me.

The whole place looked like a Hollywood set.

Any minute now, Jackson expected to see Andy Taylor and Opie strolling around a corner carrying fishing poles and whistling.

Antique globed street lamps lined tidy sidewalks. Neatly trimmed trees were plunked down at regular intervals along Main Street, and at their bases, riots of flowers bloomed in dozens of colors. Storefronts crowded together, their display windows glistening in the afternoon sunlight, beckoning the teeming visitors—carrying their bulging wallets—inside.

The perfect tourist spot, Chandler, California, was far enough north that it never got too hot and just south enough to avoid snow in winter. On the coastal side of town lay the ocean, stretching out for miles in shimmering shades of blue and green. From that direction came the deep, throaty barks of the seals and the slap of waves against the rocks. On the eastern side lay a forest, in jewel tones of emerald and deep shadows creeping back to the foot of the mountains, with the sequoias just a stone's throw away.

Overhead, the sky was a brilliant blue, the kind Jackson didn't often see back home in Chicago. A sea breeze danced in off the ocean, trailed cool fingers across his face, then raced on. Jackson tightened his hold on Reese's hand, glanced down at his daughter, then continued on down the street. His heart ached a little at the closed, distant expression on her face, but he told himself it wouldn't always be like this. He'd find a way this summer to reach her. And today was the first step in his—well, it wasn't defined enough to call it a plan. Call it a scheme. A strategy.

Hell, call it like it was.

A last-ditch, desperate attempt.

And it started now. Their first foray into Chandler required something special, he told himself. Something to get the child's mind off of visiting the puppies she hadn't been back to see in a week.

Wryly he admitted that, though she didn't speak, she had no trouble at all making her wishes known. She'd been bugging him about those dogs since that first morning. But they hadn't come here to make friends with brown-eyed, sharp-tongued women and their pets. They'd come here to heal Reese. To accomplish that task, he needed his daughter focused on talking, not puppies. He just had to get her interested in the rest of the town. The beach. The forest.

Hell.

Anything.

"How about some ice cream?" he asked, spotting the oversize, double-decker cone serving as a sign in front of the ice-cream parlor.

She looked up at him and nodded.

His heart twisted and he winced with the twinge of pain. Every time he asked her a question, a part of him still waited for an answer. A *spoken* answer. And that same part of him was disappointed again and again. It had already been a year. A year since he'd heard her voice. Now he could hardly remember the sweet sound of it. But he had no trouble at all recalling with clarity the number of times he'd asked her to settle down. To be quiet.

Be careful what you wish for.

He inhaled sharply, caught the taste of fresh bread on the air, and told himself to stop by the local bakery before going home. *Home.*

The small place that he'd rented for the next three months wasn't home. But then, their place in Chicago wasn't home anymore, either, was it? There were too many memories. Too many ghosts. Too much pain.

Maybe he'd been stupid to stay there after Diane's death. But he'd wanted Reese to have normalcy. Well, as much normalcy as he could provide, considering that she'd lost her mother. It had been so fast. So unexpected. But even as he thought that, he wondered if death was *ever* expected. Wasn't it always sudden? Even to those who were sick for a long time, wasn't death, when it arrived, a shock?

That last rainy morning with Diane rose up in his mind. He could almost hear her voice again. Hear the fear and then the anger in her tone. And he wondered again what might have happened if he'd done things differently.

But wondering, like wishing, wouldn't change anything. He quickly looked up the street and, seeing that it was clear, stepped off the curb and led his daughter to the other side. Nodding to those people he passed, he barely noticed them. His mind was too full of doubts, questions. Maybe if they'd moved out right away, his little girl wouldn't have retreated so deeply into herself. Maybe she would have turned to him as he kept hoping she would. On the other hand, he thought, throwing himself a mental bone, maybe she would have been worse off if they'd left.

Though how things could be worse, he didn't know.

Reese suddenly pulled on his hand and stopped dead.

"What is it?" he asked, looking down to see her face wreathed in the kind of smile he saw all too rarely and her right arm extended, pointing at something off to their left.

He looked and nearly sighed.

The dog.

The golden retriever sat outside a grocery store, her head tilted, ears perked as if listening to a joke only she could hear. Well, perfect. If that dog was here, the woman, Carla Candellano, wouldn't be far away. And he was in no mood for playing more word games with a female who looked too damn good for his peace of mind.

"Okay, Reese, I see it. But we're going for ice cream, remember?"

She shook her head and started for the dog. He kept a tight grip on her hand, though, and despite her small body leaning forward with all its might, she didn't move an inch. Reese looked at him over her shoulder and gave him a look that put him in mind of her mother. God. How many times had Diane shot him that same disgusted glance? It had always been enough to jump-start an argument that usually ended with muttered threats and slamming doors.

Irritation swept through him and was gone again in an instant. But this wasn't Diane, was it? This was the child he loved more than he'd ever thought it possible to love anyone. So she wanted to see a dog. Wouldn't most kids? And after all, wasn't this what he wanted? For Reese to be involved in the world outside her mind? Wasn't he praying that one day she'd care enough about *something* that she'd speak about it?

Nodding, he said, "Fine. We'll say hello to the dog, then go for ice cream, all right?"

Another smile was his reward, and he soaked it up, taking comfort in its warmth. But Reese wasn't about to stand still now that she had permission. She tugged on his hand again, and this time he let her go. As she raced along the sidewalk, he watched her like a hawk. At this one moment, she looked like any other little girl. Beautiful. Innocent. Carefree. Her small feet fairly flew across the ten feet of space separating her from the golden, and as Abbey noticed the girl's approach, she got up to welcome her.

Jackson walked slowly after Reese, giving her a moment to enjoy herself. The big dog practically quivered in delight. Her tail swept back and forth in eagerness, her eyes brightened, and damned if she didn't look as though she were grinning.

Reese threw her arms around the dog's neck, laid her cheek against Abbey's head, and then reared back, grinning when the wet, slobbering kisses started. Jackson's heart did another quick skip at the sweetness of that smile. Reese hadn't smiled again since that morning at Carla's place, and he just couldn't get enough of it.

This was good.

For about ten seconds.

Then the dog's owner stepped out of the grocer's and looked at him.

CHAPTER
FOUR

THINK OF THE DEVIL and up he walks, Carla thought. And wasn't the devil taking the time to do himself up right these days. His short-sleeved light green shirt hugged a chest that apparently spent a lot of time at a gym. Khaki slacks with a knife-sharp crease did great things for his legs, but the shadows in his eyes and the scowl on his face quickly took care of the nearly instinctual spurt of lust that erupted inside her without warning.

Just as well. The last time she'd let her hormones do the driving, she'd ended up with a broken engagement and a wedding invitation to her former fiancé's joyful reunion with his ex-girlfriend. Gee, no. Let's not.

Besides, if she wanted a summer fling, she'd go to Europe. Maybe Greece. She sure as hell wouldn't do it right here in Chandler. If she was going to have a romance that ended badly, the least she could do was get a stamp in her passport this time.

So why was she bothering with him at all? She'd spent the last two years avoiding people—deliberately distancing herself from caring. Yet here she was, ready to go where she so clearly wasn't wanted. Why? It wasn't just the fact that looking at him made her knees weak. Sure, he did great things for her insides. But she could ignore that. With practice. No, there was more here.

Her gaze drifted down to the child at his side. Those messy off-kilter pigtails and wide blue eyes drew Carla in just as they had the first time she'd seen the girl. Carla didn't want to care. She just couldn't seem to help herself. Okay, that's why.

Because of that little girl, Carla was going to ignore her own instinct to draw back and completely disregard the GO AWAY sign flashing in the child's father's eyes. After all, he didn't know it yet, but she was about to become his best friend. At least *she* wasn't trying to force-feed him Tuna Surprise.

Although maybe a heaping helping of Rachel's "specialty" might be good for him. Carla glanced again at the little girl currently having her face licked off by Abbey. Nope. She just couldn't let that happen to a kid. Especially one who looked so . . . *lost.* Might stunt her growth or something.

"Hi, kiddo," she said, and the tiny blonde looked up long enough to give her a smile. "Looks like Abbey's as happy to see you as I am."

The little girl nodded, then buried her face in Abbey's golden coat again; her smile was wide and bright and . . . silent. *Too* silent.

Glancing at the child's father again, Carla gave him a smile. If she was going to interfere, the least she could do was be friendly. "So," she asked, not wanting to leap right into a *Warning: run for your life* spiel, "what do you think of Chandler?"

"Does the word *Mayberry* mean anything to you?"

"That you're a closet Nickelodeon fan?" Which she would know, since she was one, too.

"Besides that."

Okay, yeah, it did mean something. Some big-city types meant the kind of Mayberry crack as an insult and could put Carla's back up faster than anything. Jackson Wyatt, on the other hand, actually seemed to mean it as a compliment. One point for Mr. Charm. All right, sure she was the first to admit that Chandler was no hot spot for anyone looking for a wild nightlife. But when the partying was done, this was a good place to come home to.

"Yes, I know what you mean," she said, turning for a quick look up and down Main Street. "But that's what we like about it. Small enough to get annoying but only about a half hour's ride from a city big enough to ease that itch whenever you need to."

He nodded, then gave her a look that clearly said, *Okay, conversation over. Where's the nearest exit?* She cut him off at the pass. Before he made the great escape, she had to clue him in.

Glancing over her shoulder quickly, Carla made sure the local cats were still preoccupied buying their meat from Fabulous Frank. Then she took a step closer to Jackson and said, "Actually, I was going to stop by and see you on my way home."

One dark brown eyebrow lifted. "Really?"

She drew her head back and stared at him. "How do you do that?"

"Do what?"

"Manage to inflect a whole 'Royalty to Peasant' attitude in one word?"

"Did I?"

"There it is again," she pointed out, then added, just for the hell of it, "but this time it took you two words."

"Look, Ms. Candellano—"

"Carla."

"Fine. If you'll excuse us, Reese and I were just going to get some ice cream and—"

"Excellent idea. I'll come with you." She didn't really want ice cream, but then again, she never turned it down, either. Besides, it was a lot of fun to throw monkey wrenches at a man who so clearly didn't approve of his plans being disrupted. And she still had to deliver her warning.

"But—"

"Oh, it's no bother," she said, then glanced at Abbey. "Come on, girl. Ice cream."

The dog reacted just as a pet of hers should. All quivers and drool. Hey, the words *ice cream* should always be treated with the same respect given the word *chocolate*. And for chocolate Carla had been known to make midnight trips to a convenience store more than thirty miles away, wearing nothing but her flannel jammies and a bad hairdo. When you had to have it, you had to have it.

"Don't you have leash laws around here?" he asked as they started walking and Abbey trotted happily alongside Reese.

Carla laughed and shook her head. "You really

aren't from around here, are you? Nope. No leash laws. No Super-Duper Pooper Scoopers, either. So be careful where you plant those nifty shoes of yours."

He glanced at the sidewalk, then muttered something she couldn't quite catch, which was probably just as well.

"So what were you going to stop by to see me about?"

"I wanted to warn you," she said, and enjoyed seeing his big blue eyes narrow in suspicion.

"About what, I'm afraid to ask."

"As you should be," she commented, and shifted her small grocery bag from one hand to the other. "Apparently, you've become the latest hot topic."

"What?"

"The local gossip mill is, even as we speak, planning their invasion."

He shook his head, disgusted. "Perfect."

"Hey, you said it yourself. Mayberry. Don't you remember Aunt Bee and Clara? And the telephone operator . . ." Carla frowned to herself. "What was her name again?"

"Juanita?"

"No," she said, scowling at him, "that was the waitress at the diner." Carla thought about it for a second. "Thelma Lou?"

He snorted. "Barney's girlfriend."

She looked up at him and half-smiled. Okay then. Another point for him. Who knew a guy like him would know classic TV so well? She'd gotten hooked on old reruns through desperation. All those nights of waking up in a cold sweat. Of a sad reality becoming a nightmare that haunted her into the wee hours of the morning. Whenever she woke, shaking and crying, she'd stumble into the living room, turn on the TV, and lose herself in the fictional world of Mayberry or *Lost in Space* or *That Girl*. In the darkness, with only the flicker of the screen light for company, she could forget and would, eventually, fall asleep again, sprawled on her sofa.

But she couldn't help wondering what demons prompted Jackson Wyatt to be up in the middle of the night watching television programs that had been canceled and forgotten long before either of them were born.

"Does it really matter what a fictional telephone operator's name was?" he muttered, shattering her train of thought.

"Nope," she answered quickly, though not knowing was going to drive her nuts. Still, she was glad to be rid of the sympathetic leanings she'd been about to indulge in. "Anyway, back to my original warning—around here, the names to watch out for are Abigail, Virginia, and Rachel."

"I'll make a note."

"You should," she said, since he didn't sound like he was taking her seriously. "These women make the FBI look like sissies. They can ferret out information better than an Internet hacker and they do it all without mussing their shellacked hairdos."

He frowned, looked at her, and admitted, "Okay, now you're beginning to scare me."

"Then my work here is done." She gave him an evil grin. "Better men than you have tried and failed to stand up to those three. Hell, even their husbands die off regularly just to get away."

"Jesus. You make them sound like the SS."

She waved a hand at him. "Pansies."

"Pansies?" he repeated. "The *SS*?"

Carla nodded and stopped as they came to the front door of the ice-cream shop. "Oh, yeah. *They* just used whips and chains to beat information out of you."

"And these three?" Christ, Jackson wasn't entirely sure he wanted to know. But some morbid curiosity demanded an answer.

She laughed out loud, and damned if it didn't sound good. This was no dignified murmured chuckle that could be mistaken for a discreet burp. No, this was a flat-out, loud as hell *laugh.* Her face lit up with the joy of it and her brown eyes actually *twinkled,* for God's sake. And when he noticed that she had a deep dimple on her left cheek at the corner of her mouth, he knew this was not a good sign.

His body stirred into life and, even though he knew it would lead nowhere, he enjoyed the rush of need pulsing inside him. It had been a damned long time since a woman had affected him like this.

"Oh, please," she said, and grabbed hold of the brass doorknob behind her. "Beatings, rubber hoses, and a heat lamp have nothing on Rachel's tuna-and-pineapple casserole."

Jackson just stared at her, appalled. "You're not serious."

"Oh, babe. That casserole is infamous around here." She tossed that mass of deep black curls back from her face. "Rachel makes the blasted thing every time the

Welcome Wagon rolls out." She paused, tipped her head to one side, and made a big show of thinking about that. "Really, if you stop to consider it, it's a wonder we have anyone moving into Chandler. You'd think word of that casserole would be enough to keep people out."

"It would have worked for me," he said, not too proud to admit that the thought of being force-fed such a hideous-sounding concoction was enough to make his stomach roll and pitch.

She reached out and laid one hand on his arm. A natural, friendly gesture from an obviously outgoing woman. So why did it feel like someone was holding a dryer-warmed blanket against his skin? It felt good. Too good. But it didn't mean anything. None of this meant anything. He didn't even *know* her, for God's sake.

She released him, almost as if she could hear his thoughts. Yet if she *could,* she'd do more than let go of him. She'd run like hell.

She stared at him for a long second, then shook off whatever it was she'd been feeling. "Sorry to be the one to tell you, then. Rachel's specialty is going to be arriving at your place this afternoon."

As bad as that sounded, he was glad she was talking again. Hell, he thought, talk about god-awful recipes and town gossips. Talk about anything but the near electrical zip of sensation that had just rippled between them.

"Wonderful. Maybe I'll move." He was only half-kidding.

She laughed again and Jackson enjoyed the sound so much, he basked in it for a moment or two. Until, at last, she looked down at Reese and said, "Your daddy's pretty funny, huh?"

Reese frowned, nodded solemnly, and that was enough to snuff out the small flicker of pleasure that had winked to life inside him. Strange. For a second there, he'd almost forgotten about the very thing that had brought him and Reese to this place. And that hadn't happened in . . . well, *ever*.

"You okay?" Carla asked.

No. No, he wasn't. And if things with Reese didn't change fast, he didn't imagine he'd ever be okay again. But she didn't need to hear that. And he didn't need to say it.

"Fine." He reached for his daughter's hand, gave it a squeeze, and said, "Let's have that ice cream and get back home. Apparently we're going to have company later."

Reese rubbed two fingers all around the outside of her mouth.

"Sure," Jackson told her, immediately understanding. "You can have chocolate."

She lifted her hand, dangling her fingers and wiggling them.

"With sprinkles," he agreed.

"I'm impressed," Carla told him.

He glanced at her. "With what?"

"You two have your own sign language."

Yes, they did. They got along fine, contrary to what some people thought. But he'd give anything for it to be different. "You know what they say . . . necessity is the mother of invention."

She held up one hand, smiled, and shook her head. "Oh, no. Don't get me started on mothers."

"Issues?"

"First ice cream, then tales of life with Mama. Without a layer of good, heavy ice cream, I could get ulcers and then I wouldn't be able to eat chocolate and if that happened, life really wouldn't be worth living, would it?"

"Do you always talk this much?"

"You think I talk a lot, wait'll you meet my mother."

"Back to the mother thing."

"*After* ice cream." She yanked the door open, and over the sound of the welcoming chimes, she added, "And like Reese, I'll have chocolate. With sprinkles. And hot fudge. And whipped cream."

One eyebrow lifted. "Watching your figure?" he asked dryly.

"Nope," she assured him, swinging into the ice-cream shop. "Are you?"

His gaze dropped to the curve of her butt. In those worn, faded jeans, it looked spectacular. And he had to admit, if only to himself, that chocolate looked good on her.

An hour later Carla left Jackson and Reese at the turnoff to her drive, and as the two of them walked off, she stopped to watch them. Though father and daughter were side by side, it was as if there was a chasm separating them. Even as Jackson took the child's hand, linking them, they remained independent of each other. Unconnected.

Carla shivered and tried to fight back the urge to run after them. To find out what was holding them apart and to fix it. And that surprised her. For the first time in two years, she was actually concerning herself with someone else's trouble instead of concentrating on her own. But this wasn't her business; she knew that. Heck, she didn't even have the right to ask why Reese never spoke. Why the girl's eyes carried a misery that no child should know.

But her heart ached for them and that was a sure sign that she was letting herself get too involved. She didn't want to care about another child. She didn't want to feel another parent's pain. Not again. It was enough. Done. Over.

"C'mon, Abbey."

Carla cut across her front lawn and watched Abbey sprint out ahead of her, headed for the backyard and the puppies. Her mood better now that she'd decided to butt the hell out of Jackson Wyatt's life, she kicked off her sandals and enjoyed the feel of the grass beneath her feet. The ocean's roar sounded like a distant heartbeat and the wind through the trees like a soft, vaguely remembered song. White clouds raced across a brilliant blue sky and the sun was warm but not yet hot.

In short . . . everything was perfect.

And perfect never lasted long enough to enjoy it.

"It's about time you got home."

"Beth." Her sister-in-law sat on the front porch, elbows propped on her knees. Dark auburn hair, lifted by the breeze, danced about her pale face and drew attention to green eyes that looked anything but placid. "What're you doing here? Where's Tina?" Carla glanced around for her niece, but she was nowhere in sight.

"Your brother's an idiot."

"I've got three of 'em," Carla said, though she knew damn well which one Beth was complaining about. "You'll have to be more specific."

"The one I'm *married* to."

Uh-oh. There was no smile in Beth's voice, so Carla's weak attempt at humor had obviously failed. Which meant that her idiot brother Tony was really up to something stupid. Damn it, she'd meant to see Beth earlier this week. But the days kept slipping past, and as much as it shamed Carla to admit it, she'd been too wrapped up in her own little ball of misery to pay much attention to anyone else's. So what did that say about her?

"What's he done?"

Beth jumped up suddenly and shoved her hands into the back pockets of her denim shorts. "He's driving me nuts, Carla."

"Yeah, he's pretty good at that." Vivid memories of Tony scalping her Barbie doll rushed to the surface of her mind. She took the steps to the porch, opened the front door, and nodded to Beth. "It's a gift. But to be fair, most men are pretty gifted in that area."

Beth followed her inside and stayed just a step or two behind her as she walked through the living room and into the kitchen. Carla went straight to the fridge, opened it, tossed her white butcher-paper-wrapped package inside, then slammed the door closed again. "What'd he do?"

Her sister-in-law pulled out a chair and dropped into it. Slamming her elbows onto the tabletop, she winced suddenly, lifted her arms, and turned them to take a look. Grimacing, she asked, "Jesus, Carla, don't you ever wipe this table off? There's crumbs and . . ." She flicked a finger against her right elbow. "I think it's petrified oatmeal."

"Did you come over here to do an inspection? 'Cause if you did, I should warn you that Mama does that weekly and I always flunk."

Beth pushed one hand through her hair, dusted the crumbs to one side, then set her elbows down again. "I'm sorry. I'm just so pissed."

"Understandable. Candellano men aren't the easiest people in the world to live with."

"Now *there's* an understatement."

"Except for Papa." Carla just couldn't lump her father in with the meatheads who were his sons.

Beth nodded. "True. Except for Papa."

Carla grabbed a bag of Oreos off the counter and took a seat opposite the other woman. Offering the opened bag, she waited until Beth had grabbed a couple before taking one herself. "So. Tell me."

Beth twisted the Oreo expertly, ate the white icing first (as any good American should), then nibbled at the cookie. "Okay," she finally said when Carla started to fidget. "But first, I have to tell you that my old boss called last week."

"Really?" As she remembered getting a call herself, Carla had to wonder if last week had been national Reach Out and Touch a Former Employee Week. "What'd he want?"

"Me."

"What?" Both eyebrows shot up and Carla choked on her cookie.

"Not that way. Jesus, get your mind out of the gutter."

"It's happiest there."

"Briefly, then." Beth shook her head, grabbed another Oreo, and said, "Victor wants me to come back to work."

"Ahhh. . . ." Carla nodded. "If we were in a cartoon, a lightbulb would now be flashing over my head. So what did you tell your boss?"

Beth sat back in her chair and sighed. "I told him I'd have to think about it and get back to him."

"By when?"

She shrugged. "A week or two."

"But you want to go back."

"Oh God, yes." Beth took another cookie. It wasn't that she didn't love being a mom. She did. More than she'd ever thought possible. But there had to be more to life than wiping up spills and singing along with Elmo on *Sesame Street*. Jesus. There *had* to be.

Besides. She'd really enjoyed selling homes. Finding just the right place for people anxious to put down roots. She'd always felt as though she'd had a hand in building their futures and, darn it, she missed that feeling.

"So go."

"Easy for you to say," Beth muttered, lifting her gaze to meet Carla's. "You don't live with Tony."

"True, thank God. But you guys have been together since you were kids. You've always known how to handle him."

"Until now." Beth shook her head. "His head's like a rock on this subject."

Not a good sign, Carla thought, reading more misery in Beth's face than anger—and that was saying a lot, since she was so clearly furious. And rightly so, in Carla's opinion.

"He doesn't want you to work."

"Exactly." Sighing, Beth munched at her cookie, muttered, "Got milk?," then swallowed hard. "Your brother is going ballistic because he wants me to stay home full-time. Be a professional mother and housekeeper like Mama."

"Ah, the Neanderthal approach to marriage. Guess he never bothered to notice that that's how Mama *wanted* it." God, Tony. Where did your brain go? Carla half-turned in her chair, whipped open the fridge again, pulled out two cans of Diet Coke, and set them on the table.

Beth grabbed one of them, took a long drink, then jumped up from the table to stalk around the kitchen. Her steps short and furious, the heels of her sandals clicked against the floor. Two *quacks* sounded out as the rubber-ducky clock struck the hour.

"He was so pleased when I quit work after Tina was born." Now she was talking as much to herself as to Carla and the words kept bubbling out as though they'd been simmering for ages. "I never meant it to be a permanent thing. I just wanted to spend time with Tina before going back. But I know Tony had visions of me being Superwife. Though whatever gave him that idea, I don't know. I don't *want* to bake bread from scratch. That's why God invented grocery stores!"

"Amen."

But Beth wasn't listening. She was too busy pacing and muttering and making karate chops with one hand, and it was pretty easy to guess just who she was pretending to chop.

"And for Pete's sake, why in the hell would I make my own pizza when Papa John's delivers right to my door?"

Since Carla had Papa John's listed first on her speed dial, she was forced to agree. Hell, even Mama didn't make her own pizza! So exactly when had Carla's oldest brother become a caveman?

"This is just weird," she finally said.

"You got that right. It's like . . ." Beth shook her head, took another drink of soda, and said, "I don't even know him anymore."

A spurt of worry shot through Carla, pushing her to her feet. Okay, this wasn't right. Beth and Tony having an argument was one thing. A speed bump in an otherwise pristine stretch of road. But it was something else to watch a "happily-ever-after" unravel.

"Of course you know him. He's the idiot making you nuts. The moron who loves you."

A sad twist of a smile touched Beth's lips briefly, then disappeared. She looked down at her hands, and seconds ticked past before she whispered, "The job thing isn't all of it. I think he's having an affair."

Tony, you son of a bitch.

A moment later, though, Carla reminded herself just who they were talking about here. Tony. Mr. Upstanding Sheriff. Mr. Happily Married Man and Ace Father. She was the first to admit that any one of her brothers could do something stupid. But she just couldn't believe that Tony would risk everything he'd ever loved for a quick roll in the hay.

She shook her head. "No way," Carla said flatly, firmly, putting every ounce of conviction she possessed into the words. "He wouldn't do that. He loves you."

"Yeah." Beth studied the red-and-white can in her hands as though it held the secrets to the questions plaguing her. "That's why he disappears three nights a week and won't tell me where he's going."

"There's got to be an explanation."

"There is. I just don't like it."

"And I don't believe it."

Beth lifted her tear-blurred gaze to Carla's. "You're not taking his side, are you?"

"Hell, no." Carla dropped one arm around her shoulder. "In this kind of fight, it's X chromosomes versus Y." They clicked their soda cans together in a silent salute. And Carla silently vowed to get to the bottom of this or beat her brother senseless.

Whichever came first.

CHAPTER
FIVE

"TUNA AND PINEAPPLE," JACKSON muttered, clapping one hand to his growling stomach. "Those women ought to be arrested."

True to Carla's warning, the Terrible Three, as he'd thought of them almost instantly, had rolled out the Welcome Wagon, then backed it right over him. And he wasn't at all sure he was going to recover anytime soon.

He sat down on the uncomfortable Victorian-style sofa, laid his head on the back, and tried to settle his stomach through sheer willpower. But no one's will was that strong.

Thank God he'd gone with his instinct and prevented Reese from tasting that casserole. She was way too young to be expected to live through it. He closed his eyes and saw those women again. All smiles and interested eyes, they'd kept him talking for an hour. They'd cooed over Reese until the girl had escaped to her bedroom, and then the inquisition had begun.

"Where did you say you were from?" Abigail, clearly older than dirt, inquired oh-so-politely.

"Chicago," he said.

"Ha!" Virginia said. "Told you. Everyone knows Chicago is a Mafia town. Al Capone."

He just stared at the woman with strangely unmoving hair, who looked at him as though she expected him to pull a "gat" out from under the sofa. Although the idea of jumping to his feet brandishing a Gatling gun was somehow comforting.

"Hush," Rachel told her, and leaned into him, offering her poisonous casserole. "I insist you taste this, straightaway. It's best when served hot."

He'd dutifully choked down a bite and vaguely wondered if this was tuna/pineapple at its best, what in the hell could the worst taste like?

"How long are you here for?" Abigail again.

"Three months."

"Hiding out until the coast is clear."

He gave Virginia another look, but no one else paid any attention to her mutterings. They were apparently used to her. Though clearly, *she* was watching way too much HBO.

"And I also make a delicious strawberry jam and chocolate banana cake," Rachel was saying.

Oh, he didn't even want to consider that. Especially with the smell of tuna and pineapple practically surrounding him.

"Where's your wife?" Apparently being the oldest living human gave Abigail the sense that she was allowed to ask rude questions.

"I'm a widower."

"Gang revenge," Virginia muttered, nodding and scooting just a bit farther away from him.

Fine with Jackson.

"What do you do for a living?"

Back to Abigail. Man. Carla hadn't been kidding about these women. "I'm a lawyer."

"Concilierge, you mean," her friend piped up. "To a Don."

He gaped at her.

"And then," Rachel was saying, reaching out to dig her long talons into his forearm, "for special occasions, I make my famous beef-and-garlic-parsnip hash."

His stomach rolled at just the thought of that hideous concoction. He still wasn't sure how long the inquisition had lasted, though God knows, anything over five minutes would have seemed like an eternity. But at last, it had ended.

"Well," Abigail announced, "we don't want to over-stay our welcome."

Too late, he thought. He jumped to his feet and all but raced them to the front door to see them out. As they left, they stayed in character.

Abigail nodded regally.

Virginia walked a wide path around him.

And Rachel actually giggled.

Almost before the door had closed behind them, he was headed to the kitchen, where he gave Rachel's specialty the burial it so richly deserved.

Yet here he sat, hours later, still paying the price for being polite. Clapping one hand to his rumbling stomach, Jackson stretched out on the sofa and wished to hell there was Alka-Seltzer in the house. But a moment later, his churning guts were the furthest thing from his mind, when he heard the first soft cry come from Reese's room.

"No way is Tony having an affair."

"That's what *I* said," Carla muttered. "But Beth's convinced."

"Bullshit." Nick's voice came across the phone line loud and clear, despite a roaring, swishing sound in the background. "He wouldn't do it. Tony's so straight-arrow, it wouldn't even occur to him."

Carla plopped onto her couch, leaned back into the pillowed corner, and propped her feet up on the back. She studied the chipping pink nail polish on her toes as she asked, "Then where's he going three times a week?"

"I don't know. Sheriff's school?"

"Hello?" She held the phone out, glared at it, as if Nick could see the action, then slapped it back against her ear again. "*Sheriff's school?* He's already a sheriff."

"Fine. So I don't know where he's going. I *do* know he's *not* going to some babe's bed, though. Tony wouldn't do that."

Carla didn't think so, either. Which only left a puzzle. If he wasn't cheating, what was he doing and why couldn't he tell Beth? For God's sake, didn't he know what she'd be thinking? Feeling? Worrying about?

"Crap. Are all men this stupid?"

"I refuse to answer that on the grounds that it might incriminate me, and by the way, on behalf of my gender, knock it off."

"Well, come on. If he's not screwing around, why doesn't he just be honest with Beth about what's going on?"

"Gee, I don't know," Nick said. "Why don't you ask him?"

"Maybe I will."

"No, you won't," Nick said. "Stay out of it."

"How can I do that? Beth already dragged me into it."

"Well, back out quick." He paused and Carla could almost see him scrubbing the flat of his hand across his head in frustration. "You don't want to get into the middle of a marriage, Carla."

"This is family."

"All the more reason to keep out."

"Coward."

"Damn straight."

She scowled at the ceiling and blindly studied the lamplight shadowed in a golden arc across the pale cream paint. A moth circled slowly, as if doing a dance in a spotlight, and she followed the bug's progress as though she were watching a Broadway play.

"Carla . . ."

"Hmm?"

"You're planning something."

"Nah." She smiled. "Would I do that?"

"Hell, yes."

The roaring sound quieted suddenly and the cessation of noise was startling.

"What was that?" she asked, pleased to be able to change the subject.

"Oh. The whirlpool shut off."

"Your knee again?" Carla straightened up on the

sofa, curled her legs up under her, and winced as she remembered how, just last season, Nick's kneecap had been popped clean off in a play gone bad. It was his first major injury since signing with the San Jose Saints, but it had been a beaut. Through surgery and rehab, he'd been fighting his way back to the football field. But at thirty-two he was already getting old to be a professional running back.

And suddenly she wished he wasn't living in San Jose. She wanted him closer. So she could help more. Not that he'd take her help, but at least she could offer.

"It's fine." His tone told her he didn't want to talk about it. Naturally, she ignored that.

"No, it's not."

"Carla, I take back everything I just said. Go. Interfere in Tony's life. Stick your nose in. Just stay the hell out of mine."

"What are you gonna do, Nick? Keep playing until you can't walk anymore?"

"Oh, hey!" he said loudly. "Look at the time! Gotta go."

"You're not going to get out of this that easy, you know."

"Bye, Carla."

"I'll see you Sunday at Mama's," she said quickly, and was pretty sure she heard a muttered, "Damn it," just before she hung up.

Tossing the phone onto the sofa cushion beside her, she looked down at Abbey and asked, "Is it just me? Or are men totally aggravating?"

The dog gave her a long thoughtful look and Carla took that as a sign of agreement. Of course, the fact that Abbey was female might have prejudiced her vote, but still.

"I mean, it's not just the men in my family. There's Mike." She shook her head. "He keeps coming after me, trying to get me to go back to work. There's Mr. Charm over there—" She hopped up from the couch, walked across the living room, and stared out at the house on the point. "He gives me looks that could kill, then laughs at my jokes and—" She glanced over her shoulder at the dog who sat there, head cocked, ears pricked, as if listening to every word she said. "I *saw* him checking out my butt at the ice-cream shop today. So what does that mean? Stay away? Or hello, honey?" Sighing, she admitted, "No offense, Ab, but I really miss having Stevie to talk to. Wish she'd get home already." Carla's best friend was still lounging on a Caribbean cruise while meanwhile, back at the ranch, things were really starting to suck.

Carla stared out at the Garvey house and wondered why she cared what Jackson Wyatt was thinking about her. Why she even wondered if he *was* thinking about her. For God's sake. He's a summer renter. He'd be gone in a couple of months and everything would be back to normal.

Except now, normal looked like Nick was in trouble and Tony was in even bigger trouble. And God help both of them if Mama got wind of what was going on.

Man. What had happened to her world? First she had crashed and burned two years ago. Now it looked as though the rest of her family were lining up to take the same hit. Strange, though, she thought, turning around and heading back to the couch. Carla realized that she'd been so busy today, what with Beth and Tony and Nick and Reese and Jackson, she hadn't had *time* to feel sorry for herself.

Had she really been so self-involved the last two years? She shifted uncomfortably on the sofa as an inward cringe took hold. Good God. She had. Guilt reared up and took a bite out of her heart. One thing Mama and Papa had drummed into them from childhood: *Family comes first.* But she'd been so busy hugging her own hurts and failures to her chest, she'd actually forgotten that.

"Oh, crap."

Abbey put her head on Carla's lap and looked up with soulful brown eyes. That solid, heavy weight felt good. Comforting. And as she stroked her hand along the dog's head, Carla promised, "It'll be different, Ab. You'll see. We'll help Tony and Beth. Take care of Nick. Check on Paul. God knows what's going on with him." She smiled, sighed, and said, "And who knows? Maybe if we're on a roll, we'll be able to get through to Mr. Charm and Reese."

A big, slobbery doggy kiss was her reward, and Carla laughed, hugging the golden tightly before letting go. Then she grabbed the bowl of popcorn off the coffee table. Settling back, she pushed PLAY on the remote, then laid one hand on Abbey's head. The dog turned to look up at her, and Carla said, "Don't worry. We'll find out what's going on with Tony. And Nick, too. But for now, we're gonna watch a movie." Abbey yawned. "Hey, you'll like it. Well, maybe not the end. But up until then, *Old Yeller*'s a classic."

Jackson stood in the doorway of Reese's room and watched her sleep. A Cinderella lamp at her bedside shone golden, its twenty-five-watt bulb dim enough to allow sleep and bright enough to hold the shadows at bay. For the last year Reese hadn't been able to sleep without that light on. She feared the darkness as much as she feared the nightmares that accompanied it.

Her small body twisted and shifted on the sheets, searching for a peace she never found. Her legs kicked and churned as if she were trying, futilely, to run from the memories chasing her.

She whimpered softly and everything inside him tightened, squeezing down around his heart, closing off his throat, until breathing became something like an Olympic event. His hands fisted at his sides, Jackson desperately wanted to help her, and knowing he couldn't was enough to torture him. All he could do for her was be close. Be nearby. Be there to hold her when the dreams had her jerking from sleep, tears raining down her face, her eyes filled with the misery she hadn't been able to speak of. It wasn't much, he knew, this standing guard. It wasn't enough. But she wouldn't let him inside far enough to do more.

Sighing, Jackson leaned one shoulder against the door jamb, closed his eyes, and remembered the scene he knew his little girl relived every night in her dreams.

Rain splashed down around him, falling in sheets from a steel gray sky. Cold rippled along his spine, but dread chased it, making him feel a chill that had nothing to do with the driving Chicago wind pushing at him.

Red and blue lights spun on the tops of the gathered patrol cars, flashing beacons into the rain-soaked morning. Weird stained-glass shadows danced on the grim faces of the officers who studiously avoided looking at Jackson.

Each step he took splashed more water into his shoes. His hair felt plastered to his head. His sodden clothes clung to him, weighing him down. But the real heaviness went deeper. His heart. His soul. Blackness crouched in his belly, preparing to strike. Getting ready to rip what was left of his world to shreds.

Around him, muttered conversations came to a stop as he walked closer to the jagged, torn crush of metal that had once been a Lexus sedan. Through the gloom and the haze blurring his vision, he saw a yellow tarp draped over a shape stretched across the steering wheel and dashboard. Rain pummeled down, needling through the smashed windshield to spatter on the tan leather seats. It bounced off that tarp and made a distinct tapping sound that reached him clearly, despite the roaring in his ears.

Then he heard the scream. It tore into his body with a knifelike slash. He spun around, searching, and it went on and on, rising higher and higher and—

He came out of the memory with a jerk and realized it wasn't the screaming rattling around him now but the telephone. Heart pounding, pulse racing, he turned and headed down the short hall to the living room. Pushing one shaking hand through his hair, he struggled to control his uneven breathing as he snatched up the receiver.

"Hello?"

"Hello, Jackson," a cool, deliberate female voice said, enunciating every syllable. "This is Phyllis."

His hand tightened on the phone, fingers gripping the molded plastic until he wouldn't have been surprised to feel it turn into dust. Of course. Why not? Why wouldn't she call now? Did she have a sixth sense? Did she know, even at a distance, when he was at his most vulnerable? "Hello, Phyllis." Good, he told himself. Voice even. Calm. Unthreatened.

She got right to business. "How is my granddaughter?"

So much for calm. A thread of anger whipped around his insides. This woman and her husband had been using Reese in a game of tug-of-war for months. Ever since the night of the accident. "*My* daughter is fine."

"And mine is *dead,* thanks to you." Her voice was a slap, delivered coolly and efficiently from two thousand miles away.

Jackson reeled and clenched his teeth to keep from defending himself, *again*. He'd said it all before. For all the good it had done him. His in-laws had never been big fans of his. They'd done all they could to keep their daughter from marrying a man with no past and a future they'd thought wouldn't be nearly good enough for their only child.

They'd expected Diane to marry a man with blood as blue as their own. The idea of a Barrington marrying an *orphan,* for God's sake, was just too much to bear. When she'd first shown up with Jackson in tow, her father had taken Jackson aside and offered him fifty thousand dollars to just . . . *go away.*

Hell, he thought now, listening to Phyllis's voice take on that sharp, knifelike edge. Maybe he should have taken it. Diane would be alive. But then, he wouldn't have Reese, either. No. He didn't even like the *sound* of that. His daughter was the one good thing he'd done in his life. The one decent thing to come out of a marriage that had been empty from day one.

Besides, he wasn't a man to be bought. And he never had taken orders well. So instead, he'd stayed. He'd put up with the thinly veiled insults, figuring that sooner or later they'd get used to him. Until the night he'd overheard his father-in-law, talking to a business associate, refer to Jackson as "the mongrel."

After that, all bets were off and open enmity was declared between him and his in-laws. Diane, he was pretty sure, had enjoyed ruffling her parents' feathers. She hadn't given a damn about his pedigree as long as he kept her in Manolo Blahnik shoes. Until the novelty of marrying a peasant had worn off. Then she'd wanted out as much as her parents had wanted it for her.

And after Diane's death, the battle had kicked into high gear. The Barringtons had already made a try for custody of Reese, and even losing the first round hadn't convinced them to retreat. No. His in-laws were just regrouping. Planning a bigger, more thorough attack. They'd pulled out the big guns, too, getting Reese's doctor to side with them against him.

Which was what had brought him here. To Chandler. In a last-ditch attempt to reach his daughter.

"Phyllis," he said tightly, wanting to get the woman off the phone as fast as possible, "what do you want?"

"You know perfectly well what I want," she told him. "I want Reese to be given the care she so obviously needs."

"I'm taking care of her."

"Yes, I'm sure." She didn't even bother to disguise the sarcasm.

"She's fine," he said, willing Phyllis to believe him. Hell, willing *himself* to believe it.

"We both know that's not the case."

"She just needs time," he argued, clutching the receiver tightly in his fist.

"It's been nearly a year. Too long already."

"How much time will it take then, Phyllis?" he demanded, moving now, needing to let some of the pent-up rage and energy course through him and out. He stalked around the living room, crossing to the wide front window, and stared out into the night. "You seem to be so sure of yourself, how much time exactly do we give a six-year-old girl to 'get over' losing her mother?"

"Don't take that tone with me." Steel rang in her voice and a part of Jackson celebrated the fact that he'd managed to crack her icy facade. But another part, the more rational part of him, warned not to push her too far.

He couldn't afford to piss her off any more than she already was. Not yet. Not until Reese was well and he could tell the Barringtons to go to hell.

"You're right," he said, swallowing back the anger nearly choking him. "I was out of line." Nearly killed him to say those words, but a man did what he had to do. Right?

Mollified, she said, "Thank you. Now. I've spoken to Dr. Monohan and he's reserved a bed for Reese at Fair Haven."

His spine stiffened. Son of a bitch. Give her an inch and she'd take his child. "She won't need it."

"That's to be seen," Phyllis said. "As it is, her place there is waiting for her. I've told the doctor to expect Reese by September fifteenth."

September. It was already the middle of June. And the three months that had looked like such a long stretch of time to him before were suddenly reduced to no more than the blink of an eye. How had it all come to this? he wondered. His life . . . Reese's life . . . would be decided this summer. And he didn't have the first clue how to go about making this work.

When Phyllis hung up, he threw the phone down onto a chair and concentrated on the soft distant glow shining from Carla's windows. To a man standing in the dark, those lights looked like the only safe haven around.

Squinting, Carla stumbled down the hall toward the kitchen, following the scent of freshly brewed coffee. She didn't even stop to wonder who'd made it. It was more than enough to know it had been done. Who knew? Maybe the coffee fairy had stopped by. Besides, it was tacky to question a gift. And this was most definitely a gift. From the coffee gods.

"Damn it!" She stubbed her toe against the doorjamb as she came around the corner and hopped the last few feet into the too-bright kitchen.

"What kind of good morning is that?" Mama asked.

"The only kind you should expect when you pop in at—" She shot a look at her wall duck. *"Six-thirty?"* Swinging her bleary gaze back toward her mother, Carla said, "Jesus, Mama. Are you trying to kill me?"

"Coffee first," her mother said wisely. "Then we'll talk."

Coffee. Yes. Everything looked better when seen through a caffeinated filter. Wincing, Carla limped on her sore toe, took the steaming mug her mother handed her, and buried her nose in the scent of it. Small capillaries opened up. Blood rushed through arteries. Heartbeat quickened in anticipation. She took a swallow and damn near sighed. One thing you had to give Mama. She made a great cup of coffee.

"You know," Carla said, hobbling over to the closest chair, "this is almost orgasmic."

"What?"

"Never mind." Whoa. Engage brain before speaking.

"This is how you sleep?" her mother demanded, waving one hand at her daughter's ensemble. "And if there's a fire, this is all you'll have to wear? What will the firemen think?"

Carla looked down, blinked, focused, and shrugged. Nick had gotten her the football jersey—with his number on the chest—and the boxer shorts were comfortable. "If there's a fire," she promised solemnly, "I'll remember to put on my prom dress before running for my life."

Mama sniffed. "Drink more coffee."

"Good idea." Another blissful swallow and she almost felt strong enough to ask, "What in the hell are you doing here before the crack of dawn?"

Her mother whisked a dish towel across the countertop, then ran her finger across the same surface, checking to make sure every crumb had been obliterated. Naturally, it had.

"I was up fixing dinner . . ."

Carla opened her mouth, realized she hadn't had

near enough coffee to go *there,* and snapped it shut again.

"And I saw you had company."

What? Pushing her hair back from her eyes, she stared at her mother and repeated, "Company?"

"Outside."

Dutifully Carla pushed herself to her feet and, carrying the mug full of morning courage, wandered to the window and peered out. She smiled. Heck, how could you do anything else?

Inside the puppy pen, Reese Wyatt sat in the dirt with six puppies crawling over her lap, climbing her chest, and tugging at the ends of her hair. Abbey, of course, was there, too, her head on Reese's lap, patiently ignoring the clambering paws of her litter.

It was a picture-perfect scene. The kind you saw on commercials airing around Christmastime. The first tentative rays of sunlight poked through the trees and dropped dappled shade. A happy kid. Cute puppies. Faithful dog. Carla half-expected a swell of music to rise up out of nowhere as an anonymous announcer urged people to "phone home for the holidays."

But this was real life, not TV. And in real life that happy kid had a usually cranky father who would, no doubt, be bursting onto the tranquil scene at any moment, ready to drag said kid away. Just then, a flicker of movement at the corner of her eye drew Carla's attention.

Jackson Wyatt was already here. Standing in the shadowy overhang of the eaves, watching his daughter among the dogs she so clearly loved. Carla's heart ached just a little as she studied his expression—a mixture of pleasure and pain. What was he thinking? Feeling?

Even through the closed door, Carla heard the puppies' excited yips and barks, but over and above all that was another sound. One she hadn't heard before. The little girl was actually *laughing,* the sound rising up and up like soap bubbles drifting free in the air. But Carla didn't look at the child. Instead, her gaze locked on the unshed tears glimmering in Jackson Wyatt's eyes as he listened to his little girl's laughter, and Carla's throat tightened.

CHAPTER SIX

IT HAD BEEN SO long, Jackson thought as the sound of Reese's unrestrained giggles washed over him. Like a soothing balm, that laughter eased his tortured heart and gave him the first real hope he'd known in almost a year. If she could laugh, she could talk. If she could talk, she could come all the way back to him.

He blinked back the moisture in his eyes, clearing the image in front of him. He wanted always to remember this moment. This picture of Reese, with small white fur-ball puppies clambering all over her as she took her first hesitant step out of the shadows.

Shrinks be damned.

It was just as he'd thought. Hoped. Reese would come back when she was ready to come back and not before. All the doctors in the world wouldn't change that. *Couldn't* change it. What she needed was her father.

And, apparently, puppies.

To his left, the back door opened and he frowned to himself, resenting the intrusion. Which was nuts, since he was standing in someone else's backyard. *He* was the intruder here. Well, he and Reese. Though he couldn't be sorry about it, now. When he'd first realized his daughter was gone from the house, instant irritation and fear had swept him. He didn't want his daughter running off to Carla's house every chance she got, and he'd been damn sure that's just where she'd gone. After all, the pull of puppies wasn't something that any kid could ignore.

But to get to this house, she had to cross a street that, all right, wasn't exactly the Indianapolis 500, but the occasional driver zoomed down that road. And a short six-year-old wasn't going to be easy to spot when you were doing fifty.

Even as he thought it, though, he admitted silently that wasn't the whole reason he resented Reese coming here. She was probably safe enough crossing the street—especially at the crack of dawn. But her coming here ensured that he'd have to come after her. Which meant seeing the woman who lived here. The more time he spent with Carla, the more he enjoyed it, and damn it, he couldn't afford to enjoy a woman at the moment. In *any* way.

Yet here he stood, in Carla's yard, with a soft morning breeze rippling through his hair and his daughter's laughter singing to him. So how in the hell could he be angry about any of it?

"Good morning!"

An older version of Carla poked her head out the opened door. Graying black hair framed a round face with snapping brown eyes and a wide smile. She stepped out onto the porch, wiping her hands on a pristine apron tied around her middle. "So, you want some coffee?"

"Excuse me?"

"Coffee," she repeated, a little louder this time, as if he were deaf and she was determined to make him understand. "My Carla, she's having some now. Best not to talk to her until she's finished, so you can talk to me."

Words. Coming too fast to be understood this early in the morning. Besides, if he went inside, he'd only be dragged deeper into the Candellano family. Best to escape now. "I'm sorry," he said, "but I think Reese and I—"

"What?" She slapped her hands on her hips. "You have somewhere else to be before the sun comes up?" Tilting her head to one side, she asked, "You're a vampire, maybe? I read about vampires and—"

"What?"

"Jesus, Mama." Carla's voice, blurred, indistinct, came from inside the kitchen. "Stop reading already."

"I'm kidding." She turned and glanced briefly toward her daughter. "Only you can make jokes?"

"Oh, Mama, it's way too early for this."

Jackson agreed. He hadn't planned on running into anyone at this hour. He'd hoped to just pick up Reese and get back home before anyone knew they'd been there. Best-laid plans. "We'll just be going. . . ."

The older woman ignored that completely. "You come in. You'll have coffee. You'll talk."

Not an easy woman to argue with. At least he knew now where her daughter came by her bulldozer personality. "Reese—"

"Is fine," the woman interrupted with a fond look at the child across the yard.

Reese might be fine, but she was silent again, now that she knew she had an audience. Already she was pushing herself to her feet and ignoring the jumping puppies. Abbey, though, was not to be ignored. The big dog simply pushed her head beneath Reese's hand until she got the stroking and petting she so obviously wanted.

Disappointment swelled inside him. His heart twisted and that old familiar ache shimmered through his body. For one all too brief moment, his little girl had shone brightly again. Now that moment was gone and the silence was back.

"Come inside," the woman on the porch insisted, kindness rimming her voice as if she knew exactly what he was feeling. "We're all wide awake." She tossed a cautious look back into the house and amended that statement slightly. "Most of us, anyway." She shrugged. "My daughter, we give her more coffee, she'll be all right."

As if responding to a cue, Carla stepped out onto the porch beside her mother. Clutching a cup of coffee in both hands, she squinted at him, and even at a distance Jackson felt the tug of her gaze. Not many women could pull off a football jersey and a pair of boxer shorts. But damned if she didn't make the outfit look good.

Which only served to remind him exactly *why* he shouldn't be here.

"Hi." Her voice sounded gravelly with sleep.

"Sorry about this," he said. "Reese got out on her own again."

"Cell block D needs better guards."

He stiffened. Apparently, she really wasn't a morning person. Fine. Just as well. He didn't need a friend. He didn't need a woman. Hell, he didn't need any of this.

"Come in for some breakfast," the older woman urged.

Carla rolled her eyes.

"Thanks, but we'd better go."

Her mother gave her a not too subtle nudge in the ribs and Carla winced. "Have some coffee," she said, and considered that more than gracious. Heck, she was offering to share her morning potion. What could be friendlier?

"I've got some at the house."

"Who doesn't?" she countered. "Mine's closer."

He looked from her to the girl, still standing in the puppy pen, and back again. Indecision warred on his features and sympathy welled up inside Carla until it nearly choked her. Remembering the look on his face as he'd watched his daughter's laughter opened her heart to him, and that wasn't something she'd counted on. Lust was one thing. Caring quite another. But the poor man had already had plenty of emotional turmoil this morning. Now he was being asked to face down Mama Candellano before 7:00 A.M. Who *wouldn't* feel sorry for him?

"You come," Mama piped up. "Have coffee. Ignore my daughter's foul temper—which she got from me, because, God rest him, her papa never got angry; he only got quiet—not like the rest of us, Carla's three brothers included, well, except for Paul; he's like his papa with his quiet all the time."

Carla blinked, shook her head, and stared at him. "Can she cram a load of words into one sentence or what?"

"Impressive," he said, remembering now that Carla had warned him ahead of time about just how much her mother talked.

"I told you so."

"You told him what?" Mama demanded, flicking a dish towel at Carla's hip. "You've been talking about me?"

She leaned down and planted a quick kiss on her mother's forehead. "Sure. I gave an interview on CNN. Didn't you see it?"

"Smart mouth. That's what you are." Mama clucked her tongue, waved a beckoning hand at Jackson, then turned into the house, obviously expecting him to follow.

Jackson looked back at Reese.

"She'll be fine," Carla said, pausing for a gulp of coffee. "She'll just play with the puppies, won't you, Reese?"

The little girl nodded and eased back down to the ground, delighting the puppies, who immediately began to scale Mount Reese again.

"When Mama's got breakfast ready, we'll call her in." He still didn't look convinced. "Come on; be a hero."

"What?" He looked up at her.

Carla glanced into the kitchen and whispered above the sounds of pots and pans clanging together, "I haven't had nearly enough coffee yet to deal with Mama. If you're there, she'll pester you instead."

Great. Jackson had the distinct feeling Mama would be a more formidable presence then the three women who'd descended on him yesterday, bearing salmonella.

Run, Forrest, run. That one line from a movie rattled inside his head like a warning bell. Jackson knew he should turn and leave. Knew he should get Reese and go back to the silent house across the way. But suddenly *silence* seemed more like an enemy rather than the companion it had become over the last year. But then, had it really been a friendly thing? Or was it always an enemy and he simply hadn't noticed that until today?

Whatever the answer, he didn't want to face the quiet alone. Not right now.

When he started for the house, Carla smiled, and damned if it didn't feel good to have that smile aimed at him.

A half hour later, the scent of bacon hung in the air, dirty dishes lay scattered across Carla's kitchen table, and he knew more about the Candellano family than he would have thought possible.

Morning sunlight poured through the windows, lying golden across the counters and floor. Reese sat beside him, surreptitiously handing Abbey bits of bacon under the table. On the wall opposite him, the ridiculous duck clock quacked seven times, and he told himself he and Reese should be going.

But he was reluctant to leave the warmth of this place for the cold emptiness waiting for him across the street. So instead, he nursed his third cup of exceptional coffee and watched as Carla and her mother waged a friendly war of words. Even through the bickering, though, he saw the love binding the two of them. Amazed, he felt drawn to it at the same time he admitted silently that he knew nothing about this kind of bond. This kind of unconditional acceptance. This family tie that wound deep enough to hold but not strangle.

He leaned back in his chair and remembered the string of foster homes he'd grown up in. Bounced from place to place, he'd never belonged. Never felt a part of anything. He'd thought that marrying Diane would fill that cold, dark spot inside him. Stupid, when neither of them had been in love. So it was hardly surprising that marriage hadn't given him a sense of family.

Until Reese.

Until he'd looked into his daughter's face when she was only moments old. In that one instant, Jackson had finally found the love that had eluded him all his life. One tiny girl had seemed to hold all the mysteries of the universe for him. He still remembered the swell of emotion that had risen up in him when the nurse placed his daughter in his arms for the first time.

His gaze shifted to her now, and despite the ache for what he'd lost, what they'd *both* lost, he knew that he would do whatever he could to make her whole again.

That was family, right?

"I saw on *Oprah*," Mama was saying.

"Run," Carla said, giving him a warning look. "Run fast and run far."

"What kind of thing is that to say?"

"Compassionate," Carla said, brown eyes snapping and a small twist of a smile curving her mouth.

"Pay no attention to her," Mama countered, waving a hand at her daughter and turning her gaze on Jackson. "Oprah's a smart cookie."

"I'm sure."

"See? *He* agrees."

"He's polite." Carla grinned and took another sip of coffee. Really, he thought, it was incredible the change in her personality a little caffeine could manage.

"Carla?" A man's voice, followed by the slam of the front door and quick footsteps crossing the living room. By the time they all turned around to face the doorway, the sheriff was standing there, looking grim enough to give any criminal second thoughts.

"Tony!" The older woman paled and pushed halfway out of her chair. "Beth? Tina?"

"They're fine," he said quickly, and Jackson watched color rush back into Angela Candellano's features. Then the sheriff nodded and acknowledged, "Wyatt," before turning on his sister. "Carla, we need your help."

She was already shaking her head. "No way."

Her eyes looked suddenly flat and bleak. Her face paled and Jackson had the weirdest urge to jump to his feet and put himself between Carla and her brother. The impulse to protect was so strong, so unexpected, he didn't know what to make of it.

But then Carla stood up and moved away and the moment was lost.

Tony'd known coming over here that this wouldn't be easy. His sister had a head like a rock when she wanted to. And in two years, no one had been able to talk her into doing what she did best. But today he wasn't going to give her a choice. There was no time. And no one else to ask.

"We're organizing a search—"

"I don't want to hear it," Carla said, walking to the window. She deliberately stared out at the sun-drenched yard, keeping her gaze on anything but Tony.

"Too damn bad," her brother said sharply, and Carla turned to look at him.

"Don't think you can bully me into this," she snapped. "You know why I won't."

"Yeah, I know."

"Then don't ask."

"I don't have a choice and neither do you."

She moved back to the table, set her coffee cup down with a *thunk,* then wrapped her arms around her middle. "Sure I do. And I choose no."

"Damn it, Carla—"

She snapped him a glare that would have fried a lesser man. "I'm not real happy with you anyway, Tony. So don't push me."

"What the hell are you talking about?"

Carla's gaze flashed to their mother, then back to him. Now wasn't the time. But when she got him alone, she was going to ream him a new one.

"Tony," Mama interrupted, "maybe it's not a good idea to . . ."

He only glanced at her. "There's a man missing, Mama. He's fifty-five years old. An Alzheimer's patient."

She crossed herself and muttered a fast prayer.

Tony went on, shifting his gaze back to Carla and staring her down, silently daring her to refuse. "Plus he's got heart problems. He needs to take medication for it. He wandered off from his family's campsite last night. They looked for him for hours before alerting us. We're rounding up everyone we can." Briefly he shot a look at Jackson. "We could use your help on this, too. The more searchers we have, the better."

Jackson stood up slowly, glancing from Tony to Carla and back again. "I'd like to help, but my daughter—"

"Will be with me," Mama interrupted him neatly, and looked at Reese. "We'll bake cookies. Would you like that?"

The child stared at her father for a long moment, then turned back to the older woman and nodded.

"Good," Tony said. "That's settled. You can go with Carla. One more set of eyes, plus you're new around here. We don't need you getting lost, too."

Jackson arched one eyebrow in silent insult.

"Carla's not going," she said.

"Oh, yes, she is," Tony countered.

"You'll find him." Her voice sounded hollow, even to her own ears.

"Damn right we will," Tony said, crossing to his sister and laying both hands on her shoulders. "But it'd be a damn sight easier with you and Abbey looking, too."

"We're retired." She slipped out from under his grasp and backed up a step.

"Fine. Look today; retire again tomorrow."

Carla felt the walls closing in on her. Just moments ago, she'd been laughing, and now she felt nothing but cold. Breath caught in her throat and her stomach churned. A search. She hadn't been on one in two years. Not since . . . An invisible fist squeezed her heart and she winced with the ache of it.

Two long years, and that day still hovered at the edges of her mind like a shadow clinging to her heels on a hot summer day. Always there, whether she chose to acknowledge it or not. She remembered it all. The hope. The misery. The soul-crushing pain. If she allowed herself, she would remember the scream that seemed to echo over and over again until the sound became a part of the day, etching itself into her heart.

Her pulse pounded, thundering in her ears. Tears stung the backs of her eyes and Carla swallowed the cold knot of regret lodged in her throat. She couldn't think about that now. Couldn't remember his little face. Couldn't let herself recall the sound of his laughter or the shine in his eyes or the strength of his hugs.

Because then she'd have to remember that he was dead, now.

"I can't." She shook her head, looking up at her brother, willing him to listen. To understand.

But Tony wasn't going to let her off. "Yes, you can, damn it. That's why I need you."

Carla's stomach pitched as she let her gaze slide from Tony, to Mama, to Jackson, and even to Reese, who watched her with solemn eyes. Abbey was on her feet, moving closer to Carla, as if offering silent support. She reached down and smoothed the dog's soft golden hair and knew that Tony was right. She didn't have a choice. Not today, anyway.

Ignoring pleas for help was somehow easier when they came from a distance. When Mike was on the phone talking about some far-flung place, she could tell him no, because she didn't have to look into his eyes. She didn't have to live with the people she'd refused to help. But here, standing in her own kitchen with her brother asking for help, it was a different matter entirely.

She fought down a rising tide of nausea and nodded. "Fine. Where do you want us?"

A strong, cold wind whipped in off the lake and eased the warmth of the sun. Jackson looked around at the area and wondered how in the hell they'd ever find one lone man. The lake itself was huge—he even noticed a few whitecaps dancing across the surface, pushed by the wind. A semicircle of forest backed up onto the lake and looked dense enough to hide an *army* of men, let alone one poor guy. And that wasn't even counting the open meadow laid out in front of them. Dips and gullies in the land were hidden by the high grass, and for all they knew, the man could be stretched out in one of them.

It looked hopeless.

But that fact didn't seem to bother Carla. She hadn't wanted to help—she'd made that clear. But once she'd agreed, she'd been all business. In less than a half hour, she'd been dressed and ready to go. Now he stood beside her and Abbey, watching the two of them become a team.

"What's that for?" he asked as she laid a neon orange vest with the word SEARCHERS emblazoned in black across Abbey's back, then snapped it shut beneath her belly.

"Two things," Carla muttered, not even looking up at him. "Number one, it tells Abbey we're about to go to work. And number two . . . it tells any yahoos she might run into that she's a search dog and they should leave her the hell alone." She spared him a quick look. "It also makes her easy to see in case there are hunters wandering through the woods."

"Hunters?" He glanced toward the tree line. Hell, the missing guy's family didn't have to worry only about him being lost. They had to worry about some other guy mistaking him for a deer.

"Don't worry about it," she said, as if knowing exactly what he was thinking. Nothing's in season right now."

As soon as that vest was snapped on, the golden retriever's attitude seemed to change. She stood a little straighter. Lifted her nose into the air. Her ears perked up as if listening for something they'd never be able to hear.

"She's done this a lot."

Carla nodded and stood up. "She was raised to it. And she's the best, aren't you, Ab?"

The dog continued her silent study of the terrain.

"What's next?"

Carla pulled a plastic bag from the backpack slung over her shoulder. Inside the bag was a crumpled shirt. She pulled it out, let the dog take a few good sniffs, then stuffed it back into the bag and closed it tightly. She flashed him a look. "Got to keep the shirt sealed. Otherwise, the scent would just confuse her." She reached down, rubbed the dog's head, and said, "Abbey, *find.*"

The golden barked once, then took off like a shot, loping across the meadow, her lithe body slicing through the high grasses with speed and grace.

Carla started running, too. A slow jog that gave her no chance at all of keeping up with the dog. Jackson moved alongside her, silently giving thanks that he'd been pretty good about visiting the gym in the last year.

"She's already out of sight," he said.

"She'll be back." Carla didn't sound winded at all—annoying. "She'll keep coming back to me. Then, if she finds something, she'll take me to it."

"Smart dog."

"Great dog," she said, and flashed him a smile that didn't go anywhere near her eyes.

That was the last time they spoke for nearly three hours. The only sounds were their feet thundering across the ground and the occasional crackle and spit of the walkie-talkie Carla carried. Jackson ran when she said and rested when she said. He couldn't tell one part of the forest from another. One tree looked pretty much like another to him. But Carla seemed to know where she was going. And she trusted that dog.

They were good. Hell, *she* was good.

Why had she fought her brother so hard about taking part in the search? She was clearly an expert. Why back away from the very thing that you were best at?

And why did he care?

Sunlight splintered through the leaves of the trees, looking like golden sparks in the darkness. He eased down onto the closest rock when she called a rest, and watched as she pulled a water bottle from her pack and poured some into a small bowl she'd brought along for Abbey before offering him a drink.

He handed Carla back the bottle, scrubbed both hands across his face, then studied her for a long minute before asking, "So, are we going to find him in all this?"

She looked up at him and her eyes shone darkly. She took a long pull at the water bottle, then said, "God, I hope so. I can't lose another one."

CHAPTER SEVEN

G OD.

The very thought of failing again was enough to send a bone-chilling cold racing through her. Carla wiped damp palms against the legs of her jeans and leaned back against the tower of boulders known as Castle Rock. She shifted her gaze to sweep the surrounding forest. Splotches of sunlight dazzled the darkness but did nothing to ease the blackness crawling around inside her.

Two years.

Two years since she'd done this. She would have thought she—and Abbey—would have been a little rusty. But instead, they'd come together as the team they'd always been and gone right back to business. Maybe she'd just been kidding herself about being retired. Maybe Mike, her old boss, had been right after all.

They hadn't retired. They'd just been hiding. And damn it, she wanted to be hiding *now*. Back at the house. Back where it was safe. Where no one was depending on her. Counting on her. Back where she could pretend that none of this bothered her anymore. That she wasn't haunted by the face of one little boy and the knowledge that she'd failed the one person she shouldn't have.

Abbey lay at Carla's feet, steady gaze locked on her. The dog's eyes were bright, almost energized, and Carla realized guiltily that Abbey'd missed this. Missed being out in the field, doing what she did best. But then, Abbey didn't experience success or failure. Abbey simply did the job she was asked to do. If she found the missing person alive, that was great. If she found them dead . . . well, at least she'd *found* them. Some Search and Rescue dogs, after prolonged searches, had been known to become depressed at finding only death. But that hadn't happened to Abbey . . . yet.

It was Carla who had to live with the memories. Another chill raced down her spine and she shivered as she tried to push those memories away again . . . and failed.

"What did you mean?"

She shot Jackson a look and something inside her staggered under his steady gaze. In the indistinct light, his blue eyes seemed as deep and cool as the lake. His hair fell across his forehead as he leaned forward, bracing his arms on his knees. That now-familiar stab of sweet, hot lust slammed home, but since this really wasn't the time, she ignored it. Still, ignoring it didn't lift the haze from her brain.

"Huh?"

"When you said you couldn't take losing another one. What'd you mean?"

"Oh. Did I say that out loud?"

He snorted a choked-off laugh. "In the short time I've known you, I've discovered you say everything you're thinking out loud."

Oh, not everything. If she had, he'd already know that she'd pictured him in his underwear a couple dozen times. Boxers, she was pretty sure. And if he turned out to be a briefs man, she was going to be heartily disappointed.

"Yeah, well," she said, pushing that image out of her mind *again*, "you don't have to listen."

"Hard *not* to."

She smiled in spite of herself. "Okay. Have to give you that one. Candellanos are pretty hard to overlook."

"So tell me."

"It's a long story."

"Do I look busy?"

The walkie-talkie clipped to her belt crackled and hissed with the muttered voices of the other searchers. She listened with half an ear, as she'd trained herself to. Probably something like being a cop, she guessed. You could pay no attention at all to the radio traffic and then instantly be aware when someone called *you*. And she was stalling. She knew it. No point in lying to herself when she already knew the truth.

Carla gave some serious thought to lying to *him*, though. After all, why should she tell him? She'd only known him a week. Plus, he was temporary. He'd be gone by the end of summer. It wasn't as if she had to bare her soul, here.

So why dredge it all up again?

Because it's already dredged, you idiot. Being here,

in the woods, on a search, had brought it all back more clearly than she'd allowed herself to remember it before. And judging by the look in his eyes, he wasn't going to let this go.

Nosy.

She smiled to herself. Hang around with the Candellanos long enough and you pick up some of their most irritating habits.

Nodding, she let her gaze drift from his. She'd tell him, but she wouldn't look at him while she did. She didn't want to see sympathy, or, worse yet, accusation in his eyes.

"It was two years ago. Up around Tahoe."

"Yeah?"

She scratched behind Abbey's ears and took just as much comfort from the action as the dog did.

"I was living up there then. A small town, sort of like Chandler. Surrounded by mountains and trees. I loved it." She pulled in a deep breath and let it go again. "My neighbors had two kids. A girl about three and a boy, Jamie. He was ten." She smiled as that dimpled face rose up in her mind. "He used to come over every day after school. He'd play with Abbey and ask me questions about my job and tell me about how he was going to be a search-and-rescue man when he grew up." *Oh God.* Carla swallowed hard again and lifted one hand to brush a tear away. "He was a Boy Scout, too. And one day, his troop got lost in the mountains." She shrugged. "Doesn't matter where. Mountains are mountains, I guess."

He didn't say anything and she realized he was a pretty gifted listener. Knew when to prod and when to shut the hell up and let the person talk. Although right now she desperately wished *someone* would interrupt. Would keep her from saying it all out loud. But there was no last-minute reprieve headed her way, so she went on.

"After the kids had been missing twelve hours, Searchers was called in." She shot him a quick look before returning her gaze to Abbey's understanding eyes. "That's the company I—*we* used to work for. We'd been all over the world together. Going from one disaster area to the next. Working in mud slides and snow, complete with avalanches and earthquake rubble, terrorist attacks, and even once the aftermath of a volcano eruption."

"Sounds dangerous."

"It can be." She shrugged that off, though, as if it didn't mean anything at all. But he felt a wild mixture of admiration and fear. For her. She'd been in some very hairy places, and yet she dismissed it all with a casual shrug. She had strength. Maybe more than she knew.

Jackson watched her as she seemed to pull further away from him and this place, spiraling down into her memories.

"Anyway," she said, continuing in a voice so soft, it was nearly lost in the gentle wind rippling through the trees, "by the time Searchers arrived, Abbey and I were already looking for the kids." She shot him a quick look. "It was Jamie, you know? I couldn't wait. I had to find him. God, his parents were frantic—but so sure that I'd find him. Bring him home. They knew I—" Her breath caught again. "They knew I loved him, so they were counting on me. And it should have been a simple search. Half the town had turned out to help."

"Like today."

"Yeah." She never lifted her gaze from the dog, but he knew she was looking at something else. Something only she could see. Pain seemed to radiate from her—like the waves of heat that pulsed off a road baking under a desert sun.

"Those of us with dogs were each given a shirt that belonged to one of the missing boys. I had Jamie's." She sighed a little, remembering. "Abbey and I worked the mountain, just as we always had. We picked up scents that dead-ended. We followed trails that seemed to go nowhere. Hours passed." A brief gust of wind kicked up, tousled her curls, then slipped away again. "And still, I figured it would turn out all right. It was summer. Weather was good. The boys had already been lost overnight, but with the mild weather . . ."

She paused and the static from the radio bristled in the air.

"It should have been easy. Well," she added, "comparatively speaking anyway." She shook her head and the black curls about her face trembled. "But it wasn't. Abbey wasn't getting a good scent. We heard on the radio as the other boys were located, one by one. But still, Jamie was out there somewhere. Missing. Scared. And we couldn't find him."

Jackson knew what was coming. Regret pooled inside him. He shouldn't have asked. Shouldn't have prodded her into reliving this. He could see what it was costing her, but now he wasn't sure if asking her to stop would be the right thing to do, either. Damn it, he knew what it was to live with guilt. To wonder about the what ifs. *What if I'd done that differently? What if*

I'd taken a right turn instead of a left? What if I'd been driving the car that day?

Quickly, though, he closed a mental door on those questions. This wasn't about him.

"I should have been able to find him," she murmured, more to herself than to him. "I know he must have been waiting for me—hoping to see Abbey and me come walking up. And I *couldn't* find him." Carla lifted her gaze and looked directly into Jackson's and he felt the impact of her pain slam into him. "None of it should have happened, damn it. He was only *ten*. They were on a camp-out. A fun trip with his buddies that turned into a nightmare."

"Carla . . ." He reached for her, but she shook her head and inched back.

Her fingers curled around Abbey's collar and she hung on as if depending on that grip to keep herself steady. "Oh, Jamie must have been so scared. He kept moving. Even though we always talked about what people did wrong when they were lost. He knew he should stay in one place, but he walked. And walked. Trying to find his way out. His way *home*." A single tear trickled down her cheek, but he didn't think she realized it. "Abbey and I covered miles that day. And at every turn, I told myself, This time. We'll find him here. Or here. Or here." She shook her head again. "But we didn't. Not until much later."

"What happened?" he asked when she was silent for so long, he wasn't sure she was even aware of his presence anymore.

She turned her head to look at him and he saw those beautiful brown eyes of hers shimmering with tears that he somehow knew were always near the surface. Something inside him shifted, tightened, and the instinct to protect reared up within him again. He wanted to hold her. To soothe her tears and tell her everything would be all right. Which was ridiculous, since he knew by looking at her that *nothing* was all right.

She sucked in a breath, released it in a rush, and said, "Just at nightfall we found him." She looked away again and stared off into the shadowy forest, as if it was just too much to meet his gaze. "It wasn't a big creek," she said, her voice soft, wondering. "Nothing more than a stream, really. The kind you go wading in on a warm summer's day. Something a kid would leap over without a second thought." She cleared her throat, uncurled her fingers from Abbey's collar, and took another deep breath. "But Jamie must have fallen. Hit his head on a rock." Cupping one hand across her mouth, as if she could keep the words from being said even as she spoke them, she finished. "He fell face-first into that damn creek and he drowned. In a couple of inches of water."

"Jesus." In a quick flash, Jackson felt pity for that kid and what his family must have suffered. But looking at the woman who'd tried so hard to save the boy, he also felt a wave of tenderness that surprised him with its strength. It had been a long time since he'd felt sorrier for someone else than he did for himself.

Lifting both hands, she scraped at her face with her palms, rubbing away the last of the tears. But she didn't quite succeed in wiping the pain out of her eyes. It still shone in those brown depths with a brilliant clarity. And he knew she lived with that memory every day. Despite the wiseass comments and the ready laughter, she harbored this dark knot of old pain with her wherever she went.

But then, everyone carried their own crosses, didn't they? It was just that some people made more noise about the size and weight of theirs than others did. Carla, on the other hand, spent most of her time trying to convince everyone around her that she didn't have a cross at all. Intriguing woman. One who could slide into a man's soul.

If a man *had* a soul.

"*He* didn't have anything to do with what happened."

"What?" He looked at her, found her gaze fixed on him, and told himself to get a grip. This sure as hell wasn't the time to go getting philosophical. "What?" he repeated.

"Jesus," she said. "God. He wasn't involved that day. That day it was just me, Abbey, and Jamie. That little boy needed me. Was counting on *me*. And I failed. All the times I'd saved strangers . . . people I didn't know, people I'd never see again. And the one time I desperately needed to succeed, to bring some-one safely home, I couldn't do it. He died on that mountain, when he should have been at home."

"It wasn't your fault." It came instinctively. Yet even as he said the words, he knew she wouldn't hear them. Hadn't people been saying the same damn thing to him for the last year? And he hadn't believed it any more than she would.

"Right." She nodded, stood up, and slung her back-pack over her shoulder. "Jamie's parents even said that to me, y'know? After the screams and the tears and the wailing, they thought of me. They knew what losing him did to me. And even in their pain, they tried to make it easier for me. But that only made it worse. I let him down. I let *them* down." She sucked in air and blew it out again. "Nobody's fault. Just a tragic accident," she said, in a singsong voice that mimicked everyone who'd ever said the words to her. "Sometimes these things happen. The Lord works in mysterious ways." She flipped her hair back from her face and gave him a long, steady look. "Jamie was *ten*. He liked baseball and jelly sandwiches. He loved Abbey and he trusted *me*. He was my friend. He hated girls yet doted on his baby sister. He was his parents' pride and joy. And he *died*. If I'd moved faster . . . worked it harder . . . found him just a little sooner . . . I *loved* him. And I couldn't save him because I just wasn't good enough."

"Carla—" Jackson stood up and faced her. Reaching out, he laid both hands on her shoulders and felt the tension coiled there. A part of him wished she'd kept quiet. Hadn't brought him closer. But another, stronger part wanted to somehow comfort her. And God knew he wasn't used to those kinds of impulses.

But she didn't give him a chance, anyway. She shrugged him off, gave him a smile, and said, "Glad you asked?"

"No."

"Well, that's honest." She sighed and glanced down. Abbey's head swept back and forth between them like she was watching a fascinating tennis match. "Can't blame you, though. Not a pretty story."

"It's not that." He reached for her again. But before he could actually touch her, he let his hand fall to his side. Probably not a good idea to touch her again just now. "I just . . . didn't mean to bring it all back." To make you feel so crappy, he added silently.

"It didn't have to come back," she said sadly. "It's always there."

Jackson nodded. Just as he'd thought. "I know what that's like."

She laughed shortly, but the sound carried no humor in it. "Right. Sure you do." She blew out a breath that ruffled the curls lying on her forehead. Then she gave him that smile that seemed to hit him a little harder every time he saw it. The fact that today he saw the grief behind it only added to the punch. "Okay," she announced, "self-pity party officially over."

Carla wanted to get moving. Get back to the search. Heck, anything was better than standing here, watching him watch her and wondering what he was thinking. For chrissakes. What had *she* been thinking? Why did she have to go and open her big mouth?

Because you're a Candellano and it's genetically impossible to keep your mouth closed.

Plus, she was female. If pushed or offered the slightest bit of encouragement, a woman will confess her deepest, darkest secrets. A man, on the other hand, was somehow able to hold back—at least until after sex. At which point, men did one of two things. They either opened up and shared, or they ran for the hills and all you saw of them was the soles of their feet.

Hmm.

Maybe they were on to something.

She snapped her fingers and Abbey jumped to her feet, muscles bunched and ready to work. She pushed her nose into Carla's thigh as if reminding her that the clock was running.

"Carla . . ."

"Hey, I'm okay. Honest." Embarrassed but okay. Usually she managed to keep memories of Jamie locked up tight inside her—at least until the dreams came. The dreams where she saved him. Where she found him in time and she could feel his tears on her neck and his sturdy arms wrapped around her shoulders. Every damn night, she saved him. She just hadn't been able to do it when it had mattered. "Don't know why I spilled my guts like that, but rest assured, that'll be the end of the spillage for today."

"You're back to your old self, aren't you?"

"Damn straight." Pulling the walkie-talkie from her belt, she held up a hand for silence, then punched the button. "Tony?"

A second or two of static, then, "Carla. Find anything?"

"Not yet." She turned her head and gave a good look around. "We're about a mile east of the lake at Castle Rock. We'll check out the rest of the woods here, then circle back around."

"Got it."

Carla clipped the radio back into place on her hip.

"What do we do now?"

"Now," she said, "we work." And try to forget, for a little while at least, that some sort of bond had been formed between them, here in the forest. It wasn't something she'd been expecting, and trying to deal with what it meant right now would be useless. Better to work. Looking down at Abbey, she whispered, "Find."

And they were on the run again.

Tony scanned the map in his hands for the dozenth time in twenty minutes, then lifted his gaze to the blue sky. At least they had several more hours of daylight left. With any luck, they'd find the man and be out of here by suppertime.

Of course, lately, luck was in short supply.

He yanked off his hat, swiped the back of his hand across his forehead, then jammed that hat back on again.

It was days like this that made him wish he'd become—hell, *anything* other than the sheriff. Even Nick's job looked good to him right now. And ordinarily he wouldn't have considered being attacked by three-hundred-pound middle linebackers a wise career choice.

"Sheriff?" his deputy's voice came over the radio, clouded by a burst of static.

Tony snatched up the handheld, walked off a few paces, and turned in a tight circle until the interference eased up. "Yeah, Dave. What've you got?"

"Our missing guy. Walked out of the woods, went right up to Joe Hauser, and asked for a scotch, straight up." Laughter rang in his tone and Tony couldn't blame him. It had been a long day.

"Good news." Hell, best news he'd had in a while. He looked around the busy base camp they'd set up and mentally started closing up shop. "Call everyone in and let's pack this up."

"You got it, Sheriff. We ought to have him back to you inside a half hour."

When he signed off, Tony stared at the radio for a long minute before punching it up again to contact his sister.

"Carla?"

"What's up?"

"We found our man."

"How is he?"

Tony winced at the question, asked in a breathless, worried voice. Okay, he knew what he'd asked of Carla to come out and join the search. She never talked about what had happened two years ago. But then, with family, she didn't have to, did she? They all knew what losing that boy had cost her.

Still, seeing her lock herself away was driving Mama nuts—which meant everybody suffered.

"Alive," he answered, "and looking for a bartender."

What might have been laughter rustled through the radio and he smiled. "You okay?"

"Yeah. I'm good. So. I'll see you at Mama's."

"What?" He stared at the radio, as if it could explain exactly why in the hell he'd be going to his mother's house after the day he'd had.

"It's Sunday."

"Shit."

Jackson had never had a meal quite like this one before. Noise rocketed around the dining room, bouncing off the soft yellow walls lined with china cabinets that were stuffed with glassware and what looked to be the world's largest collection of bells. The oak table they sat at was old, but the wood fairly gleamed from years of careful polishing. From the kitchen came scents that would have graced any four-star restaurant, and blasting in from the living room came the practiced voice of a professional announcer calling the play-by-play on a baseball game.

The whole Candellano clan was gathered around that table and Jackson still wasn't sure why *he* was there.

All he knew for certain was, he'd entered Angela Candellano's orbit and been sucked in. He glanced up as she bustled in and out of the room, carrying bowls of fresh garlic bread and steaming pots of spaghetti sauce that smelled good enough to make him grateful for the invitation to dinner.

The noise level, though, was incredible. There was no give-and-take conversation. This was a free-for-all. Every Candellano talked at the same time, as if they were afraid they wouldn't get a chance otherwise. Even the toddler, Tina, was banging her spoon on her high chair and babbling loud enough to prove she belonged. The shouting, he guessed, was a by-product. You had to shout just to be heard.

"The hospital says the guy checked out fine."

"It's good you found him," Mama said, passing by Tony and giving him a loving pat on the shoulder.

"Wasn't me," he admitted. "The man just walked out."

Paul pulled a small calculator from his shirt pocket. "Do you know what the odds of that were?"

"Don't care," Tony told him. "It's over."

"Astronomical," Paul muttered, punching in a few more numbers.

Tony looked at Nick. "So are you going to start this season? Half the town's asked me how you think the Saints are gonna do this season."

Nick scowled and rubbed his knee. "Don't know about starting, but the team looks good."

"Your leg," Mama asked. "It still hurts?"

"I'm fine."

"The hero of Chandler speaks," Paul said with a grin.

"Anyone want iced tea?"

"Mama," Carla ordered, "sit down already and eat."

The older woman waved her off. "In a minute. More pasta?" she asked, strolling around the edge of the table like a fussy waitress, making sure everyone had everything they wanted even before they wanted it. She laid one hand on Jackson's shoulder. "You should eat. Have a sausage. You're too thin."

"According to Mama," Paul told him, pushing his glasses higher on the bridge of his nose, "you have to eat twice your body weight daily just to keep from wasting away."

"You should eat more, talk less. And put your little toy away," Mama told him before turning back to Jackson. "So, you're a lawyer?"

"Yes, ma'am."

"Good manners," she said, beaming at him like he was a child winning a spelling bee. "That's nice."

"Mama . . ."

She frowned at Carla. "What? I say something nice

and I'm in trouble?" Without waiting for an answer, she asked Jackson, "You make a good living?"

"Oh, for God's sake," Carla muttered.

"Uh . . . yes. I do fine." Jackson glanced around the table, noticing that all eyes were on him now, and he suddenly felt like a dancing bear.

"Good, good." Mama nodded, smiling. "So, Wyatt. Is that Italian?"

"I don't think so." Where was this going? he wondered, and had the uncomfortable feeling he was being interviewed for a job.

"That's a shame." She clucked her tongue.

"*Lots* of people aren't Italian, Mama." Paul said it, then ducked his head when his mother shot him a look.

"Catholic?" she asked.

"Don't answer that," Carla told him.

Stunned, Jackson just stared at the older woman, but one of Carla's brothers saved him from answering.

"Jesus, Mama," Nick teased, "why don't you check his teeth while you're at it, too?"

"Was I talking to you?" she asked, then frowned when she saw Nick shift uncomfortably on the chair. "You all right, Nicky?"

"I'm *fine.*"

"Is it your knee?" Carla leaned over the table toward him.

"No, it's not my knee."

"Thought the knee was better." His twin sounded more curious than worried.

"It *is* better!" Nick shouted. "Jesus, can't a man move around a little without everybody thinking something's up?"

"I was wondering the same thing myself," Tony muttered, and threw a glance at his wife. Beth, though, didn't take the bait, just kept her gaze fixed on her untouched plate of pasta.

But Carla heard him and Jackson saw the glare she shot her older brother just before she kicked him.

"Hey!" Tony looked at her. "What was that for?"

"Gee," Carla said, blinking innocently, "was that your knee? I'm *so* sorry."

Beth smiled faintly, but Tony grumbled a minute or two before scooting his chair farther away from his sister.

Nuts, Jackson thought. The whole family was crazy. In a weird, warm, wonderful sort of way. He wondered what it must have been like growing up in this house. With these people, who so clearly loved one another despite the shouts and carrying-on.

Then he looked down at his daughter, sitting on the chair beside him. A smile curved her mouth as she happily ate up every bit of the pasta in front of her. Naturally, Abbey was right beside the little girl, head in her lap, soulful brown eyes locked on Reese's fork, hoping for a spill.

Reese had spent the day here, with Angela, baking cookies. Probably eating half of what she'd made. But she was happy. Relaxed.

For the first time in as long as he could remember, Jackson felt the tension that had become a part of him begin to slip away. Carla glanced at him and gave him that smile again.

And this time, he gave it right back to her.

CHAPTER EIGHT

"Congratulations," Carla said, glancing up at him as they walked across the lawn an hour later. "You survived Sunday dinner."

"It was good."

"Well, sure it was good. The food is your reward for living through the rest of it."

He shook his head. "Your family is a little . . ."

"Nuts?" she supplied.

"Overwhelming, I was going to say."

"Ah, that polite thing, that was so popular with my mother again."

Reese, half-asleep, cuddled in close, wrapped her arms around Jackson's neck, and rested her head on his shoulder. With the warm, solid weight of his child pressed against him, Jackson kept his steps slow and even and tried to avoid tripping on Abbey as she walked right in front of him and Carla.

Above them, the night sky was star-swept, points of light glittering in the blackness. An almost full moon outshone the stars, though, and laid silver-cast shadows across the yard. The quiet was damn near eerie. He still wasn't used to it.

Hell, he was accustomed to the wail of sirens, the shriek of car alarms, and even the occasional shout from one of his neighbors down the hall. Back home, the silence in their apartment was almost a relief—escape from the noise of the outside world. But here . . . the utter stillness only emphasized his daughter's muteness.

And made him loathe the idea of returning to that empty house. Especially after having been surrounded by Candellanos all evening.

To get his mind off the solitude waiting for him, he spoke up. "Your mother liked me."

She chuckled. "Don't take it so personally. Mama's got her eye out for husband material."

"Well," he said, "she's a great cook."

Carla stopped dead, knocked the heel of her hand against her right ear, and stared up at him. "Humor? Is my hearing okay? Was that actually a smartass remark?"

A smile twitched at the corner of his mouth, but Jackson managed to hold it in. "Hey, I've been hanging around with you. Must be contagious."

"Wow. Another one." She grinned up at him, and even in the soft moonlight, she was absolutely amazing-looking. Her black curls flew and danced about her face and she pushed them back with an impatient hand—that he suddenly wanted to grab and cling to. A flash of desire that he was becoming all too familiar with rushed through him again and he called himself an idiot. Hell, he was *carrying* his sleeping daughter, for God's sake.

"Actually," Carla was saying, "Mama's trying to fix me up and the pickings around here are pretty slim. Until you showed up, her prime prospect was Frank Pezzini."

Stunned, Jackson just stared at her. "You mean the guy at the grocery store? The butcher?"

"That's Fabulous Frank."

"Jesus."

"Pretty much my reaction."

"So, do you want one?" he asked a moment later, when they'd started walking again.

"One what?"

"Husband."

"Is that an offer?"

"No."

She laughed shortly and he wondered if she found everything so damn funny. Then he remembered that just a few hours ago she was breaking his heart by stoically accepting the complete blame for the loss of a child. No, she wasn't all laughs. But she damn sure knew how to compartmentalize her life.

"Just checking," she assured him before saying, "and to answer your question . . . no. Much to Mama's everlasting frustration, I'm *not* in the market for a husband, thanks."

Now that should make him feel better. But for some reason, it didn't. His own marriage had been a disaster, but maybe the cards had been stacked against him right from the beginning. After all, what had he known about family? Someone like Carla, on the other hand, should have every reason to want what she'd grown up with.

If he'd come from the kind of family she'd known, maybe lots of things in his life would have been different. He shifted Reese into a better position, enjoyed her sigh of warm breath on his neck, and asked, "Any particular reason why?"

Carla shrugged and bent down quickly to pluck a blade of grass from the lawn. As they walked, she shredded the single blade with a concentrated effort.

"Well, I'm lousy company in the morning—before coffee, that is."

"I noticed."

"Gee, thanks." She shook her head, lifted her gaze to study the sky briefly, and suggested, "I don't play well with others?"

He smiled but shook his head. "Not buying that one."

"No, huh?" Fingers busy, she thought for a minute or two. "Okay, I confess. I was almost married, once."

"What happened?"

She tossed the remnant of grass aside, tucked her hands into her jeans pockets. "He decided to go back to his former fiancée instead."

"Busy guy."

"Yeah." She looked up at him. "But he was polite, too. Sent me an invitation to his wedding."

"Thoughtful."

"Oh, yeah. I declined."

"Don't blame you."

"Passed on the baby shower invite, too."

"What an idiot."

Clearly offended, she demanded, "Why would I want to go to his wife's baby shower?"

"Not *you* idiot. *Him* idiot."

"Ahh . . . in that case, you may continue to live."

"Good to know." They were close now to her driveway. Too close. He wasn't really ready to say good night yet. So he kept talking. "I'm guessing the end of your engagement didn't go over well with your mother?"

She laughed and God, he loved the sound of it. Even Reese didn't seem to mind, since she slept on, completely comfortable in his arms.

"Being a good mother, her first instinct was to go kill him for me."

"Understandable." Hell, Jackson wouldn't mind taking a punch at the guy himself. No matter how she was making light of it, he knew that the man's betrayal must have cut at her. She was going to marry the man, for chrissakes. She must have loved him.

"But, when she calmed down, she went into a period of mourning eclipsed only by the time Nick first broke it to her that he didn't want to become a priest." Carla stopped at the edge of her drive and tipped her head back to stare up at him. "And she's been on a search for a replacement fiancé ever since."

"Determined woman."

"Oh, you have no idea." But there was a smile in her voice when she spoke. And that's what he responded to.

"Must be nice."

"What?"

"Being loved like that."

"I always sort of took it for granted," she admitted.

"But yes, it is. Annoying sometimes, too. Your family isn't close?"

He hitched Reese a little higher in his arms and laid a protective hand against the small of her back. "She's my family."

Carla studied his features in the soft, pale light and wondered what had put the flash of pain in his eyes. It was brief. Hardly noticeable. And if she hadn't already been watching him closely, she probably would have missed it.

As hard as it was to deal with her family at times, she couldn't imagine having a life without them. Just as she couldn't imagine what Jackson's life was like. The silence. With only him and Reese in the house, the quiet must be crushing.

"My folks died when I was a kid," he said, his voice a soft rumble that whispered through the air and seemed to attack the hairs at the back of her neck. "Went into the system then and got bounced around until I was eighteen."

She didn't know what to say. *I'm sorry* didn't seem appropriate.

"I know what you're thinking, and don't worry about it. It was a long time ago."

Distance. They might be standing right next to each other, but there was a distance in his voice that clearly said, Don't go there. So she didn't.

Instead, she glanced up the drive toward her own house, where the front porch light shone like a lighthouse standing on a rocky shore. Ordinarily, after dinner with the Candellanos, she'd be more than ready to crawl into her own nest and veg out with Abbey. The dog, as if reading her mind, trotted halfway up the gravel drive, turned around to face Carla, and sat down, head cocked as she waited.

Tonight, though, Carla wasn't as eager as usual to be by herself. Jackson seemed to be feeling the same way, since he made no move to start walking again.

"You were really impressive today," he said finally, just when she thought they were going to stand in the moonlight in silence forever.

"What?"

"You and Abbey. The way you worked together." He paused and her stomach rolled over as his gaze locked with hers. "It was amazing. Especially knowing why you didn't want to be out there."

Okay. Now she was ready to go inside. She didn't want to talk about that again. In fact, she'd like to pretend she hadn't told him about it in the first place. She still didn't understand exactly *why* she'd told him. Sure, it had felt good at the time, unloading those feelings. Hearing herself talk about it for the first time. But that didn't change the outcome. And it didn't change how she felt about it.

Late at night, when she couldn't sleep, she knew that boy's face would still swim to the surface of her mind. She'd still see his parents, clinging together, his mother weeping, his father stoically trying to bear the burden no one should have to carry.

That wouldn't change. Would *never* change.

She shifted slightly and the soles of her boots scraped across the asphalt, sounding like a dry nervous cough.

"We didn't find the guy, remember?"

"You looked."

She'd looked for the boy once, too. For all the good it had done anyone.

"Only because Tony bullied me into it." And at the thought of Tony came the reminder that she still had to get to the bottom of what was going on with him. Good, she told herself. Focus on your idiot brother. Much better.

"Bullshit."

"Excuse me?"

He shook his head as he watched her. "I saw your face when your brother showed up wanting your help. You said you didn't want to go. But everything inside you was *eager* to go." He reached out to touch her and she almost held her breath, waiting for the brush of his hand against her cheek. But he stopped short, disappointing them both. "I saw your face. Your eyes. It was all there, plain for anyone to see."

"No," she argued, even though she remembered clearly that rush of adrenaline. That had just been instinct. Like a firehouse dog reacting to the sound of the fire alarm. "I—"

"Carla," he interrupted, "it's what you do. It's who you are."

"Not anymore." It used to be. It used to be everything to her. But times change. People change. She wasn't that girl anymore. She wasn't wide-eyed and filled with the conviction that she could make a difference. She couldn't cling to a ratty thread of hope anymore. It had frayed in her grasp when she'd needed it most, and there was no getting it back.

"Who're you trying to convince?" he asked. "Me? Or you?"

A spurt of irritation flickered up inside her, then flattened out again. She tossed her hair back from her face and met his gaze squarely. "I thought you were a lawyer, not a shrink."

He stiffened. "You don't have to be a shrink to see the obvious."

"Really?" she countered. "Good at that, are you? Seeing the obvious?" Carla didn't wait for him to answer before adding, "Then maybe you can see that I don't want to talk about this."

"Prefer to ignore it and hide?"

She looked up at him and gave a short, harsh laugh. "Hello, Pot? This is Kettle. You're black."

"What's that supposed to mean?"

Maybe she shouldn't have said anything, but she was damn tired of everyone and their uncles offering her advice on how to "get over it." So she did what any good Candellano would do when attacked.

She fired back.

"I mean, you've got a helluva nerve accusing me of hiding. Keeping your daughter tucked away isn't the key to bringing her back into the world."

Fury pulsed inside him. Carla could almost feel the heat of it. Okay, gloves were off now. This could get ugly. A muscle in his jaw twitched and he planted his feet wide apart, as if slipping into a battle stance. She saw in his face just how much he wanted to yell. But his sleeping daughter apparently gave him enough reason to keep his voice low. As if to calm himself as much as comfort his sleeping child, he stroked Reese's back in long protective strokes.

"You don't know anything about my daughter. Or me."

"You don't know me, either," she pointed out, "but that didn't stop you from offering advice I didn't want."

"That's different."

"Of course it is," she muttered. "You're a *guy*." She wondered idly where all of the nice warm fuzzies had gotten to. How had their friendly conversation dissolved into this?

For the first time in two years, she'd been actually enjoying herself. Talking with Jackson did as much for her bruised heart as it did for her hormones. But there was a wall separating them that neither of them was willing—or able, obviously—to cross.

"Look," she said abruptly, interrupting the war with what she hoped would be accepted as a truce. "We had a good day. Let's leave it at that, okay?"

And before he could respond one way or the other, Carla stepped around him and headed up the drive. Abbey leaped to her feet and bounded toward the house, trusting that Carla would be following. Her footsteps crunched on the gravel drive as she walked away, feeling considerably lonelier than she had been only a few minutes ago. She felt his gaze locked on her back, and a part of her burned with the heat of his stare.

Hormones, she told herself.

That's all it was.

Hormones.

Lust. Pure and simple.

In all its glory.

"Carla?"

His voice, low and intimate, stopped her. She steeled herself, then looked back at him over her shoulder. He and his daughter were spotlighted in the moonlight, standing as he was, between the patches of shade cast by the nearby trees. They looked so alone that a twinge pinged around Carla's heart before she could tell herself that it didn't matter to her. That they—*he* was only a summer neighbor. A temporary blip on her radar screen.

Yeah, right.

"What?"

"You were right, you know."

"Ah," she said, loving the sound of those words, "the way to a woman's heart." She smiled in spite of the turmoil within. "Right about what?"

"It *was* a good day."

Then he smiled a little sadly, walked off, and the two of them disappeared into the shadows.

Her morning ritual was ruined.

And it was all his fault.

Grumbling, Carla pulled another Oreo out of the bag, dipped it into her coffee, and took a bite. Abbey looked up at her, hopeful as always.

"Well, *you* still love me, anyway." Carla popped the last of her cookie into her mouth, then picked up a dog biscuit and flipped it to the golden. Abbey caught it midflip and crunched contentedly. "Of course, do you love me for my wonderful self, or for my biscuits?" The dog just stared at her. "Never mind," Carla said. "Don't answer that."

Then her gaze went directly back to the view that had now effectively ruined her little wake-up ritual.

Jackson's house.

Funny, but she no longer thought of it as the Garvey place. Now it was his. And not just for the duration of the summer, either. Carla had the distinct feeling that from now on she would be looking at that house and wondering what he and Reese were doing. What *he* was doing. Hell, admit it.

She'd be wondering *who* he was doing.

Her body reacted to that thought as she'd known it would. Getting all warm and soft in places that had gone too long *without* being warm and soft. For all the good it was going to do her.

A hell of a thing, she thought. Being raring to cha-cha, so to speak, and having no one to cha-cha with. And dancing alone didn't sound like much fun.

She propped her feet on the railing in front of her and took another long sip of coffee. The familiar swirl and rush of caffeine buzzed through her system, opening her eyes and shouting, *Wake up!* at her brain.

Shaking her head, she looked down at Abbey and said, "You wouldn't think it would be so hard to wake up if you never really slept."

Abbey closed her eyes at that, obviously unmoved by Carla's predicament.

"Well, sure. *You* can sleep. You don't have one brother cheating on his wife and another brother hiding something about his medical condition." But even as she said the words, she knew it for the lie it was. Okay, fine. She was worried about her brothers. And she was currently hatching a plan to get to the bottom of Tony's trouble. But it wasn't thoughts of her brothers that had kept her up all night.

"Nope. It was *him*. Mr. Charm. Or lack thereof." Her gaze locked on the silent house across the way from her as if she could see through the wood siding and straight into Jackson's heart. Her dreams had been filled with him. The way he'd been earlier yesterday. When he'd listened to her and sympathized without pitying. When he'd touched her and made her want more. When he'd smiled and she'd read the shine of want in his eyes.

And while she was willing to admit that dreams of Jackson Wyatt were certainly better than nightmares about failing Jamie, neither of those options made for good sleeping.

So she supposed it was a measure of just how on edge she was that when the phone rang she reacted with gratitude rather than the snarl she would usually have felt.

Stepping over the dog, she hurried across the porch, coffee cup in hand, opened the front door, and snatched up the receiver on the second ring.

"Hello?"

"Carla . . ." A soft, feminine voice, filled with tears. "It's . . . Beth. . . ."

"Beth, are you okay?"

"No. Can I come . . . over?"

The little gaps between her words were filled with half-sobs that told Carla her sister-in-law was crying. Which meant Tony was still being an idiot.

"Of course you can come over," she said, her hand tightening on the receiver as if it were Tony's neck. "I'll put fresh coffee on."

When Beth hung up a moment later, Carla just stared at the silent phone for a long minute. *Oh, man.* Her back teeth ground together and every muscle in her body tightened into fighting stance.

Okay. Here was the solution to her current misery. Instead of concentrating on her own problems, she'd focus on someone else's. She'd get details from Beth, then hunt Tony down like the dog he was and give him both barrels.

That was sure to cheer her right up.

CHAPTER NINE

"You're through." The doctor's words were simple. Final.

Morning sunlight sifted through the tinted windows, making the view of downtown San Francisco look as though it were encased in some weird shaded fog. Which was just how Nick Candellano felt. As if his brain were shrouded in mist. He'd heard the other man's words; they just weren't completely registering.

Because he didn't want them to.

But he couldn't ignore the situation forever.

Nick looked up at his doctor and saw something in the man's eyes he didn't want to see. Pity. Well, shit. A cold, hard knot formed in his guts and he fought to keep it from spreading. Hell of a way to start off a morning. He scraped one hand along the back of his neck and stalled for time. Time to adjust to the reality that was about to deliver a sucker punch to his life. He'd known this was coming, though, so it really wasn't a sucker punch, was it? More like a body slam.

Somehow he'd just known it. His knee didn't feel a hundred percent, despite the physical therapy.

Still, it was a hard thing to face. Deliberately misunderstanding the man, Nick gave him a winning smile and said, "Through, you said. For this season, right?"

"For good, if you're smart." The orthopedic surgeon shook his head, took a seat behind his desk, and folded his hands atop the file folder that contained Nick's life. "Look, Nick, your knee, to put it simply, is more plastic than bone, now. Take a hit the wrong way and you're in serious trouble. You blow it out again and best-case scenario, you're looking at using a cane for the rest of your life."

Unconsciously Nick reached down and rubbed his kneecap protectively. It felt okay at the moment. *Sure. While you're sitting. What about running downfield with some three-hundred-pound maniac chasing you?* Different story. Hell, he'd been taking hits on the field since junior high. But the thought of taking another hit to a knee that had already been blown out was enough to make him cringe. And a man who didn't want to be tackled had no business being on a football field.

But Christ, he'd been playing to a crowd since Pop Warner football. How would he live without that? Without all of it? The sound of applause, the jolt of excitement he got every damn time he walked into a football stadium, the slaps on the back and the looks of pride that followed him whenever he went home.

Man, just listen to yourself.

Damn, but he was a petty man.

Nick's gaze settled on the doctor's face and he realized there was more the other man wasn't saying. Hell, what else was there? But he had to know all of it. It was like staring at a traffic accident. You didn't really want to see anything, but you just couldn't stop yourself from looking. "And worst-case?"

"Wheelchair."

Instantly an image of himself, freewheeling around Chandler, snarling at people who had the nerve to remind him of his heydays, kids throwing sticks into the spokes of his chair, filled his mind. Hell.

Sinking back into the rich leather armchair opposite his doctor, Nick scraped both hands across his face, took a deep breath, and mentally said good-bye to professional football. Though he'd known this was coming eventually, it didn't make it any easier to swallow now that it had. On the other hand, he wasn't a kid anymore. He was thirty-two, right? He'd had a good career. Made a lot of money. Traveled. And running backs didn't usually have too long a life span anyway.

The knot in his guts twisted a little tighter. He could paint this any way he wanted. Bottom line, though . . . somebody'd just pulled the rug out from under his life. And he didn't have a clue as to what he'd do next.

Looking at the doctor, he said, more to himself than the other man, "So. What exactly does a pro ballplayer do when he can't play ball?"

Beth sat at the kitchen table, wadded up her third Kleenex, and tossed it at the trash can. Neat. Even in her misery, Beth's personality shone through. She had always been a woman who believed in a place for everything and everything in its place.

Unlike Carla, who believed that wherever something landed, that obviously was its place.

"So tell me," Carla said, and pushed the cookie bag closer to her sister-in-law.

"We had a horrible fight last night." Then she thought about that for a minute, raised teary eyes to look at Carla, and amended, "Well, *I* had a horrible fight. Tony just stood there. He wouldn't even yell at me."

A bad sign.

When an Italian didn't yell, that was not good.

Carla sat back in her chair and folded her arms across her middle. Fingers plucking at the material of her sweatshirt, she kept quiet, with difficulty, and waited for Beth to continue. It didn't take long.

"I told him I wanted to know where he was going three nights a week." She snagged a cookie, took a bite, chewed, and swallowed. "Told him that I wasn't going to let him make a fool out of me."

"All good," Carla assured her.

"Yes, but he didn't say anything." She tossed the cookie to the table, jumped up from her chair, and paced the kitchen. The heels of her sandals clicked furiously on the linoleum. "Nothing important, anyway."

"What *did* he say, exactly?"

"He said I should trust him."

"Ah, the standard return-fire volley."

"What?"

"Never mind. Anything else?"

Beth pushed one hand through her auburn hair, and when that hair then fell back into place perfectly, Carla felt an inward sigh of admiration.

"He said he loved me, but he wasn't going to explain himself. That he shouldn't have to."

"Oh, that's great." Carla shook her head and sat forward again, leaning her forearms on the table. "And if it was *you* taking off three times a week, he wouldn't ask questions? He'd just trust you? Not expect an explanation?"

"That's what *I* said."

"Of course you did!" Carla nearly shouted. "It's logical. Reasonable."

Beth came to a stop beside the sink. Curling her fingers around the edge of the counter, she held on tightly, her knuckles whitening, as if her grip on that chipped Formica was the only thing holding her on to the planet. She stared out the window at the yapping puppies and said quietly, "Then he left."

Carla simmered quietly inside. Looking at the other woman's pain was enough to make her want to strangle the big brother she'd always loved so much. How could he be such an idiot? And what was she going to do about it?

The phone rang and Carla jumped, glaring at it. Now was not a good time. Her sister-in-law turned and looked at the ringing phone as if it were a snake poised to leap across the room and sink its fangs into her. Carla knew how she felt.

"God, I hate that thing. Just a minute, Beth. Whoever it is, I'll get rid of 'em." She stalked across the room, snatched up the receiver, and snapped, "What?"

"Carla? This is how you answer a phone?"

She sighed and turned around, shrugging helplessly at Beth. "Hi, Mama."

Beth's eyes went wide and she shook her head, pointing at her own chest. Thankfully, Carla was an expert at desperate pantomime. Beth didn't want Mama knowing she was there.

"Was that a sigh?" her mother's voice demanded.

"What?"

"You sighed. I heard you."

"Ears like a hawk," Carla muttered.

"What was that?"

"Nothing." She pushed one hand through her hair. "What's up, Mama?"

"Is Beth there? I thought I saw her car."

"Beth?" Carla shot the other woman a look and winced as she shrugged and said, "Yes. Beth's here."

Her sister-in-law threw both hands wide and looked toward heaven for help. Carla could have told her from experience that it wasn't coming. The only one "up there" who would be interested in helping any of them was Papa—and he was too busy enjoying the distance between him and Mama to leap into the fray.

"I'm coming over to see the baby."

"What?" Carla shook her head and reminded herself to pay attention. When talking to Mama, it paid to have all your marbles lined up straight. If her mother showed up and saw Beth crying, there'd be no stopping her from jumping in and running down to the sheriff's office to slap Tony upside the head. Which wasn't altogether a bad idea, she told herself. But before she brought in the big guns, she wanted to know exactly what was going on. Key to that was stopping Mama.

"No," she said quickly, "Tina's not here. She's with—" Carla looked to Beth.

"Debbie," the other woman muttered.

"She's with Debbie."

"That teenager with the headphones?" Mama's voice went up a notch. "All the time she's listening to singers. How can she hear Tina if she cries?"

Carla sighed again.

"I heard that."

Carla's forehead hit the wall. "Mama, Tina's fine. I'm fine. Beth's fine."

Her mother sniffed. "So fine then."

Great. She had one woman in her kitchen, crying and another woman on the phone, offended. Well, if she had to pick one to deal with at a time, and she definitely had to choose, she'd pick the one standing in front of her.

"Did you want something, Mama?"

"I wanted to tell you I like your young man."

Instantly worries about Beth slipped to second place in her mind as Carla saw where her mother was headed. "He's not my 'young man.' Heck, he's not a young man, period."

"He's too old for you?"

"I didn't say that, I—"

"It's because he has a child you don't want him?"

"Of course not." Insulted, Carla stood up straighter and tightened her grip on the phone. "Reese is a sweetheart."

"So why don't you like him?"

"I *do* like him—" Carla shot a glance at Beth and didn't know whether to scream or be grateful. For the first time since walking in the front door, the other woman was smiling. All it took was Carla being tortured to ease Beth's misery.

"Good. I'm having him over for dinner tomorrow night. You should come."

"Mama, don't invite him for dinner." She reached up and rubbed her forehead, but it was like trying to fight off a nuclear missile attack with a fly swatter.

"He has to eat."

"Not with me."

"Why not with you? You need a man; he needs a woman. . . ."

Oh, for God's sake. "Well what're you waiting for? Book the church!"

Behind her, Beth snorted out a laugh.

"Don't be smart," Mama said.

"Mama, I don't need help finding a man. I just don't *want* one."

She heard her mother take in a long, protracted breath before releasing it again in a rush. "You told me you weren't gay."

Help me. Mentally, she screamed. But somehow, she managed to keep her voice steady and even as she said, "Mama, I have to go."

"Go where?"

Anywhere.

"Beth and I . . ."—her mind raced, then settled on an acceptable excuse— "are going shopping."

"Fine. So buy a nice dress to wear for dinner."

Her mother hung up before she could argue again, and a dial tone told Carla that Mama had won that round.

Carla actually winced as she pulled her fingers back from the phone. But problems with Mama could come later. Right at the moment, there were other pots to stir.

Turning around, she looked at Beth, and the other woman said, "Looks like we've all got our troubles."

"Don't even go there," Carla told her. "I'll worry about Mama later. Have you ever considered following Tony when he leaves?"

Beth shook her head fiercely and folded her arms across her summer yellow tank top. "No way. I don't want to *see* him with his girlfriend, the home-wrecking, husband-stealing bitch. It's hard enough to imagine it."

Carla guessed she could understand that. However, *she* wouldn't have any trouble at all facing down her brother and whatever female he was doing whatever he was doing with. "All right," she said, "*I'll* follow him. What nights does he go out and what time does he leave?"

Jackson stared down at his daughter's mutinous face and held back a groan of frustration. For such a little thing, she could really put a lot of disapproval into a glare.

"Reese baby," he tried again, still futilely hoping that a six-year-old could be reasoned with, "we can't go see the puppies."

Her little arms snapped across a narrow chest and her brow furrowed. She sighed heavily, unwound her arms, and mimed picking up a puppy and holding it to her face.

"I know you want to see them, but they're not *your* puppies. We can't just go over there anytime you want to."

She nodded so vigorously, one of her pink barrettes flew out of her hair and clattered on the wood floor.

"Fine. I know Carla said you could come and see the dogs, but—" He was talking to the back of her head as she walked toward the front door. Two long steps and he'd caught her. Taking her arm in a gentle grip, he turned her around to face him. Jackson went down on one knee so they were at eye level, and he studied those solemn but determined blue eyes so much like his own.

She was in there. God knows she had no trouble making her wishes—well, *demands*—known. Why wouldn't she talk to him? Why wouldn't she let him inside, beyond the walls that she'd built since that night a year ago?

Reese laid her small hands atop his and tugged. Jackson's heart ached, and not for the first time a thread of panic unwound inside him. If he couldn't reach her . . . if he couldn't get her to talk to him . . .

Resolutely he pushed those thoughts to the back of his mind where they simmered constantly, occasionally erupting into a froth of desperation. He *would* get through to her. He couldn't lose Reese. Time was running out. Just last night, his mother-in-law had called again, reminding him that if he didn't find a way into Reese's silence, she might be lost to him forever.

"Ah, baby, why won't you talk to Daddy?" he whispered, and he watched her eyes darken. Secrets lurked in their depths and he wished to God she'd let him help. Pain rippled through him. He sighed, swallowed, and said, "It's okay, Reese. It's okay. You can talk to me when you're ready. I'll be here. Always."

She nodded slowly, keeping her solemn gaze locked with his.

He only hoped she was ready to talk before the end of summer.

Reaching out, he swiped his fingers across the silky strands of blond hair lying across her forehead. She gave him a tentative smile as if she knew he was weakening. And, damn it, he was. That smile alone should have been enough to convince him to race his daughter across the road. A smile. Laughter. Hell, she'd reacted more to the puppies—and to Carla—than she had to anything else in the last year. So if he had any sense, Jackson told himself, he'd be using whatever he could in his campaign to bring his daughter back to him.

Even if that meant spending time with a woman who touched places inside him he'd thought were long dead.

Two hours later, Carla tried to reclaim some of her morning. But not even playing with the puppies could completely ease the turmoil raging in her brain.

When had her world shifted so out of control?

It was as if she were living in one of those little glass snow globes and some unseen giant hand had given it a good shake. And she didn't like it. She preferred things as they'd been for the last two years. Predictable. Safe.

But instead, she had her brothers worrying her, and a little girl with lost eyes, and the girl's father—who managed to light wildfires in her body with a glance. And then there was Mama. "She told me to buy a dress. I don't *do* dresses. And she knows it." She looked over at Abbey. "Why me?"

Disgusted, Carla plopped down onto the wet grass, drew her knees up to her chest, and focused her gaze on the puppies, splashing through the sprinkler. Bath time always began with a free-for-all. The puppies got to play and she got them all wet at once. One thing about goldens—they loved water. Despite her whirling thoughts, Carla laughed as the puppies tripped over their own feet and climbed all over one another and her to get closer to the water source. Abbey sat to one side, like a canine lifeguard, watching her children with a patient eye.

"Morning."

Her stomach jittered at the sound of his voice. Well, this is good, she thought. Nothing like having a gorgeous man see you when you're soaking wet and covered with muddy puppy paw prints. Sure. Why not? The morning was on a downhill slide already. Facing the inevitable, Carla glanced over her shoulder at Jackson and his daughter, right beside him.

Her heart did a weird little bump and roll and she wasn't sure if it was caffeine deprivation or the sight of Jackson Wyatt. She hadn't had nearly enough coffee this morning, but she had a feeling this particular reaction was pure Jackson. His dark hair was windblown and he wore a forest green T-shirt that clung to the chest that only last night had had a starring role in her dreams. His blue jeans were well worn and did amazing things for his long legs.

Blood pumped, breath staggered, heartbeat trip-hammered.

Oh, yeah. She was in fine shape. She blew out an unsteady breath and told her hormones to take a nap. Or a cold shower, whichever was quickest. A sense of self-preservation had her shifting her gaze to the child standing alongside him. Her little Scooby-Doo tennies practically danced in place in her eagerness to get to the puppies. Her hair still looked bedraggled, but there was a shine in her eyes that hadn't been there just two weeks ago.

Dogs. Little miracles, Carla thought. Without even trying, they gave love that reached out to whoever needed it most. And Reese obviously needed it. She still wasn't speaking, but since that first magical morning when she'd laughed, she'd seemed a little less shut off. A little more "connected."

No wonder her father was warming up to the idea of allowing the kid to play with the dogs—despite the fact that it meant spending time with Carla. Even he could see that the pups were making a difference in his daughter's life.

"Hello?" Jackson said. "Earth to Carla."

She blinked up at him, laughed, and said, "Sorry. Zoned out there for a minute."

Jackson didn't mind. Her distraction had given him an extra minute or two to simply look at her. No woman had a right to look that good wet and muddy. She smiled and her face lit up, her dark brown eyes sparkled, and something inside him yearned to be there in the mud beside her. Preferably naked.

Diane never would have rolled around in the grass with a cluster of puppies climbing all over her. But then, Carla Candellano was unlike any other woman he'd ever met.

Which was as good a reason as any for him to keep his distance. Yet here he stood. He couldn't seem to stay away from Carla any more than his daughter could bear to be separated from these puppies. And that probably explained why he'd agreed to have dinner with the Candellanos again tomorrow night. It was simply another excuse to be near Carla.

Reese tugged at his hand, trying for freedom, but he held her tight. "Your mother came over this morning."

Carla's chin hit her chest. "I know. She called. You know, you don't have to say yes when she comes up with one of her plans."

"I wanted to say yes. I like your mother." *And you,* he added silently.

"Oh."

Not exactly an enthusiastic response. A little uncomfortable now, he said, "Look, I'll understand if you're not exactly pleased to see me today, but I'd appreciate it if you'd let Reese and me help with"—he waved a hand at the puppy balancing itself against Reese's right leg—"whatever it is you're up to."

She flipped her hair behind her back. "It's bath day."

Reese pulled away and this time he let her go. He watched as she dropped to the ground and gathered the puppy in close, laughing as the tiny dog wriggled its wet little body against her.

"For them or you?" he asked, smiling at the sound of his daughter's laughter. But as he studied Carla, that smile faded. Her long dark curls were gathered into a ponytail on top of her head, but the ringlets hung wet and black down to her shoulders. Her T-shirt clung to her breasts, outlining the lace of her bra and molding itself to her figure. Her gray sweat shorts were soaking wet and those long legs of hers looked tan and luscious enough to fuel daydreams designed to taunt a man.

And that silver toe ring seemed to wink at him in the sunlight.

She pushed a long wet strand of hair out of her eyes and said, "I'll answer that, wise guy, as soon as you tell me why I wouldn't want to see you today."

One eyebrow lifted. "Well," he said, remembering how it had been when he and Diane had had their legendary arguments, "I figured after last night, you'd need some time to cool down." Diane had always needed *days*. And expensive presents.

Carla laughed. "Are you serious?" Shaking her head, she set the puppy aside and reached for the hose. Scrambling to her feet, she added, "For an Italian, yelling just means you're *alive*."

"Is that right?" Tension he didn't know he was carrying unwound inside him, and he smiled as he watched her waving the sprinkler end of the hose.

"Oh, yeah. So." She swung the sprinkler closer toward him and asked, "You alive?"

"You wouldn't." But he backed up a step just in case.

Carla laughed. "Never dare a Candellano."

He closed his eyes as the water hit his face.

That night, Carla prowled restlessly through her house. Her nuked half-eaten frozen dinner sat abandoned on the kitchen table and the TV sounded from the living room. Some game show host was snidely pronouncing her contestants Too Stupid to Live and Carla didn't care enough to go in there and shut the rude woman off.

She turned her back, leaned one hip against the counter, and stared at the kitchen. "I guess I could clean." Abbey cocked her head as if surprised by the suggestion. Carla laughed. "Yeah. I'm not *that* bored."

And it wasn't really boredom clawing at her anyway. It was something else. Something she hadn't felt in way too long. Heat pulsed inside her, warming her blood and clouding her mind. That had to be the reason why it suddenly seemed like such a good idea to run across the road to ask Jackson if she could borrow a cup of sex.

"Oh, man."

A knock at the door brought her upright. Hey. Maybe it's him. Maybe he's just as needy as she was right now. Maybe—"Hell, Carla," she muttered, stalking across the kitchen, "just open the door."

"Well, it's about time," the woman on the porch announced. "Is this any way to treat the bearer of coconut rum?"

"Stevie!" Stephanie Ryan, girlfriend extraordinaire. Tall, blond, with a great body, which was, just now, sporting a gorgeous Caribbean tan, she was the kind of woman other women usually hated, just on general principles. But Stevie was also the best kind of friend. She'd tell you exactly what you needed to hear. Whether you wanted to hear it or not. "You're back!"

"Well," she said, "to coin a phrase, *duh*."

Stevie leaned forward, gave her a quick kiss, then carried her bag of goodies straight through the house to the kitchen. "Hi, Ab. I brought you a present, too."

The big dog woofed, then snatched the squeaky rubber palm tree out of the air when Stevie tossed it to her.

"And what'd you bring me?" Carla asked, watching her friend pull bottle after bottle out of her bag. God, she'd missed having Stevie to talk to. But with Jackson here, Carla had to admit the two weeks her best friend had been gone had passed a lot faster than they would have without him around.

Stevie flashed her a wicked smile. "I picked up a new favorite drink on that cruise. And being the wonderful human being that I am, I've decided to share. I brought coconut rum and all the fixings for a fabulous girls' night in."

It did sound fabulous. "Just what I need."

"That's not what I hear," Stevie said, uncapping the first bottle.

"Huh?"

"Good one." The tall blonde grinned and said, "I wasn't home fifteen minutes and I was hearing all about you and Mr. Wonderful across the street."

"Oh, crap."

"Virginia says he's a Mafia informer."

"Perfect."

"Rachel says he loved her tuna-pineapple slop."

"Uh-huh."

"And *your mother* says he's your new boyfriend."

"Good God."

"So which is it?"

"Would you believe none of the above?"

"Nope." She reached down Carla's blender from the top shelf. Then, walking to the fridge, she opened the freezer, took out the ice bucket, and plunked some into the blender. "Girl, any man who can get all these women talking is one I've *got* to meet."

"Why?" Carla asked, suspicion coloring her tone.

"Oooh," Stevie countered, smiling, "territorial. So tell me, have you two done the ugly yet?"

"No," *damn it,* "and we're not going to."

"Uh-huh. That was convincing. How bad do you want him?"

"Oh," Carla admitted, "*bad,* Stevie. I want him really *bad.*"

CHAPTER

TEN

CHAPTER
TEN

CARLA SLIPPED THE STICK end of a tiny purple umbrella into her hair to join the others already nestled there and leaned back on the couch. She took another drink of the frothy concoction in her icy glass, then looked at Stevie. She blinked once to clear the image of her friend.

"My tongue ith numb."

Stevie tried for a sip of her own cocktail, but her swizzle stick nearly blinded her. So she plucked it out and tossed it onto the tabletop. It landed right beside her crossed ankles. She grinned as if she'd made a three-point basket from the free throw line and took a swallow of her drink. "Whaddayou care? You're not usin' it for anything."

"A perthon needth a tongue," Carla argued, and used her thumb and forefinger to try to shake some life into hers. It didn't work.

"Some of us more than others," Stevie agreed. "Long tongues are nish . . . *nice*."

Carla grinned at her friend, then laughed. With all of the paper umbrellas sticking out of her upswept blond hair, Stevie looked like she was wearing a hydrangea bush on her head. "Thath what I like about you," Carla said, nodding. "You thay, *say,* jus' what I'm thinkin'."

"Long tongues?"

"Here'th ... *here's* to 'em," Carla said, and lifted her glass in a mock salute.

They sat in the middle of the couch, their feet propped up on the table in front of them. Across the room, their favorite movie, *Practical Magic,* was playing on the TV, more for background noise than anything else. And Abbey lay curled up on the floor where she could keep an eye on both of them.

"So tell me about Mr. Hot to Trot," Stevie demanded, jabbing Carla in the ribs with an elbow.

"Mmmm ... he is, ya know." She clucked her tongue a time or two, to ease up the numbness. "Hot, I mean. He looks at me and I'm ready to lay down and whimper. Plus, he has great hands."

"Long fingers?"

"Oh, yeah."

"Thass good. Gynecologists and lovers should always have long fingers."

Carla snorted a laugh. "Eww."

"I'm right. You just don't wanna admit it."

"I don't mind admittin' that I'd like to give those fingers of his a try."

"So, how come you're not doin' a mattress dance?"

Carla shifted uncomfortably and stalled by taking another long drink. That rum was really good. "'Cuz I don't want to care."

"Then don't," Stevie polished off her drink and pushed herself far enough forward to reach the frosty blender sitting on the table. She poured herself some more, topped off Carla's glass, then set the pitcher down before leaning back comfortably again. "I need another umbrella."

"Take one outta your hair."

"Nah. So anyway, back to your sex life."

"What sex life?"

"Essackly." Stevie shook her head, paused and waited for her head to settle back on her neck, then said, "Carla honey, I love you. But you need to get laid."

"I know." Just the thought of hitting the sheets with Jackson Wyatt was damn near enough to make her climax. Just not quite. "Believe me, I know. But I can't jus' hop in the sack and then say, 'Thanks for the orgasm; gotta run.' "

"Why the hell not? Guys do it all the time." Stevie took another deep swallow and shivered as it slid down her throat. "The creative ones even throw an 'I love you' in there somewhere."

Despite the alcohol-induced haze in her brain, Carla heard the tinge of old pain and enough bitterness in her best friend's voice that it made her own heart ache. Reaching over, she took Stevie's hand and squeezed it. "He was a jerk."

"True." Stevie's mouth twisted into a smile filled with regret. "But a cute one."

"Oh, yeah. Cute, but stupid."

"I didn't say stupid. Jus' a jerk."

"Hey," Carla said, "he's my brother; if I want to call him stupid, I will."

Stevie returned the hand squeeze and muttered, "Thanks, pal."

Four years ago, Nick and Stevie were the couple being talked about in Chandler. That is, until Nick had made first string on the team and let all of the media attention go to his head. Of course, it was being named one of *People* magazine's Fifty Most Eligible Bachelors that had really ended everything between Carla's brother and her best friend. Women had come out of the woodwork going after Nick—and being a man, he'd let his penis do the thinking for him.

And with the Little General in charge, he'd forgotten all about Stevie.

Idiot.

"All men are idiots," Carla announced.

"Amen."

"Including my brothers. Well, except for Pocket Protector."

Stevie chuckled. "How is Paul? Haven't seen him in a while."

Carla shook her head and was appalled when the room tilted. "Whoa." She took a deep breath. "We hardly shee him, *see him*, either. 'Cept on Sundays. He's workin' on somethin', I guess."

"Uh-huh, back to your stud."

She laughed. "Stud." Her eyes closed and instantly an image of Jackson rose up in her woozy mind and smiled at her. Her voice went wistful. "Wonder if he is."

"Want me to find out and report to you?"

Carla gave her a good-natured shove. "Hell, no."

Stevie shoved right back. "Thass what I thought. So all you hafta do is pretend you're a guy. Use him and discard him."

That was certainly an idea, Carla told herself. The problem was, if she used him, she had the distinct feeling she wouldn't *want* to discard him. And then where would she be?

"Could always go for Mama's pick," she muttered, more to herself than to Stevie.

"Who?"

"Frank."

"Good Christ!" Appalled, Stevie stared at her. "Honey, *nobody's* that drunk."

Carla laughed again. Damn, things were funnier when looked at through the bottom of a rum bottle. And God, had she missed having Stevie around to talk to. "Yeah, you're right."

"Damn straight I am and—hey!" Stevie yelled suddenly and jumped to her feet, where she swayed unsteadily for a long moment before reaching out a hand to Carla.

"What?"

Abbey shot to her feet, too, poised to protect.

"Dancin' time!" Stevie shouted, and pointed at the television.

On-screen was the best part of the whole damn movie. All of the female stars were drinking midnight margaritas and dancing through the house. With Carla and Stevie it was tradition to join right in.

"Back it up!" Carla called as she pushed herself off the couch.

Abbey barked and ran around the room.

Stevie grabbed the remote, pushed REWIND, and held it until she hit the scene right at the beginning. Then the two of them, grinning like idiots and singing at the top of their lungs, forgot all about men and sex and the hangovers that were sure to follow tonight's revelries. Instead, they put their problems on hold and danced along to "Put de Lime in de Coconut."

Across the road, Jackson stood in the open doorway of his house and stared at Carla's place. The hours he'd spent with her earlier that day hummed through his mind with a sweet insistence. He couldn't seem to stop thinking about her. Hearing her laugh. Seeing her smile. Watching her patient tenderness with Reese.

He leaned one shoulder against the door frame and remembered how it had felt to see Reese turning to Carla. To see the little girl smile up at someone other than him and be welcomed with open arms. A few weeks ago, he might have been threatened by his daughter's growing affection for Carla.

Sure, that sounded petty and small, but it was true. Over the last year, it had been just him and Reese, clinging together on a flimsy life raft being slapped around on a choppy sea. Coming here had been a last-ditch attempt and he knew that. He'd hoped to find his daughter again, and instead, they'd both found Carla.

What that meant—to either of them—he wasn't sure. All Jackson knew for certain was, he liked being around her. Liked knowing she was right across the street and that he'd see her again tomorrow.

And he wanted her.

With every breath.

His gaze narrowed at the thought. What kind of self-ish bastard did that make him? His daughter was locked in a world of silence and he was thinking about getting Carla between the sheets. Real Father of the Year material.

He rubbed his eyes with his fingertips, then stared at the house across the way. Her drapes were open. Light beamed from every window in the place, but it was the front window that claimed his attention.

Through the glass, he watched Carla and a blond woman dance. And though there were two of them, he saw only Carla. Arms high, hips swinging, head thrown back, she moved with a wild abandon that made him hot and hard—and he wished to hell that blonde wasn't there.

"You bitch."

"Quiet," Stevie whispered. "I'm dying."

Carla sat in her usual post, feet propped up on the porch rail in front of her. Alongside her sat Stevie, wearing sunglasses in a futile effort to block out the brightness of the morning. When you had the hangover to end all hangovers, sunshine was an evil thing.

Easing her head down, Carla rested it along the top of the chair back and hoped that, if she was very careful, the pounding might ease off sometime next week. "You had to bring *two* bottles of rum?"

"Have you no respect for the dead?"

"You're talking. You can't be dead."

"Damn." Stevie took a tentative sip of coffee, whimpered as it went down, then said, "You don't mind if I just stay here, do you?"

"At the house?"

"On the porch."

"How long?"

"Forever work for you?"

"In a big way. I'll stay with you."

"A true friend." Stevie sighed. "Man, it's been a long time since we drank that much."

"I know," Carla agreed, thinking back. God, it was hard to make the brain work. She could almost *feel* her brain cells dying. "The last time was . . ." Oops.

A smile twitched at one corner of her friend's mouth. "Relax. I remember. It was the night I found Nick in bed with that Chargers cheerleader."

"Yeah, it was." And Stevie had come running to Carla, sobbing, her heart broken—and that was the first time Carla had wished she was seriously big enough and strong enough to beat the crap out of one of her brothers.

"Her pom-poms weren't real," Stevie muttered.

"Huh?"

"The cheerleader. Double D pom-poms jiggle. Hers didn't. And the way she was riding Nick, if they'd been able to, they would have."

"Gee, thanks for the image."

"What're friends for? Do we have aspirin?"

Carla reached for the bottle. "How many? Three? Four?"

"Would a dozen be too many?"

"Too many and yet not nearly enough."

"Oh well, four then, I guess, and—" Stevie sat up a little straighter. "Well, hel-lo, Hot and Tasty!"

Carla shook out the aspirin before looking up. "Hello, wh—" She shut up as she followed Stevie's open-mouthed stare.

Jackson walked down the slope of lawn from his house, carrying a white trash bag. Carla's gaze locked on the wide expanse of his chest. He wasn't wearing a shirt, God help her, and watching the play of his muscles as he walked was enough to make her mouth water. He wore a pair of jean shorts that dipped low around his narrow hips, displaying a flat abdomen, and made her daydream about what was hidden beneath the denim material. He lifted the lid of the trash can, tossed the bag inside it, then paused and looked across the street. His gaze went directly to hers, and Carla's breath hitched in her chest. Even from a distance, the power of that gaze hit her with a strength that would have knocked her on her ass, if she hadn't already been sitting on it.

Then he lifted one arm and waved before turning around and walking back up the slight hill to his house.

And Carla had to admit, the view of him leaving was just as good as the view of him coming.

"Wow."

When she could breathe again, Carla shifted a glance to her friend. "Tell me about it."

"How is he close up?"

"Way better."

"What's he do?"

"Lawyer."

"Nobody's perfect."

Carla laughed and let her gaze slide back to the house across the street. God, this was pitiful. If she wasn't careful, she'd become twelve years old again and start walking back and forth in front of his house waiting for him to come outside and notice her.

"Oh, yeah," Stevie said, "I'd be happy to try him out for you."

"Not a chance, blondie. You can have Frank, instead."

"Gee, thanks," she said dryly.

"Hey," Carla said, smiling as she reached for her coffee, "what're friends for?"

"And this is Carla when she was a tree in the second-grade Christmas play."

Mama's voice stabbed through Carla's head like a dagger, only, unfortunately, not as lethal. They'd made it through dinner—of course she'd shown up. It was eat at Mama's with Jackson or nuke another grim pot pie. But with there only being Carla, Jackson, and Reese for her to dote on, Mama had taken her act up to new levels.

Not only had she pointed out that her only daughter was getting old and should hurry up if she ever wanted to have children . . . now she'd hauled out the family photo albums. Thank God that when she was only seven, Carla'd had the presence of mind to burn the naked baby pictures of herself.

Well, she'd actually done it so Nick would stop embarrassing her by showing them to his friends. Still, in the long run, that act had been worth the spanking she'd received.

"She was a good tree," Mama insisted to Jackson. "Very convincing."

Lord, isn't a hangover enough punishment for one day?

"She looks very . . . *leafy,*" he finished, and flashed Carla a commiserating smile.

"Mama." Carla looked across the dining room table at the woman she dearly loved and yet wanted to strangle. "I'm sure Jackson doesn't want to look at old pictures."

"Why wouldn't he?"

"Sure," Jackson said. "Why wouldn't he?"

"You're a big help."

He smiled at her again, and damned if her internal organs didn't start sparkling. Not a good thing. She couldn't do this. Couldn't not do it, either, apparently. But the point was, she had to find a way to stop indulging in fantasies about him. Despite Stevie's insistence that it would be easy to sleep with him and move on, Carla was pretty sure that wouldn't be an option for her.

Damn it.

Reese flipped through the pages of the photo album, under her father's indulgent gaze, until suddenly she stopped and pointed to one particular picture. She smiled and stroked her fingertip across the glossy surface of the photo and Carla glanced at it only long enough to know she didn't want to talk about it.

Naturally, her mother didn't share her reticence.

"Ah," Mama said. "You like that, eh? That was three years ago."

Carla's insides tightened.

Jackson watched Carla's reaction to the photo of her and Abbey and couldn't help being intrigued. But he didn't have to ask any questions. Angela Candellano puffed up proudly and volunteered the information he wanted.

"My Carla, she got a medal that day. From the mayor." She looked at her daughter and practically beamed. "For being brave and finding a little lost girl."

"Really?" Jackson prompted, wanting more. Needing to know more about this woman who'd devoted so many years to something that she now didn't even want to discuss.

"Her papa"—she crossed herself—"God rest his soul, was so proud. I have the medal framed, if you want to see it, and—"

Carla pushed up from the table. "Another time, okay, Mama?" she said, and her voice was tight despite the forced smile curving her mouth. "It's late and—"

Her mother shook her head and clucked her tongue. Setting Reese onto her feet, the older woman stood up and walked around the table to stand in front of her daughter. Despite the age and height difference between the two, Jackson was struck by how much alike the two women were. Reaching up, Angela cupped Carla's cheek in the palm of her hand and, ignoring her audience, said softly, "You should stop this, Carla. You worked hard. You tried."

Memories crowded to the front of her mind. The boy she'd failed. The misery of his parents.

"Mama, I don't want to—"

"Talk about it," Mama finished for her. "I know. But

it's a sin to turn your back when so many people need your help."

"Nobody needs me, Mama," she said just as quietly, and looked into the brown eyes that still shone with the same steady love and understanding Carla had known and counted on all her life.

"Don't be foolish, Carla," her mother said. "Open your eyes. Your heart."

She couldn't. When you opened your heart, it got broken. And she didn't think she could stand that kind of pain again. Mama meant well, but she didn't know. Didn't know what it had been like to stand in front of that boy's parents and witness their misery. To offer apologies and know it would never be enough. To realize that if she'd only been a little faster, a little better, that child would have been going home to pizza and ice cream.

Instead of being zipped up into a dark green body bag.

She swallowed hard, pushed the images away, and said only, "Thanks for dinner, Mama."

"Stubborn. Like your papa."

She smiled. "Like my mama."

"Stubborn? Me?" She sniffed, waved a dismissive hand, then turned to Jackson. "You'll take some cannoli home for dessert." Glancing back at Carla, she added, "You? I don't think so."

On the moonlit walk home, it took all of Jackson's willpower to keep from bringing up the very subject she'd been so eager to change back at the house. But only last night they'd argued about it, and he just didn't want to go there again.

The ocean's distant roar pounded like a heartbeat on the cool night air. Reese walked between them, holding their hands, and Abbey strolled alongside, as if she were a nanny keeping an eye on her charges. And Jackson realized it felt . . . *good* to be here. Like this. With Carla and Reese. He glanced down at his daughter and warmth spread through him as he realized again how much she'd gained in the few short weeks they'd been in Chandler.

And looking at Carla, he silently admitted how much *he'd* gained, too.

Hell, he'd never even been around a family like the Candellanos. Growing up in a series of foster homes hadn't taught him a damn thing about how people who loved one another lived. Then he'd met Diane, but the Barringtons were as far removed from the Candellanos as . . . well, Chandler was from New York City. They weren't even similar. The Barringtons lived by a set of rules, first and foremost of which was: *Appearances are everything.* And he had to give them credit. From the outside looking in, they seemed to have everything. It wasn't until he'd actually married Diane that he'd seen past the carefully constructed facade the Barringtons presented to the world. And discovered that there was nothing at all behind it.

"Silence is an unfair weapon."

"What?" He glanced at Carla and felt the now-familiar kick-start to his bloodstream. Moonlight really did amazing things for her. Even the ends of her hair seemed to shine.

"Silence," she repeated. "You're being even more quiet than usual. Which tells me that, thanks to my family, you're seriously regretting your idea to spend the summer in Chandler, or . . ."

"Or," he prompted.

"You're trying to figure out a way to keep my share of the cannoli."

"Your share?" He grinned. "I'm sure I heard your mother say you didn't get any."

"She didn't mean that."

"She sounded serious."

"Trust me," Carla said. "My mother's always trying to feed me. She thinks I'm too skinny."

"You're not."

"Gee, thanks. Okay, maybe I can do without the cannoli."

A woman's weight. A wise man never opened that door. Even accidentally. "I didn't *mean* that; I just meant—"

"Feeling guilty?"

"A little, and I'm not sure why."

She laughed shortly. "Welcome to my world."

Between them, Reese jumped up, letting the two of them take her weight. Carla staggered into Jackson and felt the near electrical shock of heat splinter through her body. It had been way too long since she'd felt anything remotely like this. And damned if she wouldn't like to feel more of it. Actually, what she'd like to do was get Reese home and tucked into bed—and then, after an hour or two of foreplay, take the girl's daddy to bed.

But the hard reality was, she had to go home, hop in her car, and spend the night trailing Tony to wherever he was disappearing to. Another reason to be mad at her brother—besides the obvious, him making Beth miserable—now Carla could add the crime of ruining her own potential sex life.

And man, did he have potential.

Jackson looked down at her, still smiling, and everything inside her lit up with an eagerness that shook Carla right down to her bones. Gazes locked, neither of them said anything. Seconds ticked past, slowly, slowly, as he lowered his head toward hers. His smile faded, his eyes went dark and smoky in the moonlight, and Carla tipped her head back, waiting for that first brush of his lips against hers.

When it came, it was better than she'd hoped. And less than she wanted. A soft, brief kiss that wouldn't have satisfied a teenager on her first date. Yet it sizzled through Carla's body with enough power to weaken her knees and make her yearn for more.

"Whoa."

"Yeah," he said, and his gaze moved over her face as if burning her features into his memory. "That was . . . good."

"I was gonna go with 'great,'" she said, "but okay."

"Carla—"

Headlights sliced through the darkness like twin laser beams, shattering the intimate spell and canceling whatever it was he'd been about to say. Which was probably just as well, Carla thought with the last rational brain cell she had. This was going nowhere fast. Especially with a six-year-old still standing between them. Literally and figuratively.

Each of them keeping a tight hold on Reese's hands,

they took a couple of steps back from the road, just to be safe. But the car didn't race past. Instead, it slowed, then stopped alongside them.

A rental, it was a top-of-the-line black sedan, and for one brief moment Carla actually considered Virginia's opinion that Jackson worked for the mob. If this wasn't a "Godfather" car, she'd eat it.

But one glance at him and she knew he was as confused by all of this as she was. So apparently this wasn't a clandestine prearranged meeting between Jackson and the local Mafia.

Just then, the passenger side window slid soundlessly down and Carla saw an older woman with perfectly styled hair and grim, straight lips staring at them. She was still pretty, in that tight-faced way that always indicated at least one major face-lift. But even in the moonlight, Carla could see the flash of indignation in her pale ice-colored eyes.

"Jackson," the woman said, her tone frosty with disapproval as she gave Carla a quick once-over, then dismissed her, "*this* is how you're planning to 'cure' my granddaughter?"

CHAPTER
ELEVEN

REESE SHIFTED POSITION SLIGHTLY, edging herself just behind Carla's left leg. She felt the child's uneasiness as if it were a palpable thing—which told her exactly what Reese thought of the older people in the snazzy car.

Grandparents, huh?

Carla's gaze slid back to the woman still glaring daggers at Jackson. Oh, yeah, she looked like the "have a chocolate chip cookie; come and climb on Grandma's lap" type. God. The look on that woman's face was enough to freeze your blood. Any kid would have backed up. Hell, it was all Carla could do not to cross herself.

"Well, Jackson?" the woman snapped, sparing Carla another quick look. "Nothing to say for yourself?"

"Hello, Phyllis. This is a surprise."

And not a pleasant one, Carla thought. His voice sounded tight, and she heard the anger in its undertones. But she was pretty sure the older woman hadn't. Or if she had, she obviously didn't care. Carla had the immediate urge to turn around, go back to her mother's house, and apologize for every crappy thing she'd ever said or thought about her.

The older woman turned to the man behind the steering wheel, hidden in the shadowy interior of the car. "Now do you see why I insisted we come, Walter?" she demanded.

"Why *did* you come?" Jackson asked, and the woman looked directly at Carla before answering.

"That is *family* business, which I believe I prefer to discuss in private. And certainly not on a public street."

Christ. Carla half-expected the woman to lunge out of her car, screech at the sky, and call down her flying monkeys.

If possible, the temperature dropped another ten degrees. Jackson went absolutely rigid. His features looked as if they'd been carved in stone, except for a telltale muscle twitch in his jaw.

"Fine." He waved one hand. "The first driveway on the right. We'll be right there."

"Reese can ride with us." She moved to open the car door, but Jackson was too quick for her. He laid one hand on the door and kept it closed.

"We'll be there in a minute." Clearly he wasn't going to budge on this one, and apparently even the woman in the car realized it.

"Oh, very well." The window hummed back up and the car took off.

Once they were gone, Carla gave Reese's hand a quick squeeze, then turned the girl over to her father. Mindful of the fact that the child was standing right there, she said only, "Wow, feel the warmth."

He gave a quick look at the daughter now clinging to his thigh. "Yeah, the Barringtons are real charmers."

"Reese's grandparents?"

He nodded. "My late wife's parents."

"They seem . . ." she let the sentence trail off, since her mother had always told her if you can't say something nice, don't say anything at all.

"Lethal?" he finished for her, with a quick look over his shoulder at the black car parked in his driveway. "They are."

Worry creased his features and Carla had the urge to reach out and touch him. To reassure him that everything would be all right. Which was ridiculous, since she didn't know that anything was wrong. And if it was, she had no idea what it was and how to fix it. Still, the impulse was there, and that was something she hadn't felt in a long time.

A car horn beeped.

They looked and saw the woman standing beside the car, watching them. Even from a distance, Carla felt the icy stare directed right at her. And she could almost understand it. Their daughter, Reese's mother, was dead. And when they come to visit, they find their former son-in-law kissing someone else.

Not much of a kiss in the grand scheme of things, Carla told herself, but given time, it might have been. It had sure gotten off to a good start. But she and Jackson wouldn't be picking up where they'd left off. Not with the sentinel standing in the driveway watching their every move.

"I guess you'd better go."

"Yeah." He looked at the driveway again before

turning back to Carla. "Look, I'm sorry she was rude to you."

She shook her head and that wonderful hair of hers fell in wild curls around her face, making Jackson want to reach out and thread his fingers through them. To see for himself if they were as soft as they looked. And then he wanted to kiss her again. Deeper, longer. He wanted to feel her warmth snake through him until it filled him, easing away all the dark, cold corners inside.

The car horn beeped again and this time it served as a reminder to Jackson that he didn't deserve to lose those cold, dark places. Hell, he'd earned every one of them. Diane might have paid the price, but he was carrying the scars.

"Hey, no biggie," Carla said with a shrug.

"Yeah, it was." Phyllis could be as smug and vicious with him as she wanted to be. She had her reasons and he couldn't blame her for them. But she'd had no right to turn those glacier eyes on Carla.

"I'll survive." She smiled at him. "But I won't be giving back the ruby slippers. And that goes for my little dog, too."

The reference hit him instantly. *The Wizard of Oz.* The wicked witch. Appropriate. And Carla'd only seen the woman for a couple of minutes. Apparently, though, she was an excellent judge of character. He laughed shortly, then glanced at the star-swept sky overhead. "Never a falling house around when you need one."

Abbey leaned in to Carla's left leg and the heavy, solid weight felt comforting. Almost as if the golden knew Carla was having a couple of lousy minutes and was trying to help. But she wasn't the one who really needed the assistance, she told herself. Heck, *she* didn't have to go over to that quiet house and face those people. It was Jackson and Reese she felt sorry for.

Well, mostly the little girl. After all, Jackson had willingly married into that family and she had to guess he'd met Diane's parents before he'd married her. But Reese . . . poor thing, she still held a fistful of her daddy's slacks and was trying to be as invisible as she could be. Heck, Carla even felt a momentary flash of sympathy for Diane, the child's late mother. Being raised by that cold fish of a woman couldn't have been a picnic.

But she couldn't offer comfort to a dead woman, so instead, she gave it to Reese. Going down on one knee, Carla hooked one arm around Abbey's neck and avoided a sloppy doggy kiss while she looked directly into Reese's eyes. "I know you have to go and see your grandparents now," she said, and inwardly winced when the girl nearly cringed. "But tomorrow, how about you come over and help me take the puppies to the vet for their shots?"

Instantly Reese's eyes went wide with excitement. She nodded hard and even let go of her father long enough to reach out and hug Carla. Stunned, she didn't even react for a minute. The child was usually so reserved, so locked up tight, that this spontaneous hug was completely out of the blue. But as those little arms went around her neck, Carla felt them snake around her heart just as tightly.

Such a tiny thing to be so alone, she thought, enjoying the feel of the little girl's face buried in the curve of her neck. But she wasn't really alone, was she? She had a father who clearly adored her. And grandparents, such as they were.

Sighing to herself, Carla hugged Reese back, then eased away and stood up. Looking from the child to the man beside her, Carla realized that in spite of her best efforts, she was being drawn into Jackson and Reese's life. It had happened so slowly, in such tiny stages, that she hadn't really noticed until just now. And she didn't know how to back out again. Or even if she wanted to.

Oh, yeah. This is good.

"Come on, honey," Jackson said softly, taking his daughter's hand in his. "Let's go." Then he looked at Carla for a long, slow minute and she felt her toes curl. "I, uh—"

"See you tomorrow," she said abruptly, cutting him off just in case he was going to say something stupid like, *Sorry about kissing you.* Heck, she was going to dream about that kiss tonight, and having him apologize would only ruin what could be a great little fantasy.

"Right," he said. "Tomorrow." Then he turned and he and Reese headed for the house where the wicked witch still stood like the gatekeeper to hell.

"You should have called," Jackson said as he and his in-laws entered the quiet house. He hit the wall switch beside the door and three lamps in the living room flashed into life.

"So you could tell us not to come?" Phyllis countered as she walked past him, leaving a trail of White

Shoulders in her wake. She stroked her bejeweled fingers across the entry table, then rubbed them together in distaste at the dust she'd picked up. "I think not. Walter?"

Her husband followed her into the living room without even glancing at Jackson. No great surprise there, he thought, rubbing his mouth in an attempt to hold back words that would only make things worse. Walter Barrington had never made a secret of the fact that he considered Jackson some kind of bad seed upstart. Even his signing the prenuptial agreement the man's lawyers had insisted on hadn't convinced Walter that Jackson wasn't after Diane's money.

And it frosted the old man's ass to have to deal with Jackson, rather than simply dismissing him as a social-climbing upstart.

Jackson hadn't wanted the damn money, of course. What he'd wanted from Diane was something more ethereal than that. He'd made his own fortune, with no help from Walter Barrington or anyone else. No. It wasn't money that had drawn him to Diane. She'd had something else that Jackson had always craved.

Roots.

She'd once told him that she could trace her family back to the fifteenth century. He still remembered how awed he'd been at the statement. For a man who'd never even seen a photo of his parents, that kind of family history was staggering. And a part of him had wanted to share in it. Sure, there'd been more to it than that. Diane had been beautiful. And sophisticated. Everything he'd convinced himself he needed in a wife.

He'd never said anything about love. For that matter, neither had she. Theirs was a marriage made on Wall Street. Two portfolios becoming one. A true merger in the most clinical sense.

But then Reese had come along and everything changed.

At least, for him.

Walter glanced around the room with a dismissive snort. Shorter than his wife, Walter carried himself like a king and expected people to treat him as such. The whole Short Man syndrome thing had probably been coined after a psychiatrist had bumped into Walter. What the man lacked in height he more than made up for in arrogance.

Jackson still suspected that Walter was more pissed than grieved over the loss of his only child. Because by dying, Diane had done something he couldn't control. And that just didn't happen in Walter Barrington's universe.

Phyllis sat down gingerly on the edge of the sofa, as if she expected to pick up grime on her sleek lavender Chanel suit.

"Who was that woman?"

"A friend," he said, and knew there was so much more to Carla than just that. How much more, he didn't know, but either way, it was none of Phyllis Barrington's business.

One dark eyebrow lifted and her red-lined lips curved into something that on someone else might have been called a smile. "Do you always kiss your friends on the street? In front of your child?"

"Yeah," he said tightly. "Always."

That fiction of a smile disappeared. "Come here, Reese."

The little girl didn't leave Jackson's side.

"Has she gone deaf as well as mute, now?"

"No," Jackson snapped, resting one hand on the back of his child's head. "She can hear just fine."

"If that's true," the woman said, lowering her gaze to fix on Reese, "then please come here when Grandmother asks."

With a last look at her father, Reese did as she was told, and it tore at Jackson just to watch her slumpshouldered pace.

"Stand up straight," Phyllis said as she watched the same thing and came away with a completely different reaction. "A lady does *not* slouch."

Reese did what was expected of her and stopped directly in front of her grandmother.

"Your hair is a mess." Impatient fingers twitched at a stray hair and flicked it off the girl's forehead. "Walter, look at her."

Walter never took his gaze off Jackson.

"Why are you here?" Jackson asked, meeting the older man's gaze with a steady look.

"That's perfectly obvious, I should think," Phyllis said as she brushed at the front of Reese's overalls with the flat of her hand.

A headache thrummed behind his eyes, but irritation quickly outpaced it. "If you were worried about Reese, you could have called."

"That's hardly satisfactory," she muttered, clucking her tongue over the Scooby-Doo tennis shoes. "Walter, we must buy this child some decent shoes."

"She *likes* those shoes," Jackson told her.

Reese threw him a grateful look and Jackson forced a smile for her.

"What she likes isn't always best for her, now, is it?"

"What is this about?" Jackson demanded, sure they hadn't flown two thousand miles to discuss Reese's footwear.

Before answering, Phyllis looked at her granddaughter and said, "Go to your room, Reese. Grownups have to talk for a while."

Don't piss them off, Jackson reminded himself when he wanted to shout at the woman that Reese was *his* child and to kindly not order her around. It took a second or two, but he managed to tamp that anger down, and when he looked at Reese, he was almost calm.

"It's okay, honey. Go ahead."

She nodded and mimed sticking her hand into a bag.

He smiled wearily and nodded. "Yes, you can have two cookies."

She scuttled out of the room before he could change his mind, and she'd hardly rounded the corner to the kitchen before Walter grumbled, "She's like a damn monkey, gesturing like that."

Jackson took a half-step toward the other man before he could stop himself. Hands fisted at his sides, he ground out, "She's communicating. The only way she can right now."

"Well, that's the problem, isn't it?" Walter countered. "Phyllis, tell him."

"Tell me what?" He swiveled his head to look at the woman who'd stood up to tower over her husband.

"That Dr. Monohan has found room for Reese earlier than we'd planned."

Panic reared up inside him and Jackson had to fight it back down before he could speak. "*We* didn't plan anything. You did."

"Someone has to think of the child's best interests," Walter said.

"I'm her father," Jackson reminded him. "I know what's in her best interests."

"Really?" Phyllis tugged at the hem of her short jacket, making sure the fabric fell precisely into line. "And that would include dressing her like some homeless person?"

"She's dressed like a child."

"She *mimes* like some damned carnival act," Walter grumbled.

"That won't be forever," Jackson snapped.

"Then how long?" Phyllis demanded. "Just how long are we supposed to stand by and watch our only grandchild drift into mental instability?"

"She's not *crazy*!" Jackson shouted before he could stop himself. "She's just a kid. Trying to deal with something no kid should have to worry about."

"You have to nip these things in the bud," Walter said before Phyllis could open her mouth again. And Jackson was just as glad. He'd as soon yell at another man than at a woman, thanks. "Stop this nonsense now, before it gets so out of hand, she'll be like that trained gorilla, only talking in hand signs."

The urge to defend and protect roared to life so ferociously it nearly choked him. Jackson had to struggle to draw air into heaving lungs. Damn them for coming here and ruining the only sanctuary he and Reese had been able to find in the last year. Here, in this place, he and his daughter had begun to reach for each other. Here she'd laughed for the first time. Here she'd found people who simply accepted her . . . they weren't constantly trying to analyze her or look for incipient madness. They offered her love, friendship, and she'd begun to respond to it.

And he'd be damned if he'd let these two ruin his daughter as they'd ruined their own.

"I think you should leave," he said tightly.

"You're actually trying to throw me out?" Walter asked, clearly amused.

"Bodily, if I have to," Jackson assured him, and was pleased when he noted the man's gaze narrow thoughtfully.

"I won't stand for it," Phyllis said, ignoring her husband and coming to within an arm's reach of Jackson. "I lost my daughter because of you. And I will certainly *not* lose Reese."

"Diane's death was an accident."

"Perhaps. But what you're doing to Reese is not."

"What am I doing?"

"You're ignoring her silent call for help."

"I'm reaching her," he argued, staring down into eyes so pale, they looked like the ghosts of eyes that *used* to have life in them.

"Oh, yes," she said snidely. "We saw what great strides you've made."

"She laughed the other day," he told them, and waited for their reaction. Phyllis's eyes went wide, but

Walter paid no attention whatsoever. "That's right. Laughed. Out loud. For the first time in nearly a year."

"Then we have to move quickly," the woman said, and opened the black leather bag that hung from her right wrist. Delving into it, she came back up with a slip of paper and clutched it tightly. "This is Dr. Monohan's private number. He can be reached day or night. I'll call him now. Tell him of the breakthrough and let him know we'll be on the first flight back to Chicago."

She moved for the phone, but Jackson's voice stopped her midstride. "No."

"No?" Phyllis slowly turned to face him, astonishment clearly etched on her features. "Why on earth not?"

"Because we're not going to Chicago. You two are."

"But Reese—"

"Is making progress," he finished for her. "Just as she'll continue to do, here."

"You don't know that," Walter said.

"I believe it."

The other man snorted.

"You're doing this to spite us, aren't you?" Phyllis asked.

"Believe it or not," Jackson told her, throwing his hands wide and letting them slap back against his sides again, "not everything is about *you*. I have to do what I think is best for *my* daughter." Pulling in a long, deep breath, he let it out again before saying, "We agreed that I would have the summer with Reese to try to reach her without Fair Haven Clinic."

"But she laughed," Phyllis reminded him, and Jackson thought for a moment that he saw genuine concern in the woman's eyes. And for that reason, he softened his voice when he spoke up again.

"Exactly. That's why we're staying. If she can laugh, she can talk. If she can talk, she can come all the way back."

"And if she doesn't?" Phyllis prompted.

Oh, he didn't want to think about that. Because if she didn't, he would lose her. To Fair Haven. To doctors and tests and locked rooms with visitation rights. He knew it. He could fight the Barringtons—and he would. But he'd also lose. Going up against one of Chicago's most prominent families was a losing proposition from the beginning. The Barringtons had already brought pressure to bear. They knew too many influential people to be stonewalled by him. They could call in favors from judges and have Reese taken from him in a heartbeat.

If Reese were her former cheery self, her grandparents would have continued to hate him, but they would have been content to leave the day-to-day child care to him as long as they had optimum visiting rights. But her withdrawal had not only scared them, it had also embarrassed them. A Barrington—even a six-year-old one—never showed weakness. And if they had to take custody of the child to have her "cured," then that's what they would do.

"If she doesn't," he said quietly, "we give Fair Haven a try."

The two older people looked at each other for a long minute before Phyllis nodded. Slipping the piece of paper back into her purse, she snapped the bag shut and said, "Fine, then. We'll expect you back in Chicago by the first of September."

They headed for the door, but Phyllis stopped short. "We're staying at the Hyatt Regency in Monterey, but we'll be leaving for home tomorrow morning."

Unbelievable. They'd flown halfway across the country to come and give him crap for an hour. But then, he reasoned, when you had your own jet, you pretty much treated the open skies as your own private freeway.

Walter stood with the door open, checking his watch.

Phyllis kept talking. "Tell Reese we said good-bye."

Since he'd won this round *and* they were leaving, Jackson felt magnanimous. "Why don't you say good-bye for yourself?"

Phyllis looked as if she wanted to, but Walter snapped, "Let's go. You can call her from home. Not like she's going to speak to you."

The woman inhaled sharply, nodded, and said, "Good-bye, Jackson."

When they left, he leaned against the closed door for a long minute, just enjoying the fact that they were gone. But the threat they'd brought with them hovered in the air like some bad-smelling cloud.

It was the end of June. He had only two months left to find his daughter. And suddenly two months didn't seem like nearly enough time. Fury pulsed inside him. He didn't like feeling helpless. Didn't stand for it usually. There was always something he could do. Some trick he could pull in court. Some smooth move that would throw the opposition off their stride and give him the edge he needed.

Until now.

In this situation, he was as lost as Reese. He didn't have a clue how to get through to her. He was doing everything he could. Wasn't he? Or had he missed something? Reese's face blossomed in his mind and his heart ached at the thought of losing her. He couldn't let that happen. Somehow, someway, he had to pull off a miracle.

Shoving one hand through his hair, he walked through the entryway into the living room and didn't stop until he was in front of the wide front window. Staring out at the darkness, he watched the black sedan pull from the drive and barrel off down the road. Then his gaze shifted to Carla's place and focused on the one light shining in the window, like a candle left burning for some lost wanderer. He stared at it and wished it was meant for him.

CHAPTER TWELVE

CARLA FELT SLEAZY.

And a little queasy.

She grimaced and rubbed the flat of her hand across her stomach. A half a bag of Oreos and two Hershey bars didn't come close to making up for missing out on Mama's cannoli. But she'd had to have *something*. Although now it seemed even chocolate was turning on her.

Of course, she could be wrong. Could be that it was just nerves hitting the pit of her stomach and stirring things up. Nodding to herself, she unwrapped another Hershey bar and took a bite, figuring that if she got her stomach full enough, there'd be no room for nerves to stir.

Shaking her head, she stared through the windshield, down the familiar street toward the blue-and-white house with the wide front porch. Tony and Beth had bought the place four years ago and then spent the next three years redoing it. Carla remembered all the weekends when the family had come together helping to build that Victorian-style porch. Naturally, the combined Candellano forces had driven Beth nuts during the painting. She'd kept giving advice on how to *neatly* detail all of the gingerbread trim with the tiny brushes she'd purchased specifically for that task.

And as far as Carla knew, those tiny brushes were still sitting unused in their little packages. No Candellano man was going to use a tiny brush when a big one would do the job faster. She smiled to herself. Beth had been outgunned, but despite her worries the porch looked terrific. Well, better from a distance than close up, but that was another story.

The family had built the porch swing, potted enough ferns to make a simulated rain forest, and drunk champagne together when it was finished. Later they'd gathered on that porch when Papa died, when Nick made the All-Star Team, then again the night Tina was born. They'd laughed and cried and held one another and built memories that were now threatened because of Tony.

"He's an idiot," Carla muttered. This was all his fault. Her upset stomach, and the fact that not an hour after leaving Reese and Jackson, she was sitting in a dark car, dressed like a burglar. With her black jeans and long-sleeved black T-shirt, Carla felt hot and uncomfortable and, well, the word came to mind again. Sleazy.

"You know," she told Abbey, after popping the last of the Hershey bar into her mouth, "being a PI ain't all it's cracked up to be." She slouched a little lower in the driver's seat and tried to pretend she was anywhere but where she was. Sneaking around after one of her brothers was not her idea of a good time.

No, the good time would be back at her house. Or rather, across the road from her house. With Jackson. She reached up and rubbed the tips of her fingers across her mouth as if she could still feel the pressure of his lips against hers. That had been over way too quickly.

Carla wasn't exactly a vestal virgin or anything, but that one kiss with Jackson had been enough to convince her that he was different from anyone else she'd ever kissed. Which naturally led her to wonder how much better . . . *other* things would be with Jackson. She sighed and shifted in her seat again. It was a good thing she led such a full and lively fantasy life. Though she couldn't help imagining what might have happened if Jackson's in-laws hadn't decided to swoop in at precisely the wrong moment. At the thought of those two, she scowled and reached for another candy bar but stopped herself before she could unwrap it. Heck, another hour or two in this car and she'd weigh three hundred pounds.

Sitting up straight again, she rolled the windows down and let a cold cross-breeze drift through the car, carrying the scent of the ocean and just a hint of someone's barbecue grill. Abbey pushed herself up on the passenger seat and stared at Carla, head cocked.

"What?" she asked. "Bored? Yeah, well, me, too."

The dog looked back at her and Carla could have sworn there was disapproval in that steady brown stare.

"Hey, it's not like I *want* to sneak around following Tony. But I promised Beth."

Abbey turned her head and leaned out the passenger-side window, to better enjoy the food smell.

Okay, Carla thought with disgust. She was headed for the deep end, now. Making excuses to her dog. That was pitiful. She tapped her fingers against the steering wheel, shifted in her seat until her too-tight jeans eased up enough to let her breathe comfortably, and focused her gaze on the house down the street again. Minutes slipped past, and just when Carla began to think that maybe Tony wasn't going to do something stupid tonight after all, their front door opened and he stepped out.

Her fingers curled around the leather-wrapped wheel, and as her palms began to sweat, her mouth dried up. Yeah, she'd been born for intrigue. Should have been a spy.

She watched as Beth came out onto the porch and folded her arms across her chest as if giving herself a comforting hug. Scowling now, Carla saw Tony climb into the squad car he routinely drove, leaving the family minivan parked in the driveway.

"Okay," she muttered, "maybe this isn't too bad after all. At least he doesn't mind being seen in the patrol car. He can't be doing anything illegal then, right?"

Abbey didn't voice an opinion.

"Right," Carla said as she fired up the engine, "not illegal. Just immoral. Idiot." She pulled away from the curb, and keeping her headlights turned off, she followed along at a safe distance behind her oldest brother. Too close and he'd recognize her car. Too far away and she'd lose him.

Following people wasn't as easy as it sounded.

He turned right at the end of the street, and once Carla had made a "Hollywood stop," tapping the brakes and rolling on through, she followed him. Streetlights were haloed in the first wisps of fog stretching in from the ocean. An older woman sat hunched on a bus bench; a group of kids on skateboards hooted and laughed as they rolled along the sidewalks. A few cars dotted the parking area in front of the shops on Main Street, but Tony went right on past the open slots, so she knew wherever he was headed, at least it wasn't downtown Chandler. Good. That was something, anyway.

All Beth needed was for Virginia, Abigail, and Rachel to get hold of the news that Tony was doing . . . whatever he was doing.

Carla kept him in sight but stayed far enough back that she congratulated herself on her very first attempt at stalking. When Tony's car took the freeway on-ramp, Carla had to flip on her headlights to join him. She didn't want to take the chance of being stopped by the Highway Patrol.

"Where's he going?" she wondered aloud, but Abbey was too busy enjoying having half her body out the side window to worry about the reason for the trip.

Carla braced her elbow on the car door, kept one hand on the wheel, used the other to scrape her flying hair out of her face, and kept her gaze fixed on her brother's distant car. Her stomach churned, but now it wasn't the chocolate bothering her. It was the thought of what she might find when Tony finally stopped driving.

For all of her big talk, Carla really didn't want to walk in on her brother and his sleazeball girlfriend.

He took the next exit and Carla stepped on the gas pedal, hurrying to keep up. As much as she regretted having to do this, she couldn't stop now. Not without some answers, whether she liked them or not.

At the end of the off-ramp, though, she was alone. Leaning on the steering wheel, she looked first left, then right, and didn't see a damn thing. Not a taillight. Not a headlight. The long dark road stretched out in both directions, the only sign of life an old gas station with flickering fluorescent lights. There were no cars at the pumps, though, and if she hadn't known better, Carla might have thought she was alone in the world.

"What the hell do you think you're doing?"

"Jesus Christ!" Carla jumped straight up, nearly strangling herself on the shoulder strap of her seatbelt. One hand clapped to the base of her throat, she swiveled her head to the left and saw Tony, glowering at her through the driver's-side window. "Damn it! Are you trying to kill me?"

"Don't tempt me."

When her grandparents left, Reese let out a long, deep breath and snuggled down under her blanket. She didn't like all the yelling, and her grandpa's mean face scared her sometimes. But as long as her daddy was close, she knew everything would be all right. He wouldn't make her go away.

She didn't want to go to that doctor place. Her fingers plucked at the smooth top of the blanket and she bit at her bottom lip as she thought about leaving here. She didn't want to go. She liked the puppies. And Nana

Angèla. But best of all, she liked Carla. She smelled good, and when she smiled, her eyes did, too.

Reese turned over onto her side and closed her eyes. Her Cinderella light glowed just beside her, softening the dark, keeping all the scary shadow places far away from her bed. And her door was open a little bit, too, so the hall light spilled into her room. Her daddy always left the light on and he never said she was a baby like Mommy used to.

Mommy.

She squeezed her eyes tighter shut and tried not to think about Mommy. 'Cause when she did, she remembered that last day. And she remembered why the car crashed. And why Mommy died. And why she could never tell anybody what happened.

'Cause if she did, then her daddy wouldn't want her anymore and Grandma and Grandpa would send her away to that doctor place.

"God, you shouldn't sneak up on people like that." Heartbeat racing, head spinning, Carla tried to catch her breath, then gave up on it and just went with the wheezing and gasping. She shot Abbey a quick look and muttered, "Some watchdog you are."

"You should talk about sneaking around," Tony griped. "You were following me, Carla."

"Well, duh."

"Why?"

She flicked him a furious glance, then looked up into the rearview mirror as a blast of reflected headlights shone in her eyes. "I have to move. I'm blocking the exit, here."

"Fine," he snapped, stepping back from the car. "Pull over to the left and park by me."

"Park by you *where*?" Carla looked to where he pointed and still didn't see the squad car.

"Just around the incline, there."

Her gaze finally picked up the slope of green grass that, in the darkness, had pretty much disappeared until Tony had pointed it out. Damn it. She threw the car into gear, whipped a quick left turn, then pulled around behind the small ridge of land to park alongside Tony's patrol car.

Yeah, she should give up raising search dogs and become a detective. This was obviously where her true calling lay. Her first stakeout and she'd not only been caught red-handed but had also been damn near scared to death by the guy who wasn't supposed to see her in the first place. Grumbling to herself, Carla shoved the gearshift into PARK, turned off the engine, and set the brake. Looking at Abbey, she muttered, "You were no help at all. The next time I try to be stealthy, I'm leaving you at home and bringing Stevie instead."

Abbey woofed, then wiggled a greeting at Tony as he stepped up to the car and yanked open the driver's-side door.

"So," he demanded, wearing the sternest "cop face" she'd ever seen on his features. "You want to tell me why my *sister* is tailing me?"

She unsnapped her seatbelt and turned to face him. "It's your own fault."

"Oh," he said, folding his arms across his chest, "this should be good. How is this *my* fault?"

"Because you made Beth cry," she snapped. Planting both hands on his chest, she gave him a shove that backed him up far enough that she could climb out of the car and fight standing on her own two feet.

A cold wind slapped at her, tugging at her hair, whipping it across her eyes. She tipped her face into the wind, pushed her hair aside, and glared at her brother. It was dark but for the slanting beams of the headlights she'd left on. As they stared at each other in silence, his squad car's police radio hissed and crackled like an angry crowd.

Now that the adrenaline in her body was easing down to levels low enough to allow her heart to slide back from her throat to her chest, Carla was ready to face down her older brother. And the longer she stared up into his angry face, the more furious she became. Where did he get off being mad? He was the one screwing up. "What the hell are you up to, Tony? What's going on?"

"You mean besides being stalked by my little sister?" He glared at her. "This has nothing to do with you, Carla."

"We're family."

"Which is the only reason I'm not arresting you."

"For what? Driving?" She snorted at his cheap attempt to scare her again.

"For following me."

"That's not illegal."

"Hey, I'm the sheriff. It is if I say it is."

"Damn it, Tony, what are you up to?"

"It's none of your business, Carla. Butt out. And go home." He turned around and walked toward his car.

Carla wasn't about to let him get away with that, though. She wasn't going to be put off. She wasn't going to go back to Chandler and tell Beth they still didn't know what was going on. "No way, big brother. I'm staying right here until I get an answer."

"Hope you brought a sleeping bag." He glanced at her as he opened his car door.

"You can't just walk away from this."

"Watch me."

With no other choice left, she pulled out her big gun and fired. "I'll tell Mama."

He slammed the door and turned around to face her. "That's a low shot, Carla."

"So talk to me."

"Can't you just trust me?"

"Not after listening to Beth." Carla walked closer, laid one hand briefly on her big brother's arm, and looked up into his eyes. "Tony, you're scaring her. And trust me, no woman—not even a sister—is going to be on a guy's side in a situation like this."

"A situation like what?" His brow furrowed, he threw his hands high as if surrendering to the inevitability of his sister's interrogation.

"Like you boinking some airhead when you should be home with Beth and Tina, and I swear to God, Tony—"

"What?" His roar drowned out the police radio and seemed to rattle the leaves of the trees surrounding them. Carla blinked and shook her head to get rid of the ringing in her ears.

"You heard me." She didn't back up, not even from the grizzly bear look on his face. Now that it was out in the open, it was better for everyone if they just said what they had to say now.

"Yeah, I heard you, but I don't believe you said that."

"Join the club. I couldn't believe you would do something so tacky. So low. So . . ."

"Finished already?" he prodded quietly. Now this was the Tony she knew. When he got mad, he went quiet, like their father always had. Oh, he shouted occasionally. He was Italian, after all. But when he was pushed beyond his limits, the shouting stopped and the silence began.

His lips thinned until his mouth was a grim slash across his face. His gaze narrowed on her and Carla almost told him just how much he looked like Papa the night Paul confessed to blowing a hole through the back of the garage with his chemistry kit.

But that was off the subject.

"Give me a minute," she told him. "I'll think of a few other things to call you. Like a son of a bitch. A bastard. A low-down, lying, weaselly, good-for-nothing, cheating—"

"I didn't cheat."

"Huh?" He said it so quietly, so evenly, she had no choice but to believe him. If he'd tried to stall her or evade the subject or even ranted a little, it would have been different. But his simple denial came from the heart and carried the ring of truth. And while that made her feel a hell of a lot better about her brother, it still left too many unanswered questions.

Muttering under his breath, he turned away from her, reached up, and shoved both hands through his hair with a viciousness that should have snatched him bald. When he whirled around to face her again, his features in the headlights reflected a wild mixture of astonishment and fury.

"I can't believe you think I'd—"

"Well, what else were we supposed to think?"

"We?"

Well, he picked right up on that one, didn't he? she thought. "Beth and I."

"Beth?" He snorted a choked-off laugh that sounded as if it were strangling him.

"Great. So Beth asked you to follow me around like some third-rate PI."

"She didn't have to ask. I volunteered. And excuse me?" Carla demanded, just noticing that veiled insult. "Third-rate?"

"I caught you, didn't I?"

"It was my first time."

"Last time."

"Yeah. Not to change the subject or anything, but just how did you catch me?" Carla planted both hands on her hips and tipped her chin up. "I thought I did a pretty good job, considering."

A derisive laugh shot from his throat. "You did a lousy job. I noticed a car driving without headlights. Then I noticed it stayed behind me—always the same distance."

"Oh."

"*Then* I noticed the make of the car."

"Ahh . . ." Well, she'd known that was a possibility. "I should have rented a different car."

"Then I saw my 'shadow' follow me off the freeway. Figured it had to be you."

"So you decided to scare me to death to pay me back."

"I wasn't trying to pay you back, I was *trying* to get rid of you."

"So you could go meet the cheerleader."

"What cheerleader?" he demanded.

"Whatever babe it is you're meeting."

"You really think I'd do that to Beth?"

"Beth thinks so."

"Well, that's perfect. Great. My wife thinks I'm cheating on her."

"What's she supposed to think, Tony?" Carla demanded, stomping over to stand directly in front of him. "You leave three nights a week. You won't tell her where you're going, what you're doing."

"And that adds up to 'boinking a bimbo'?"

"Pretty much."

"That's nice. Nice to know how much my family thinks of me."

"Isn't it kind of nice to know that your family cares enough about you to hunt you down like a dog?"

"That's supposed to make me feel better?"

"Yes. At least it shows we care."

"I'm all warm and fuzzy here." He leaned one hip against the front fender and folded his arms across his chest. In the headlights, he didn't look angry anymore. Just tired.

And her heart reacted. This was Tony, after all. The big brother who'd defended her against Nick's and Paul's teasing. The one who used to buy her popcorn at the movies. The one who taught her to ride a bike. Years of love, of admiration, rolled through her, but before she could give in to the need to try to make him feel better, she remembered why she was there in the first place.

"So," Carla asked after a long moment of quiet that dragged at her last nerve, "are you going to tell me what's going on?"

"No."

"Tony . . ." Frustration rippled through her.

He looked up at her. "But I will tell Beth."

"Deal." Carla smiled at her big brother and tried to get a grip on her own curiosity. After all, Beth would tell her, eventually. As long as he wasn't cheating—and she believed him on that score—then he and Beth could work everything out. They'd been together too long to settle for anything less.

One corner of his mouth turned up in a begrudging smile as he reached for her, drawing her close enough for a brief, hard hug. "Now will you go home? Or do I have to arrest you for harassing a police officer?"

She went.

It was late, she was tired but too full of chocolate and irritation to sleep, so instead, she parked her car and took Abbey for a walk. The night was quiet but for the murmur of the low-tide ocean. She listened to the whisper of water on sand, felt the cool fingers of wind tug through her hair, and headed for the beach by the closest route.

Which took her across Jackson's front yard. Not that she was doing that on purpose or anything. That would be way too elementary-school. But could she help it if his house lay between hers and the shoreline?

Abbey, free of the confines of the car, darted ahead of Carla but always trotted back as if making sure that she was coming. Her tennis shoes slid on the damp grass, and she tucked her hands into her pockets for warmth. Tossing a glance at the house as she passed, Carla noticed that the evil in-laws' rental car was gone and was glad for Jackson.

At least his night had improved.

"Hi."

"Jesus!" Carla shouted, and grabbed at the base of her throat. Whirling around, she spotted Jackson, standing in the shadowy corner of the house, where he could look out on the ocean. Once again, her heart was in her throat and her breath pounded in and out of her lungs. Shaking her head, she asked of no one in particular, "Is there a contract out on me? Does somebody want me dead?"

"Bad night?" he asked.

"Interesting night," she amended. "But at least I know my heart's strong." And as that organ slipped back into a more normal beat again, she whistled for Abbey and turned to walk up the incline toward Jackson.

Though he stood in deep shadow, Carla had no trouble seeing the remnants of anger still etched into his features. His mouth looked tight and his eyes . . . well, face it, his eyes looked good. Angry but good.

"So," she asked, keeping her gaze fixed on those eyes, "how'd it go with the wicked witch?"

"Ugly."

"Want to talk?" she asked, and wasn't sure if he'd take her up on it or not. And while he thought about it, she filled the lingering silence. "Hard to believe, since I talk so much myself, but people tell me I'm a good listener. And sometimes it helps to talk to a stranger and—"

"You're not a stranger, Carla."

A ripple of something warm and luscious rolled up her spine at just the way he said her name. Silly. Schoolgirl silly, yet there it was. Man, she was in some potentially deep trouble here.

"So," she said, clearing her throat, "a friend, then?"

He laughed shortly, but she didn't hear the slightest hint of laughter in his tone. "I don't usually think about kissing my friends."

"No?"

"No."

Well, that settled that. "Then I don't want to be your friend."

CHAPTER THIRTEEN

SHE WAS A GIFT, Jackson thought.

One he didn't deserve.

But one he wanted more than he'd ever wanted anything or anyone.

Just looking at her, standing there in the shadows, with ghostly fingers of fog drifting around her, was enough to bring him to his knees. Her long-sleeved black T-shirt clung to her figure, outlining every curve. Her worn blue jeans skimmed along her rounded hips and long legs like a lover's touch. The cold ocean wind lifted those black curls of hers and twisted them about her face in a wild dance. Her skin seemed luminescent in the weird lighting, and her eyes shone with the same desire pulsing through him.

He'd been standing here, thinking about her, trying not to think about her, for what felt like hours. Jackson couldn't afford to get involved right now. If nothing else, his in-laws' visit had reminded him of that. They'd made it clear countless times that unless he pulled off a miracle this summer, he would lose Reese forever. And that's all he should be concentrating on. Finding a miracle. Making it happen.

Instead, there was Carla, infiltrating his life, his dreams. Images of her laughing, shouting, taking care of those puppies, playing with Reese, they all tumbled over and over again through his mind, chasing away the shadows, the dark corners that had become such a part of him during the last year.

But if the shadows left his soul, wouldn't he just be . . . empty?

Abbey raced back from wherever she'd gone to and plopped herself down in front of him, apparently waiting for a little attention herself. He kept his gaze focused on the woman watching him while he stroked the golden's head.

"So?" Carla asked when the silence stretched on toward eternity. "Are you gonna kiss me or what?"

He grinned and realized that he hadn't laughed or smiled so much in years as he had since meeting Carla. His gaze shifted briefly to her mouth and everything inside him tightened. But it wasn't just the physical urge to kiss her that had him wanting to grab her and hold her and bury his face in the sweet curve of her neck. It was Carla herself.

Brash and honest and outspoken, she was different from every other woman he'd ever known. Her family was as much a part of her as her brown eyes, and yet she was a strong, fiercely independent woman. She sparked things in him he hadn't even been aware of. She made him laugh, despite the ax hanging over his head. With gentleness and kindness she'd begun to reach Reese when no one else had been able to come close.

And she set his blood on fire just by breathing.

"Hello?" Carla asked, taking a step closer. "You taking a nap?"

"Nope."

"Great. So are you?"

"Going to kiss you?"

"Yeah," she said, drawing that one word out into two or three syllables.

"I'm thinking about it." He eased away from the wall, moving toward her.

"Well then, I'll think about letting you." She pushed a windblown strand of hair out of her eyes.

"You'll let me."

"Is that right?"

"Oh, yeah."

"What makes you so sure?"

She was just an arm's reach away. He swore he could smell her scent on the ocean-flavored air and it swirled down inside him, spreading like a fever.

"Because you liked our first one."

Carla gave him a slow smile. "I do love a cocky man."

"Not so cocky," he said, finally reaching for her, pulling her close, wrapping one arm around her middle. His right hand swept up her body to cup her cheek, tipping her face up until he could look down into her eyes. Desire shone there, along with something else. Something deeper, stronger, and he had to look away before he saw too much, felt too much. His gaze moved over her features, even as his fingers stroked her smooth, soft skin. He traced his thumb across her cheekbone and felt the warmth of her rush into his bloodstream. She touched him. Her hands splayed open against his chest, and heat swam from his brain straight to his groin.

Better. Much better. Want, hunger—those he could deal with. Anything else wasn't an option.

As he slid his hand from her face to the back of her head, his fingers slid through her hair, loving the silky feel of it against his skin. "Not cocky," he whispered, lowering his head to hers, "just hungry for you."

His words sent a ripple of excitement dancing along her spine. His voice, a whispered hush of need, seared her blood and she knew that despite everything else that had been going on tonight, this moment had been in the back of her mind. Since that first too-brief kiss hours ago, she'd been wanting another shot at it. Another taste of the sweet, hot rush of desire that she hadn't felt in far too long.

It didn't seem to matter that this was nuts. She didn't care that there was no future here. After all, if no promises were made, then no promises could be broken. They couldn't let each other down if neither of them expected anything more than a kiss. And with that thought firmly in mind, Carla leaned in toward him, going up on her toes, tilting her head, and holding her breath as his mouth claimed hers.

The first flush of heat swept through her with the force of storm-tossed waves. Her knees weakened, as if she were trying to hold her balance in an undertow, but that didn't seem to matter, since he was holding her tightly enough to cut off her air. Which she didn't mind in the slightest.

Who needed air when you could have lips?

His mouth moved over hers in a fury of dazzling need and she responded, parting her lips for his invasion, welcoming the wild ride of sensations. His tongue swept into her warmth, and with his first caress he stole her breath and sent fiery explosions splintering through her brain.

Cold air and warm hands touched her, held her, teased her, and Carla wasn't sure if the shivers wracking her body were from the damp or from his touch. And she was way too involved to try to figure it out. Her fingers speared through his hair, holding his head to her, silently demanding more of his mouth, his taste.

Her blood danced, her body throbbed, and she had an incredible urge to yank his shirt off just to feel his skin beneath her hands. And while he kissed her, plundering her mouth with fevered deliberation, she realized with a shock that her reaction to Jackson had nothing to do with how long it had been since she was kissed last. This was all him. No one else had ever done this to her before. No man had ever been able to light up her insides like a bonfire on the beach with a single kiss.

Later, she told herself, think about it later. Right now, just enjoy. Her hands fell to his shoulders and her fingers dug into the fabric of his shirt, digging right down for his skin. His hold on her tightened, his arms flexing around her middle, squeezing her, holding her tightly to him, molding her body to his. The world fell away. The roar of the ocean faded away. They were alone. Just the two of them. Just—

Ninety-five pounds of golden retriever hit them both hard enough to end the kiss and send them staggering.

Abbey, reared up on her hind legs, planted one forepaw on each of them and stuck her head between theirs, licking and sniffing in delight at this new game.

Jackson grunted.

Carla laughed, loud and long, then released Jackson so she could catch Abbey. "Feeling left out, were you?" she asked. The dog gave her a slurping kiss, then aimed one at Jackson.

"Thanks," he muttered, wiping one hand across his jaw.

Abbey wobbled a little on her hind legs, then dropped to sit at their feet, turning her head to watch one, then the other of them. Jackson could have sworn the dog was smiling.

And hell, he should be grateful to the canine chaperone. Another minute or two of that kiss and he'd have had Carla stretched out in the damp grass. He could almost see her there now, naked and willing, and everything in him yearned to feel that. To lose himself in her touch as he'd lost himself in her kiss.

But now that the spell was broken, that wouldn't be happening tonight. And it was probably just as well. Carla wasn't the kind of woman a man walked away from easily. And he would *have* to walk away. Better to just leave that kiss a stand-alone incident. Better for both of them.

"Well, that was way better than the first one," she said, and he lifted his gaze to her smiling eyes. "We must get better with practice."

"Yeah," he said, wanting to taste her again and knowing he couldn't. He shoved both hands into his jeans pockets, stared at a point just over her head, so he wouldn't have to look into those dark brown eyes, and said, "Carla, look, I—"

"Right." She held up one hand and he looked at her in time to see her shake her head, a wry twist of a half-smile on her face. "No, no. Wait. Let me guess. You're about to say, 'We have to talk.' "

"What?" His body still humming with the near electrical charge of excitement she'd stirred inside him, he only stared at her.

She laughed shortly, harshly, and it sounded as though it had scraped across her throat. She pushed her windblown hair back from her face. "Oh, hey, don't worry about it. I've heard this speech before."

"What speech?" he demanded as she backed up a step, her features going as cold and unforgiving as the wind whipping in off the ocean. "What the hell are you talking about?"

"You just kissed me like you were a man dying of thirst and I was the only drinking fountain in hundreds of miles," she said. "And now you're about to tell me that it won't happen again."

Guilt jabbed at him, along with a little irritation. Okay, sure, he had been about to say pretty much just that. But he didn't care for the way she was lumping him in with whoever had given her the speech last.

"I knew this was gonna happen, you know," she was saying as she paced in short angry steps back and forth in front of him. "I even told myself to steer clear. To never mind those eyes of yours. To forget about the broad shoulders and the nice butt."

He straightened up a little, grinning. "Nice butt?"

She glared at him, and with her eyes narrowed, she looked damn dangerous.

"See," Carla went on, warming to the subject as she talked, "I've been down this road before. I even recognized the road signs." She kept pacing, her steps quickening, and Abbey jumped up to pace with her, four feet matching steps with two. "Remember the fiancé I told you about?"

"Yeah, but—"

"That was a rhetorical question," she snapped. "Anyway, he's the one who was still so hung up on the former fiancée, he wound up going back to her?"

He stepped in front of her to slow her down, but she just swung wide around him, her tennis shoes squeaking slightly on the damp grass. Abbey pranced and jumped alongside her as if enjoying this new game.

"Yeah, I remember you telling me about him, but what's he got to do with this?" he demanded.

"It's the same damn thing all over again," she muttered, more to herself than to him. Carla wanted to laugh. Or cry. Or scream. No, she didn't want to cry. She'd done enough crying over the last couple of years to last her a lifetime. What she really wanted was to punch him in the nose, but she'd probably break her hand.

She should have known. Damn it. He'd even told her flat-out that his wife had died only a year ago. Of *course* he would still be in love with her. And wouldn't be interested in anybody else. Although why that should bother her so much she didn't know, since she didn't want a relationship, either, right? Right. But still, she'd been dumped for a former fiancée. She didn't especially enjoy being dumped for a dead wife, too.

"You know, when you moved in, I told myself . . . summer renters. Temporary. Butt out, Carla. But did I listen?" She didn't wait for him to answer. "Hell, no, I didn't listen. I'm a Candellano. We don't listen to anybody!"

He grabbed her as she passed him again, dropping both hands on her shoulders and holding on. "You're going to listen to me."

"Why should I?" She pulled free. "I've heard it all before."

"I don't know what the hell you're talking about," he muttered, fixing his gaze on hers. "But I'm going to say what I started to say."

"Fine. Go ahead." She crossed her arms over her chest, cocked her head, stared at him, and tapped the toe of her shoe against the earth.

He let her go, took a step back, and said, "When you showed up tonight, walking out of the fog like that, it was—" He looked at her. "Like I'd willed you to come to me. And I wanted you more than my next breath."

"Hmm. Past tense. That's nice."

"Damn it, Carla. This isn't just about me. Or you. I'm only here in Chandler because of Reese. And she's the one I have to think about now. Not myself. Not what I want or need, but what *she* needs."

"And it should be," she snapped. "Your daughter should come first, I get that. I approve, even. Heck, I'm not looking for a husband, remember?" She reached down and laid one hand on Abbey's silky head as if needing to be grounded. "I don't even know why I'm so pissed. I mean, Stevie told me I should use you, then discard you—"

"Discard me?" he asked. "Who the hell is Stevie?"

She ignored him. "But that's not me, so that wasn't going to happen. And I know damn well that summer renters are temporary, so this wasn't going to go anywhere anyway . . ."

Jackson tried to keep up with the stream of words pouring from her.

". . . but then there was Reese and she was so cute and so lost and before I knew it, I was being sucked in and there was no way out again." She threw her hands high and let them slap against her thighs. "So it's my own fault and I really shouldn't be mad at you at all, so don't worry about it, by tomorrow I'll probably be fine and we can forget all about this whole miserable little scene."

"Forget it?" he asked as she walked past him, obviously in a hurry to get away from him. "Carla, that kiss is going to haunt me."

She stopped dead, looked back over her shoulder, and gave him a small smile. "That's kind of a booby prize," she said, "but I'll take it."

She walked away from him, her and her dog, and in a few steps they were swallowed by the mist and Jackson was alone in the cold, damp fog.

The rain wouldn't stop.

It slammed into him, dragging him down, pushing at him, and every step was a labor. The scream came again and his blood went like ice. A child's voice. Horrified.

The scream tore at the air like fingernails on a black-board and Jackson followed it, heart pounding.

Firemen hovered around the back of the car, prying at the passenger door with the Jaws of Life. Machinery hummed, metal screeched, and still that scream went on, ripping at his heart, chipping away at his soul.

Reese.

Alive.

Thank you, God.

He pushed past the uniforms standing between him and the car. He had to reach his little girl. He had to get to her. Stop her screams. Help her. Save her. Please, Reese.

Daddy's coming.

Daddy's here.

And a movement caught the corner of his eye.

He turned his head, looked at the tarp-draped bundle in the ruined front seat.

It moved.

The tarp shifted, sliding back. Rain pounded through that broken windshield, chasing the yellow plastic as it fell away.

Breath caught in his lungs.

He stared at Diane's face, torn by the glass, her long blond hair matted with blood.

Her eyes opened. She stared at him. And smiled.

"You did this," she whispered.

And Jackson woke in a cold sweat, heart hammering in his chest.

CHAPTER
FOURTEEN

IT WAS LATE BY the time Tony got home.

He pulled into the driveway, turned the engine off, and simply sat there in the dark. Everything Carla had said to him still echoed in his mind, taunting him with the knowledge that he'd really made a mess of things. He stared at his house and thought about the people inside. Tina, his baby. From the moment of her birth, Tony had been a goner where she was concerned. She'd opened her eyes for her first look at the world, fixed those dark brown eyes on her daddy, and stolen his heart in the space of a breath.

And Beth.

He'd loved her since freshman year of high school. Her smile had drawn him in and her soul had captured him forever. He couldn't imagine his life without her. And that's what scared him.

Things were changing.

She was changing.

And it terrified him to think that he might lose her.

The front door opened as he watched the silent house and a spear of lamplight sliced through the encroaching fog. His breath caught in his chest. Beth stepped out of the house, wearing that floor-length white cotton nightgown and robe set that she liked so much. Her auburn hair hung loose down past her shoulders, ending with a soft curl just above her breasts. He swallowed hard but couldn't tear his gaze from the woman who was his wife. His everything. With the lamplight glowing golden in the fog, she looked like an angel stepping out of the mists.

And just as unreachable.

He climbed out of the car, walked across the grass that needed mowing, and climbed the set of five steps to the wide front porch that ran halfway around the house.

"You're back," she said.

"You sound surprised." God, he wanted to touch her. To pull her close as he'd always been able to. But there was a distance between them now, brought on by too many harsh words and cold silences.

She swung her hair back over her shoulders and Tony's gaze dropped to the tiny ring of embroidered pink rosebuds lining the scoop-necked collar of her nightgown. How many times, he wondered, had he run his fingertips across those roses before sliding his hand beneath the fabric to cup her breasts? An ache he recognized and yearned to satisfy clawed at him, but there were things that had to be said. Things that had to be settled, first.

"Every time you leave I'm not sure if you're coming back. At least, not lately," she said, and the words cost her.

He heard the tremor in her voice and her pain jabbed at him. "How can you even think that?" he asked, honestly bewildered. Surely she knew that she was as much a part of him as his own heart. Did years together, years of loving, trusting, laughing, and loving, mean nothing? Did you suddenly wake up one morning and say, *Okay, that's it; I want something new*? Could you really turn love on and off like a faucet?

"How can I not, Tony?" Her bottom lip trembled and she made a Herculean effort to steady it. It almost worked. She shook her head and her mouth worked a time or two as she tried to regain control, but finally she gave it up and spoke anyway, letting the sound of tears color her voice. "I don't even know you anymore."

"I'm still me," he said, stepping closer and reaching for her. When she stepped back, out of reach, it almost killed him. "Beth, you know me better than anyone else on earth. You always have. Even when we were kids."

"But we're not kids anymore, Tony." She reached up and rubbed her hands across her face, wiping the glistening tracks of tears from her cheeks. "I'm not stupid. I know men get . . . *bored*. When wives become mothers, they're just not sexy anymore."

"Bullshit."

Her gaze snapped to his.

For the first time in his life, he wanted to grab his wife and shake her. "I haven't changed, *you* have," he countered, and kept his teeth gritted to avoid shouting as loud as he really wanted to. Amazing how quickly a man could move from sadness to fury.

"How have I changed?" she demanded, moving

farther away from him and the lamplight, walking down the porch toward the swing that drifted lazily in the soft wind. Pale tendrils of fog reached for her, snaking around her legs. "I'm still here. Night after night. I'm not the one running around God knows where doing God knows what."

"You're not happy anymore. Don't you think I noticed?"

"It's not that I'm *un*happy. I'm just . . ."

"What?"

"Tony, I tried to tell you this before and you didn't want to hear it."

"Try again."

"I just . . . need more."

"And that's what I'm trying to give you."

She laughed shortly, a hollow sound that rippled around him. "You're trying to give me more by never being around?"

He followed her, moving into the shadows until he was standing right beside her. Staring down into her face, he said, "You think I *like* being away from you and Tina? You think I'm enjoying myself here? I'm only doing this for you!"

Beth jerked her head back and stared at him in stunned surprise. *Her sake?* "What the hell are you talking about?" Her voice went up a notch.

Across the street, a light flashed on in an upper window.

He saw it, muttered a curse, then lowered his voice to a furious whisper. "Keep it down. You want to do this in front of *Abigail*, for God's sake?" The old woman had ears like a bat and there was nothing she'd like better than to have a fresh piece of gossip to report the following morning.

Beth cringed and lowered her voice. Fine. She'd be quiet, but she was going to have her say. Right here. Right now. Ever since Carla had offered to spy on Tony for her, Beth had been ashamed of herself. She should have confronted Tony the minute he'd started acting so weird. Waiting for a situation to get better only made for ulcers and profits for the Mylanta people.

"That's really good, Tony," she said, and punched his upper arm with a balled-up fist.

"Ow."

"You're doing this for me. Right. Gee, thanks so much." She hit him again. "Hey, it isn't every cheating husband who tells his wife that he closed his eyes and did it for her!"

"I'm not *cheating*!" he yelled, and instantly regretted it.

Down the street a dog barked, a window sash was thrown open, and someone yelled, "Keep it down!"

"Perfect," Beth muttered. "Think Abigail heard that all right or would you like to repeat it for those in the back of the audience?"

Dropping into the swing, Beth gave it a push with her foot, and the chains creaked as it slid into motion. Usually she loved sitting out here in this swing. She could watch her neighbors, play with Tina, wait for Tony to come home from the station. It was a place built with love. But tonight she only wanted to rock it hard enough to shake the misery out of her bones.

Tony, though, had other plans.

He snatched her up out of that swing, dragged her up close and tight to his chest, and wrapped his arms around her in an iron-hard grip. She shoved at his chest, hating that her body responded to his physical nearness even as her heart was aching. She shoved again but didn't move him an inch. He was the proverbial unmovable object.

"I have *never* cheated on you," he said, his voice a low rumble of sincerity.

Beth looked up at him, and even in the strangely distorted light, she saw his gaze, clear, straightforward, steady. He stared right into her eyes, and if he was lying, then he was a better actor than she'd ever given him credit for being. The ice around her heart thawed just a bit, weeping into her soul with a profound sense of relief.

But he wasn't finished.

Tightening his grip on her even further, he held her pressed close, her body aligned with his. She felt every solid, strong inch of him, and just as it had the first time he'd kissed her, when she was fourteen, her blood did a slow, thick dance through her veins.

"How could you even consider that?" he asked, his breath dusting across her cheeks, his voice scraping along her spine. "Damn it, Beth, you know me better. You know that I've never loved anyone the way I love you."

She dipped her head and stared at the vee of flesh exposed by the open collar of his shirt. "I didn't say you loved the bimbo, I said you were having sex with her."

He squeezed her tighter and the air left her lungs in a rush. "There *is* no bimbo." Lifting her clean off the porch, he drew her up until they were eye to eye. "And why in the hell would I want to go *have sex* when I could be here *making love*?"

Her stomach did a quick pitch and roll and her throat closed up. Love shone in his eyes. She felt it in his touch, heard it in his voice, and basked in it briefly. But there were still unanswered questions hanging in the air between them.

"If all of that's true—"

"*If?*"

"Then where are you going three nights a week? Why won't you tell me?"

Fog swirled in deeper, thicker, cloaking them in a misty blanket of gray, binding them together with filmy, damp fingers.

Sighing, Tony knew the only real way back to the closeness they'd always shared was the truth. Maybe he should have been honest from the get-go, but it wasn't easy for a man to admit to letting his wife down. Swinging her up into his arms, he sat down on the swing, held her close, and let the chains creak in accompaniment.

"I've been working," he said finally, and even then had to squeeze the words out like choking up something bitter.

"No, you haven't," she said, and tried to push off his lap. "I've called the station to talk to you and you're not there."

"I took a second job," he said, and watched her eyes widen, then narrow again in suspicion.

"Where?"

"At the community college."

"Doing what?"

"Teaching a course on criminal justice."

For several long seconds the creak of the swing was the only sound as Beth just stared at him.

"You're teaching."

"Yeah."

"Why?" she demanded, then took his face between her palms and forced him to meet her gaze. "And why didn't you tell me?"

"I should have." A rush of air left his lungs in a heavy sigh. "But it's not easy to admit that you're doing such a crappy job of supporting your wife that she wants to go out and get a job herself to take up your slack."

"Oh, Tony," she said, leaning forward until her forehead rested on his. "You really are an idiot."

"Thanks. Just what I needed to hear to make the night perfect."

Shaking her head, she pulled back, stared him directly in the eye, and said, "Me wanting to go back to work isn't about money. It's not about there being something wrong with *us*. It's about *me*." Her hands skimmed across his face, her fingers tracing the familiar pattern of his features, and when he turned his head to kiss her palm, goose bumps skittered along her spine. "Don't you get it? It's not that I don't love Tina. And you. I *do*. But I need to talk to grown-ups during the day. I need to use my brain for more than playing sing-along with Elmo and Big Bird."

He gave her a wry smile and she hoped she was

getting through. Staring into his eyes, Beth felt love pool inside her and overflow for this man. He'd tried to fix what was wrong—bungled it, sure, but he'd tried. And for that, she loved him. For that and so many other things.

"Tony, I love you. I just need to—"

He stopped her, placing his fingertips across her lips and smoothing them gently over her skin. "It's okay, baby. I think I get it." His gaze moving over her face, his hands followed, smoothing back her hair, skimming the line of her jaw, and tracing the length of her throat. When she shivered and moved closer, he whispered, "I love you so damn much that it scares me sometimes."

"I know; me, too." Her words were hushed, slipping into the surrounding mist and disappearing.

"I want you to be happy, Beth." He leaned in and kissed her neck, running the tip of his tongue across the pulse point at the base of her throat.

"Mmmmm. . . ." She tipped her head to one side and closed her eyes as his touch lit up the darkness inside. "Keep doing that," she told him quietly, "it's a good start."

"I've missed you, baby."

"Oh, God, Tony, me, too." She shifted on his lap, sliding around until she was straddling him, knees on either side of him. Hooking her arms around his neck, she kissed him, then ground her hips against him, loving the feel of his erection pressed tightly to her.

The fog swirled deeper, thicker, wrapping them in a soft, quiet world where only they, and the creak of the chains, existed.

He slipped his hands up, beneath the hem of that nightgown, and up and up until he could cup her breasts and finger her taut nipples. She moaned in a deep-throated sigh that rippled through him and ignited the fire he carried only for her. Watching her expression shift, tighten, he whispered, "Just how strong do you think this swing is?"

She looked him in the eye as her hands dropped to his belt buckle. In an instant, she had it open and was busily working the button and zipper on his khaki trousers. When her fingers curled around him and squeezed, she said softly, "I think we're about to find out."

"Noisiest night I've ever lived through," Abigail complained over a cup of herbal tea the next morning.

"Whatever was it?" Rachel asked, leaning across the table for a packet of artificial sweetener. She tore the pink paper open, dumped the contents into her tea, and stirred with one hand as she picked up her hot cinnamon roll with the other.

"Probably gangs," Virginia muttered, throwing cautious glances over her shoulders.

"Don't know what it was," Abigail said, "but the screeching and moaning damn near kept me up all night. And that blasted fog. Couldn't see a thing."

Stevie came out from behind the counter of Leaf and Bean, her coffee/tea shop, carrying a carafe of steaming coffee in one hand and a pot of hot water in the other. Offering refills to her customers, she listened in on the conversations as she passed.

". . . high school football team really needs help if we don't want to get laughed outta the league."

". . . there's a sale down at Hastings."

". . . Mike lost his paycheck at the Indian casino."

Smiling to herself, she threaded her way through the tables, topping off coffee cups and refilling tiny silver teapots. This was what she loved. Being here. In her own place, keeping up with the news in Chandler. Oh, she enjoyed traveling—seeing the world—but she loved coming back here. Home. Because *this* was the world that held her heart. Sooner or later, everyone in town came through her shop. A pastry and a cup of coffee—or tea, for the wimps—could solve most of life's problems.

Coming up on the Terrible Three, she heard Abigail again.

"It's a terrible thing when a person can't sleep at night."

Rachel piped up, talking around a mouthful of cinnamon roll. "The sheriff lives right across the street. Why didn't you call him?"

Abigail leaned in close and used her best theatrical whisper. "He was gone most of the night again. Looked out my window before I went to bed at eleven and he *still* wasn't there."

"A shame." Rachel clucked her tongue. "Such a nice couple."

"He's probably working for the Mob," Virginia said.

Irritation swept through her as Stevie stopped alongside their table and tried to remember that the old biddies spent nearly every morning in her shop. Steady customers. Everyone knew they were gossips. No one really paid attention. But hearing them go after her friends was just—*Oh, what the hell.*

Giving them a wide smile, she refilled teapots and said, "Abigail, you must be so proud. I hear your great-grandson checked into rehab on his own, this time."

The old woman sniffed and her rouge-filled cheeks looked even redder than usual.

"And, Rachel," Stevie continued, starting to enjoy herself, "you know, I wouldn't pay attention to what anyone else says. I think the face-lift turned out great."

Rachel sucked in air like a vacuum and huffed it out again with a muttered, "I never!"

"Gossips can be so cruel, don't you think? 'Morning, Virginia!" Then Stevie moved on, duty to friends done. As she crossed to the counter again, the bell over the front door sounded out and she turned to see Carla walking into the shop. Abbey, her faithful shadow, was just a step or two behind her, prancing, while Carla looked to be dragging.

"Coffee. Quick." Carla leaned on the polished wood counter and moaned helplessly. "My coffeemaker died this morning."

"God, it's an emergency." Grinning, Stevie hurriedly poured fresh coffee into a thick white ceramic mug.

Carla cupped it between her palms, inhaled the fragrance slowly, deeply, then sighed as she took her first sip. "You saved my life."

"My pleasure." Setting the coffeepot down on the hot plate, Stevie gave her full attention to Carla. "You look like shit."

"Gee, thanks." Though she didn't want to hear it, Carla knew it was the truth. Just taking a brief glimpse into her mirror this morning had damn near turned her into a pillar of salt. She didn't have bags under her eyes. She had luggage.

But then, what can you expect when you're up all night watching old reruns on Nickelodeon? Still, staying awake on purpose was better than being chased out of sleep by dreams.

And such dreams, she thought, taking another deep gulp of coffee. This time, it hadn't been nightmares of past failures that had tortured her. This time, it had been Jackson. His image. His kiss. Although she was forced to admit that waking up horny was better than waking up crying.

But torture was torture, right?

"Do you have any Oreos around here?"

"Good God!" Stevie looked at her, appalled. "I don't do Oreos, remember?"

"And you call yourself a friend."

"Biscotti?"

Grumbling, Carla said, "I guess that counts as a cookie."

"Peasant."

"Snob."

Stevie sighed, slid a chocolate-dipped biscotti under her friend's nose, wiped an imaginary spill from the counter, and asked, "What's up, Carla?"

"Nothing." She didn't want to talk about it. Didn't want to think about it, either, but she didn't seem to have a choice about that. That one stinking kiss had messed up her mind and set off a buzz in her body that was still humming twelve hours later.

She really needed a life. Someone else's, preferably. Because lately, her own really sucked.

The everyday chatter surrounding her was comforting somehow. She'd really missed dropping in here during the two weeks Stevie had closed up shop for a vacation. Shifting her gaze to take in the room, Carla looked quickly past the Threesome up front and instead enjoyed the look and feel of the Leaf and Bean.

Cream-colored walls, studded with the occasional dark wood beam, were hung with ferns and baskets of petunias that seemed to flower for Stevie no matter the time of year. Small tables and ladder-back chairs crowded the shining wood floor, and along one wall stood glass cases proudly displaying the baked goods that drew customers from as far away as Monterey.

"Grace," Stevie called out to the girl at the end of the counter, "I'm taking a break. You watch the place, okay?" Then she picked up a pot of coffee and told Carla, "Come on back."

Following the pot of coffee as much as anything else, Carla stepped behind the counter, snapped her fingers for Abbey to follow, and walked into the tiny cubbyhole Stevie referred to as "the office."

Basically the size of a small closet, the room held one desk, two chairs, and a file cabinet. A state-of-the art computer sat atop the gleaming desktop, and a poster of Paris hung on the wall. The one window looked out over the patio area and, beyond, the ocean. Plopping down into the chair behind the desk, Stevie pointed at the other chair and ordered, "Sit."

Too tired to argue, Carla did. "If you're going to lecture me, at least give me more coffee."

Refilling her cup, Stevie tossed a plain biscotti to Abbey, who lay down to crunch contentedly. Then, sitting back, Stevie crossed her feet on the corner of the desk and asked, "Okay, what's the what here?"

Hell, she'd come here knowing that Stevie would ask questions, Carla thought. So she might as well talk and get it over with. Staring into the black coffee, she said, "You remember Mr. Hot and Tasty?"

"Oh, yeah." When Carla said nothing, Stevie gasped, dropped her feet to the floor, and leaned forward. "You slept with him."

"Nope. Close," *oh God, so close,* "but no cigar."

"Well, damn."

"You could say that."

"What else could I say?" Stevie asked quietly.

"Oh, you could say that I really, really . . . like him."

"Like?"

"That's as far as I'm willing to go," or, at least, admit to, Carla told herself. She wouldn't have been stupid enough to fall in love with the wrong man again, right? No one was dumb enough to fall in love with a man who was still in love with his dead wife. A man who was here only temporarily. A man who turned her knees to butter and her blood to boiling.

"You're in love with him, aren't you?"

Carla lifted her gaze to look at her best friend. "Not yet. But God help me, it wouldn't take much."

"And that's bad because . . . ?"

Leaning back in her chair, Carla tightened her grip on the coffee cup and shook her head. "How many reasons do you need?"

"What've you got?"

"Let's see. . . ." She held up one hand and lifted one finger for each reason as she ticked them off. "He's only here for the summer. He's got a daughter with a problem that terrifies him. He's still in love with his dead wife. He's only here for the summer."

"You said that one already."

"It's a big one. Deserves to be counted twice."

"Uh-huh. And how do you know he's still in love with his wife?"

"When he kissed me"—she sighed and thought about it—"it was great for a couple minutes there. Then he backed off so fast, it was like he was Dracula and I was wearing a garlic corsage."

"He kissed you?"

"Oh, yeah."

"A friendly peck on the cheek?"

Carla shook her head. "No, more of a close examination of my tonsils."

"This sounds promising."

She grumbled, "Then I'm telling it wrong."

"Carla, stop thinking so much, will you?" Stevie topped off her coffee again. "What do your instincts say?"

Well, that was easy. Her whole body was screaming at her to go over to Jackson's place and kiss him again. But her instincts were telling her to back off. To let this go before she got hurt again.

And if she had any sense at all, she'd listen.

Damn it, she hadn't wanted this. Hadn't counted on it. Sure, she made jokes now about her fiancé dropping her and running back to his old girlfriend. But that was simply a good Candellano diversionary tactic. If you laughed first, then people were laughing *with* you. Not *at* you. But the real truth, the one she hid even from herself most of the time, was that she'd been humiliated when the man she'd agreed to marry had packed up and taken off.

Her pride had taken a beating and her heart had been kicked around until it still ached at the oddest moments. So now, she had to wonder . . . did she really want to set herself up for another fall? Especially when she had the distinct feeling that if she lost again, the pain this time would be soul-shattering? She'd already lost one man to a former love.

Did she really want to lose one to a ghost?

CHAPTER FIFTEEN

"No." JACKSON LOOKED DOWN at his little girl and sighed. Damn. She was still wearing the expression that clearly said, I hate my completely crappy father. He'd been looking at that fierce, silent, temper tantrum for the last hour. Ever since he'd had to stop her from going over to Carla's house.

And in a weird sort of way, he was almost enjoying this show of emotion. Even if it was negative and aimed directly at him. For a solid year now, Reese had been more or less drifting through the world. She touched nothing and allowed nothing to touch her. She ate and slept and went through the motions of living, but she'd only been a spectator in her own life.

Jackson's own life had changed drastically, too. He'd cut back on work over the last few months until he was now a rare visitor in his own office. He'd shifted so many of his clients to other lawyers that the only person who would really notice his absence this summer was his secretary—and he was pretty sure her résumé would be making the rounds while he was gone.

And he didn't give a damn.

For years he'd focused on nothing but the law, his career. Success had become the only goal worth striving for. In his desperation to prove to himself and everyone else that he was more than an orphan in an expensive suit, he'd lost everything that should have been important. He'd married the wrong woman for the wrong reasons and then resented the demands she'd made on his time. They'd had a child Diane hadn't really wanted, fought more than they'd talked, and then finally, in the space of one rainy morning, he'd become a single parent with no clue at all about how to do the most important job he would ever have.

What the hell did he know about families? Little girls? Oh, he loved Reese. Had from the moment of her birth. But was love enough? Didn't she need more, and if she did, would he be able to give it to her?

Jackson still remembered the panic he'd felt the first time he and Reese had been left alone. Diane's funeral service barely over, the mourners had left as quickly as was socially acceptable. And the Barringtons hadn't stayed much longer. Then it was just him and Reese. As it had been for the last year.

And despite everything, this time with her had been precious. He'd gotten closer to her than he probably would have been if tragedy hadn't dropped into their laps. He knew firsthand what it was like to supervise bath time. To see her smile when she woke up—before she remembered to shut herself down. He held her when she cried and soothed her nightmares. He'd found the person inside his little girl and life would never be the same for him—no matter *what* happened.

But now things were different. Things were changing. Here, in this place, with these people, Reese was beginning to find her way back. And for that he was more than willing to put up with her anger. Who knew? One of these days, she might actually open her mouth and argue with him. And there probably weren't many parents who would admit to looking forward to that.

Reese crossed her arms over her narrow chest, stuck her bottom lip out, and glared at him.

He almost smiled. "You can make that face at me all day and it's still not going to change anything."

Her bottom lip jutted out just a bit farther. The little girl took a deep breath and huffed it out, clearly disgusted. She pointed across the street, at Carla's house, then made a giant *X* over her own heart.

Jackson sighed and tossed a quick glance at Carla's place himself before looking back at his daughter. "Honey, I know Carla promised you could go with her to take the puppies to the vet today."

Reese planted both hands on her tiny hips and tapped the toe of one Scooby shoe against the grass.

"But," Jackson pointed out, "she's not there. You can see that her Jeep's not in the driveway. She must have already gone."

Reese shook her head furiously.

"She probably just forgot," Jackson tried to ease the sting of being left behind, but it wasn't easy. Especially since he had the feeling *he* was the reason behind Carla's early-morning escape. No doubt after what had happened between them the night before, she hadn't wanted to be bothered with him *or* his daughter. And he really couldn't blame her for it. Though how he was supposed to make Reese understand it all was beyond him.

"Look, sweetie," he said, going down on one knee in front of her. "Why don't you and I go down to the beach? Build a castle or something in the sand?"

Her mouth screwed up and she heaved a sigh worthy of Sarah Bernhardt. Clearly, he was no substitute for a cluster of puppies. But at last, she seemed to decide that he was better than nothing, and nodded.

"Good." Pulling her into his arms, he held her close and patted her back. He should have kept his distance from Carla. All along, he'd known and told himself that any attempt at a relationship would be a mistake. In too many ways to count. And now because of him, his daughter was disappointed and hurt. "You'll see," he said, keeping his voice a lot more cheerful than he felt. "We'll have fun."

She stiffened in his arms and he drew back, to see her staring off down the street. It was only then he heard the muffled roar of a car engine and half-turned to watch Carla barreling down the street and then pulling into her driveway. Car parked, she climbed out, with Abbey jumping to the ground right beside her.

Carla sighed as she stared across the street at the man and his daughter. She pushed her hair back out of her eyes and told herself that she had to get used to being around them. Whatever happened—or didn't happen—between her and Jackson, he and Reese were an undeniable part of her life, at least for the rest of the summer. She couldn't ignore them. She couldn't avoid them. She could only try to keep her feelings as protected as she could.

Then Jackson stood up, shoved one hand into his pocket, and laid the other on Reese's shoulder. The wind ruffled his hair and Carla knew it was already too late. Her feelings were involved. For better or for worse, Jackson Wyatt had slipped into her life, and getting him out again wasn't going to be easy or painless.

He shifted position slightly, moving his long jean-clad legs into a wide stance. His dark blue T-shirt strained across a chest that was too broad to be ignored. And even from across the street, she felt the heat of his gaze lock on her and dip inside where that heat bubbled and frothed, demanding to be noticed.

Whoa. She hadn't had *nearly* enough coffee at Stevie's place.

Beside her, Abbey quivered in eager anticipation, wagged her tail, and took a step or two down the drive. Then the dog looked back at Carla as if asking permission to continue.

"You, too, huh?" Heck, even her dog had adopted the Wyatts, most especially the little girl who so clearly needed the unconditional love that Abbey offered. And what, Carla wondered, did the girl's father need? There was something in his eyes that called to her. Something in his touch that made her want more, despite the trouble she knew it would cause. But it was more than hormones. Like she'd told Stevie . . . it wouldn't take much to make her love him. But if she did, what then? He didn't want love. He'd had it. And, with his dead wife, had lost it.

Besides, it wasn't just Jackson staking a claim on

her heart. There was Reese, too. If she allowed herself to love them . . . then when they left, her heart would be broken twice over.

Call her coward, that just didn't sound like a good time.

Abbey woofed, dragging Carla's attention back to the moment at hand. "Right," she said. Giving a quick glance at the road to make sure there were no other cars around, Carla smiled and said, "Go ahead."

Abbey took off like a shot, golden hair flying, legs sprinting her toward the little girl she loved. Across the street, Reese opened her arms and laughed as Abbey rushed to her.

Carla kept her gaze locked on the scene as she crossed the street, then slowly walked up the incline toward Jackson. All she had to do was get a grip. And not on him, despite how much she wanted to. Briefly, she wished she could take Stevie's advice. Use him and move on. But she couldn't. Heck, even Stevie couldn't do it. She talked a good game, but when it came right down to it, her friend was no different from Carla when it came to the basics. Sex without emotion . . . some kind of connection just wasn't an option.

Damn it.

When she finally shifted her gaze away from the love fest that was Abbey and Reese to look at Jackson, she almost wished she hadn't. Staring up into his deep blue eyes, she felt that now-familiar lurch of hormone juice scuttling through her body. She locked her knees and walked the last few steps like Frankenstein.

Embarrassing but preferable to melting into a puddle at his feet.

Oh, man.

"I didn't expect to see you this morning," he said, his voice a low scrape of sound in the otherwise still air.

"Yeah, well," she said with a shrug that belied the turmoil within, "I'm a constant source of surprises."

"So I'm finding out."

That flash of interest in his eyes set off a like flash in her bloodstream that Carla really didn't want to think about at the moment. So she didn't.

"Anyway," she said, a little louder than she'd planned, "I'll be ready to leave for the vet's in a few minutes. Reese?" She waited until the little girl tore her attention from Abbey to look up at her. "You still want to come with me?"

The child nodded so fiercely, one messy pigtail swung hard against her face, slapping her in the eye. Carla grinned. Impossible not to. Were all kids this great? "Okay then. I'll load up the puppies and then pick you up, all right?"

Reese nodded again, a bit more carefully this time, then buried her face in Abbey's golden hair.

Carla started back down the incline, and before she'd taken more than a couple of steps, she heard Jackson's footsteps behind her. But then, she didn't have to hear him to know he was there. She *felt* his presence in every corpuscle. Oh, for God's sake. She was beginning to sound like a soap opera. He laid one hand on her arm and she stopped, braced herself against the ribbon of warmth unfolding inside her, then turned around to look at him.

"Thanks," he said.

"For what?"

He let his hand drop and she missed the feel of his fingertips on her skin. Yeah, she was dealing with this really well.

"For taking Reese with you," he was saying. "She was really looking forward to it."

Carla just stared at him for a long minute. Well, that was insulting. He hadn't expected her to come through, she thought, just a little disgusted. Who was he used to dealing with that he would assume she would go back on her word? To a *kid*, no less. Well, fine, it wasn't easy to face him again this morning, but that didn't mean she was going to hide. Although, an annoyingly honest, quiet little voice in her mind whispered, she had hidden from other things before.

That was different, though. That was—never mind. The point was, she wouldn't hide from a man just because she was embarrassed. Hell, she was a Candellano. She'd been embarrassed regularly since she was a kid.

"And just why was it I was supposed to not show up?"

"Well," he said softly, tossing a quick glance at his daughter to make sure she wasn't listening before looking back at Carla. "Last night . . ."

"Last night was last night. No biggie." *Liar. Hell, if she tried, she could probably still taste him.* "Look, it was a kiss. Okay?"

"It was more than that," he muttered, keeping his voice pitched at a level low enough to rumble along her spine.

"Yeah, you're right," she said. "It was a kiss and a brush-off all in one move."

"I wasn't dumping you."

"I didn't say dumped."

"Fine. I wasn't brushing you off."

"Gee, and it felt so familiar."

"Christ, you could drive a man nuts."

"It's a gift."

"One of many."

"Uh-huh." Carla tossed her hair back out of her eyes and told herself not to listen to the nice stuff. Not to notice how good he smelled or to recall how it had felt to be held against that broad chest and caressed by those hands. Better to remember that this was a man on the rebound from a dead wife. And there was no way she could win against that kind of competition. Time to get the hell out of Dodge.

But before she did, there was one thing she wanted clear. Lifting one hand, she shielded her eyes from the morning sunlight that seemed to outline his silhouette in a bright gold that sizzled around him. Squinting slightly, she met his gaze squarely and said, "Whatever else is going on here, Jackson, there's one thing you should know. I always keep my promises. No matter what."

"I'll remember that."

She nodded, licked her lips, and rocked on her heels. "Okay then. Good."

"Fine."

"Wonderful."

He studied her for a long minute or two, his gaze hot and dark enough to fuel countless daydreams. And all she could think was, *Breathe, Carla. Breathe.*

· · ·

Less than a week later, it was the Fourth of July and the town of Chandler was geared up for its annual celebration. Red, white, and blue bunting draped across Main Street and American flags fluttered from every lamppost. Kids on skateboards rode sidewalk waves as they slipped in and out of the holiday crowds, laughter drifting in their wake. A few half-hearted shouts from their deftly avoided targets followed them, but no one paid much attention.

At the edge of town, a traveling carnival beckoned, with rainbow-colored tents and tinny circus music blasting from overhead speakers. A Tilt-A-Whirl, a mini–roller coaster, and a carousel for toddlers, made up of a circle of grinning dolphins wearing chipped blue paint, were like a siren's song. Small children tugged impatiently at parents who moved too slowly, older kids raced toward the promise of fun, games, and maybe a little adventure, and teenagers strolled hand in hand, young love on parade.

Carla grinned and sucked in the smells of the Fourth; burning popcorn, roasting hot dogs, and suntan lotion. *Life is good.* The sun shone down from a brassy blue sky, and a stiff ocean wind kept the heat from settling long enough to be annoying. Thanks to all of her good Italian blood, her shoulders, bared in her hot pink tank top, weren't turning red, and her denim shorts showed off her legs and her tan to perfection. Crepe paper was stuck to the bottom of her right sandal, courtesy of the cotton candy she'd stepped in earlier, but hey. Could've been worse. She might've been barefoot.

God, she loved the Fourth of July celebrations in

Chandler. On this one day of the year, she delighted in living in a Mayberryesque town.

Neighbors cheered when the tiny parade moved down Main Street and waved to this year's Queen of Chandler as she rocked unsteadily on her flower-bedecked throne. They took off their hats and solemnly saluted the American flag as it was proudly carried by members of the VFW. They laughed when the 4-H Club's pig scampered off into the crowd and cheered when the high school band made it through "God Bless America" without hitting one sour note. They shared memories of past parades and came together in a way that citizens of a bigger city would never understand.

Nearing the edge of town, Carla smiled at the tiny flag jutting up from Abigail's lacquered hairdo. But when she noticed Rachel carrying a covered dish, Carla gave silent thanks that she wouldn't be forced to eat whatever ptomaine specialty lurked within. Keeping one hand on Abbey's collar, she slipped behind Frank Pezzini as he turned his dubious charm on a female tourist who looked desperate to escape.

"Better you than me," Carla murmured, and headed past the entrance to the carnival with a reluctant glance. But she knew the rules. Had known them since she was a child. First lunch with the family. *Then* the carnival.

"I know what it is to lose someone you love," Mama Candellano was saying. "When Carla's papa died"—she crossed herself quickly—"God rest his soul, I cried enough to float the house away. But time passes. And the tears don't come all the time anymore."

She meant well, Jackson told himself, and wondered briefly what this nice woman would have to say if she guessed that he wasn't mourning Diane. That he'd never really even missed her. They'd been too separate. Too distant when she was alive for him to pretend devastation once she was gone.

That kind of marriage just didn't exist in Angela Candellano's universe, and damned if he didn't envy her that. But then, he thought as he looked around, he envied the Candellanos quite a bit in general.

Around him, the family, minus Carla, was busily digging into the picnic lunch they'd set up only minutes before. Submarine sandwiches, potato salad, and, of course, pasta salad were spread out in a banquet like he'd never seen before. They laughed at the same jokes, teased one another, and he'd even caught the worried glances being tossed at Nick, who was already on his third beer in less than an hour.

Jackson had been glad of Mama's invitation to join them for the Fourth. It was good for Reese to be around them. To feel, even briefly, what it was like to be surrounded by a happy family. *That's a damn lie.* Hell, it wasn't because of Reese he wanted to be here. He wanted to see Carla. He wanted to be near her. Around her. *In* her.

Damn it.

Jackson scraped one hand across his face and focused his attention on the woman still talking to him.

"So I say," Mama wound up what must have been a long speech, "you have to get back on the horse." She paused for a second, then leaned in and looked him in the eye. "By this, I don't mean get on my daughter, you understand."

Jackson choked on a gulp of lemonade and just managed to keep from spitting it out.

"Jesus, Mama," Nick blurted, "why don't you just slap Carla's picture on eBay and see how much you can get for her?"

"Now you eavesdrop?" Mama demanded, completely glossing over the question.

"Hard not to," Nick pointed out, and took another long pull on the beer bottle. Then he looked at Jackson and said, "My sister's not up for grabs."

"I didn't say she was." Hell, he wasn't sure how any of this had happened.

"Just so you know."

"Nicky, what's the matter with you?"

"With *me*?" he countered.

"Shut up, Nick," Tony ordered from across the blanket.

"Ah, the voice of reason. Yes, sir, Sheriff." Nick saluted his brother by tipping the neck of the bottle to his forehead.

Mama snatched the bottle from his hand, then slapped the back of his head with her fingertips.

"Hey!"

"Enough, Nick," she said, and the flash in her eyes was clear even to Jackson. "Before you embarrass me."

"Oh, great. Now I'm embarrassing."

Paul piped up, "Give it a rest, Nick."

"You, too?" He looked at his twin. "Hell, you should be on my side."

"You're drunk."

"Not yet," he said, "but the day is young."

"Had enough of the happy family routine?" Carla asked as she strolled up.

Jackson's gaze slammed into hers, then slowly drifted down to enjoy the picture she made. Her family and everyone else faded away. All he could see was her. Long dark curls tossed by the wind, her tank top and shorts exposed plenty of sun-kissed skin the color of warm honey. Brown leather sandals were strapped to her slender feet, and that silver toe ring of hers glinted in the sunlight. Her brown eyes shone and damn near sparkled as she looked at him, and he felt the solid punch of hot frenzied need stab into his stomach.

"Huh?" he said when he could make his voice work again.

"Smooth talker," she countered, and smiled at him.

Damn it, she had weapons and wasn't afraid to use 'em. The scoop neck of her tank top dipped dangerously low over the tops of her breasts, and as a cool wind shot past them, he noted, with some inner pain, that she wasn't wearing a bra, either.

The last few days had been a kind of living torture. Reese had completely adopted herself out to Carla and those puppies. And naturally, where his daughter went, he went. He'd spent every day with Carla, and yet apart. There'd been no more kisses. No more touching. Just the sound of her voice, the music of her laughter, and the constant niggling ache to have more. And he'd spent every night thinking about what that *more* would be. What he'd like to be doing to her. With her.

He was really getting sick of midnight Nickelodeon.

"Carla!" Mama beamed at her as though she'd just flown in from Paris and hadn't been seen in ten years. But in the next instant, that smile faded. "You're late."

"I know. Wanted to miss the work."

Reese, cuddled up on Mama's lap, grinned brightly, then jumped up, ran around the edge of the blanket, and threw herself at Carla. When those small arms wrapped around her waist and squeezed, Carla felt her heart clench. Amazing what power this child had gained over her. And seeing the little girl sitting on Mama's lap, being cooed and fussed over, had felt . . . *right*. The child had become a part of the Candellano family, and Carla knew that when the Wyatts eventually left, she wouldn't be the only one to miss them.

Still, they weren't leaving today, so she refused to think about the emptiness looming ahead. Smiling, she smoothed her hand over the girl's head and said, "I'm glad to see you, too, sweetie. You look so pretty today."

Reese preened and stepped back from Carla so that she could fully appreciate the blue-flower-sprigged yellow sundress she wore. She gave a slow twirl and Carla smiled in approval. "Gorgeous."

Reese pointed to her shoes.

Carla checked out the white leather sandals with garish paste gems glued to them. "Wow," she said admiringly, "princess sandals!"

Reese grinned again and did a brief two-step, the better to flash those jewels in the sunlight.

Carla shot a glance at Jackson, and the expression on his face as he watched her and Reese was so tender, she almost felt guilty for noticing him in an unguarded moment.

"You're the prettiest girl here," Carla proclaimed, though her throat felt tight.

"I told her that, too," Mama said. "The prettiest six-year-old and Tina is the prettiest two-year-old. Aren't we lucky?"

"Yeah," Carla murmured, stroking the girl's hair back from her face. "Lucky." Then inhaling sharply, she said, "Why don't you give Abbey some water, sweetie?"

Reese nodded and hooked her fingers through Abbey's collar to lead the dog around the blanket.

"Good call on missing the work," Nick told his sister in the silence that followed. "You missed the auction, too."

"Auction?"

"Yeah, Mama's taking offers and—"

Mama slapped the back of his head again.

Nick sighed and picked up his sandwich.

Something was going on and Carla wasn't entirely sure she wanted to know what it was. On the other hand . . . she looked at Jackson. "You're Switzerland here."

"I am?" Those blue eyes of his widened with feigned innocence and one corner of his mouth twitched into a brief half-smile, and damned if Carla's stomach didn't do the now-familiar pitch and roll.

"No family ties or allies," she pointed out. "So what's going on?"

Jackson glanced at Nick, then Mama, before answering, "Switzerland claims neutrality."

"Big help."

"Smart man," Tony muttered.

Conversation rose up around them again and Carla

sat down between Nick and Beth. Close enough so that she could see Jackson clearly but not close enough to drive herself insane. She'd expected to find Jackson and Reese here. Of course her mother would invite them. Mama would never stand for anyone being alone when they could be in the middle of the Candellanos.

It's all right. She could do this. Hadn't she and Jackson been getting along perfectly well in the last several days? Reese spent most of her time with Carla and the puppies, who were growing so fast, it was hard to believe just a couple of weeks ago they were nothing more than fur balls. And with Reese at Carla's house, it was only natural for Jackson to be around, too.

And it was probably natural that she'd done enough daydreaming about him that her blood seemed to be on continual boil and her shower massage was starting to look better and better.

"You okay?" Beth whispered.

"Terrific."

"Good." Beth's gaze shot to her husband and a slow smile curved her mouth. Carla grabbed another carrot and wished it were a cookie. Wasn't it bad enough she had to sit here horny and alone? Did she have to watch her sister-in-law's obvious satisfaction on top of it?

Ever since she and Tony had straightened out their problems, they'd been downright sickening.

"Jackson seems nice."

Carla stared at her. "Not you, too."

"What's that mean?"

"You're siding with Mama?" Carla kept her voice low, not wanting him to overhear anything.

"Hey, he's better than Frank."

"*Dead* is better than Frank."

"Good point." Beth leaned back, bracing her palms flat behind her.

"Change of subject," Carla announced, and reached for half a sandwich. "When do you start work again?"

Three boys about twelve years old ran up to the blanket and stopped next to Nick. Holding out football cards with his picture on them, they asked for autographs, and thankfully, Nick was sober enough to comply. Carla frowned as she watched her brother smile weakly and wave to the kids as they left, then nod to the adults, who gave him a hearty thumbs-up. For a hometown hero, Nick didn't look too happy.

But Beth was talking and Carla turned her head to look at her.

"Next week," her sister-in-law said, "I'll be going into the real estate office three days a week. Not full-time, but a little more than part-time."

"Who've you got to watch Tina?"

Beth laughed and tossed her auburn hair back from her face. "Mama volunteered before I could finish asking her."

Nothing Mama would like better than baby-sitting her granddaughter. "So everything's worked out?"

"Oh, yeah," Beth said, practically purring. "Things're great." Then she took a good long look at Carla and suggested, "So now that we've got *my* life straightened out, what're we going to do about yours?"

"We? Who's *we*?"

Beth grinned. "I was talking to Stevie and—"

"Don't tell me." Carla held up one hand. "Use him and discard him."

"Use him, at least," Beth said, glancing at the man in question. "I mean, Carla, *look* at him."

"I have."

"So do something."

"Okay," Carla said, dusting her palms together. "Get everybody off the blanket."

"Funny."

"I try."

Thankfully, then, Tina distracted Beth, and Carla was left to her own thoughts. And God knew she had plenty of them. Too many, really. She'd argued with herself so much lately that she was beginning to feel like Sybil.

There were lots of things she'd *like* to do. But she'd just be lining up to have her heart stomped into the dust. Would the pain be worth the pleasure?

Two hours later, Carla and Jackson wandered through the carnival area, watching Reese as she stopped every few feet to inspect something new or interesting. They'd played the ring-toss game until Jackson had won Reese a lop-eared stuffed panda. They'd eaten cotton candy and popcorn, had their pictures taken with Zippy the clown, and watched an absolutely disgusting pie-eating contest.

Jackson was having as much fun as Reese.

"You act like you've never been to a carnival before," Carla said, taking a bite of her cherry Sno-Cone.

"I haven't," he said, glancing at her long enough to notice the cherry syrup had painted her lips a deep, tempting red. "Never had time, I guess. And Diane wasn't a carnival kind of person."

"I'm guessing the grandparents aren't, either."

"No." He actually chuckled at the thought of the Barringtons wandering through a sawdust-littered field, eating cotton candy.

"They seem scary."

"They *are* scary," he admitted, hating the fact that just the thought of those people was enough to toss a wet blanket on a great day.

"What do they want?" Carla asked.

He looked at her. "Reese. They want Reese."

Appalled, she glanced at the child feeding Abbey a handful of popcorn. She stiffened in outrage and a swell of gratitude filled him as she said, "Well, they can't have her."

"That's what I've been saying."

"Keep saying it."

They walked again, with Reese leading the way toward the mini–roller coaster. Jackson shoved his hands into his pockets and realized how good it felt to have someone on his side. To see that he couldn't possibly turn his daughter over to people as cold and distant as the Barringtons.

Frustration rose up inside him. Shaking his head, he stared at Reese as he said, "They want to take her from me and put her in a hospital. Fair Haven Clinic. Twenty-four-hour-a-day therapy."

"Jesus," Carla whispered with a shudder. "Seems a little extreme."

"They're not patient people. They say it's been a year and she should be talking."

"And locking her away is the answer?"

"No. It's not." He shook his head and pulled one

hand out of his pocket to wave at his little girl. "Look at her. She's doing great here. She's happy. She's . . . she's going to talk soon. I know it."

Jackson handed the man in charge a ticket and Reese clambered into a seat on the mini-coaster. As the ride chugged off on its rail, Carla said, "It's none of my business, I know, but—"

"But?" He looked down at her as he curled his fingers over the hot bright orange metal railing.

"Maybe therapy's not such a bad idea?"

"We already tried it," he said, cutting her off. "Three weeks they worked with her and nothing changed."

"Three whole weeks, huh?"

He shot her a glance. No one understood. But three weeks had felt like three years. "Reese hated it. She cried." He closed his eyes at the memory and saw his child again as she'd been. Withdrawn. Sad. So damn sad. "Big, silent tears rolled down her face every time she had to go." He opened his eyes again and looked at Carla, whose eyes shone with a sympathy and understanding that warmed him. "I couldn't do it anymore. Couldn't make her go. Couldn't put her through it."

Circus music drifted down around them. People pushed past them, laughing, talking.

"What happened to cause this?" she asked, and he realized that he'd never really told her. Funny. Most people, when they met Reese, immediately wanted to know what was behind her behavior. Not Carla, though. She just loved. And he was humbled by the gift this woman had given his child. In return, he thought, the least he owed her was an explanation.

He inhaled sharply, then blew it out in a rush. Best to get this said before the ride was over and Reese rejoined them. "It was a car accident. Reese had a doctor's appointment. Nothing serious. Just a checkup. Her mother was driving. In the rain. A truck pulled out in front of her and Diane drove right into it."

"Oh God, Jackson."

She laid her hand atop his and he turned his hand so that he could link his fingers through hers and hold on.

"Reese was trapped in the wrecked car with her mother's body for nearly two hours before the firemen could get her out."

A whisper of pain, of tender sympathy, gushed from her, but he kept talking, wanting to get it all said.

"She was screaming when I got to the scene. Diane died instantly, but Reese was screaming." He shoved his free hand through his hair, then wiped his palm across his face. "I can still hear her," he murmured. "I close my eyes and I can still hear her."

"Jackson—"

He shook his head and watched as the roller coaster came to a jerky stop right in front of them. Reese, sitting in the third seat, beamed at him, her face filled with childish excitement and the kind of joy he'd almost given up on seeing ever again. As the carnival worker went along the coaster, unfastening the safety straps, Jackson finished his story, never taking his eyes off Reese.

"When the firemen finally pulled her out of the car and I could reach her . . ." He swallowed hard. "She looked at me through big, teary eyes and the screams stopped. I haven't heard a sound from her since—not until the day at your house, when she laughed." He turned then to look at Carla, and the tears in her eyes seemed to overflow into his heart, his soul. "You reached her, Carla. When no one and nothing else had, *you* reached her."

"It wasn't me," she said, blinking back the tears and holding tightly to his hand. "It was the puppies."

"And you." He glanced down at their joined hands and smiled as Reese ran up to them and laid both of her hands atop theirs. "You touched us both, Carla. And damned if I know what to do about it."

CHAPTER
SIXTEEN

At dusk, the dancing started.

One section of the grassy field was staked out and claimed as a makeshift dance floor. Strings of tiny white lights reached out from the nearby trees and crisscrossed the area, shining like lines of low-hanging stars. Someone had hooked a stereo system up to the speakers and a wildly diverse selection of rock and roll, Frank Sinatra, and country music poured out over the crowd.

And as Ol' Blue Eyes sang about doing it "his way," Tony and Beth whirled through the ankle-high grass, eyes only for each other. Nick stood to one side, beer in hand, watching all of the couples. Paul did a slow waltz with baby Tina cradled in his arms and Jackson swayed in time to the music, with Reese standing on the tops of his feet and grinning up at him.

A sunset that looked as if it had been painted especially for the occasion hung out over the ocean, turning the water into a shimmering surface of gold and crimson. A soft wind rippled through the crowd, and as the first stars peeked through the black velvet sky Carla draped an arm around Stevie's shoulders and watched the party.

"What a great day, huh?" she asked.

"Terrific," her friend agreed. "Did you hear? Rachel's Fiesta Platter Surprise caused a minor outbreak."

"Of what?"

"Food poisoning."

"Serious?"

"Nobody died," Stevie assured her. "But by now they're probably wishing they had."

"Good God. Wonder what the 'surprise' in Fiesta Surprise was?"

"As far as I'm concerned," Stevie said, "the surprise is that anyone'll eat anything that woman cooks."

"They don't want to hurt her feelings."

"So instead they end up worshipping at the porcelain altar."

Carla's mouth twitched, and when she looked at Stevie, they both gave in to the laughter nearly choking them.

"Ah," Carla mused, "life in Chandler. Always interesting."

"Some times more than others."

"Huh?"

"You should be out there dancing," Stevie told her.

"I don't see you out there."

"Strictly supervisory position this year, thanks."

Frowning, Carla studied her friend for a long minute. "You're not still hung up on—" She jerked her head in her jerk of a brother Nick's direction.

"Nope," Stevie assured her. "But my body . . ." she sighed. "Remembers. Though it's been two years and the memory's vague."

"Oh, crap." Carla hated thinking of her best friend still hurting over Nick's betrayal.

"Hey, chill out." The blonde smiled and shook her head. "I'm over it. Probably all I need is another man. Quick." Cocking her head, she asked, "Wanna lend me yours?"

"He's not mine," Carla said. "And *no*."

Stevie's gaze shifted to the dance area and locked onto Jackson, smiling down at his daughter. She'd finally had a chance to spend some time with the man who was so occupying her best friend's thoughts and feelings lately. And she liked him. Which was both good and bad, Stevie figured. Good because Carla surely deserved a break. Bad because Jackson Wyatt was going to be leaving real damn soon. Still, the summer was young yet, and there was a lot to be said for taking advantage of the here and now.

"He's a good one, Carla."

"Yeah, I think so." Hell, Carla *knew* so. She'd spent too much time with him in the last few weeks not to have noticed. His tenderness with his daughter. His desperation to reach the child before he lost her forever. He was giving his all to that little girl and it touched Carla deeply to be a witness to it. But it was so much more than that, she thought. It was little things. Like the way his cold, standoffish facade had melted during the time he'd been in Chandler. How he smiled when he saw her. And the way his slightest touch made her tremble.

Okay, that last one wasn't a "little" thing. It was pretty damn big. And getting bigger all the time. She seemed to be in a constant state of arousal these days. Lately she'd watched more late-night TV than she had in years. Even her nightmares hadn't chased her from sleep as often as thoughts of Jackson did.

"Then why," Stevie said, "don't you get out there and—oops. Never mind."

"What?" Carla asked, coming up out of her thoughts like a swimmer breaching the surface of the ocean after a particularly long dive.

"Listen," her friend said.

She did. The music had changed; the slow, smooth strains of Frank Sinatra gave way to a pulsing beat and a deep, throbbing voice.

A slow smile curved Carla's lips even as she shook her head and started backing up. "Oh, man. . . ."

Stevie laughed and grabbed Carla's arm, holding her in place. "It's no use," she said. "Here they come."

Sure enough, Tony, Paul, and Nick were heading right for her, silly grins on their faces.

"Let's go, little sis," Tony said, taking one of her hands in his.

"Tradition," Paul said simply, snatching her other hand.

"We're bigger than you," Nick warned, and stepped behind her to give her a push.

"Help?" Carla said, looking back at Stevie.

"You don't *want* help and you know it," her friend said on a laugh, moving closer to the dance floor for a good view.

No, Carla thought, she didn't want help. And she

only pretended to protest. The real truth was, she'd be devastated if this particular tradition ever ended.

Van Morrison's song, "Brown-Eyed Girl," blasted across the crowd as the Candellanos moved to the center of the grass. Tony, being the oldest, claimed the first part of the dance and swept his younger sister into a fast-paced whirl. He was stalwart, brave, and proud. The strong one. The one everyone depended on. And she loved him fiercely.

She laughed up into his eyes and remembered every other year when her brothers had claimed this dance with her. From the time she was a kid and thought her three brothers were the most fabulous people on earth, this song had been *hers*.

The Candellanos' own "brown-eyed girl."

And every time she heard it played on the radio, it brought back wonderful memories and a sense of warmth that had seen her through some very dark times.

Tony grinned and handed her off to Nick with a flourish. Nick led her in a half-assed jitterbug that had her laughing so hard she could hardly keep up. Again and again, he spun her around the grass, singing in a slightly slurred, very off-key voice that still touched her heart. Nick, the show-off. Nick, the supremely confident one, the one who made them laugh and kept them guessing. And even when she wanted to drop-kick him, she loved him so much it hurt.

Then it was Paul's turn and Carla's heart squeezed painfully. Paul was so reserved, so quiet, so the opposite of every other Candellano, that when he really smiled, as he was doing now, it took her breath away. The tender one. The brother who protected his heart as carefully as he did his computer calculations. And though all three of her brothers held a piece of her heart, Carla sometimes thought she loved Paul best of all.

For the last chorus of the song, the four of them draped their arms around one another and moved in a wild, fast circle—as if they were at a Greek wedding. Linked, joined by blood and love and memory, the Candellanos formed a tight bond that locked enemies out and drew those they loved even closer.

"They're really something, aren't they?" Stevie asked, loud enough to be heard over the music, as Jackson came up to stand beside her.

"Yeah. I don't think I've ever met anyone like them." He turned back for another quick check on his daughter and wasn't at all surprised to see her sitting on Mama Candellano's lap again. Reese seemed to have claimed the older woman for her own, and Jackson couldn't really blame her. To be offered nothing but warmth and acceptance and love? What kid wouldn't respond? Let alone one with a wounded heart like Reese's.

"Not surprising," Stevie was saying. "The Candellanos are one of a kind."

"All of them?" he asked, swinging back around to watch as Carla and her brothers danced, laughing, together.

"Every last one," Stevie said.

Jackson tore his gaze from Carla in time to see a brief flash of pain dart across the surface of Stevie's eyes, and he knew there was a story there, somewhere.

Instantly he shifted his attention back to Carla. He had the distinct impression Stevie wouldn't appreciate him noticing her pain.

Funny, there were dozens of people dancing beneath the strings of tiny lights, but he saw only Carla. Her body swayed in time to the music. She tossed her head and her dark curls flew about her laughing face in wild abandon. Her long, bare legs flashed honey brown and his gaze locked briefly on that damn silver toe ring, winking in the lights. Everything about her was so *alive*. So vital. So . . . *immediate*. And he wished for nothing more than to be out there himself, dancing with her in the soft light. He could almost feel her in the circle of his arms, and knew that their bodies would meld together perfectly. He wanted to hold her, caress her, feel her heart beating against his. He wanted to whirl around beneath the stars and lose himself in the shine of her eyes.

God, he wanted her more than anything he'd ever wanted in his life.

The last pulsing beats of the song were fading when the blonde beside him reached out and tugged at the sleeve of his shirt to get his attention.

"What?" he asked sharply, reluctantly turning his head to look at her.

"Color me curious," she said, glancing to one side, to make sure Carla was still out of earshot, "but I want to know what you're up to."

"Up to?"

"With Carla."

His back teeth ground together. Christ. What was this? Another inquisition? More veiled threats? Carla's brothers had been hinting at dismemberment all afternoon—now he had to take it from Stevie? "Watching her dance, mainly," he managed to grind out.

"Cute," she said. "But not the answer I was looking for."

"It's the only one you're gonna get."

"Is that right?" Stevie cocked her head and looked up at him. "Look, H and T," she said, and Jackson frowned. What the hell did that mean? "She might look to you like a great way to kill a summer, but there's more to Carla than that."

That was the problem, wasn't it? She was way more than a summer fling. Too *much* more, for a man who carried around enough baggage to fill a cargo ship. Hell, if she were easy, he'd have been able to scratch his itch a long time ago.

"Trust me, I've noticed."

She laughed, loud and long. "Oh, honey, I *don't* trust you. That's why we're talking."

He lifted one eyebrow in a manner that he knew damn well usually served to terrify clients and opponents alike. Stevie wasn't impressed. And he wasn't the least bit surprised.

"And before you say it," she went on, "I know this is none of my business. Hell, Carla'd kill me herself if she could hear me. But I'm going to say this anyway."

He flicked a glance at the dance area and noted that the Candellanos had stopped dancing and were headed his way. "Then you'd better say it fast."

She looked, too, then turned to meet his gaze again. When she spoke, the words came fast and furious, tumbling over each other in her haste to get them said.

"Fine. Carla's had a rough couple of years. Maybe she's told you and maybe not. Also not my business. And I don't know what's between you two—but I'm telling you here and now. You deliberately hurt her . . . leave her heart all cut and bleeding . . . and I will personally scoop *your* heart right out of your chest—with a garden rake."

"Jesus!" Jackson winced at the imagery. And staring into her pale blue eyes didn't make him feel any better. She looked about as friendly as a mother grizzly bear about to defend her cubs from intruders. This was one dangerous blonde. But he respected her for trying to protect Carla. Hell, wasn't that exactly what *he'd* been trying to do, by keeping his distance?

"Well, good," Stevie said, smiling. "I believe we're clear."

And terrified, he thought, but he wasn't about to admit that.

"I don't want to hurt her," he said, and knew that much, at least, to be the truth.

"You know what?" she said, studying his eyes as carefully as if reading the fine print on a contract. "I think I believe you."

"Gee, thanks."

"Hey," she said, giving his shoulder a friendly slap, "don't bother to thank me. I do what I can."

"What you can do about what?" Carla asked as she walked up to join them.

Her brothers, Jackson noted, had split off from her, Tony going back to his wife, Paul, reaching for his Palm Pilot, to sit beneath a tree, and Nick to fetch yet another beer. Briefly Jackson wondered what had spurred the other man's drinking binge today, but in the next instant he returned his focus to Carla.

"Oh," Stevie said, "I decided to let Jackson dance with you."

Carla laughed, but he saw the quick, uncertain glance she shot him. "Decent of you."

"I'm a swell person."

"So I've heard."

"Well," Stevie announced a bit too loudly, "you kiddies get on with it. I'm heading over to Mama for another bite of that strawberry cake of hers." But before she left, she gave Jackson a long, steady look and muttered, "See you around, H and T."

He felt immensely safer the minute she left. Any woman who could come up with such inventive threats was *not* a woman to cross.

"Getting to know Stevie, huh?"

Jackson turned back around to look into Carla's beautiful dark brown eyes. "A little too well, I think," he said, then dismissed thoughts of the blond entirely. "She did have one good idea, though."

"Yeah?" she asked, tipping her head to one side and smiling up at him. "And what's that?"

In the soft glow of the overhead lights, her eyes looked deeper, darker, than ever before. Her skin warm and golden, her hair seemed as thick and smooth as heavy silk and he wanted—no—*needed* to touch her.

Now.

He held his hand out to her. Jackson said, "Dance with me."

"Oh," she said, shaking her head, "you don't have to—"

"*Dance* with me, Carla."

Her gaze locked with his and Jackson could have sworn he was falling into the warm depths of her eyes. And damned if he wasn't enjoying the plunge. When she laid her hand in his, he closed his fingers over hers, wanting to feel her skin against his. He smoothed the pad of his thumb across her knuckles and delighted in the shiver of appreciation he saw tremble through her.

Keeping a tight hold on her hand, he led her into the center of the grassy field. Around them, couples, young and old, moved in tandem to Faith Hill's throaty, sexy voice reminding them to "Breathe." The music swelled as he drew Carla tightly against him and slid one arm around her waist. She pressed close, laid her left hand high on his shoulder, and swayed in time to the music, moving her hips in a way that made him want to grab her and make a run to the closest bed.

Get a grip.

Carla's blood pumped furiously and she was pretty sure her knees were turning to water, but she held on anyway and enjoyed the ride. God, it felt good, just being here, this close, feeling his body pressed along the length of hers. Who knew dancing could feel so sexy? His thighs brushed hers; the button snap on his jeans dug into the soft skin of her belly, where her tank top pulled up. His hand dropped from her waist to just above her butt, and she held her breath, hoping he'd explore a little farther south. But even as that hope presented itself, she knew it was futile. They were in the middle of a dance, surrounded by the citizens of Chandler. No way was he going to grope her—heck. Her mother and his daughter were just a few feet away.

Okay, that was as good as a bucket of ice water dumped on her head. She pulled back a bit and tried for some conversation. Anything to keep her mind too busy to think about what she *really* wanted to think about.

"So did you enjoy the Fourth?"

"Yeah," he said, making a tight turn so that he could watch her hair fly off her neck. "I really did."

Safe territory. Go for it. "It's my favorite holiday."

He looked surprised. "Better than Christmas?"

"Uh-huh. The Fourth is easy. It's fun and relaxed and warm and, big plus here, fireworks. I'm a fireworks freak. Christmas is nice, but it's crazed, too." She shook her hair back out of her face and saw his eyes darken. A quick flash of something warm and liquid shot through her and Carla had to swallow hard before talking again. "Um, you know . . . everyone running around. Buying presents. Worrying about what to buy. And in my family, there's *a lot* of buying." She smiled, despite the warmth still trickling through her bloodstream. "Christmas Eve dinner's the tradition with us, and it's a nuthouse."

"You guys are big on tradition, huh?"

"Tradition: good. Change: bad." She shrugged. "It's a Candellano way of life."

"Like dancing with your brothers?"

Her hand slid up his shoulder, and without really thinking about it, she ran her fingers through his hair at the back of his neck. Soft and thick. She felt his jolt of reaction to her touch as it slammed through her as well. But she kept talking. Not too hard for her, under most circumstances.

"Yeah. Dancing." She inhaled slowly, deeply, and saw his gaze drop to the dip of her shirt. Her nipples peaked. Oh God. "Dancing. With my brothers. It's the"—she closed her eyes; maybe if she didn't look up at him, she'd be able to think and even, in a stretch, form a complete sentence—"song. 'Brown-Eyed Girl'? They've always danced with me to that song. It's kind of . . . *mine*." *Mine. Oh, that was brilliant.*

Faith Hill reminded her again to just breathe and Carla did her damnedest to follow orders. But it wasn't easy.

"It *is* your song," Jackson whispered, and she opened her eyes to find his locked on her. His gaze moved over her features like a caress. Excitement spilled through her, pouring down along her limbs, then climbing back up her legs to settle in one particular spot that immediately started throbbing in time to the music.

"Jackson . . ." There was more she wanted to say, but with her throat closed up tight, it seemed impossible at the moment.

He swept her into a slow turn that dizzied her as completely as the Tilt-A-Whirl would have.

"Whenever I hear that song, Carla, I'll remember tonight. And how you looked." His gaze drifted over her again and she felt as though she could dance forever, as long as his arms were around her. As long as he kept talking, letting his voice ripple along her spine. As long as he kept looking at her as he was now. "I'll remember how the lights sparkled in your eyes. How your lips were stained red from that cherry Sno-Cone. How your legs looked long and lean and silky."

"Jackson," she said his name again, mainly because she liked the sound of it. Her hand cupped the back of his neck, fingers wrapping around until she could almost feel the pounding pulse point at the base of his throat.

Something sizzled and she was pretty sure it was her.

The music ended; couples began to drift out of the arena, back toward their blankets to get a good seat for the coming show. But she and Jackson just stood there, still wrapped together, still swaying, as if to a tune only they could hear.

He opened his mouth to speak again, but whatever he was going to say was lost in the first *boom* and crash of the fireworks overhead.

Carla tipped her head back in time to see an explosion of blue and white stars that skittered off into the blackness and winked out of existence. "Oh, look," she whispered, and Jackson turned her in his arms so that she could lean against his chest. Her breath caught as, one after another, rockets raced into the sky, burst open, and spilled dazzling light against the dark backdrop. Gold, red, silver, chasing each other through the stars.

The crowd "oohed" and "aahed" at all the right places and Carla lost herself in the crashing beauty overhead. She felt Jackson's arms wrap around her middle and she laid her hands on his forearms, loving the feel of him, so close. So warm and strong.

And she wanted to lay him down in the grass and make love under the shadows of man-made rainbows splintering across the sky.

Jackson couldn't remember ever feeling this . . . content. To be here. On this grassy knoll overlooking the black ocean, with this woman in his arms. He glanced toward Reese and saw her, still cuddled on Mama's lap while the older woman pointed at the fireworks.

Clouds of smoke drifted through the night, carrying the scent of gunpowder. Children darted across the grass, holding sparklers high, dropping trails of bright embers behind them, like high-tech bread crumbs. Old people cuddled on blankets as they'd probably been doing for years. Teenagers used the distraction of the fireworks to get some serious necking done. And the younger kids fell asleep, safe in the arms of those who loved them.

Chandler.

Mayberry.

Good.

His arms tightened around Carla, pressing her tightly to him. The scent of her hair drifted to him and slipped inside, filling him, until she was all he could think of. Her warmth pushed into him, easing away the chill he'd carried inside him for far too long. And as the cold eased, he wondered how he would ever be able to go back to his old life. How would he face the emptiness of his condo? The sterile world of the city? How could he be the man he'd been when he hardly remembered him anymore?

Distant roars sounded out, thundering across the crowd as dozens of rockets shot heavenward at once for the grand finale. Blossoms of color erupted against the darkness, one on top of the other, crashing, shattering, spilling blue and green and gold and silver until the colors became one, bleeding into one another, dazzling the crowd.

"Isn't it beautiful?"

He looked down at her as she stared up at the sky and Jackson saw the fireworks reflected in her eyes. Bright color dazzled those brown depths and drew him in, welcoming him into a world he'd never known before.

It was magic. The whole damn night.

Hell, this place.

This woman.

Magic.

And he had to have her.

Had to claim, just once, a piece of the magic for himself.

"In my whole life," he said softly, staring into those star-sprinkled eyes, "I've never seen anything *more* beautiful."

And then he kissed her while the sky exploded.

CHAPTER
SEVENTEEN

FIREWORKS.

And *not* the ones in the sky.

Brilliant bursts of color flashed behind her closed eyes and Carla knew she was getting a much better show than everyone else was.

Jackson Wyatt had a *great* mouth.

His breath dusted her cheek. His right hand inched higher from her middle to rest beneath the underside of her breast, and everything in her ached for him to keep going. To touch her. Cup her.

But even while her blood boiled, Carla had enough brainpower left to be grateful for the crowd's distraction. While they were watching the sky, they weren't watching her and Jackson.

His mouth moved over hers with the tender expertise of a concert pianist playing a Steinway. Tender yet firm, hard yet gentle. He held her closer, tighter. The kiss deepened and she tasted him, drank him in, and gave as good as she got. The world spun crazily out of control and she didn't really care.

Then the crowd applauded the end of the fireworks display and the moment was lost as Jackson pulled his head back to stare down at her.

He sucked in a gulp of air like a drowning man surfacing for the third and final time. She knew how he felt. Every inch of her body was burning and sputtering like a slow-burning sparkler. Her knees did that jelly dance that she was getting so used to when she was around him. And other parts of her were absolutely vibrating.

Ooh. Vibrating. Good word.

"Carla," he said softly, "are you thinking what I'm thinking?"

"Depends," she said on a sigh. "Does it have anything to do with being naked and rolling in Jell-O?"

He blinked, grinned, and snorted a laugh. "Green or red?"

"Oh," she said, "red. Definitely."

His smile faded. "This would probably be a mistake."

"Absolutely." Hadn't she been telling herself that for weeks?

Lifting one hand, Jackson cupped her cheek, then smoothed her silky hair back from her face. God, he wanted her. He wanted his hands on her, sliding over smooth skin and discovering every curve and valley. His gaze followed the motion and he told himself that if he was smart, he'd stop. If he was smart, he'd forget this moment had just happened. If he was smart, he'd collect Reese and head back to the empty house he'd rented.

Reese.

Amazing just how fast thoughts of your kid could put an end to other thoughts.

Tossing a glance at the blanket where the other Candellanos were packing up the remains of the day, he stared for a long minute at Reese. The little girl was helping Carla's mother and the smile on his daughter's face was almost enough to ease the pain of having to forget all about hot, steamy sex.

Almost.

No way was he going to be waiting for his kid to fall asleep so he could sneak Carla in. Christ. Just thinking about it made him feel like some sleazeball renting a room at a pay-by-the-hour motel.

Carla followed his gaze, watched Reese for a long minute, then patted his arm in understanding. "Hey," she said, "Jell-O's not all it's cracked up to be anyway."

He glanced at her. "Liar."

"Yeah, well, it makes me feel better." She smiled and started walking toward her family, with Jackson just a step or two behind. Which, unfortunately, gave him a great view of *her* behind. Were the shorts she was wearing getting shorter?

"Beautiful, Tony," Mama was saying. "Nicer than last year."

"I didn't do the fireworks, Mama," Tony said, draping one arm around Beth and pulling her close.

Mama waved both hands in the air as if wiping that statement away. "You're the police. You're in charge, right?" She glanced around. "Where's Nicky?"

"He wandered off a while ago," Stevie said, then looked at Tony. "Don't worry; I've got his car keys."

Paul shot Stevie a quick look as he folded the last of the blankets. "I'll take these home for you, Mama. Then I've got to get back to the office."

"You work too much."

"Fog's comin' in," Tony noted.

"At least it waited until *after* the fireworks this year," Carla said, snatching up the now-empty food basket.

"Reese," Jackson said quietly, reaching for her, "it's time to go home."

Instantly the little girl shook her head fiercely and threw her arms around Mama's waist.

"Ah. . . ." Carla's mother looked up at Jackson and smiled. "Is my fault. I told Reese that Tina is staying the night with her nana tonight and I thought maybe she would like to stay with me, too."

Burrowing even closer to the older woman, Reese nodded and looked up at her father with huge pleading eyes.

"She'll be fine," Tony said.

Jackson nodded but didn't answer.

This was a moment, too, he thought, staring at his child. In the last year, she'd hardly been able to bear being away from him. Yet here she stood, wanting to be a normal little girl and spend the night with the closest thing to a *real* grandma she'd ever known. A sweet ache settled in his chest as Jackson went down on one knee so that he and Reese were eyeball to eyeball.

"Are you sure, honey?" he asked, trying to see past her excitement to how she might react later tonight. But there was no fear in her eyes. Just anticipation and a contentment that he certainly wasn't used to seeing.

Reese smiled, nodded, and let go of Mama long enough to throw her thin arms around his neck and give him a brief, hard hug. Then she stepped back, moving close to Mama Candellano again.

"Okay," he said, standing up. He looked at Carla's mother and said softly, "She's afraid of the dark, so I always leave a light on and—"

Mama held up one hand. "It's okay." She laid one hand on Reese's head. "Everybody's afraid of the dark, right? So we don't be in the dark."

The little girl grinned.

So easy, he thought. When the Barringtons made a fear of the dark seem like cowardice.

"Don't worry so much." Picking Tina up, Mama plopped the toddler onto a well-padded hip, then took Reese's hand. "We're gonna have a party. We'll have ice cream and popcorn and maybe watch a Princess movie, huh?"

Reese nodded as they walked away and Jackson noticed his daughter making the hand sign for sprinkles.

"Sure, we'll have sprinkles," Mama told her. "What's ice cream with no sprinkles?"

Jackson shook his head in wonder. In just a few weeks, Carla's mother had found a way to communicate with Reese. The woman understood his daughter's little hand signs and didn't pressure her for more. She'd given his daughter the warmth and acceptance and love that Jackson so wanted for her. Without even trying, Mama made the Barringtons look even worse than before.

Abbey stared after the girl, then threw a quick look at Carla. Didn't take a genius to interpret it. "Go ahead," Carla said, knowing her mother was just as nuts about Abbey as Reese was. The dog bounded after Reese, and she and Jackson were alone.

Carla stepped up beside him and laid one hand on his arm. "My mother adores her. Reese really will be okay. Don't worry."

"I know. And she's *happy*." He looked down at Carla's hand on his arm, lifted it, placed a soft kiss on the inside of her wrist, then met her gaze again. "I'm not worried. I was just standing here thinking I should feel guilty for being glad Reese is out of the house for the night."

Well, apparently the fire in her blood hadn't been put out completely . . . just banked down to embers. Embers that were now suddenly flaring back into life. Around her, people moved off, their celebration over.

Hers was just beginning.

"Feel guilty tomorrow," she said, leaning into him. "I'm Italian *and* Catholic, so I know. Trust me on this: there's *always* time for guilt."

"Yeah?" One corner of his mouth lifted into a twitch of a smile and Carla's stomach flip-flopped. "Maybe if I kept busy enough tonight, I wouldn't have the time for guilt."

Promising.

"So what's going on with Carla and the new guy?" Tony crawled into bed and stretched out atop the fresh, sweet-smelling sheets.

"Butt out, Tony!" Beth called from the bathroom.

"She's my sister."

"Uh-huh."

"She's had a rough couple years."

"And she's a big girl," Beth assured him. "She knows what she's doing."

"That's what worries me." He scowled toward the square of light spilling through the open bathroom door. "Since when did you get so calm and sensible?"

Beth appeared in the doorway, leaning one hand high on the doorjamb. Her pale green silk nightgown slid along her body and Tony's mouth dried up.

Stepping into the room, Beth walked slowly, seductively, toward the bed. "Since," she pointed out, "I decided to enjoy our little vacation from our daughter." She sat down on the edge of the bed and tossed her hair back over her shoulder. "Tina's with your mom and you have two whole hours before you have to go back on duty. But if you'd rather talk about Carla . . ."

He grabbed her and pulled her across his lap. "Carla who?"

Stevie let herself into the Leaf and Bean and walked across the dark shop toward the staircase at the rear of the building. She flicked the wall switch and instantly the stairwell brightened, lighting her way to the loft above her shop.

The place was too quiet.

After being surrounded by people all day, the emptiness of her home only seemed magnified. Usually she enjoyed being alone. Hearing her own thoughts. But tonight her thoughts weren't exactly worth listening to.

She should have asked Paul to come home with her to watch a movie. It had been too long since the two of them had spent some time together. And she missed his company. She could use her friend tonight.

She walked across the bare wood floors to the wide front window that looked down on Main Street. Digging one hand into her pocket, she pulled out Nick's car keys and jingled them in her hand.

"What the hell is going on with you, Nick?" she wondered aloud. He'd never been a big drinker. Today, though, he'd been sucking down beer like a man given one day to live and told to make the most of it. Why? But a second later, she tossed his keys onto the closest table and turned her back on the window. "And why the hell do you care, Stevie?" she asked herself before heading to the shower.

A half hour.

She left Jackson on the road in front of her house with the understanding that he'd take Reese's things over to her mother's house and Carla would meet him at his place in half an hour. Her stomach twisted into wild knots of expectation. Every nerve ending went onto high alert and even her breathing seemed a little forced.

And a half hour had never seemed so long.

Still, there were a few things she had to take care of before she could head across the street and, well, get taken care of. Carla smiled to herself at the prospect and, humming, walked around the side of the house to the backyard.

She went straight to the puppy pen. The little guys tumbled all over themselves in their eagerness to greet her. Their yips and high-pitched barks drowned out the calming sound of the burbling water fountain.

"Well, hi, fellas," she crooned as she unlatched the gate and stepped inside the enclosure.

Instantly what felt like dozens of tiny paws leaped at her. Carla squatted, taking the time to pet each of them in turn before checking their food and water bowls. Then she gave them a few more pets and kisses before saying good night and leaving the pen.

Hurrying into the house, she took the fastest shower on record but spared an extra moment to shave her legs again. Then she quickly dried off, slathered Sweet Pea body lotion on every inch of skin she could reach, and stepped into a pair of lacy panties before pulling on one of the few dresses she owned. A spaghetti-strapped sundress of pale yellow, it set off her tan and made her feel all girlie. And a little silly. Here she stood, dressing up, when all she wanted was to get *un*dressed. With Jackson. But what the hell, she went for it. She whipped a brush through her hair, then gave it up as useless. There was just so much you could do with a headful of curls. Slapping some lip gloss on and giving her eyelashes a couple of quick strokes with the mascara wand, she stood back to inspect her reflection.

Her cheeks were flushed, her eyes sparkled, and she could practically see excitement outlining her body like some sexually charged aura.

"Oh boy," she whispered, and her mirror self grinned. She wouldn't think about consequences. She wouldn't think beyond tonight. The moment. The need hammering at her until she could hardly see. No . . . she'd take Stevie's advice. She'd make love without hanging all of the extras onto it. She'd accept it for what it was—well, what it was going to be: blindingly good sex—and let it go at that.

She bolted out of the bathroom, snatched up her sandals, and hopped across the living room, putting them on and moving at the same time. Heck, the end of celibacy at least called for her to be on time.

Grabbing the doorknob, she threw the door open and smacked right up against Jackson's broad chest. Pushing her hair back out of her eyes, Carla said, "I was just coming over and—"

"I couldn't wait," he said, his voice thick, his blue eyes smoky with a need that slammed into Carla with the power of a velvety fist.

"I'm glad." More than glad. Delighted. Excited. Hungry. They both knew damn well they'd been building toward this moment for the last few weeks. And now there was no time for thinking. No time for worrying about whether this was the right or wrong thing to do.

For right now, it was the *only* thing to do.

"Nice dress," he said, his gaze raking her up and down, quickly, thoroughly.

"Thanks." Her gaze locked on his mouth. God, that was one great mouth. All she could think about was their last kiss . . . and their next one. And where else that mouth might go.

"How fast can you get out of it?"

"Speed of light mean anything to you?"

"My kind of woman." He grabbed her and Carla fell into his embrace. His arms swept around her middle, holding her tight, lifting her feet right off the floor. She wrapped her arms around his neck and planted her mouth on his. He took a step farther inside and kicked the front door shut. Then he slammed her back against the wall, and pinned her in place with his body, like a butterfly in a glass case.

His mouth claimed hers in a deep, hungry kiss. He drank her in, his tongue exploring her warmth, her heat. He stole her breath, then gave her his own. She took it, swallowing it, holding it deep within as his hands prowled her body. Roughly, frantically, he touched her, grazing his palms over every inch of her that he could reach. The soft cotton of her dress rubbed with every stroke he made, heightening the sensations. Her upper thighs tingled as she lifted her feet and hooked them around his waist. Her center pushed against his abdomen and she rocked into him, desperate to feel him touch her there. To take her higher, faster, than she'd ever been before.

He cupped her breasts, his thumbs and forefingers peaking her nipples until she moaned into his mouth with a wild screech of pleasure she hardly recognized as her own voice. Tearing his mouth free of hers, he trailed damp kisses along her jaw, her throat, and the base of her neck. He pushed her higher on the wall, unwilling to let her go. Unwilling to move. He had to have her. Here. Now.

Carla tipped her head back and stared blindly up at the ceiling. Her body swirled with so many sensations at once, it was impossible to separate one from the other. Heat spiraled through her, searing her blood, scorching her soul, and melting her heart. She felt herself winding tighter and tighter as he touched her, sliding his hands up to her shoulders. His thumbs hooked those narrow strips of fabric and pushed them down. Carla shifted in his arms, helping him, pulling her arms free of the straps, letting the dress fall to her waist. Chilly air kissed her flesh and Carla shivered. Then Jackson's hands cupped her breasts and she gasped, arching into his hands.

"Oh God. . . ." Her body ached and throbbed with a need so deep, so primal, that she writhed against him, looking for a peace only he could give her.

Jackson reacted. He shifted his hands from her breasts to her waist and lifted her high enough to taste her nipples, one after the other. His tongue circled each pebbled tip, tasting, savoring. His breath dusted her skin, and chills snaked along her spine.

"Jackson . . ."

"God, you taste so good," he murmured against her flesh.

Her fingers clutched at his shoulders as she braced herself on his strength, and she knew if she didn't have him soon, it would kill her. Tension raced through her. She felt the heady rush toward completion begin and knew that the slightest intimate touch from him now would set her off.

He let her slide back along the wall, keeping his hands at her sides, steadying her, holding her, as if he would never let her go.

And that worked for her.

Then he shifted one hand, sliding it between them, slipping his fingers beneath the fragile silk barrier of her panties. She'd wanted to wait until she held his body within hers. But it was too late. Now she needed it. Needed that pulse-pounding crash of release. She moved into his touch and he dipped two fingers inside her. "Jackson!" she cried out as her world splintered into thousands of tiny jagged pieces. She shook and trembled in his steady grip, riding the explosion that threatened to tear her in two and welcoming it like a long-lost friend.

Before the last of the tremors had faded away, Jackson tore his hand free and said, "Bed," congratulating himself on getting his voice to work. Hell, he felt as tight as an over-tuned guitar string. Watching her climax claim her had damn near killed him with a ferocious want that was like nothing he'd ever known before.

Carla'd been in his thoughts, his dreams, for weeks, and now that they were finally together, he needed to be a part of her so badly, it was an ache that went far deeper than just physical need.

He wanted to feel the warmth she offered and surround himself with it. He wanted to give her the same kind of pleasure she gave him. He wanted to watch her eyes go soft and hazy with completion again and he wanted to be inside her when that moment came, this time.

And he couldn't do all that standing up in the foyer, fully clothed.

"Oh, wow. Definitely bed," she agreed, threading her fingers through his shower-damp hair.

"Where?" he groaned.

"The hall." She dipped her head to kiss his neck, his throat, her lips moving over his flesh, her words muffled. "Through the living room."

Jackson braced her behind with his forearm and carried Carla across the small cluttered room in a few long strides. She pressed herself close to him and he felt her nipples, peaked and hard against his chest. His heartbeat thudded painfully and his breath jammed solid in his lungs. She tightened her legs around his waist and dug her heels in as she moved against him.

"Hurry," she whispered, and that one word echoed inside him over and over again.

Hurry. God, yes. No time for niceties. No time for soft music and sweet-smelling flowers. No time for romantic words or slow, languid caresses. Need pushed them both and Jackson surrendered to it, knowing it was give in or go crazy.

Only three doors led off the tiny hall. One opened into a bathroom where wet towels littered the floor and makeup paraphernalia lay scattered across the sink and counter. He ignored it. Another door was closed, but the third stood ajar and he spotted the clothes she'd worn earlier that day, tossed across the foot of the bed. He stepped inside. Curtains over the window that opened onto the backyard were open, and moonlight spilled into the room like a silver river.

Holding her tightly, Jackson bent down, grabbed the edge of the quilt, and tossed it aside and out of his way. Then he dropped Carla onto the mattress and heard the old springs scream in protest as she bounced. While he tore at his clothes, he watched her shimmy out of her dress, then slide her panties down and off.

His mouth watered.

His throat tightened.

And an erection that was already painfully hard throbbed with an ache only she could ease.

Dropping onto the bed beside her, Jackson claimed her mouth as his hands roamed her body, stroking, rubbing, exploring. His palm skimmed across her nipples, one after the other, then down her rib cage, across her flat abdomen to the nest of dark curls that guarded her secrets. He dipped first one, then two fingers into her liquid heat again and sucked in a gulp of air when her hips lifted into his hand. Ready for more, she rocked her body against him, taking him deeper, demanding his touch.

His tongue entwined with hers, he drove her higher, refusing her air, refusing her anything but the sensations he caused. He wanted everything else to fall away for her. He wanted her mind emptied of anything but passion, and that was only for him. This woman, this moment. He wanted her, needed her, so desperately, his heart twisted painfully in his chest.

Carla loved the feel of him. She skimmed her hands along his back, down his hips, and back up again. The clean, male scent of him drove deep within her and she clung to it. Want and heat and a deep ache that pulsed along with her rapid heartbeat pushed her to feel him, all of him. She shifted just enough that she could take him in her hand. He groaned as she rolled her fingers over his erection and stroked him in as tender and intimate a way as he did her.

"You're killin' me here," he whispered against her neck, his breath dusting her skin, sending shivers of delight coursing through her.

"Oh, not yet," she promised, and rubbed the pad of her thumb across the tip of him.

"Carla." Her name was a groan, a harsh plea just before he kissed her again. He touched her deeply, pushing his fingers inside her, stroking his thumb over the core of her until the small, delicious spirals of completion gathered on the horizon like storm clouds in the distance. It was coming again. She felt it. Knew it was there, waiting for her.

Carla planted her feet on the bed and rocked her hips over and over again into his touch. Tearing her mouth from his, she cupped his face with one hand as the tension within mounted. She looked up into his eyes and saw desperation shining there.

She stroked him harder, stronger, glorying in the hard, thick feel of him. Loving the knowledge that she was bringing him to the brink.

"Say my name," she whispered brokenly.

"Carla," he said, dipping his head for a brief hard kiss that tasted of frenzied passion. "Always, Carla."

Her breath hitched. She fought for air. Fought to find the words she needed so desperately. "I love it . . . when you call . . . my name. I—oh . . . *God,* Jackson. I'm coming now." She shook her head, fighting it. "Too soon. Want you . . . inside me this time. Want to feel—"

"Come, baby," he crooned, letting his voice ease her over the precipice. "There'll be more. Much more. Come now and let me see you."

Her eyes squeezed shut as the tremors claimed her, but she forced them open—she wanted to watch him this time. Wanted him to see what he did to her with a touch. Wanted him to know what it meant to have his fingers inside her.

She rode the wave of pleasure, higher than before, groaning his name, digging her nails into his shoulders, holding on to him even as he pushed her over the edge.

As the last of the tiny ripples of satisfaction died away, he shifted position and pushed himself deep inside her.

Strong. Deep. So deep.

A sharp, sweet sting of renewed glory burst within her and she lifted her hips to meet his first thrust. Again and again, they moved together, racing toward the finish line. He threaded his fingers through hers. Planted their hands at either side of her head and stared down into her eyes, her bottomless, warmth-filled eyes, and lost himself in all that she was . . . in all that she offered him.

And when soul-rocking pleasure crashed down around them, he called her name—a raw, powerful shout that dragged at his heart. This time, when she came, Carla wrapped her legs around his middle and pulled him in so deeply he'd never be able to leave.

"Shtevie?"

She shoved her hair back from her face, squinted at her bedside clock, and groaned. *One A.M.?* Who the hell?

"Hello?" Her voice was a croak of sound and she cleared her throat, swallowing hard. "Who is this?"

" 'Sme, Nick."

Stevie pushed herself up in bed, reached to the nearby table, and flicked on a light. *Good God. No one should be awake at this hour.* And certainly no one should be making a phone call—unless there was an earthquake or similar natural disaster. She squelched a groan and blinked. "Nick, you idiot. Why are you calling me?"

"You gotta come get me."

She pulled the receiver away from her ear, stared at it for a long minute as though she could actually *see* the moron on the other end of the line, then slapped it back to her head. "What are you talking about? Get you from where? Where are you?"

"Jail."

"What?" She stared blankly ahead, then automatically reached for the TV remote that she'd left on her bedside table. Once again, she'd fallen asleep with the TV on, wanting the sound of voices in the empty loft.

"Jesus," Nick mumbled. "Do you hafta shout?"

"You jerk, you woke me up and now you're complaining?"

"C'mon, Shtevie, be a pal. Tony won't lemme out 'less shomebody comes to get me."

"You're drunk."

"Thass wha' Tony says."

Irritation rushed through her, quickly replacing any concern she might have had a minute ago. Arrested by his own brother for being drunk. She was willing to bet there weren't many men who could claim that honor.

"I'm not coming to get you," she said, even though her body apparently disagreed. Her legs were hanging off the side of the bed, and her feet were already scooting into a pair of sandals. Old habits were hard to break. Even after two years. Deliberately she kicked them aside.

"Dammit, Shtevie, who else'll come for me?"

"Why should anyone have to?" she asked, and hung up before she could get sucked back into Nick's orbit.

Big lie.

She was still in Nick's orbit. Probably always would be. Because she loved the Candellanos too much to distance herself.

Damn it.

Flopping backward onto the bed, she folded her arms around her middle and hung on. But it didn't seem to help. Loneliness curled up inside her chest, took hold of her heart, and squeezed until a single tear rolled down the side of her face and disappeared into her hair. She wasn't crying for Nick . . . the tears were for what-might-have-beens.

"She not comin'," Nick muttered, and hung up the phone.

"And this surprises you?" Tony demanded. Grabbing his brother's arm, he half-dragged him out of the office and down the hall to one of the two empty jail cells. Giving Nick a shove into one of them, he slammed the iron door and locked it.

"I'll go home wi' you," Nick decided, squinting at his older brother through the one eye that wasn't swollen shut. "We're *family*."

"No, you're not comin' home with me. And yeah, we're family. Why do you think I'm so pissed?"

"Eye hurts."

"You're lucky that's all that hurts."

"C'mon, Tony, lemme go."

He shook his head. "Drunks sleep it off here. In jail."

"Not a drunk."

"You drove your car onto Reverend Michaels' front lawn and destroyed his wife's garden goose."

"Damn thing ran out in front'a me."

"It's plaster."

Nick laughed. "Nope. *I* am."

"Nope," Tony replied, turning his back on his younger brother, "you're an idiot. Stevie took your keys for your own good. Did you *have* to hot-wire the car?"

Nick lay back on the cot and tossed one arm across his eyes. "Sheemed like good idea at th'time."

"Yeah? Wait'll Mama finds out."

Nick groaned.

"Wow."

"That about sums it up," Jackson agreed.

"That was . . ."

"Amazing? Incredible?"

She turned toward him, running her hands up and down his chest until his body stirred and he issued a muffled groan. "I was thinking more like . . . *foreplay*?"

Jackson slid one hand down the side of her body, along the curve of her hip, and down her thigh before going back up. He was hard again.

"Lady," he promised, determined to enjoy every minute of this night with her, "you ain't seen nothin' yet."

"Surprise me."

Obliging both of them, Jackson flipped her over onto her back and trailed his mouth down the front of her, sucking on one nipple, then the other, while she writhed beneath him. Then he moved again, laying a trail of damp heat down the center of her body, licking, tasting, exploring until finally he settled between her thighs.

"You're really good at this 'surprise' thing," she said as she licked dry lips.

"Here comes the best part," he murmured, and slipped off the bed to kneel beside the mattress.

Carla's stomach whirled. God. She knew what was coming. *Her.*

He pulled her toward him, drawing her close until her rear was on the edge of the bed. Then he lifted her legs and laid them across his shoulders.

"Oh, God. . . ." Carla pushed herself into a sitting position and looked down at him. "Jackson, you don't have to—"

His eyes gleamed with passion when he looked up at her. "Surprise," he whispered just before his mouth covered her.

Carla gasped and looked down at him as he worked her body in the most intimate way possible. Her fingers dug into his hair and hung on. Her breath strangled in her lungs. And she watched him as his tongue took her on a roller-coaster ride of sensation.

CHAPTER EIGHTEEN

REESE'S TUMMY HURT.

But it was a good kind of hurt. Like when you're going somewhere special and you get all excited and everything inside turns into knots and your tummy aches 'cause you just feel so good.

She liked it here at Mama Candellano's house. No, she thought, *Nana's* house. Reese smiled. Nana had said *all* of her grandchildren should call her Nana, and then she had kissed her and said she would be Reese's Nana, too. Nana smelled good and she always smiled and never got mad or sad or made Reese feel bad about not talking. And she cooked popcorn on the stove in a big pot.

In the crib beside Reese's bed, Tina was sleeping, holding on to a tiny stuffed bear, and the sound of the baby's breathing was kind of nice. Like company. But best of all was Abbey, lying beside Reese in the bed. The big dog's head rested on the child's chest and she stroked her fingers gently across Abbey's soft golden hair.

Reese took a deep breath and released it again on a sigh. Lamplight streamed in from the hallway, lying across the floor and the foot of her bed like the yellow brick road. And when that thought came in, it brought with it the thought of wicked witches and scary monkeys and mean wizards and . . .

Abbey lifted her head and looked, ears pricked, at the open doorway. Reese held her breath. Then Nana was there, smiling, stepping into the room and tsking her tongue as grown-ups did.

"Is a good thing I don't see a dog on the bed," she said, petting Abbey as she sat down on the edge of the mattress. Still smiling, Nana glanced at Tina, then turned back to Reese. "Not sleeping?"

She shook her head.

"You want Nana to tell you a story?"

Reese nodded.

"Ah, good." She reached out and smoothed Reese's hair back from her forehead. "I tell you a story about a little princess and her golden dog."

Reese smiled and as Nana's whispered voice hushed into the room, she closed her eyes and began to dream of grand adventures as she and a brave Abbey saved a kingdom.

When Reese was finally sleeping peacefully, Nana leaned forward, kissed her forehead, then sat back again, giving Abbey an extra pat. "Abbey, you watch over our girl. Sweet thing has too much pain for one so small."

As Nana left the room, the dog cuddled beside her charge and slept.

"I think I'm paralyzed."

Jackson chuckled. "Not a minute or two ago, you weren't."

"Oh," Carla assured him, lying flat on her back and staring blindly at the moonlit ceiling, "it was worth it. But now I'm finished forever."

The last few hours had been incredible. Her whole body ached from the near gymnastic exertions, yet still hummed with an almost electric pleasure. And something else. Something warm and tender and so beautiful, she felt the ache of it at the backs of her eyes.

Despite her resolve to keep emotions out of this, it had happened. Just as, she was forced to admit, she'd known it would. Her heart *was* involved and there was just no denying it—at least to herself.

Even as she basked in the wonderfully languid sensation creeping through her body, her mind raced from one dark thought to another. There'd been no mention of love while his hands stroked her skin and his mouth teased her into oblivion. He hadn't whispered of forever. Hadn't made promises. There was no talk of tomorrow. He'd kept part of himself locked away from her even while his body lay cradled deep within her own.

Jackson, though lying naked beside her in the moonlight, already had one foot out her door. And it wasn't just the fact that he was leaving. This went far deeper. She felt it. Maybe this was about his dead wife.

Maybe he still loved her. But she couldn't know for sure because he wouldn't let her in. He had his heart so firmly packed away, she'd never be able to reach it.

Acknowledging that fact brought a misery so deep, Carla nearly wept.

"Ruined for any other man, eh?" he asked, a knowing gleam in his eyes.

She forced herself to smile in spite of the disquieting thoughts racing through her mind. She wouldn't let him know just how right he was.

"Don't sound so proud." Although he had a right to be. No one else had ever touched her so deeply. Made her feel so much. Made her want to feel even more. There was a magic, a kind of oneness, between them that she hadn't expected, and she didn't really know what to do about it.

Because, she realized, there was a word to describe what she was feeling. *Love.*

And she knew she couldn't tell *Jackson.*

Hell, she could hardly force herself to face it. She'd done it. Fallen in love with the one man she shouldn't have. Damn it. Carla wasn't sure when it had happened. When she'd taken that one step too many and waltzed blindly from attraction straight into trouble. But there was no going back, now.

She loved his smile, his voice, his touch. She loved his tenderness with his daughter and the way his rare smiles lit up his eyes. She loved that he argued with her, talked with her, and had the ability to kiss her into a coma.

She loved him.

Stupid, she told herself, and fisted one hand on the

sheet beneath her. She'd thought this one night would be enough. She'd fooled herself into believing that somehow being with him would ease the ache and satisfy the need. But it hadn't. All it had done was create a deeper need.

To be loved back.

A need, she knew in her heart, that wouldn't be met.

Just like before, her mind taunted. When her fiancé had left her to go back to his old girlfriend, Carla had lived through the pain and the humiliation by promising herself she'd never make such a stupid mistake again. Now she'd not only gone and done it; she'd multiplied the problem by caring more for Jackson than she ever had for ol' what's his name.

Misery was waiting just around the corner, gleefully rubbing its hands together, waiting for the perfect moment to pounce. And she didn't have a clue as to how to avoid it.

"I don't know about proud," he said, shifting to one side, needing a little space. Damn, the connection with her was still humming through him. He'd felt more a part of her than he ever had anyone else. And it was humbling and downright staggering. But damned if he wasn't thankful for her. For everything she'd shown him and given him over the last few weeks.

Jackson couldn't give her what she wanted from him. What he instinctively knew she needed right now. But at the least, he could give her this. "No, not proud. Just . . . grateful."

Just like that—Misery jumped at her.

He rolled over a bit, putting some distance between them, and a deep, cold chill washed over Carla as what was left of her balloon popped. He was already pulling away from her and they were in the same bed. Any minute now, he'd be bolting for the door.

"Grateful?" She nearly choked on the word. Hell, he hadn't even let her keep her illusions for long. What was he saying? Had she done him a favor? Was he going to offer her a tip next? Carla squeezed her eyes tightly shut, but it didn't help. Well, he'd made himself pretty clear, hadn't he? She might be more than a casual one-night stand, but she was considerably less than the love of his life. Pain rippled in and blended with the anger beginning to churn her stomach into tight knots of discomfort.

This just gets better and better. Or worse and worse.

It was downright humiliating to realize that she didn't mean a damn thing to him. *Grateful?* What a hideous word.

Gritting her teeth, she turned her head on the pillow and locked her gaze with his. "Is this where I say, *'You're welcome'*?"

Surprise etched his features. "That's not what I meant."

"It's what it sounded like."

He pushed himself up onto one elbow and looked down at her. "Damn it, Carla, I only meant—"

" 'Wham, bam, thank you, ma'am'?" Oh, man, if she weren't at home, she'd be picking up her clothes, gathering the tattered remnants of her pride, and leaving about now. But then, even if she could run away, his words would come with her. The sad truth that she loved someone who didn't love her in return would race alongside her, taunting her no matter how far she managed to get.

"You're putting words in my mouth."

A strangled laugh shot from her throat. "Trust me, if I was going to do that, I'd do a better job."

"Carla . . ."

She groaned as she sat up. Muscles she hadn't used in far too long screamed out at her. Okay, fine. So she wasn't paralyzed. Only wounded. Not in body.

In soul.

In heart.

But she wouldn't let him know that. Couldn't stand the thought of him feeling sorry for her, for God's sake. She had a *little* pride left, thanks very much. So she did what any self-respecting Candellano would do when attacked. She fought back.

"You're right," she said, swinging her legs to the floor and standing up. Stark naked, she ignored the ripple of gooseflesh that erupted along her spine, and glared at him. "This was a great way to spend an evening. Better than renting a movie, but nothing special."

"Bullshit."

She laughed again, and this time the tight sound sliced along her throat like a piece of jagged glass. "Just call me Dr. Carla. Give me your poor, your miserable, your horny. I'll straighten 'em right out and make 'em fit for civilization again."

"What the hell are you talking about?" He sat straight up and the sheet covering him fell to his lap. Carla's gaze raked across him, and even as miserable as she felt at the moment, her pulse pounded and her fingers itched to touch his broad, bare chest again. *Christ, you're hopeless.* God, she needed air. She couldn't breathe. She felt as though a giant invisible hand were squeezing her lungs, making it impossible to draw a breath.

Good. Maybe she'd pass out. And when she came to, he'd be gone.

No such luck.

"Talk to me, damn it."

"Me," she muttered, shaking her head as she tossed her hands high, then let them slap down against her bare thighs again. "I'm talking about *me*. And my incredible ability to make the absolutely *wrong* move at the wrong time. It's a gift, that's what it is. A gift." She folded her arms across her middle and hung on tight. "I swear, if I could figure out how to do it, I'd kick my *own* ass."

Oh God, she should have known better. She'd told Stevie that it wouldn't take much to push her over the edge. Then what does brilliant Carla do? She doesn't wait to be pushed. She *jumps*.

Head first.

Jesus, you'd think she'd have better survival skills.

Disgusted with herself and suddenly feeling *way* too vulnerable, Carla grabbed up her clothes from the floor and tugged them on. With her tank top and jean shorts acting as armor, she felt a little less inclined to run screaming into the darkness. Though that definitely remained an option. Standing in a shaft of silvery moonlight, she turned around to look at him. Man, he looked good. His hair tousled, his naked chest dusted with hair that only moments ago she'd been threading between her fingers, he looked like the poster boy for a *Sex Is Good* campaign. She swallowed hard and tried to get a grip.

"It's okay," she lied, determined to find a way out of this minefield. "I'm a big girl. I knew this was going nowhere. I knew we were just scratching a mutual itch."

"A mutual— It was more than that, damn it." He practically leaped off the bed, took a few long steps, and grabbed her upper arms.

"No, it's not," she said, hating that it was true. Hating that she loved and he didn't. She pulled free of his grasp and desperately missed the warmth of his hands on her body. "Can't be. You're leaving the end of summer. Nothing's changed."

He reached up with both hands and shoved them through his hair. Carla watched the play of muscles across that broad chest, and despite the situation, she wanted to wrap her arms around him and beg him to stay. But she didn't; it wasn't her call.

Besides, what would be the point? If she asked him to stay, he'd only go into a long explanation about why he couldn't. No, thanks.

God, she was cold.

Jackson looked down into her eyes and saw the hurt and the confusion written there, and knew he was responsible. Just as he'd been responsible for the passion and pleasure he'd seen in those dark brown depths only moments ago.

He wasn't entirely sure how he'd fucked this up, but he'd done a damn fine job of it.

Her pain echoed inside him and he wanted nothing more than to turn the clock back. To the beginning of the night, when need and passion had driven thoughts of reality out of his head. When he'd allowed himself to believe for a while that there might be more here for him. More than just taking and giving comfort and sweet release. That for once in his whole miserable life, he wouldn't be at the wrong place at the wrong time.

But it was useless and he knew it. They couldn't go back. She stood there looking at him through those dark brown eyes of hers and he actually *felt* her withdrawal. But then, he couldn't really blame her, could he? He'd done the pulling away first. The moment he'd realized that he didn't have the right to claim a love that he'd never dreamed of.

He let his hands fall to her shoulders, and just the feel of her skin, soft and warm beneath his touch, made him want her again. But it was more than sexual need. There was an emotional draw that tore at him. One that he'd never expected to find. One that he didn't know what to do about.

She was right. He *would* be leaving. Tonight hadn't changed that. Except in one way—his departure now would be more painful than he wanted to think about.

Was he a selfish bastard? Yes, his child deserved 100 percent of his attention right now. But when the hell was it going to be *his* turn? Life with Diane had screwed him over so many times, he'd hardly known up from down for years. Now, he'd found Carla, a caring, loving, generous woman, and he had to look away when all he wanted to do was grab her, crush her mouth under his, and toss her back onto the sex-rumpled sheets. He wanted to lose himself in her warmth, her body. He wanted to hold on to her and never let go.

God, I need you, Carla Candellano. "I *am* grateful," he said, despite the way she winced at the word.

"Jesus, will you stop saying that?"

She stepped back from him and his hands slid free. Surprising how cold he felt now that he couldn't touch her. Methodically he grabbed up his clothes and pulled them on in silence. The rustle of fabric sounded out like a scream in the stillness.

Then, taking a few steps past her, he stared out the window at the moonlit darkness beyond the glass. Black silhouettes of trees danced lazily in a soft wind. Across the yard, the puppies lay in a tangled heap of gold. The burble and slap of the water fountain reached him through the closed window. From his left, he heard Carla's breathing, deep and steady.

Reaching out, he curled his fingers over the windowsill and stared into the reflection of his own eyes in the glass. When he spoke, he didn't look at her. Couldn't afford to.

"I came to Chandler for Reese," he said.

"I know that."

"She's my priority."

"She should be," Carla said, and he heard the distance in her voice. Probably just as well, he told himself. Better for both of them. But God, how he missed the comfort of her in his arms. The magic of touching her. The warmth of her heart beating against his.

"The thing is," he continued, and now he chanced a quick glance at her. Those dark curls fell around her pale face. Her brown eyes looked wide and haunted. Her lips, still puffy from his kisses, worried together nervously. And he wanted to grab her. More than anything in his life, he wanted to reach out, drag her close, and wrap his arms around her. He wanted to bury his face in the sweet curve of her neck. He wanted to inhale her scent, that soft, tantalizing mix of woman and flowers. But he couldn't. Not now. Not again. Jesus, admitting that was killing him. "It stopped being *just* about Reese a couple weeks ago."

She bit down on her bottom lip and he winced. Shit. Perfect. He was doing great here.

"See . . ." He shook his head and looked away from her wounded eyes, back into the glass. Back where he was forced to stare into his own eyes and see the misery there. "I found something here, too. Something I hadn't counted on. Planned for." His jaw clenched, he admitted, "I found you. And for the first time in too long a time, I felt . . . *happy*."

"Well, hell," she muttered thickly, "can't have that."

"That's right," he snapped, shooting her one quick look. "*I* can't have that. I'm not allowed."

She shook her head as if she hadn't heard him right. "Excuse me? You're not allowed to be happy?"

"Don't you get it? How in the hell do I let myself be *happy* when my little girl is trapped inside her own head and it's all my fault?"

"What?"

He pushed away from the window and reached up to viciously rub one hand across his mouth, almost as if he could wipe away the words he'd just said. But there was no point in that, was there? Ignoring the facts wouldn't change them. She had to know. Had to know why, no matter what he might feel for her—and he wasn't about to explore *that*—he couldn't act on it.

Not when Reese was still so hurt.

Jackson inhaled sharply, deeply, then started talking again before he could change his mind. "I told you. About the accident. When Diane died and Reese—"

"Yeah," Carla said quietly. "You told me."

"Well, there's more."

"Tell me."

Tell her? Why? So she could look at him with the same disgust he gave his reflection every morning when he first faced a mirror? Did he really want to tell her this? Did he want to open this all up? No. But he also needed Carla to understand exactly why he couldn't stay. Why he couldn't accept what she offered. What they might have found together. Even though he wanted it more than anything in the world.

"I *mean* it's my fault that accident happened. *My* fault Diane's dead." Christ. That was the first time he'd said that out loud. What the Barringtons wouldn't have given to have heard him say it. His chest ached. Breath strangled in his chest and he felt as though his skin were too tight for his bones. "I'm responsible. It was *my* fault that my daughter is too far away to find her way back to me."

"It was an accident," Carla argued, and it struck him that she was the only person in his life—ever—to try to defend him. And it surprised him just how touched he was by the attempt. As for the accident . . . everyone else avoided talking about it or, like the Barringtons, was all too eager to lay the blame at his feet.

A small curl of warmth sputtered to life in the pit of his stomach. He shoved one hand through his hair, then scrubbed that hand across his mouth again. A tightness in his chest squeezed his lungs. He needed air.

Turning around, he grabbed the window sash and threw it open. The wood scraped against its frame, like fingernails down a blackboard. Instantly a cool ocean-kissed summer breeze rushed in and flooded the room, carrying the combined scents of sea and pine and the jasmine bush at the edge of Carla's yard. He inhaled it all, taking it inside him, making a memory of this moonlit night when the magic ended.

"Diane and I weren't happy," he said, and almost laughed at the pitiful understatement. *Weren't happy.* That didn't go anywhere near describing the fights, the slammed doors, the whispered insults, and the icy chill that had settled over their apartment. "We hadn't been for a long time." Shaking his head, he let the night air brush past him and studied the darkened backyard as if he could find answers in the shadows. "Got married for all the wrong reasons and couldn't find enough good ones to stay married." He threw Carla a quick glance, then turned away again. "She was talking to a lawyer. Told me that last morning that she was going to file for divorce."

She looked confused. "I'm sorry. . . ."

Jackson didn't even acknowledge her. Sympathy for a long-dead marriage wasn't important. What was important was that she understand why he wasn't doing what his heart wanted him to do right now. Why he couldn't. "It was raining. I mean *pouring.* The sky was black and the rain was hard, falling down so thick it was like some bucket in heaven had been upended." His hands tightened on the window frame, his fingertips digging into the old, worn wood. "Diane was afraid to drive in the rain. Didn't like it. Said the slippery roads scared her. Asked me to drive her and Reese to the doctor."

He nodded to himself as he saw that morning all over again. His memory was crystal clear. He saw Diane's face again and the angry tears gathered in her eyes. And he saw himself, dismissing it.

"But I had a big meeting," he told Carla, snorting now at the stupid excuse that had seemed so important at the time. "So I told her to grow up. Told her that once we were divorced she'd have to drive herself, so she might as well get used to it."

"Jackson—"

"I told her she was being ridiculous!" his voice boomed out, smothering hers and forcing Carla to really *hear* him. "It was just *rain,* for God's sake."

And Diane had screamed at him. Her society friends probably wouldn't have recognized her with her features twisted and red with anger. She'd called him a few names—nothing he hadn't heard from her before— then she'd taken Reese and slammed out of the apartment.

It was the last time he saw Diane.

Until the cops pulled back that yellow tarp and he stared into her open, lifeless eyes and saw guilt staring back at him.

"An hour later," he said abruptly, closing off that particular memory, "she was dead." He pushed away from the wall and forced himself to turn and look at Carla again. "My wife was dead and my little girl went from screaming for her dead mother to absolute silence in the blink of an eye."

One tear rolled down Carla's cheek and shone silver

in the moonlight until she brushed it away. It touched him that she would cry for him. For Reese. And his insides raged because the one woman who had ever given a damn about him was the one he'd have to walk away from for the sake of his child.

He'd failed Reese once.

He wouldn't again.

"I can't even imagine how terrible that was to live through," Carla said, her gaze locked with his, "but how was it your fault?"

"Are you serious?" Dumbfounded, he just stared at her for a heartbeat or two. He'd confessed his deep dark secret and she still didn't get it? Didn't she understand the torment he'd been living with for the last year? Throwing his hands high again, he asked, "Didn't you hear me? Weren't you listening?"

"Yeah, I was." She took a step closer. "I heard you describe a terrible accident. I didn't hear where you caused it."

"Christ, Carla. Diane was scared. She asked for help and I turned her down. If I'd been driving, it wouldn't have happened."

"You don't know that."

"That's the point," he snarled, angry at himself, not her. "I'll *never* know that."

"This is nuts," Carla said, and followed him as he walked out of the bedroom. She was only a step or two behind him when he entered the kitchen. "You can't blame yourself by playing the 'what if' game."

He grabbed a glass off the counter, turned on the water tap, and filled it. Then he shut the water off, drained the glass in one long gulp, and set it back onto the counter. He didn't look at her. "What ifs are all I've got left."

Carla's mind was spinning. Yes, it was terrible. A hideous accident. Diane died and that was tragic. What had happened to Reese was horrible. But the fact that he was going to punish himself for the rest of his life was ridiculous.

"Only if you let them be."

"You don't understand."

"Oh, yes, I do," she said. "What if you'd been driving? Well, gee, Jackson, what if it hadn't been raining? What if Diane hadn't been afraid to drive in the rain? What if Reese's doctor's appointment was for the following day instead? What if you hadn't lived in Chicago?"

He shot her a dismissive glance, then stomped past her to pace the living room. "That doesn't even make sense."

"And your scenario does?" She went right after him.

"I was there. I could have helped. I didn't."

"And if you hadn't been home, then what?"

"But I was."

"Maybe if you'd been driving, you all would have been killed."

"We don't know that, though, do we?"

"That doesn't change the facts, Jackson." She reached out, grabbed his arm, and tugged until he turned around to look at her. "You can play 'what if' forever, but it's useless. You can't change what happened, and torturing yourself won't make it any easier."

"It shouldn't *be* easier."

Carla drew her head back and looked at him. He

wanted to suffer. Thought he deserved it. And wouldn't settle for less.

"I get it," she said softly. "You have to be a martyr."

"I didn't say that."

She choked out a short laugh. "Sure you did. But for how long, Jackson? One year? Five? Ten?"

"I—" He shook his head and clamped his mouth shut. She saw a muscle in his jaw twitch.

"You're hiding from the past," she said, "but you're going to miss the future."

"Yeah?" he snapped, whipping his head around to pin her with a steely blue gaze. "Look who's talkin'."

"What's that supposed to mean?" She played dumb despite the fact that she knew darn well where he was headed with this.

"You've been hiding, too, Carla. Running from the one time you weren't able to help. You took all the blame for that, didn't you?"

"I didn't—"

"I know," he said, his voice soft, his words decisive. "You didn't find the boy. Neither did anyone else who was looking for him. You know what the difference is?" he asked, closing the gap between them. "The difference is, you're the only one who quit. Everyone else who was there that day is still working, aren't they? They're going out on other searches, helping when they can. You walked away from something you were meant to do. That only a handful of people in the world are capable of doing." He reached out and tilted her chin up with the tips of his fingers.

Her gaze met his and everything inside Carla went still. Even her heartbeat seemed to stop.

"You quit rather than help others who might need you." He shook his head and smiled sadly. "So don't stand there and tell me not to live on 'if I'das.' You're doing it yourself."

Tears stung the backs of her eyes and she blinked frantically to clear them. She wanted to argue his point. She wanted to remind him that the others who'd been looking for Jamie hadn't loved him. She wanted to say that her failure had been more than messing up on her job. It had been losing a little boy who was a part of her life, her world.

Carla choked back the tears crowding her throat. She wanted to tell him all of that. But she couldn't. Because he was right. Damn it, he was right. For two whole years, she'd clung to her failure and hugged her hurts close. She'd taken the blame for Jamie's loss, though she was no more culpable than any of the other searchers out there that long, miserable day.

"Oh God." Carla clutched her fingers together in front of her. Looking up at him, she said softly, "Good shot, Jackson. You hit your target dead center."

"Carla, I wasn't trying to hurt you, just—"

"To make me understand." She pulled in a long, shaky breath and felt it shudder through her. "Well, congrats. You did it. You scored where no one else has been able to. Not Jamie's parents, not my family." Her bottom lip trembled and she bit into it briefly. "I have been hiding. From the pain? From the failure? I'm not sure which." Carla walked past him, kicked a fallen throw pillow out of her way, and stopped at the wide front window. "I'd never failed before. Not at anything that was important to me. And it shames me to think that maybe it was my own failure and not the loss of Jamie that's kept me hiding all this time."

"Carla, that's not true—"

She lifted one hand to cut him off. "It's not the point right now, anyway," she said. "That's something I'll have to figure out on my own." Turning around to look at him, she studied him as if it was the last time she'd ever see him. In the dim light, his features were drawn and tight and looked as though they'd been clawed out of marble. "The point is, Jackson . . . that I'm at least willing to admit that I've been wrong. You won't. Instead, you're going to live with a guilt that isn't yours and let it punch you in the heart every time you look at your daughter."

He swayed as if her words had hit home.

"I can't put myself first, Carla. Not now. Not when Reese needs me so much."

"I love her, too, Jackson," she said. "And I want her to be healthy and happy again. But tucking her—and yourself—away isn't the answer."

"Do you know what is, then?" he asked, his voice a low growl in the silent room. "Because I've been looking for that answer for a year now and I haven't been able to find it."

"Maybe," Carla said softly, "it's because you've been looking in all the wrong places."

CHAPTER
NINETEEN

"YOU DID IT, DIDN'T you?" Stevie demanded, and tightened her grip on the phone.

"I don't know what you're talking about."

"Nice try, Carla. I know you better than that. And you've been crying." Damn it. He'd made her cry. That son of a bitch. Stevie picked up a pen and stabbed it at her desk blotter.

She usually liked the early-morning hours at the Leaf and Bean. It was quiet, just a few regulars at their favorite tables. But this call from Carla had blackened her mood in an instant.

"I knew it last night," Stevie said tightly, and took another stab with the pen, pretending it was going straight into Jackson Wyatt's black heart. Just wait until she caught up to him. "When you guys left the picnic I knew you were headed for bed."

"Gee," Carla said, "a psychic."

"Fine. The signs were there for anybody to read. But I also knew you'd gone and fallen in love with him."

On the other end of the line, Carla sighed. "I'm an idiot."

"No, you're not," Stevie defended. "*He* is." Damn it. Hadn't she warned that bastard what she'd do to him if he hurt Carla? Hadn't her threat been clear enough?

"Look," Carla said on a heavy sigh. "I didn't call to whine or to sic you on him. I just called to say I'm going to skip out on our lunch today."

Understanding, Stevie said, "Okay, you're excused."

"Thanks, Mom."

"For one day," Stevie told her, standing up in her office as if Carla could see her making the point. "I give you one day to feel sorry for yourself. Tomorrow I want you fighting mad."

"I'll work on it."

"I'll call you later." When Carla hung up, Stevie replaced the phone in the cradle and gave serious thought to hunting down Jackson Wyatt. But as soon as the urge presented itself, she realized she'd be better off waiting until she'd cooled down a little. Going after the man while her best friend's teary voice still rang in her ears almost guaranteed that *somebody* was going to get hurt. And it wouldn't be *her.*

Grumbling under her breath, she left the office and went out into the shop. She checked her regulars, refilled coffee cups, served some cinnamon bread, and kept repeating, *Stay busy. That's the secret. Stay busy.*

Naturally, the rest of her morning was shot to hell when the front door opened and Nick walked in. And as much as she hated to admit it, even to herself, thoughts of Carla flew out of her mind the minute Nick showed up.

He paused on the threshold as if unsure of his welcome. Stevie took that moment for a good, long look at him. Nick Candellano looked like thirty miles of bad road.

His hair stood on end; his clothes were wrinkled as if he'd slept in them—which she was pretty sure he had done, since jails seldom furnished jammies. His cheeks were covered in black stubble, and one of his eyes was swollen shut and blossoming purple like an overblown hydrangea.

He caught her gaze, winced with his one good eye, and sheepishly made his way over to the counter. The few people in the shop insisted on stopping him to talk football, which gave her a long opportunity to observe him. Those long legs of his moved with an easy grace that made her think he really belonged swaggering on board a ship. A pirate ship. She could see him, hair flying in the wind, barking orders to his men, sailors scrambling to comply—and some dumbshit woman standing beside him, gazing up at him adoringly.

Oh, good God.

She was just a touch crankier than usual when she greeted him. Planting one hand on her hip, she said, "Well, hi, *Dick.* I mean, Nick."

"Funny," he said, and his voice sounded low and raspy. "Real funny."

"Who's making jokes?"

"Gimme a break, will you, Stevie?" He planted his elbows on the counter and cupped his head in his hands. "It's been a rough morning."

"Preceded by a crappy night." God, he looked miserable. By all rights, she should be happy about that.

But she wasn't. Nick had been the one big heartbreak in her life, but she still didn't hate him.

"Pretty much," he agreed, then added, "Don't talk so loud, okay?"

Stevie buried the smile twitching at her lips. He surely wouldn't see the humor in it. "Whose door did you walk into?"

"Huh?" He lifted his head to stare at her.

"Your eye, dumbshit. How'd you get that black— excuse me, *purple*—eye?"

"A present from my brother."

"Intriguing. Which one?"

"Which one has the key to the jail cell?"

"Ahh. . . ." Reaching behind her, Stevie grabbed the coffeepot and an empty blue ceramic cup. Filling it, she set the cup in front of him, right under his nose. "Well, you could always sue him for police brutality."

Nick choked out a harsh laugh and made a grab for the coffee. "You want him to *kill* me?"

When she opened her mouth to speak, he cut her off.

"Never mind. Don't answer that." He rubbed one hand across his whiskery jaw and said, "I came to get my car keys. Tony said you have them."

Nodding, Stevie reached for the hook beneath the counter. Picking up his key ring, she set it down in front of him. "You didn't need your keys last night, apparently."

"Don't remind me."

"What is up with you?" she asked when her curiosity overrode her common sense. "Drinking and driving?"

"I know," he muttered, and cradled his coffee cup between his palms. "Stupid."

"Beyond stupid."

He lifted his bleary one-eyed gaze to hers and Stevie saw real misery—not just the pangs of a hangover. A flicker of worry sparkled to life inside her before she could stop it. "What's wrong?"

He almost told her. She could see the words hovering on the tip of his tongue. Then for some reason, he changed his mind. Nick lifted the coffee cup and paused to inhale the rich, full scent of the hot brew before taking a deep gulp. "God," he said on a heavy sigh. "That's good. I may live after all."

Stevie smiled and pushed her curiosity aside for the time being. "Glad to hear it."

He flicked her a wary glance. "You are? That's a switch."

"Believe it or not, Nick, I'm over you." Stevie set the coffeepot back down onto its warming plate, then leaned her forearms on the counter. Staring directly into his one good, but bleary eye, she said frankly, "Who would I torture if you were gone?"

Carla *had* been crying.

But she was finished now.

Jackson was right about one thing, anyway. For two years, she'd moped and cried and felt sorry for herself. She'd mourned sweet Jamie and her own failure. She'd run home to Chandler, with a figurative tail between her legs. She'd hidden away, refusing to risk failure again, even if it had meant turning her back on the chance to help those who needed her.

Jamie's parents had grieved with her, never blaming, never accusing. Her own family had tried to make her see. They'd tried to tell her exactly what Jackson had only a few hours ago. Apparently, though, she hadn't been willing to listen until she had the chance to be completely humiliated. Okay, not completely. At least she hadn't confessed to being in love with him. She'd been spared his pity, if not his anger.

"Small consolation," she muttered as she paused on the back porch long enough to scrape the soles of her tennies on the mat, "but it's better than nothing."

The question was: What did she do now?

Keep moping?

Yeah, that was an attractive idea.

Just a few hours ago, she'd been arguing with Jackson, telling him that he was using what had happened in his life as an excuse to stop *living* his life. If she continued to do the same thing, what did that say about her?

Stepping into the kitchen, she threw a quick glance at the wall duck. Six forty-five. Mike wouldn't be at Searchers' office yet. If she called now, she could leave a message and not get dragged into a conversation she wasn't up to having at the moment. Plus, she told herself as she marched through the kitchen and into the living room, once she left the message, there'd be no going back. She'd be committed.

Grabbing up the phone, Carla stared at the receiver for a long minute, thinking about this. Was she ready? Could she do it? And if she couldn't, did she have any right to criticize Jackson?

Her fingers tightened on the steel gray phone. She bit her bottom lip, inhaled sharply, deeply, and then, before she could think any more about it, hit the number three speed dial button.

She waited, stomach churning, palms dampening. This was a number she hadn't dialed in two years. A number she'd told herself she'd never call again. Her mouth went dry. Seconds clicked past and then her call connected and the phone in LA was ringing. She waited again. Four rings before the answering machine kicked in, then Mike Shaner's deep, gravelly voice came on the line.

You have reached Searchers. If this is an emergency, hang up and dial three-two-three five-five-five seven-oh-oh-oh. Otherwise, please leave a message and we will return your call as soon as possible.

One long beep sounded and Carla hesitated—but only briefly. "Mike, it's Carla." She closed her eyes, took a deep breath, and said what she had to say quickly, before she could change her mind. "If you still want us, you can put Abbey and me back on your list of searchers. We're ready to go back to work."

She hung up quickly and waited for the panic to crawl through her. But it didn't come. Her stomach was still a mass of knots, but she also felt a sense of . . . purpose, for the first time in two years. She'd done the right thing. It had taken her too long to do it, but the point was, it was now done. And she owed that to Jackson.

Despite the sting of his words, he'd at least given her the truth—as she'd done for him. The question was, Carla thought as she stared out the front window at the house across the street, what would Jackson do about his own truth?

"I know you don't want to leave," Jackson said, bracing himself against the flash of anger in his daughter's eyes. It seemed all he did lately was annoy or disappoint the females in his life.

Starting last night and going right through this morning, when he'd picked Reese up from Mama Candellano's house. His daughter and the older woman had been busily making chocolate chip pancakes when he'd arrived. Though he'd given Reese time to eat her creation and had a cup of coffee himself, he'd still scooted her away long before she was ready.

Funny. Just a few weeks ago, he'd been hoping that Reese would respond to him. Regain her sense of self. Communicate.

Now that she was, he was suffering for it.

Even silent, the child had no trouble at all making her fury known. One Scooby-Doo tennis shoe tapped against the driveway and her thin arms were folded across her narrow chest in a posture that had become all too familiar lately. His heart ached for her. She'd been so happy here. Come so far.

But it just wasn't far enough. And now that things between him and Carla were bound to be strained, he couldn't take the chance of Reese being affected. What if she slipped backward rather than advancing? No. He'd thought about this for hours and Jackson knew there was only one thing he could do.

He had to return to Chicago earlier than he'd planned. There was a chance, he told himself, that with Reese's recent strides, the doctors the Barringtons wanted her to see would be able to help her come the rest of the way back. And if she hated him for taking her away from the place and people she loved . . . Jackson swallowed hard. Maybe she'd start speaking sooner, if only to yell at him for ruining her life.

Determined, he ignored his daughter's mutinous glare and picked up her little tote bag, stowing it in the trunk of the car.

When her daddy walked past her, going into the house for the rest of the suitcases, Reese grabbed her tote bag out of the trunk and carried it to the side of the house.

She couldn't go away.

She didn't want to leave Carla and Abbey and Nana. She didn't want to go back to Chicago.

The wind blew hard and Reese lifted one hand to rub tears out of her eyes. Her bottom lip quivered as she wondered what to do. Where should she go? If she stayed, Daddy would make her leave. She could run to Carla or Nana. She scraped the toe of her tennis shoe across the grass. No, she couldn't. 'Cause they'd call Daddy and he'd come and then he'd take her away again.

Reese propped her back against the side of the house and slid down to the ground. Her bottom hit the grass hard and she whimpered a little. Until Abbey trotted up to her from the backyard. The big dog slipped her head beneath Reese's arm and cuddled in close, licking and sniffing until Reese heaved a sigh and hugged Abbey's neck really hard. *Don't be sad, Abbey. I won't go away. I won't leave you.*

"Where's Reese?"

Carla stepped back from the front door and waved Jackson inside. He moved past her, his gaze darting around the room, searching, even as he kept moving, walking through the house in long, hurried strides. By the time he was back in the living room looking at her, Carla had gotten over her surprise and was prepared to face him.

"Is she out back?" he demanded.

"Reese isn't here," Carla said, and for the first time noticed the fine edge of panic in his features.

"She has to be," he told her, his voice tight, thick. "She would have come to say good-bye to Abbey. She loves that dog."

"Abbey's still at Mama's. That's probably where Reese went."

"Okay, yeah. That's probably it." But he didn't move.

"She's saying good-bye?" Carla picked that one word out of the rest and focused on it. Something cold and ugly settled in her bones and sent out ribbonlike tentacles to every corner of her body.

Jackson braced his feet wide apart and shoved both hands into the back pockets of his jeans. He didn't meet her gaze but looked away, as if still searching the room for his daughter. "We're leaving. Going back to Chicago."

"It's not September yet," she said, even as a voice in her mind was shouting, *Stupid. He knows that. He just wants to get away from you!*

"I know," he said, shaking his head. "I just thought it'd be better for everyone if we left earlier than planned."

A deep, throbbing ache blossomed in her chest and Carla winced with the pain of it. One night with her and he wanted thousands of miles separating them. Well, at least she had the answer to the question she'd wondered about earlier. Jackson had decided to keep running from his truth. To stay in hiding. To continue to make himself pay for a tragic accident that he hadn't caused and was unable to prevent.

And along with the grief welling inside her came a surge of irritation. "So you were just going to leave. Without saying a word."

He sucked in a gulp of air and finally met her gaze. "I thought we'd pretty much said it all last night, Carla."

"Did you?" Tears clawed at the backs of her eyes, but she didn't—wouldn't—give in to them. "And didn't like what you heard, apparently, since you're picking up and moving back home."

"I just thought it would be easier if we didn't have to go through the whole summer seeing each other."

"Easier on who, Jackson? Me? Or you?"

"You." He yanked his hands from his pockets, marched across the room, and grabbed her upper arms. His fingers pressed into her skin, and even through the fabric of her short-sleeved shirt she felt the heat of him right down to her bones. "Damn it, Carla, do you think I *want* to go?"

She tipped her head back and stared up into his lake-blue eyes, noting the banked fury sizzling on their surfaces. But she'd never backed down from anger in her life and she wasn't about to start now. "Nobody's forcing you to leave."

"I know that. I was trying . . ." His words trailed off as his gaze moved over her, hot, hungry, furious, and yet so filled with yearning that Carla's breath caught in her chest. "I was trying to do the right thing. By you."

Again the stinging sensation of budding tears burned

her eyes. "And you think the right thing to do is leave?"

"I don't want to hurt you, Carla."

"I know that." Oddly enough, she really did know that. She felt it pouring from him in waves of concern and affection, and she wrapped those tender folds around her heart and held on tightly.

He loosened his grip on her arms but couldn't quite bring himself to let her go completely. The pads of his thumbs caressed her and a ripple of something warm and silky slithered along her spine in response.

"It's not like I want to go," he admitted, his voice a deep scrape of sound that scratched at her heart and tugged at her soul. "But I can't give you what you need. What you want."

"And you know what I want?"

"I can guess," he said, finally letting her go as if he couldn't bear to touch her when he knew it would be for the last time.

"Is that right? Well then, let's hear your best guess."

"Love." One word and it hung in the stillness between them.

Her heart bumped up against the wall of her chest and she felt its staggering beat. Carla swallowed hard and said, "Good guess."

One corner of his mouth twitched up into a brief sad smile. "I can't be what you need," he said, and she could see that it cost him to admit it.

His features tight, his eyes glittering with a pain she shared, Carla knew that no matter what he felt for her, he wouldn't allow himself to confess it. He was determined to pay for a mistake he hadn't made. And nothing she could say would change his mind.

"You're wrong," Carla said softly, with a slow shake of her head. He was going to turn his back on everything they might have had together. She stared up at him and felt that small flicker of exasperation sputter and grow as it erupted within the misery crowding her heart. "It's not that you can't. It's that you *won't*. There's a difference. We talked about this last night, remember?"

"I do care about you, Carla."

Crumbs. He was offering her crumbs, when they could have found a banquet together.

"Yeah? Well, I *love* you." *Oh, crap. Brilliant, Carla. Just freaking brilliant.* She slapped one hand to her forehead and muttered, "Is it too late to take that back?"

His eyes widened. He opened his mouth to speak, but she cut him off.

"Don't say anything, okay?" *Please don't say anything.* God, if he said something stupid like "Gee, too bad," she'd have to kill him. As it was, she wanted to find a nice high cliff and get a running start toward it. Turning away from him, she walked to the phone and picked up the receiver. Before she dialed, she said, "I didn't mean to say that."

"Carla . . ."

"It just sort of . . . popped out. But maybe it's just as well. At least now you know exactly what you're running from."

Oh, he knew. He knew exactly what he was giving up. What he was walking—not running—away from. And though it was killing him, he just didn't see another way for them. Reese had to have his complete attention. Even if that meant that he would leave his heart here, in Chandler.

Jackson watched Carla as she made her call and forced himself to stand still. He memorized the look of her, every line, every curve. He drew her image on his mind and etched it in deeply. After today, this was all he would have of her, and the realization made it even harder to keep from going to her. Especially since everything in him was screaming at him to cross the room, grab her, wrap his arms around her so tightly she couldn't draw a breath unless he did, too, and hang on to her forever.

Love.

He'd been offered the world.

And he couldn't accept.

His brain raced, his heart ached, and a roaring in his ears drowned out her voice as she spoke into the phone. Until she dropped the receiver and turned to look at him. Her face pale, her big brown eyes haunted and terrified, she said, "Reese and Abbey aren't at Mama's. She hasn't seen either of them in more than an hour."

CHAPTER
TWENTY

INSIDE AN HOUR, A search was organized.

Jackson and Carla had checked both houses, the yards, and the surrounding areas and had come up empty. There was no sign of Reese. When Jackson discovered her tote bag missing from the trunk of the car, the nightmare grew blacker. His little girl had run away.

Like father, like daughter.

The words echoed in his mind, taunting him, tormenting him. He'd been ready to pick up, pack up, and run back to Chicago, despite Reese's obvious reluctance to go. Hell, despite his own reluctance. Now, the little girl had obviously taken matters into her own hands. And beaten him to the running-away punch.

Pacing wildly, Jackson paid no attention to the people gathered with him in the sheriff's office. All he could think of was his daughter. Her face. Her eyes. The misery and anger he'd read in those blue depths the last time he'd seen her.

No. Not the last time.

He'd see her again.

All he had to do was find her. *Daddy's coming, baby.*

Guilt reared up and took a fresh bite out of him. For a year, he'd paid penance for the tragedy that had hit his child so hard. Now, once again, because of him, Reese was in danger. How would he ever be able to live with himself if anything happened to her?

"Jackson?"

Carla's voice reached through his misery and dragged him back from the darkness settling in his mind. He whirled around and immediately found her gaze in the crowded room. And even at a distance, he felt her worry, her love, her support. She'd offered him so much and he'd turned his back on all of it. Pain pinged around inside his chest like a bullet ricocheting off a rocky wall. But then, that was something he'd just have to learn to live with.

From across the room, Carla smiled at him. After everything that had happened between them, it was a wonder to Jackson that she was willing to speak to him. Let alone help him when he was at his lowest. Yet here she stood.

Undaunted, she was clearly ready to do whatever was necessary to find Reese and bring her home safely. All business now, Carla wore heavy climbing boots and blue jeans. Her faded T-shirt was tucked into her waistband and around her waist was a heavy belt with a walkie-talkie clipped to it along with a water bottle, compass, and flashlight. At her feet was a backpack that held God knew what kind of emergency equipment.

Her strength filled him and for the first time in his life, Jackson leaned on someone. He'd never really needed or even *wanted* to need anyone before. But now, knowing he wasn't in this alone meant more to him than he ever could have imagined.

Crossing the room to stand beside her at Tony's desk, Jackson looked down at an unfolded map spread atop the stacks of papers cluttering the scarred wooden surface.

Carla slipped her hand into his, threaded their fingers together, and held on tightly. He felt her warmth, the strength of her heart, flow into him, and Jackson silently returned the pressure of her grip.

"Tony and two others will take the section by the lake. You and I are taking the woods at the base of the foothills. The area we covered when we searched for the missing man. Nick and Paul," Carla said, and nodded at her other brothers, standing opposite them, "will take the beach and the coves."

"Nobody knows those coves better than we do," Nick said. His one good eye looked clear and steady as he nodded at Jackson. "If she's down there—"

Paul pushed his glasses up higher on the bridge of his nose and finished his twin's sentence. "—we'll find her."

"The others," Carla said, with a quick look around at the familiar faces, "are spreading out and working in teams to cover everything else."

"Thanks." Jackson bit his tongue to keep from shouting, *Let's get going, already!* They had to hurry. His daughter was out there. Alone. And it wouldn't be daylight forever, for God's sake. But Carla's hand in his kept him from raging. Steeling himself to patience, he listened as the townspeople gathered in the office received their instructions and he watched their faces. Everyone there was solemn, determined. Old and young, they'd turned out when Tony had issued a call for help. They'd come from the barbershop, the drugstore, the art galleries, and the diner. They'd left their businesses and their families to do whatever they could.

Stevie wandered through the room, filling coffee cups from one of the dozens of thermoses she'd filled and brought to the sheriff's office. Even Virginia, Abigail, and Rachel had turned out, bringing sandwiches that no one had the stomach to touch—but still, the effort was there. Mama Candellano muttered prayers and bounced Tina on her hip as Beth checked the batteries in the walkie-talkies.

Years of isolation fell from Jackson's shoulders like a hundred-pound weight. His gaze shot around the room and he realized that it wasn't only Carla who had invaded his life, his world. It was also her family. Her friends—now *his* and Reese's friends, too. This town had become the home he and his daughter had never known. Without ever realizing it was happening, he'd become a part of Chandler.

He'd come here hoping to heal his daughter and now found his own heart and soul restored.

But at what cost?

Carla squeezed his hand even tighter and the pressure of her grip closed around his heart as well. She tipped her face up to his, and when he felt the power of her gaze locked on him, Jackson turned to meet it. Those deep brown eyes called to him as they had since the first moment he met her. But now he saw so much more when she looked at him.

He saw a chance at a future.

If they found Reese.

"We'll find her," Carla said, reading his mind, if not his heart.

Jackson scraped one hand across his face. "She could be anywhere."

"There are a lot of us and only one of her." She picked up her backpack and slung it over her shoulder. "We *will* find her."

He hung on to her hand as if it was a lifeline tossed into a churning sea. "We *have* to."

Have to hide. So Daddy can't find me. So he can't make me leave.

Tired, Reese stumbled slightly as she walked. Her legs hurt and her toes pinched in her Scooby-Doo tennis shoes. Beside her, Abbey whined, and she turned to look at the big golden dog.

Don't be scared, Abbey. It's just trees and rocks and probably no monsters. Monsters don't come out in daytime, do they?

But if she was still hiding at nighttime, then what? Would there be monsters? Or a wolf that liked to gobble up little girls? Her tummy ached, partly 'cause she was hungry and partly 'cause she had a scary, icky feeling inside. Reese chewed on her bottom lip as her gaze moved over the trees. There was too many of 'em. She couldn't see anything but trees. Turning in a slow circle, she wondered how she'd ever find her way back to Carla's house when she was finished hiding.

Abbey poked a cold nose at her, pushing her head beneath Reese's hand, hoping to be petted. Tiny fingers stroked her while the shadows played around them, and Reese wished her daddy was there. Then they could go back to Carla's house together.

And Reese wouldn't be so scared.

Hours later, Nick squinted into the afternoon sun, pushed the button on his walkie-talkie, and said, "Tony, this is Nick. Paul and I have covered most of the beach. . . ."

Static crackled, then his brother's voice hissed at him, "Anything?"

Nick glanced up as Paul stepped out of the closest cove, shaking his head in disgust.

"Nothing." Nick looked back over his shoulder at the beach they'd already searched. He and Paul had talked to every surfer, every tourist, on the sand. They'd shown everyone the picture of Reese that all of the search teams had been given, but no one had seen her.

Paul walked up to him. "Anybody else have any luck?"

Nick shook his head. "Tony? We'll keep going. Still have some beach to cover and there's the old cave. . . ." The one where the Candellano boys had played pirate games when they were kids.

"I remember," Tony said. "Keep in touch."

"Right."

"Let's go then," Paul said as Nick hooked the walkie-talkie back to his belt. "If the tide comes in and she's at the cave—"

"I know." Nick scowled at the thought and the two of them hurried across the wet sand.

•   •   •

Tony walked the edge of the lake, wishing to hell somebody would find the kid. His walkie-talkie bristled regularly, but there was no good news.

Glancing to the edge of the water, he watched the reeds sway with the wind. Beneath the surface of the lake, he knew, the water was murky, the lake bottom covered in mud thick enough to snatch a man's shoe off.

He didn't like to think what could happen to a little girl who might stumble into it. Instantly, baby Tina's tiny face rose up in his mind and a cold chill ran down his spine. Thank God his daughter was safe at home.

Damn, he felt sorry for Jackson right now.

"Where the hell is she?"

Carla's own fears spiked at the worry in Jackson's voice. She wished there was something she could say to help. Something she could offer him. But the truth was, she had nothing.

They'd been looking for hours and hadn't found a trace of Reese. Carla'd used every trick she had at her disposal, but it hadn't done any good. She'd checked for footprints; she'd examined bushes and low-hanging branches, hoping to find a trace of fabric or a strand or two of blond hair. But it was as if Reese and Abbey had just vanished.

Damn it.

Just like Jamie, a voice in her mind whispered, and she cringed from the words. No. It wouldn't be like Jamie. Not this time. She wouldn't let it be. Her heart ached and pain seemed a part of her now. But she wouldn't give in to it. Wouldn't surrender to the desperation clawing at her insides.

She couldn't. Not if she expected to find Reese.

And she damn well *would* find her.

"I don't know where she is," Carla finally said, and came to a stop, swinging her backpack to the ground. Pulling her water bottle free of the pack, she took a long drink, pushed her hair back out of her eyes, and looked up at Jackson.

His features were tight, drawn in pain too deep for words. His blue eyes were narrowed as he continued to scan the woods even as he took a long drink of water himself.

They'd hardly spoken since they'd started searching. There hadn't been time. Or breath to waste. And really, she thought, what was there to say? *I love you?* Not the time. Also not what he wanted to hear. She'd found that out last night. No, the only important thing now was Reese. Her safety.

Wounded hearts and feelings really didn't stack up against a child's life. Carla fought down a thread of panic that began to unwind in the pit of her stomach, sending small curls of terror throughout her body. Fear wouldn't help. It would only make her second-guess herself. And she couldn't afford that.

Especially now.

Now when memories of Jamie were darting around the edges of her mind, looking for a way in.

Reese needed her.

And Carla would *not* fail.

Not this time.

"I'm going nuts here," Jackson muttered.

"I know." It had been two years since she'd done

this. Since she'd had to try to hold up a net of hope beneath a parent tumbling down a slope of misery.

And this time, she needed that net as much as Jackson did.

"It's early yet," she said, refusing to give in to the fear scratching at the base of her throat.

"Early?" He tossed the bottle back into his pack. "She's six years old. She's been missing for nearly five hours." He waved a hand, encompassing the surrounding trees, the shadowed spots beneath the low branches, the leaf-littered ground, and the seemingly endless nooks and crannies where a child could hide. "She's wandering around out here. Alone."

"She's not alone," Carla reminded him. "She's got Abbey with her, and that dog will give her life to save Reese."

"Yeah." He sucked in and blew out a breath. "That's something." His jaw twitched and she could see the effort he was putting out to keep from howling in frustration. "How in the hell will we ever find her?"

The pain in his voice, the agony in his eyes, tore at her heart. She could no more have stayed away than she could have stopped breathing. Stepping in close, Carla wrapped her arms around his waist, splaying her hands against his back, and held on until he reacted, holding her tightly to him. Resting her head on his chest, she listened to the pounding beat of his heart, savored the feel of his arms around her, and whispered, "We'll find her because we *have* to. Because she needs us."

He sighed and his breath ruffled her hair. "It'll be dark in a few hours. What then?"

"Then we use flashlights," she said simply, and tipped her head back to stare up at him. "We don't stop. Ever. Not until she's safe."

Jackson looked down into her eyes and saw the worry, the panic, shining there. But he also saw determination and a glint of pure steel. She wouldn't give up on someone she loved. It wouldn't occur to her. And he silently thanked whatever fates had sent him here, to Chandler.

To Carla.

"If I didn't have you with me right now," he admitted, releasing his grip on her waist long enough to reach up and stroke her cheek, "I'd be more lost than Reese."

"Jackson . . ."

"It's true." He'd taken from Carla, giving nothing back, and excused it all by holding Reese out in front of him like a shield. He'd hidden behind his past, his child, and his own fears.

And in that blindingly clear instant, Jackson wondered how he'd ever believed he could leave Carla. The thought of never seeing her again opened up a black, deep hole inside him that shook him to his bones. The idea of living his life without her in it was unthinkable.

Unimaginable.

Those dark brown eyes of hers looked straight into his soul and somehow saw beyond all the bullshit to the man he really was and . . . God help her, she loved him anyway.

How could he leave when the very thought of being without her was enough to steal the air from his lungs?

I love her.

Those three little words bounced in his mind like a Super Ball on steroids. Every little corner of his brain lit up when the words hit, until the inside of his head felt like a pinball machine on Tilt.

Well, he'd picked a helluva time to see the light. But now that he had, he knew he had to tell her.

"This isn't the right time," he said, his gaze moving over her features like the softest caress, "but you need to know something."

"You don't have to say anything."

"I was an idiot last night."

"That's not important now."

"Yeah, it is. You took me by surprise, Carla. I never thought I'd . . . *care* so much for someone."

She flinched at the word *care* and Jackson saw it. And he couldn't blame her. *Care* was a pretty weak word to describe how he felt about her. He hadn't meant to confess anything to her now. But suddenly, in the midst of this confusion, this worry, it seemed more important than anything to get the words said. The *right* words.

"I love you," he said, and watched her eyes widen, darken, then dim slightly with a sheen of tears she frantically tried to blink away. "You are the missing piece in the jigsaw puzzle that is my life. Without you, there's no completion."

Pulling back, she shook her head as she reached for her backpack. "Jackson, you don't have to—"

"Yeah," he said, reaching out to grab her upper arm in a tight fist. Swinging her around to face him, he said quickly, "Yeah, I have to. I have to tell you now. Before we find Reese, so you'll know that it isn't gratitude talking." She flinched at the word *gratitude* and he remembered why. "I *do* love you, you know. You sneaked up on me, Carla. I wasn't looking for you. Hadn't planned on you, God knows. But suddenly there you were and it threw me."

She inhaled sharply and blew the air out in a rush.

"I've spent the last year concentrating on Reese. And before that, there was Diane. I thought I loved her once, you know? And I watched that feeling disintegrate into nothing more than irritation."

"This isn't the time to—"

"Yeah, it is," he insisted, wanting to say it all. To make sure she understood. "Jesus, now more than ever is the time. I finally figured out how important it is to say what you're feeling when you're feeling it. When Diane died, I realized that life could be over in a heartbeat. Go out for breakfast and be dead by lunch. So whatever we say, whatever we *don't* say, *matters*. It matters so damn much, Carla. It's all that *does* matter." Grabbing her other arm, he pulled her close to him again until their bodies pressed together in a way that made him want to hold her even closer. "I *love* you and I need you to know that—before we continue this search."

"I love you, too." There were tears in her eyes as she said the words, making them that much more precious.

"I'm counting on that," he said.

"We will find her, Jackson."

God, he needed to believe her. And right at that moment, he did feel as if they could accomplish *anything* as long as they were together. "You're right. We will. And when we do, there are some things I have to do. I have to do whatever I can to help Reese."

"I know that."

"I'll still have to take her back to Chicago. To see the doctor the Barringtons have found." He shook his head. "They're rotten human beings, but in their weird way, they're concerned about Reese. They wouldn't settle for less than the best in a doctor."

She nodded. "Of course they wouldn't."

He slid his hands up her shoulders until he was cupping her face in his palms. His gaze locked on her, and he knew in that instant he would always see her as she was this moment. With tears shining in her eyes and the wind tossing her dark curls into a black halo around her head. And he made a promise, for the first time in he couldn't remember how long.

"When Reese is well . . . when she's come all the way back to me . . . to us . . . I'll be back."

She smiled up at him and nodded again. "Damn right you will."

He bent his head and kissed her gently, briefly, and even at that, a sizzle of heat shot through him as surely as a lightning strike would have.

"Jackson," she whispered, then stopped. Jerking her head around to the right, she held her breath, stared off into the distance, and listened.

"What is—"

"Shh," she ordered, then added, *"listen."*

He did, straining with everything in him, and that's when he heard it.

A dog.

Barking.

CHAPTER
TWENTY-ONE

JACKSON TENSED AND LISTENED again. A dog's bark. Faint. At a distance. *Abbey?*

Coming from where?

"Damn it." He turned his head, trying to pinpoint a direction. "Sounds like it's coming from everywhere at once."

"No," Carla said, grabbing the backpack and slinging it over her shoulders. "It's coming from there." She pointed, then set off, not bothering to see if he'd follow. She knew he would.

Grabbing his own pack, Jackson hitched it onto his back and in a few quick strides caught up to her. "How can you tell?"

"Experience?" She hurried her steps, listening, concentrating. "Instinct? I just know."

"Works for me," Jackson muttered, and focused on staying beside her when *his* instincts were screaming at him to run. Logically, he told himself that it could have been any dog. It didn't *have* to be Abbey. But it was and he knew it. Felt it. Which meant that Reese was close, too. *Hang on, baby. Daddy's coming.*

They moved deeper into the trees, where the wind didn't reach, where the air was so still, it felt as though God Himself was holding His breath. Summer heat dripped down Jackson's back in long lines of sweat, but he hardly noticed. Their footsteps beat out like crazed heartbeats against the leaf- and pine-needle-littered ground. He tried not to think about his little girl, hungry, scared, and unable to shout for help.

He shot a glance to his left and briefly studied Carla's profile. Her gaze narrowed, jaw set, she looked intense, determined, and he felt better just knowing she was beside him.

"Stop." She held her arm out to one side, slapping him in the chest.

He froze in place, bowing to her experience, though it cost him. His daughter was out there . . . somewhere, and he wanted—needed—to get to her. His arms ached to hold her again. Now. This patience thing had never been a big part of his personality and now was no different. Then again, he'd learned a lot these past few weeks with Reese. He'd learned that waiting sometimes brought you what you wanted most, so he forced himself to be still. To be patient, to see what came next, even while he mentally willed Carla to hurry.

Hurry.

His own breathing sounded unnaturally loud in the tense quiet. But then, *every* sound was magnified. The papery rustle of the leaves overhead. The slide of Carla's tennis shoe against the earth as she shifted position slightly.

"There it is again," she whispered, more to herself than him, and started moving at a fast jog. "This way."

"Right behind you."

Carla's senses were on full alert. This was different from a few weeks ago, when she'd walked around with Jackson, looking for that missing man. *She* was different. She'd faced her demons. Put them behind her instead of holding them close enough to drag her down. She'd admitted to her failures and vowed to start again. Today, she was using every ounce of her skill. Every trick she'd ever picked up on disaster sites. And making up a few new ones as she went. Today, she was searching not only with her eyes, but with her heart.

She felt Jackson's rising sense of urgency and sympathized, though she wouldn't encourage it. Right here, right now, she was the expert; he was the parent. She needed to keep him calm. Hell, they both needed to be calm. Focused. Later, when Reese was safe, *then* they could each take the time to quietly fall apart.

The distant barking was closer now, yet at the same time, it sounded fainter, weaker. And so damn familiar. *Abbey.* Another twinge of worry settled around her heart, this one not for the child, but for the dog. At her belt, the walkie-talkie bristled and hissed like a nest of snakes. But she didn't have time to snatch it free and call to anyone.

Right now, the most important thing was to reach Reese. And Abbey. Later, there'd be time to assess the situation and call in to base to alert everyone else and get help if they needed it.

Carla sprinted forward, running through the trees, not concerned at all about Jackson keeping up. His footsteps pounded out behind her like a reassuring heartbeat in the night. While she ran, her mind clicked off landmarks, pinpointing their location. She heard the dog again and turned left, heading down a leafy slope, toward the huge, jagged pile of stones known to the locals as Castle Rock. Carla gasped and stopped dead.

Jackson ran smack into her and they both staggered. Then he looked beyond her and in an instant pushed past her.

"Reese!"

The little girl looked up at them with tears streaking down her dirty face. Her overalls were ripped and torn, black dirt staining the knees. Leaves and dirt dotted her hair and her bottom lip was bleeding. She sat on the ground, at the base of the rocky structure, Abbey's head in her lap.

Abbey woofed in greeting, then lay still.

A stunning, crashing relief poured through Jackson. Reese was hurt. But she was alive.

"The rocks," Carla warned as he stepped past her.

"Yeah." He tossed a glance at the small mountain of stones, none of which looked real stable. And even as he thought it, a scattering of pebbles smacked and danced their way down the mass. "It's okay, baby," he said, keeping his voice quiet. "You're okay now. Daddy's here. Everything's fine."

Two steps, three, and he was crouching beside his little girl. His thumbs brushed away the dirty tear tracks on her face and he stared into Reese's big blue eyes as his heartbeat slowly returned to normal. Carla was there beside him, expertly running her hands over the child's head and neck, her arms, her legs.

An eternity later, Carla looked up at him. "I think she's okay, but we should move her away from these rocks."

"Right."

He picked his daughter up gently, moved her back from the rock wall, and set her down again. Then he hurried back to Carla and, after her nod of approval, helped her move the dog to safety as well.

Then he went to Reese again, wanting to reassure himself that she was fine. He knelt in front of her and she reached for him, catching his face between her small hands.

"What is it, sweetie?" Jackson covered her hands with his and gave silent thanks for the chance to be able to hold her again.

Her mouth opened and closed, slowly, awkwardly, like a creaky, rarely used door. Fresh tears coursed down her cheeks, her bottom lip quivered shakily, and she swallowed hard.

He watched her, wanting to help, not knowing what she needed. Frustration tore at him.

Then she inhaled sharply and blurted, "Daddy . . ."

Stunned to his soul, Jackson shuddered with the impact of that soft, scratchy voice. It had been so long, he'd nearly forgotten what Reese's voice sounded like. Now it was raw and unsteady and *beautiful*. And the sweet sound of it nearly broke his heart. Tears stung his eyes, his throat closed around a knot the size of Texas, and he felt as though he couldn't draw air into suddenly heaving lungs.

Miracles. He'd been blessed with miracles.

"Reese—" Grinning now, Jackson shot a fast look at Carla, saw his own surprise mirrored on her face, then turned back to his daughter. "Reese honey, you're talking." *Dumb, Jackson. She knows she's talking.* "Are you all right?"

She ignored the question. "Abbey's hurt."

"I know, honey." He glanced at the big dog and saw Carla was giving the golden the same careful check she'd given Reese. But the expression on Carla's face told him she wasn't happy with what she was finding. Torn now, Jackson's heart ached for Carla and at the same time he wanted to celebrate. His little girl had come back from the darkness.

Giving him a small smile of understanding, Carla stroked Abbey's neck, then eased backward, distancing herself from all of them as she pulled her walkie-talkie out and pressed the button.

"Daddy!" Reese patted his face insistently until he turned back to watch the sorrow in her eyes. She swallowed again and said, "I climbed the rocks so I could see. There's too many trees an' they're too big an' I'm too little so I got lost." Jackson hurt all over at those three little words, but she wasn't finished. "An' I fell down and then lots and lots of rocks started falling and Abbey pushed me out of the way and then a big rock hit her and she . . . she . . . *cried.*"

"Ah, baby . . ."

"An' it's *my* fault!" Reese wailed, and the pitch her voice reached brought a chill to Jackson's spine, lifting the small hairs at the back of his neck. "Just like when Mommy died."

Everything in him went cold and still as he stared at Reese. *Jesus*. Guilt and pain shone in her eyes and she hiccuped around a fresh batch of tears as she kept talking. It was as if, silent for so long, now that she'd started speaking, she couldn't stop. She had to say everything she'd been holding in for the last year.

"Baby, your mommy's accident wasn't your fault," Jackson broke in, but she wasn't listening.

"It was raining and Mommy told me to be quiet so she could consecrate an'"—she pulled in a jerky breath and hunched her shoulders as if trying to hide from her own words—"an' I didn't be quiet and I called her and called her and then she turned around to look at me and that big truck came and Mommy *died*. She *died* 'cause I didn't be quiet and I've been real quiet since then, but she didn't come back and now I hurt Abbey and—"

A knife blade of pain stabbed at him and Jackson pulled her close, felt her thin arms wrap around his neck and hang on as if she were dangling from a cliff. He patted her back and soothed her with the words he should have said so long ago. But he hadn't known. Hadn't even guessed that his child was torturing herself with the same guilt that had eaten away at him.

"You didn't do anything, baby," he whispered, and eased back so that she could look into his eyes and know he was telling her the truth. "It wasn't your fault, Reese. The accident. It wasn't anybody's fault. Oh, baby, you had nothing to do with it. It was a terrible thing, but you didn't cause it. Nobody did." And as he tried to help his daughter, he saw and felt the real truth himself. "It just . . . *was*. It happened, baby, but not because of you."

She let go of him long enough to run one hand under her nose. "Mommy's not coming back, is she?"

"No, baby," he said, and kissed her cheeks, her forehead, the tip of her nose. "She's not. But I'm here. I'm right here with you. And you're safe."

She pulled in another long breath and let it go in a soft rush. "I love you, Daddy."

"I love you, too, baby," he whispered, stroking her tears away with the pads of his thumbs.

She looked back over her shoulder and asked, "But what about Abbey, Daddy? Is Abbey gonna die, too?"

"I hope not, baby."

God, he hoped not. But it didn't look good. The big dog was lying still. Breath moved in and out of her lungs, but she'd made no attempt to get up. And a few feet away, Carla murmured into the walkie-talkie and paced, pushing her hand through her hair.

"We hafta help Abbey," Reese said.

"We will." He stood up and walked to Carla while Reese scooted over to take up position alongside the golden again.

Carla swallowed back her fear and said into the walkie-talkie, "Thanks, Tony. And hurry, okay?" When Jackson appeared beside her, she blinked back the tears crowding her eyes and tried for brave.

It didn't work.

"Is she hurt bad?" Jackson asked.

"One leg's broken. As for internally, I don't know." Her gaze drifted to where the little girl sat, patiently stroking the dog's head, whispering words of comfort. "I called for help. Tony's coming. Bringing a doctor. And a vet."

"Carla . . ."

It was Jackson's obvious pain that broke through her own. Even in his joy with his child, he worried about her. Taking his hand, she said, "Don't feel bad, Jackson. Not now. You've got your daughter back. She's safe. She's talking again."

"But Abbey got hurt 'cause a me," Reese said, and Carla turned to look at the little girl's tormented expression.

"No, sweetie." Drawing Jackson along with her, Carla walked toward the dog she'd loved and worked with for years and the little girl who'd become a part of her heart. Crouching down, Carla took a seat opposite Reese, and as the child stroked Abbey's head, Carla laid her own hand atop the girl's.

Abbey whimpered, flopped her tail half-heartedly, then lay still again.

An ache pulsed in time with Carla's heartbeat, but she needed to make sure Reese didn't pick up another burden to carry on her narrow shoulders. "It's not your fault." She took a deep breath, steadied her voice, and put every ounce of conviction she possessed into her words. "Abbey did what she was trained to do, Reese. What her heart told her to do."

A single tear rolled down the girl's cheek.

Carla felt Jackson's hand come down on her shoulder and she welcomed the heat of his touch. It seemed to slip inside her to where the cold, scared child within her cowered.

"Abbey saved you, Reese. She loves you. She was taking care of you. Just as she's always done." *Sweet, brave, gentle-hearted dog.* "She wouldn't want you to be sad."

"But if she dies like Mommy did then I can't see her anymore." Sorrow glimmered in the child's eyes and Carla didn't try to erase it. Even children needed to grieve. To feel pity and pain. And to become stronger for it.

"No, you won't," she said softly, refusing to lie to Reese, unwilling to give her false hope. "But you'll always remember her." *As I will. Always, Abbey.*

"Uh-huh."

"And you'll have your daddy."

"And she'll have you, Carla," Jackson said, his deep voice reverberating around them. He reached out and covered both of their hands with his. "You'll have both of us, Reese. And no matter what happens, we'll get through it, *together.*"

Carla just stared at him. Her heart breaking, mind spinning, she looked into his lake-blue eyes and saw the promise of tomorrow. "Jackson . . ."

"I love you, Carla," he said.

Carla glanced at Reese and the little girl gave her a watery smile. Then she turned back to Jackson as he went on.

"You are the best thing that ever happened to me. To us." He shifted a quick look at his daughter, then at their joined hands before shifting his gaze back to Carla's. "I'm tired of living in the past. I want a future. With you. Here, in this place."

Warmth fought past the chill in her bones and spread throughout her body, filling her with hope, love, and a joy she'd never known before. And despite the worry over her injured dog, that happiness blossomed within her.

"I love you, too," she said, wanting him to know that, believe it—yet what if he was only saying this because of the emotions in the moment? "But—"

"No," he said, and leaned forward to place a quick, hard kiss on her mouth. "No buts. No guilt. No running. Not anymore. Maybe this isn't the most romantic proposal on record. . . ."

She blinked. "Proposal?"

He shook his head. "I must really suck at this if you couldn't guess what I was trying to say. Yes, it's a proposal. Because I need you, Carla. *We* need you."

"Jackson," she said, and he cut her off again.

"Marry me."

"What?" She sat back on her heels, staring at him.

"Just say yes. Don't think about it. We've both done too much thinking in the past. This time, just trust your heart. Trust *my* heart." His gaze moved over her with a slow sweet stroke that touched her more deeply than any words could. Okay, maybe it wasn't romantic. But it was *real*. She saw it in his eyes. Heard it in his voice. Felt it in the warmth of his hand atop hers.

And that made it perfect.

"*I love you.*" He said it again, emphasizing the words. "I want to marry you and love you for the rest of my life. Say yes, Carla, and help me build the kind of family that will keep us all safe. And happy."

Carla swallowed back the lump in her throat and looked at Reese. The little girl was smiling through her tears and Carla's heart twisted. Wasn't this life, though? she thought. Reese safe, but Abbey injured. Things were so rarely good or bad, but more often a weird mixture of the two. Pain and joy came together and Carla knew it was important to grab happiness when the chance for it appeared.

In a few short weeks, her life had been turned upside down, shaken up, and finally, magically, set right.

And even a Candellano knew when *not* to argue.

She looked into those incredibly blue eyes of his and, smiling through her tears, said simply, "Yes."

EPILOGUE

Violins sang on the soft summer air.

The sun hung over the edge of the horizon and stained the afternoon sky with brilliant slashes of red and pink and purple. A soft wind rushed in off the ocean and the ripples of water slapping against the shore beat a constant rhythm that kept the crowd moving.

Well, Carla thought, smiling, the rhythm of the sea and Mama standing at the head of the buffet table. She tore her gaze from the picture-perfect sunset long enough to glance at her family. The Candellanos and most of Chandler were too busy celebrating her wedding to take much notice of the bride. Which was okay, since she was sort of enjoying this moment of solitude.

"Do you know how gorgeous you look?"

Jackson came up behind her and slid his arms around her waist. So, solitude could be overrated. Carla grinned up at him and felt her heart flip over at the smoky desire in his eyes. "Tell me."

"Later. . . ." He dipped his head to kiss the curve of her neck and smiled as her curls danced across his cheek.

"Ah," she murmured, tipping her head to give him better access. "The famed wedding night."

He glanced to one side, where their guests danced to the trio hired to play for the reception. Sand and sea and laughter and love. It was perfect. Everything a wedding should be. Filled with family and friends and so much joy, Jackson felt his heart swell to the point of bursting. "It'll be as perfect as today was, I promise."

Carla turned in his grasp and threw her arms around his neck. Smiling up at him, she said, "I'll hold you to it. But about the honeymoon—"

Jackson shook his head and laughed. "I already told you. It's no problem."

"You don't mind postponing it until I get back?"

He smiled wryly. "I think we can wait until you've finished helping out at an earthquake."

"I don't know how long I'll be gone. . . ." Searchers had called and she was back on the job. She felt whole and confident and so damn happy, it was probably illegal.

"We'll be here," he assured her. "Your husband and both of your flower girls." He slid a glance to their left, where Reese stood at the water's edge, tossing rose petals into the receding sea. Beside her, Abbey, a cast on one foreleg, barked so hard, her flower-bedecked collar slipped drunkenly to one side.

The golden was well on her way to being as good as

new. Of course, she wasn't well enough to accompany Carla on this search-and-rescue mission. Carla would have to use one of the company dogs for now. But soon, she and Abbey would be working together again.

And coming home to Jackson and Reese.

"I'll be back as soon as I can."

"You're worth waiting for. And I'll keep busy setting up my new office."

"And taking care of the puppies," she reminded him as she went up on her toes.

"That, too."

Behind him, Carla saw Abigail, Virginia, and Rachel huddled together, whispering.

Laughing, she told Jackson, "I think the Terrible Three are talking about us."

He didn't even bother to glance at them. Instead, he bent his head to hers and, just before he kissed her senseless, said, "Let's give 'em something to talk about."

CHAPTER
ONE

NOTHING LIKE A WEDDING to make you feel more . . .
single.

But Stephanie, "Stevie," Ryan wasn't complaining.
She liked being single. She was good at it. Although at
the moment, she felt about as conspicuous as a stow-
away on Noah's Ark. Everywhere she looked, there
were couples. From teenagers, clinging to each other
like survivors of a sinking ship, to the Swansons,
whose combined age would probably make a decent
SAT score. Even the grade-schoolers were paired off,
for a little hair-pulling and name-calling.

Yep, in a world of matched luggage, Stevie was a
duffel bag.

Still, she was okay with that, most of the time. It
was only on days like this when she really felt the lack
of a man in her life. Although the last time she'd *had* a
man in her life, she'd ended up wishing she'd stayed
single. So, what was the point, really?

Half the town of Chandler, California, had turned

out for Carla Candellano's wedding to Jackson Wyatt. And even though the bride and groom were long gone, off to their wedding night at a luxury hotel in Monterey, the reception had kept right on rolling.

In the open meadow at the edge of town, tiny white lights had been strung in the trees and across a makeshift dance floor in the clearing. Off to the left, the Pacific Ocean roared out a solid, steady beat as waves pounded against the shore and slammed into the rocks lining the beach. Moonlight poured down from a clear late-summer sky and the stars looked as though God had hung strings of lights through the night sky to help with the celebration.

The party was finally winding down—there were only a few diehards left out on the meadow. And though Stevie's fingers were tapping to the music, she was ready to make her getaway. All she wanted now was a pint of fudge brownie ice cream, an old movie, and her jammies, not necessarily in that order.

She glanced down the length of the white-cloth-covered table. Grabbing her chance, she stood up and slunk away while most of the Candellanos were busy talking. Quickly she made her way along the tree line toward town. Music and the noise of the crowd faded into the distance, sounding almost ghostly as she moved farther away from the party. Humming along with the music, she heard twigs snap beneath her feet as a cool evening breeze drifted in off the ocean and skittered along her skin. She shivered but lifted her face into the wind, loving the feel of the sea-scented air surrounding her.

She sighed. It had been a good day all in all. Her

best friend was married to a man who clearly adored her. And Stevie had managed to escape the maid of honor's curse of being trapped with the most boring man in attendance. Which in this case would have meant Frank Pezzini.

"Oh, man," she murmured. "Now that Carla's off the market, I wonder if this means Frank will start turning his charms on me?" A sobering thought. Another shiver rippled through her, but this one had nothing to do with the wind. Ye gods, just thinking about having to sit and chat with a man who had shined up his best white patent-leather shoes for the wedding was enough to make her run for the hills.

Stevie hurried just a bit, eager now to put Wonder Frank well behind her. An old Supremes song soared from the distance and she picked up her pace, keeping time with Diana Ross in her prime. Taking a shortcut through the trees, Stevie lifted the hem of her dress and ducked her head to avoid low-hanging twisted branches, stretched out across the path like black leafy arms. Then one of those arms snatched a handful of her hair and twisted it around a gnarly piece of bark.

"Ow." Stevie skidded to a stop, her feet sliding on the leaf-littered ground. "Damn it." She grabbed at the top of her head as she twisted to try to escape. But she only managed to knot it further. "Oh, this is perfect," she muttered, and slanted a glance toward the crowd, too far away now for her to expect any help. "This is just great. Now what do I do?" She had two choices. Stand here and become "one" with the tree . . . or rip her hair out at the roots.

Neither one worked for her.

"Come on, tree, give me a break here, okay?" She reached up and worked her fingers around the snarl, but every time she moved, she only made it tighter. So much for the "good day" theory. "Look, you seem like a nice tree, but—"

"Would you two like to be alone?"

A deep voice, familiar. With more than a touch of laughter in it. Turning as far as she was able, Stevie glanced to one side and spotted two long tuxedo-clad legs. Thank God. The cavalry. "Paul?"

The legs moved closer. "Yeah, it's me. What are you doing?"

Dumb question. She tried to turn her head farther so she could get a look at his face. But he was too tall for that and she had to settle for a glimpse of his white shirt. "Oh," she muttered. "Just hanging around."

"Very funny."

"Gee, I'm sorry I'm not at my witty best—what with being held captive by a tree and all."

"I can wait."

She kicked at him, but since she was caught and he wasn't, he managed to avoid the toe of her strappy little sandal. Probably just as well. The way she was going, she might have broken a toe.

"You're enjoying this, aren't you?" she accused.

"I shouldn't be, should I?"

"You're just gonna stand there? Is that it?"

He chuckled and she glared at his knees.

"I'm not worried," Paul said, his deep voice rumbling out around her. "I think your . . . 'bark' is worse than your bite."

"Oh, tree humor. Swell." She tugged at her hair

again and tears welled up in her eyes. "Are you gonna help me or just stand there?"

"I'm trying to decide." He came even closer and bent down, hands on his knees, so he could look her square in the eyes. One corner of his mouth lifted into a half-smile and she gritted her teeth. "You know," he said, "seeing you like this . . . it's déjà vu."

She frowned at him and seriously considered ripping her hair out. It'd be a lot less infuriating. But it would hurt, too. So she forced herself to take a deep breath, bite back her aggravation, and ask, "Déjà vu?"

"Yeah. Only the last time, your ponytail was caught in the hinge of our back door and——"

Memories flooded her brain and she nodded, then winced at the accompanying pain. "And you left me standing there, caught, while you and Bill Wilder went to the beach."

"Hey, I was seventeen."

"And I was stuck for a half hour."

"How long you been here now?" he asked.

"A couple of minutes."

He looked up at the branch where her hair was in a knot, then lowered his gaze to hers again. Grinning, he said, "Then for old times' sake, I'll be back in a half hour."

Stevie couldn't believe it when he stood up and moved past her. "Paul?" She twisted her body, trying to look behind her, but it was just too hard, what with the tree having a death grip on her head and all. "Paul, if you leave me here, I'll . . ."

"You'll what?" he challenged from behind her.

"I'll . . ." Think, Stevie. What could she do to get

back at him? Sabotage his computer? Tell his mother? Hmm. . . . "Okay, fine, I can't think of anything while my head's caught in a tree . . . but once I'm loose . . ."

"Oh, now there's incentive to help you out."

"Paul—"

"Kidding. Just kidding."

He walked back to her and stood right in front of her. Stevie's head hit the middle of his chest and she leaned into him while he tugged at her hair. The scent of Old Spice drifted to her and she smiled to herself. An old-fashioned scent—but on Paul, it worked. He was warm and solid and comforting—now that he'd finally decided to give her a hand.

"Why'd you have your hair all piled up on top of your head, anyway?"

"I am maid of honor, hear me roar. Ouch."

"Sorry."

"Uh-huh," she muttered, and winced as he pulled and tugged. "Anyway, ponytails are not the preferred hairdo for weddings."

"Your hair looks good down."

"If I have any left when you're finished, I'll keep that in mind."

"Everybody's a critic." He tugged again. "There."

"Free at last, et cetera," she muttered, and moved out from under the tree before she slowly straightened up, eyeing that branch like an enemy. Lifting one hand to the top of her head, she rubbed her aching scalp and felt where her wedding "do" had fallen apart. Fingering several long stray locks of hair hanging to her shoulders, she said, "Well, I bet this looks great."

She shifted a glance at Paul. He folded his arms

across his chest and shrugged shoulders that somehow looked a lot broader in a tux. "Wedding's over anyway; take it down."

"Good idea," she said, and reached for the remaining pins holding half of her hair up. She pulled the last few out, then shook her hair free, running her fingers through the mass until most of the bark and leaves were gone.

"More me, now?" she asked, smiling up at him.

He just stood there, looking at her. In the pale dappled moonlight she couldn't really see his dark brown eyes very well. Those wire-framed glasses he wore acted something like a shield. But then, she'd always felt as though if Paul didn't want you to know what he was feeling, you'd never be able to guess it.

Tall, dark, and gorgeous, Paul and his twin, Nick, were as different as two men could be. Paul was thoughtful, brilliant, and mysterious. Nick was loud, athletic, and in-your-face outgoing. But it wasn't just their personalities that made them different. Though both of them were total hunks, despite being twins, they looked nothing alike. Nick was a little taller, a little more muscle-bound, and had the once-broken nose of an athlete, while Paul's features were cleaner, sharper, and somehow more . . . Kurt Russellish.

"Oh, yeah," Paul said, his mouth tipping up into the crooked grin she knew so well. "This is definitely the Stevie we all know and love. Tree bark in her hair and a tear in her dress."

"A tear?" She looked down. There it was. Right at the hem. She must have stepped on the damn thing during this trek through the "wilderness." "Just . . . perfect."

"Close enough."

"What?" She looked up at him.

Paul shook his head. "Nothing. You headed home?"

"That's the general idea. I'm thinking ice cream and a movie." She started walking again and Paul fell into step beside her. "What about you? Shouldn't you be back there helping the family celebrate?"

He pushed the edges of his jacket back and shoved his hands into his pockets. "Trust me, they don't need my help."

"Uh-huh," she said, watching her step and belatedly holding the hem of her dress up a few inches. Heck, she'd only been able to make good her getaway because the Candellanos were so busy having a good time, they hadn't noticed her leaving. "So what happened to your date?" she asked. "Weren't you supposed to be bringing Sandy the Amazing?"

Thank God he hadn't, she thought. Otherwise she'd still be stuck on the tree while he danced what was left of the night away. Or, worst-case scenario, he'd have saved her while Sandy stood there watching. Oh, that would have been fun. Sandy, like most of Paul's dates, could be intimidating. They were usually brilliant *and* gorgeous, with interesting careers and fascinating lives.

But then, being the head of a computer firm that designed innovative software for everyone from Hollywood's special effects industry to the military, Paul moved in *way* different circles from Stevie. Owning the Leaf and Bean, a coffee and tea shop, Stevie usually met early-morning joggers and people with hangovers looking for a cure. Oh, yeah. Different crowds entirely.

A short, sharp laugh shot from his throat. "The Amazing Sandy. Oh, she'd like that. Yeah, she was supposed to come with me, but she had to cancel."

"Why? Did she get wind of what a Candellano party is really like?"

"Nothing so terrifying. She was the backup pilot on the space shuttle—and the scheduled pilot broke his arm in a baseball game, so . . ." He shrugged again.

"Bummer," Stevie said. "I hate when that happens."

He shot her a look and smiled. "Happen to you a lot, does it?"

"Oh, yeah," she assured him, waving one hand in the air. "Just the other day, I was having coffee with this cute guy—all of a sudden, he rushes off to a phone booth, changes his clothes, and flies off to save Metropolis. Again."

Paul laughed and this time Stevie really listened to it. A long roll of deep thunder rising up and settling down around her. Something inside her turned over. Weird. This was Paul. Her friend. Her ex's twin. For Pete's sake. Get a grip, Stevie.

"So anyway," she said, a little louder than she'd planned, but hey, a girl had to speak up when her brain went on vacation, right? "You headed back to your house tonight?"

"No," he said, and pulled one hand from his pocket to grab her arm as she stumbled over a tree root that jutted up from the ground to grab her foot. Apparently she'd been a logger in her former life and now the remaining forest was out to get her.

"Thanks." She held up one foot and pointed at the completely useless, though very pretty, silvery sandals. "These shoes ain't made for walkin'."

"I get that," he said, letting her go and shoving his hand back into his pocket. "Anyway, I don't want to drive back to the house. Thought I'd just stay at Mama's tonight. Head home in the morning."

Stevie nodded and kept quiet for a while, her brain moving along at a slow trot. She was alone. He was alone and in no hurry to make the drive to his place. Why should they be alone separately when they could be alone together? Made sense when you thought about it like that. Besides, when it came right down to it, the thought of being in her apartment alone right now suddenly didn't seem as appealing as it had a few minutes ago. Maybe it was the aftereffects of the wedding—all that eternal love stuff—but a little company sounded like a good thing.

"You interested in ice cream and a movie?" she asked.

He glanced down at her warily. "What kind of movie? A chick flick?"

She laughed but gave him a good look up and down. "Okay, fine. You do look sort of James Bondish tonight."

"Double-O Suave, that's me."

She held one hand up in surrender. "Well then, I promise you guns and stuff blowing up."

"I'm there."

The minute they walked up the stairs and into her apartment, Stevie excused herself to change and told

him to get the ice cream. While she was gone, Paul looked around the loft apartment Stevie kept above her shop, the Leaf and Bean. It was so like her. Warm, comfortable, cozy. Dark red walls with cream-colored trim. Books crowded and jumbled together in a few bookcases and were stacked on the floor and tables surrounding the overstuffed sofa and matching chair. An entertainment center stood on one wall, and on the opposite wall was a fireplace with more than its share of ashes piled under the grate. The only thing missing was the dogs.

He smiled to himself as he walked toward the small, galley-style kitchen. Stevie was the softest touch in town when it came to animals. But her heart really belonged to the stray dogs of the world. She was forever adopting one or a dozen and keeping them around until she could find them a home. And since there were no current ankle biters growling or sneering at him, it looked as though she'd been busy.

It had been a while since he'd been in her place, but he remembered where everything was. He grabbed down two bowls from a glass-fronted cupboard, then turned to the fridge. He yanked open the freezer and stood for a long minute, deciding which of the three cartons of ice cream to choose.

"Fudge brownie for me!" she called from the other room as if reading his mind.

"Got it!" he yelled back. "Hot fudge, too?"

"Is the pope Catholic?"

"Stupid question," he muttered. Stevie was the only woman he knew who kept fudge and whipped cream in the house at all times. Any other female would be

moaning about calories and her latest diet. Stevie, though, liked to eat and didn't mind admitting it.

"Damn it," she grumbled, and he just caught the frustration in her voice.

"What's wrong?" He took a step toward the nearly closed door separating her bedroom from the main room.

"The stupid zipper is stuck in the stupid fabric and I can't even tear the stupid thing off." She wrenched the door open, marched toward him, and turned her back on him. "Can you get that before I have to chew myself free?"

Paul stared down at her back. Smooth, lightly tanned skin looked like peach silk in the soft light. He swallowed hard and forced himself to focus on the pale blue zipper caught firmly in the fragile fabric. He wouldn't even notice the nude-colored bra back strap just beneath the edge of the dress. He didn't notice, either, how the dress skimmed along her body like a lover's touch—and he didn't think about how the sky blue dress made her big blue eyes look like chips of turquoise.

She glanced back and up at him over her shoulder. "Earth to Paul, come in, Paul."

"Huh? What—oh. Right."

Stevie shook her head. "You know, maybe you've been working too hard. They say the mind is the first thing to go."

"Yeah. Right." No big deal. It was a zipper, for chrissakes. All he had to do was get it moving. He didn't have to pull it all the way down and expose her

naked back. He didn't have to help her out of the damn dress. Just get the stupid zipper working again so she could go and put something on that he wouldn't be thinking about getting her out of.

A chastity belt, maybe.

He grabbed the zipper, carefully keeping his fingers from brushing her skin. There was no point in torturing himself, right? But the damn thing was stuck good. He clenched his jaw and reminded himself that he was the man who came up with the programs to run distant satellites. Surely he could figure out a zipper.

"If it won't come down," Stevie said, "just rip it off me."

"Right." An image flashed in his brain and it was one that ordinarily he'd have squashed flat. In his mind, he saw himself pull that dress off of her in one quick magicianlike move, leaving her in only a bra and panties. Then he saw her turn to him. Look up at him and open her arms. He watched her rise up on her toes, bring her mouth close to his. He damn near felt the brush of her breath against his cheek.

Shit. Maybe coming here wasn't such a good idea.

"Did you get it yet?" she asked, trying to turn around and look.

"No," he muttered thickly, his throat knotted with a desire he'd gotten used to ignoring over the years. "Hold still, will ya?"

"Sorry," she said, then gave a low whistle. "Cranky, aren't we?"

"Just frustrated," he murmured, yanking on the zipper again. Frustrated in more than one way, but she

didn't need to know that, did she? Hell, she'd never had a clue and now wasn't the time to let her find out.

He slid his fingers beneath the fabric and forced himself to ignore the feel of her satiny, warm skin against his. And in a second or two, he had it. The zipper leaped free and he let her go, taking a quick step backward for good measure.

"Thanks." She clutched the top of her strapless dress tight and turned around to look at him. Those big blue eyes of hers dazzled him as they did every time he looked into them. Her wide mouth was curved in a smile that was designed to bring men to their knees. Stevie'd never had any idea of the effect she had on men—him in particular. With her heart-shaped face, long, slender body, and a laugh that made a man think of midnight kisses and rumpled beds, she was a walking wet dream.

Yet somehow, she never seemed to get that.

Now, as he stared at her, Paul had to ask himself one very important question.

How was he supposed to get over his brother's ex-girlfriend when every time he saw her, all he wanted to do was throw her onto her back and bury himself inside her?

CHAPTER
TWO

TONY CANDELLANO TURNED A cop's eye on the last few revelers at his sister's wedding reception. Vince Halloran looked as though he'd hit the champagne one too many times, but Vince's wife, Betsy, was stone-cold sober, so there wouldn't be any trouble there. Well, Tony amended, Vince's life wouldn't be pretty come morning, but at least he wouldn't be driving tonight, making everyone else in Chandler a target.

A fierce wind off the ocean whipped across the clearing and snatched at the strings of lights, making them dance and sway until they looked like clouds of fireflies. Candle flames in the centerpieces winked out and tall white wicker flower stands bursting with roses, carnations, and daisies toppled over, littering the ground with splotches of color.

His mother's crocheted shawl flew off a nearby chair and Tony grabbed it before it could take flight. Wadding it up, he shoved it under his left arm and turned into the wind to look for his family. Squinting

against the dirt and bits of twigs suddenly pelting him, he spotted his wife, Beth, and headed for her.

"Storm's blowing in!" he shouted to be heard.

Beth looked up at him and pushed her dark auburn hair out of her eyes, only to have it slapped back across her face again. "No kidding?" She grinned up at him briefly, then reached down to pick up their daughter, Tina.

Tony tossed the shawl at Beth, then took the little girl from her. Wrapping a blanket around the child, who somehow managed to stay asleep despite the howling wind, he looked at his wife and said, "Grab your stuff. Where's Mama?"

Beth picked up Tony's tuxedo jacket, then her own purse and sweater. "She took some things to the car a few minutes ago. Reese and Abbey are with her."

"Good," he said. "We'll meet 'em there." He spared a quick glance heavenward. Clouds scuttled across the surface of the night sky, obliterating stars and swirling, crashing into one another as thunder roared in the distance. "Man, this blew up fast." He cupped the back of his daughter's head and held her close to his chest. Then he shifted his gaze back to Beth. "Have you seen Stevie? Or Paul and Nick?"

Clearly exasperated as the first cold, hard splats of rain smacked her, Beth said, "Jesus, Tony, can't you take the night off? They're adults. They know enough to get in out of the rain. Now how about we do?" Then she held her purse over her head, cradled her stuff in the crook of her arm, lifted the hem of her bridesmaid dress, and took off, sprinting toward the car.

"Right," he muttered, tugging the blanket up high

enough to cover Tina's head. "Hell. She's always right. Damn annoying."

He made it to the car just before the skies opened up and the meadow was half-drowned in a wall of water.

Stevie hit the PAUSE button, and on the TV, the movie stopped dead. A hard driving rain pounded into the silence, crashing against the roof like thousands of tiny fists hammering to get in. Setting the remote and her ice-cream bowl down onto the coffee table, Stevie unfolded her long legs and pushed herself off the over-stuffed sofa.

"Listen to that." She walked toward the wide front window overlooking Main Street.

Rain slapped at the windowpane, blurring the outside world into a wash of street lamplight that smeared gold across the glass. Overhead, thunder rolled and lightning flashed, edging the clouds with a shimmer of white-hot light that dazzled briefly and was gone.

But Paul hardly noticed. Instead, his gaze was locked on Stevie. Her ponytail dangled temptingly and bounced with her every movement. She wore a pale blue tank top over—God help him—braless breasts and blue-and-white-striped drawstring cotton pants. She was barefoot and the pale pink polish on her toes looked incredibly sexy, damn it. When she half-turned to him and smiled, Paul sucked in a breath and held it for a long moment before slowly releasing it as he counted to ten. Then twenty.

"Isn't it great?"

"Yeah," he muttered, though he wasn't entirely sure he was talking about the thunderstorm. *She* was great.

She was the sexiest woman he'd ever known. And the one woman he couldn't have.

Stupid.

But true. God knew, Stevie colored the way he looked at other women. He'd never had a hard time getting dates. The women in his life were successful, beautiful, and great to be with. He'd even had a couple of long-lasting relationships that might have led somewhere . . . eventually. Then inevitably he would start comparing those women to Stevie and they always came up short. His scientific mind chewed on that thought for a few seconds as he stared at her. There was just something about Stevie—something he hadn't found in any other woman.

Now if he could just identify it and get over it, life would be good.

She cranked the old-fashioned window open wide and stuck one hand out into the rain. Smiling, she leaned out farther and tipped her face up to the clouds. Her right leg lifted, toes pointed, and the cotton fabric of her pajamas tightened across her bottom. Paul told himself he was an idiot.

When she pulled her head back inside, her face was dotted with raindrops, sparkling in the lamplight before she wiped them away with the backs of her hands. Shivering, she cranked the window shut again and turned to look at him.

Her nipples peaked against the thin material of her tank top, but Paul refused to look at them.

Much.

"God, it's great outside. Cold," she added with a grin. "But great."

"You always did like storms," he said gruffly, and congratulated himself on getting his voice to work.

"What's not to like?" she asked, not really expecting an answer. "Loud noise, lots of rain, and bright lights." Turning back to watch the storm, she frowned a little. "It's really coming down, though, Paul. Maybe you should just camp out here tonight, huh?"

Oh, yeah, there's an idea.

"I don't know," he said. "We'll see how the storm goes." With any luck, it would dry up fast. Hell, there was only so much a man could take. Staring at the television, he felt her take a seat at the end of the couch again. But even if the sofa hadn't moved beneath her, he would have known she was close. Her perfume reached him, drifting on the chill air and teasing him into drawing several deep breaths just so he could pull that scent down inside him.

She grabbed her ice cream, wriggled around, getting comfortable, and when she was finally settled again, he picked up the remote, hit PLAY, and tried to distract his brain from her by saying, "By the way. The movie? You tricked me."

"No way," Stevie said, and licked the last drop of fudge sauce from her spoon. She sighed a little, eyed Paul's half-eaten ice cream and thought about finishing it off, then gave up the idea. Even she had her limits. "I promised you guns and bombs. Hello?" She pointed at the TV screen just as a car burst into flames.

"Yeah," Paul agreed with a wry smile. "Cars, guns, Arnold. Also a love story."

Stevie glumly stared at her empty ice-cream dish, then reached out and reluctantly set her bowl onto the

coffee table before leaning back into the cushions of the sofa. Curling one leg up under her, she stretched out her other leg and playfully nudged Paul's thigh with her foot. "So we both win a little." She shifted her gaze from Paul's strong profile to the television and added, "Besides, Michael Biehn is one hell of a kisser."

"You know this on a personal level, of course." One dark eyebrow lifted.

She wished. Heck, the only kissing she'd had in the last couple of years was on her *way* too short Caribbean vacation last month. And even then, it had been nothing special.

"You think I watch this movie for the explosions?" she asked.

Hey, she was willing to give her friend the manly flick full of destruction and mayhem. But who was to say she couldn't get a little something out of this, too? Almost every woman she knew owned a copy of *The Terminator.* Romance and bloodlust. The perfect blend.

"Just look at him," she said on a sigh, and tapped Paul's thigh with her foot again. "The way he takes her face in his hands . . ."

"Stage direction." He grabbed her foot and held it still. She hadn't even realized how cold her foot was until his large, warm hand curled around it.

"How he looks deeply into her eyes . . ."

"He's an *actor.*" Paul snorted and shook his head.

She ignored him. Men never appreciated stuff like this, anyway.

"And that line: 'I came across time for you,

Sarah.'" Stevie slapped one hand to her chest and sighed dramatically.

"The script," Paul said, his hand tightening around her foot.

"God, you're as romantic as cold broccoli."

He slanted her a slow look and dug his thumb into her arch. She tried to pull free, but Paul's grip was firm. "Hey, I don't need a writer to make my moves for me."

Stevie chuckled. "Excuse me, I've seen your moves."

One dark eyebrow lifted again. "Is that an insult?"

"An observation." She shrugged and smiled at him, and this time when she pulled her foot free, he let her go.

"Based on . . ."

"Personal experience," she countered, and scooted closer to him, forgetting about the movie for the chance to tease Paul. He looked so . . . *upstanding,* sitting there in his starched white shirt. The collar lay open at his throat and the sleeves were rolled up to his elbows, revealing muscular forearms with a deeper tan than anyone would expect a computer genius to have. His right foot rested on his left knee, and as she watched, he reached up and stabbed his fingers through his habitually too-long hair. His expression was tight and his eyes wary as she continued.

"Remember? The summer your Nana came to visit for a whole month?"

"I remember."

She could tell by his expression that he did, but that didn't stop her from talking about it. What were friends for if not to torture from time to time?

Outside, the rain pummeled Chandler with an unrelenting assault. But here, in the loft, they were warm and dry and Stevie was really enjoying herself. "You and I went down to the docks to get fresh fish for your mother, and—"

"I said I remember," he ground out tightly.

She ignored his attempt at stopping the flow of memory. "And on the way home—"

He nodded abruptly. "I kissed you."

"Uh-huh." She grinned at him. "And it was . . ." Stevie paused, rolled her eyes, and made a production out of trying to find the right word. She sensed his impatience and had to hide a smile. It wasn't often a person could push Paul out of his "Mr. Reasonable" mode. So on those rare occasions, it was something to savor.

"What?" he demanded, and shifted position on the sofa, turning to face her, forgetting all about the movie, where Arnold was even now headed for the motel where the hero and heroine were—well, they weren't thinking about the Terminator.

She looked at him and grinned. "Yucky."

Actually, that kiss had been hurried and unexpected and sort of sweet, as she recalled it now, through that cottony haze of memory that made every embarrassing moment of your life a little easier to swallow than it had been at the time. It was summer then and the sun was hot, blasting down out of a startlingly blue sky. Tourists had invaded Chandler and the screeching laughter of the crowds on the docks had vied with the cawing of the gulls wheeling in the air over the fishing boats.

Chandler hadn't changed much over the years,

though it had seemed a lot bigger when she was thirteen. She'd loved this town even then. She'd been so happy to belong. To finally have a home where people knew her, knew her father. After living like a gypsy, trailing after her mother for years, coming here and finding a home had meant more to Stevie than anything. The Candellanos had been icing on the cake, so to speak.

Even summer seemed longer, hotter, back then than it did now. Then her only worry was how to get the darkest tan possible before school started. Well, that and avoiding going to visit her mother wherever the woman happened to be living at the time.

Still, Stevie remembered that summer more clearly than any other. Because it was the last summer she'd been completely alone. The summer before she'd found love.

Paul grabbed her foot and scraped the tip of one finger along her arch just to get her attention.

It worked.

Stevie jumped, yelped, and pulled her foot out of his grasp. "Hey, tickling is *not* fair."

"All's fair, like they say. Besides, I resent the word *yucky.*"

"Yeah, well, that's how I remember it." She rubbed her foot, then curled it under her just to be on the safe side. Smiling, she looked up at him. "You bit me, remember?"

He scowled at her. "You moved."

She blew out a breath. "Didn't know you required statuary for your best work."

"A little interest, maybe."

"You caught me off guard."

"It was a spur-of-the-moment kind of thing."

"Ah . . . so you needed warm-up time," she said, remembering now how quickly that kiss had ended. And just how quickly Paul had walked away from her, leaving her standing on the boardwalk at the docks, watching him go as she rubbed the taste of him into her mouth. A young girl was allowed to romanticize her first kiss.

Paul muttered something she didn't quite catch, then said, "You know, you weren't exactly a great kisser yourself."

Okay, fair's fair, but let's be realistic. "Hey, I was a kid."

Yeah, she had been, Paul thought. But even then he'd been nuts about her. Back then, he'd considered himself light-years older than his little sister's best friend. But that hadn't meant he could avoid dreaming about sun-kissed fair skin, big blue eyes, and a sprinkling of freckles across a tiny nose.

He just hadn't admitted those dreams to anyone.

Not even Nick, his twin.

Though many times over the years, he'd wondered what might have happened if Nick had known that Paul was interested in Stevie. Would it have changed anything?

"So," she said, bringing him back to the moment at hand, "how do you get all of these dates with women like the Amazing Sandy? It's your brain they're after, right? Can't be your kissing abilities."

He gave her a tight smile. "I've improved a little over the years."

"Sure you have," she said in a deliberately placating tone.

He stared into those incredible eyes of hers and felt his blood pump expectantly as he promised, "I could curl your toes."

"Uh-huh." Her gaze drifted toward the television again, where the hero and heroine were tangling together on the bed, finding satisfaction and peace for a few wild, heartbreaking moments before running from their enemy again.

"You think I can't?" he asked, irritation coloring his tone.

"Hmm?" Stevie said, only half-listening as Michael Biehn threaded his fingers through Linda Hamilton's and took her on a slow ride toward heaven.

Stevie's body burned and she shifted uncomfortably on the sofa. A slow, sweet ache settled low in her body. Oh, wow, she'd been manless way too long. And maybe watching this movie hadn't been such a good idea after all.

"I said," Paul repeated, and stared at her profile as she watched the movie instead of him, "I could curl your toes."

"Yeah, yeah," she said, waving one hand at him.

Paul bit back a rush of frustration. "You know, I'm not that sixteen-year-old kid anymore."

This time she looked at him and smiled. But she still didn't look convinced that he was anything but "good ol' reliable Paul." Exasperation spilled through him. It was one thing to be fighting to ignore his response to her. It was quite another for her to not even admit to a *chance* that he could take her places she'd never been before.

And a purely male streak of pride rose up and refused to be quieted.

"I know that."

"Y'know," he said, studying her, "I don't think you do."

"What is up with you tonight?"

"It's not just tonight," he said, more to himself than to her.

"Paul," she said with a shake of her head. "You don't have to prove anything to me. We've known each other too long."

"Yeah. Maybe *too* long."

"What's that supposed to mean?"

"Nothing." Pushing one hand through his hair again, he muttered, "I'll bet you five bucks I can make you whimper."

"Huh?"

She looked so surprised, her expression only fed the sudden need to prove something to her—and to himself. If all they were going to share were memories, then he'd damn well give her one worth remembering.

Reaching into his pocket, he pulled out his wallet, thumbed through a stack of bills, and plucked one out. Slamming the five-dollar bill onto the coffee table, he looked at her. "Five bucks says I can make you curl up and cry 'uncle.'"

"You're crazy," she said on a laugh that bubbled from her throat and fizzed through his bloodstream.

"Probably, but that's beside the point."

She stiffened. "I'm not going to bet you. And I'm *not* kissing you."

"Chicken?" he prodded, knowing damn well that Stevie Ryan had never turned down a dare in her life.

"No, I'm not chicken," she said, lifting her chin defiantly. "But I think you're nuts."

"Chicken, like I said."

She shook her head slowly and blew out an exasperated breath. Paul was pretty sure she was going to say no after all and then he wasn't sure what he'd do, because suddenly he wanted to kiss her more than he wanted to take another breath.

Then in the next instant, her expression shifted into one of resigned submission. "Okay, fine. I don't know where this is coming from, but if it'll make you happy"—she scooted closer to him, tipping her face up to his—"go ahead. Give it your best shot."

There was nothing he wanted more. But even as he made his move, a small voice whispered in the back of his mind, sending out a warning. Which he ignored.

"I plan to," he promised, and grabbed her bare shoulders. His thumbs pressed into her warm, soft skin and instantly fires erupted in his body. Fires that had been smoldering for so long, the slightest touch was enough to snap them into an inferno.

Pulling her close, Paul took his time, letting his gaze drift across her features. Her hair was still dusted with rainwater and her eyes looked huge and surprised and so damn blue he was pretty sure he could drown in them. He slid his hands up, along the column of her throat, and he felt her shiver as he cupped her face between his palms. Her skin still felt cool and rain-damp. He speared his fingers through her hair at her temples

and slowly, slowly, lowered his head until he slanted his mouth across hers.

Her quick intake of breath was enough to feed the fires within. Relishing this long-awaited second taste of her, Paul was in no hurry to have it end. Her mouth against his was soft, pliant. Her breath puffed against his cheek and a small, faint moan built in the back of her throat.

He pulled her closer, letting his hands slide down to her back, splaying against her spine, holding her tightly enough to him that he felt the hard, rigid tips of her nipples stabbing into his chest. His body quickened, his heartbeat thundered in his ears, and Paul deepened the kiss, parting her lips with his tongue and sweeping into the warmth of her. Tasting her, exploring her, and as he did, he felt her surrender.

But he was too lost himself to savor the victory.

CHAPTER
THREE

STEVIE'S BRAIN SHORT-CIRCUITED.

That was the only explanation for what was happening inside her. Her stomach was spinning, her blood was humming, and her heartbeat pounded out a quick, hard rhythm to match the rain pelting the roof. Every inch of her body felt screamingly *alive*.

She melted into the strong arms sweeping her close to a broad chest and one small corner of her mind tried to remind her that this was *Paul*. Paul, her friend. Paul, Carla's brother. Paul, Nick's twin.

Paul, the best damn kisser she'd ever experienced.

Cells in her body that had been in a coma for too long suddenly woke up and started shouting, Hallelujah! A swirl of excitement pulsed inside her and brought a dangerous thrill that ached for more. Demanded more.

She should stop. Think. Figure out what was happening here. But Stevie didn't want to question what she was feeling. She wanted to revel in it. She wanted

to give herself over to the mind-numbing magic swamping her. And that realization shook her to her bones.

When Paul finally pulled back, breaking their kiss, Stevie looked up at him through eyes blurred with a passion she'd never known before. He looked hazy, indistinct, and so damn good it floored her.

"Toes curling?" he whispered, a half-smile curving his mouth in a way that tugged at her insides and promised secret pleasures.

She gulped. "You could say that."

"Uh-uh. I want to hear *you* say that."

"Okay," she said, and swallowed hard, hoping she'd remember to breathe again in a minute. Her head was still a little spacey and she was pretty sure it was from lack of oxygen. Which right now didn't seem like a bad trade-off. "My toes not only curled; I think my bones melted."

Something dangerously wicked and enticing flashed in his dark eyes and Stevie felt that tug again. The ache settling low inside her pulsed with a need she hadn't expected—and wasn't quite sure what to do about. This was just so out-of-the-blue. What was a girl supposed to say to one of her best friends when she was suddenly imagining him naked?

"So then," he said, his voice a deep rumble of sound that echoed the thunder and seemed to roll along her spine. "I guess you owe me five dollars."

She nodded dumbly. Five dollars. The bet he'd made. The challenge he'd thrown at her, knowing she wouldn't be able to resist the dare. It had seemed like a silly thing. A risk easily taken and disarmed. But he'd

tricked her. Tricked her into discovering a whole new side to him. And now everything was different. Before, when she looked at Paul, she'd always seen her friend. Someone to count on. Someone who was as much a part of her ordinary life as the Leaf and Bean.

Oh, she wasn't blind. She'd certainly noticed how handsome he was. How tall. How sure of himself. How good he looked in his usual jeans—and she'd for sure noticed *other* women noticing him. But she'd never felt that flash of liquid heat. The tingle of awareness a woman feels when a man is driving her crazy. The spiraling sense of desire as it rushed through her body demanding to be assuaged.

Now, though, she looked into those dark brown eyes of his and saw carefully banked passion. And she wondered why she'd never seen it before.

A part of her worried—about what they'd just done and what it might mean to their friendship—another, stronger part of her wanted to feel it all again. And to hell with the consequences.

Instantly her heartbeat stampeded into life. No more thinking. She wasn't going to question anything. God knew there'd be plenty of time for that tomorrow and the days to follow. For now, "I'll see that five and raise you five more." She heard herself saying it and still couldn't believe it.

"Yeah?" he asked, running his fingertips along her forearm. "What's the bet this time?"

Stevie trembled at his touch, felt the slow slide of his fingers against her skin, and was pretty sure she was on fire. She closed her eyes briefly, then opened them again to meet his steady gaze. Thunder crashed overhead,

rain slashed at the windows, and she heard the television, too, as a background buzzing in her head.

But none of it mattered. All she could see was Paul. All she felt was the surprisingly strong reaction to him that was still simmering inside her. And she knew that no matter what happened tomorrow, she had to have tonight. "The bet is . . . can you do that again?"

His eyes darkened even further until they looked almost black in the dim lamplight. A muscle in his jaw twitched and that incredible mouth of his tightened into a hard, thin line that defined the restraint holding him in place.

"We do that again and it won't be enough," he warned thickly.

"I know." Right now there wasn't much she was sure of, but Stevie knew without a doubt that if he kissed her again, neither of them would be able to stop. And life as they knew it would be changed forever.

Slowly, very slowly, Stevie leaned into Paul, and one heartbreaking inch at a time, she brought her mouth closer to his. When tension bubbled in the air between them, she touched her mouth to his and surrendered to the magic.

Angela Candellano went through the house she'd lived in for more than thirty years, turning off lights and moving inexorably toward her bed. At the moment, visions of that soft mattress were all that kept her moving.

"I'm getting too old for this, huh, Anthony?" She tipped her head back and smiled at the ceiling and, far above that, heaven. Her smile faded slightly as she scolded her late husband. "You should have been there.

You couldn't wait two years to die?" Starting up the stairs, she gripped the banister and kept up a steady one-sided conversation. After all, just because a person dies doesn't mean you should stop talking to him. How would that look? The only person in heaven no one talked to? People would think no one loved him. And she couldn't have that.

"Our Tony, he walked Carla down the aisle. But you know that, don't you? I felt you there. Your daughter, she did, too." She made it to the landing and paused, thoughtful. "And Nicky. Did you see him? Such misery there. He won't talk. Not to his mama anyway." She shook her head again. "Not like Nicky to be quiet. Paul, he's the one like you."

She opened the door closest to her and sneaked a peek at her two grandchildren, sleeping in Carla's old room. Little Tina was still in the family crib that had seen more than its share of babies over the years. And Reese, her newest granddaughter, was sleeping peacefully in the single bed.

Along with . . . Angela sighed and reached down to stroke the golden retriever's silky head. Whispering, she said, "Is good thing I don't see a dog in the bed."

Abbey laid her head back down atop Reese's feet and settled in for the night.

"You look after our girls, huh?" Angela walked quietly out of the room, leaving the door open just a bit in case one of the girls needed her. And with that thought in mind, she kept her voice down as she went on to her room at the end of the hall.

"You think just because you went to heaven you don't have to do anything anymore?" She walked into

her room and stopped beside the long maple dresser. There on its highly polished surface was a votive candle, a statue of the Blessed Virgin, and Angela's favorite picture of her husband. She picked up the silver-framed photo, stared into those smiling eyes she still missed so much, and said, "Talk to Nicky. Do something. You don't have friends up there?" She ran the tip of her finger across the glass and murmured, "I'm worried, Anthony. Something is wrong."

"This is crazy," Stevie murmured when Paul tore his mouth from hers. She dragged in a deep, gulping gasp of air and then let it out on a hissing moan as Paul's mouth moved down her throat and left a trail of heat behind him.

"Nuts," he agreed, his breath brushing her skin and singeing it.

"We should stop."

"Yeah, we should."

She tipped her head back and stared up at the ceiling, watching it as the wood beams began to spin. Then she realized her eyes were rolling. "Don't you dare stop."

"No problem."

He shifted, drawing her onto his lap and dipping his head lower, following the edge of her tank top along the swell of her breasts. Lips and tongue drew a line of fire across her skin that sent Stevie into a rushing whirl of sensation. She wiggled on his lap and felt him, hard and ready beneath her. Her body weakened even as her blood leaped into life.

A tingling began, low and deep within, and she gave

herself over to the glory of it. She'd never known such an amazing twist of feelings all at once. Want and need roared through her, demanding to be met. Paul's hands moved on her and she swore she felt every imprint of his fingers like a brand, burning deep, sliding down into her bones.

He yanked the hem of her top up, exposing her breasts, and she arched into him, offering herself and silently commanding him to take. His hands closed over her and she nearly splintered. His thumbs and forefingers tweaked at her nipples, tugging and pulling, sending shafts of white-hot desire ricocheting through her body with a wild abandon that forced her to move. How could she lie still and not touch him, too? Not feel his skin, flushed and warm and strong and solid. She reached for him, tugging at the buttons lining the front of his shirt and grumbling frantically when they refused to give way.

"Tear 'em," Paul muttered, too busy himself to care about the niceties.

"I'm trying."

He lifted his head and looked down at her, eyes blazing. With an oath, he ripped his shirt open, and Stevie heard buttons pinging around the room as they took off like rockets.

A short, sharp laugh shot from her throat, but then her mouth went dry. Instantly she reached for him, drawing her palms down his chest, trailing across every well-defined and very tanned muscle. She hissed out a breath when he pulled her close, bringing skin to skin, chest to chest, heartbeat to heartbeat.

Madness. Everything about this was crazy. Wild.

Insane. Stevie didn't care. All she knew was that she needed his hands on her. Needed to feel his mouth taking her. Needed to feel the rush of something fierce and raw racing through her.

Paul couldn't seem to stop looking at her. She was everything and more than he'd ever imagined. Her honey-colored skin tantalized him. Desire crashed inside him like storm waves pounding on the shore. They left him shaken, dazed, and hungry for more.

She was everything.

Everything he'd ever dreamed of. Everything he'd thought about for years. And he couldn't get enough of her. He had to have her. Now. This minute. There'd been enough waiting.

Paul dropped one hand to the juncture of her thighs and felt her melt into him as he touched her. Even through the soft, worn fabric of her cotton pants, he felt her heat and knew that she was as ready for this moment as he was.

"Paul," she ground out tightly as she moved into his touch, swiveling her hips and brushing her nipples against his chest. "I need you now. Here. Right now."

"I can do that." In one quick move, he flipped her off his lap and rolled with her onto the floor. The rag rug beneath them did nothing to soften the hardwood planks, but it didn't matter. Nothing mattered except the need to touch. To feel. To explore.

To claim.

Breathing heavily, Stevie yanked at the drawstring at her waist, then scooted out of her pants while Paul ripped at his own clothes. There was no time to enjoy the image she made, lying naked on the floor. The

roaring in his ears could have been thunder, but was probably his own blood, pounding through his veins.

In seconds, they were locked together on the floor, rolling back and forth, hands moving, touching. Mouths taking, giving. Breath burned hot and blood boiled.

His hands were everywhere at once and Stevie's mind blanked out. She couldn't think. Didn't need or want to think. All she needed was him. Inside her. This minute. Before she exploded.

"God, Paul," she managed to groan as she opened for him. "Now, now."

"Now." He pushed his way into her depths and Stevie screamed out his name.

She teetered briefly, heart-stoppingly, on the edge of completion and then with one swift, sure plunge, he took her over. Her body tightened around his, squeezing him hard, with a damp, velvety grip, forcing him to take that wild ride into oblivion with her.

And as they fell, he heard her whisper, "Paul," just before he went deaf, dumb, and blind.

"Just bury me here," Stevie murmured when she was finally able to make her voice work again.

Paul's voice came muffled against her shoulder. "Can't bury you. We're inside."

"'Kay. Cremate me. Burn down the building."

"Jesus," he said, lifting his head to look down at her. "You're real cheery after sex."

She blinked, then focused those blue eyes of hers on him. Blowing out a breath that ruffled the blond hair hanging across her forehead, she said, "Seriously. I can't move."

"Could be because I'm pinning you down." He started to roll off her.

Her hands slapped down on his back. "No. Don't move."

Paul stopped dead and looked down at her again. He couldn't believe what had just happened. His head was still pounding . . . could be the damn thunder again. His body was humming with completion and yet rarin' to go. The slightest word from her and he'd have at her again, only this time there'd be more . . . style.

Stevie smiled and winced as she shifted under him. "If you move right now, I just might splinter."

"Wouldn't want that."

"Thanks, me, neither." Her hands scraped along his back, her fingertips dancing up and down his spine until Paul had to grit his teeth to keep from groaning. "That was . . ."

He couldn't resist. "Toe-curling?"

She laughed shortly and he felt the slam of it echo inside him. "Hair-curling." One of her hands dropped to the side of his face and brushed his hair back. Shaking her head, she said, "I gotta say. I'm impressed."

A smile quirked at the corner of his mouth. "Thanks. But that wasn't my best work."

"Yeah?"

Her eyes held a speculative gleam that stirred the heat between them back into life. Paul's body tightened inside hers and she moaned, a soft, quiet sound, slipping from her throat and directly into his soul.

He slid one hand up her body, cupping her breast, thumbing the nipple until she twisted beneath him and arched into his touch like a flower turning toward the

sun. "Oh, yeah." His voice dropped to a notch just a shade lower than the crashing roll of the thunder. "That was just the five-dollar special."

Stevie laughed, as he'd hoped she would, and he listened to the frothy sound as it danced into the room and settled down around them like soap bubbles, bursting on impact.

"Then I've got to know," she said.

"What's that?"

She ran the tip of one finger across his bottom lip, tugging, smoothing, playing. Then she met his gaze squarely. "What'll *ten* bucks get me?"

His blood thickened. "Mmm. A big spender."

"Hey, you get what you pay for."

"I even offer a money-back guarantee."

"I'm hard to please."

"I'll take that as a challenge."

"Good."

Then he kissed her, a long, sweet savoring that slowly built until Paul was diving into her depths, exploring every secret that had haunted him for years. She gave as good as she got, making him tremble with need, shaking his world to its foundations.

And as the last of summer died in the onslaught of the first real storm of the season, they rode out the fury, locked in each other's arms.

The alarm went off at four-thirty and Stevie lunged for it. Instantly she moaned as muscles long ignored ached and screamed in protest. She rolled off the bed, swinging her feet to the floor. Bracing her elbows on her knees, she cupped her head in her hands and for one

incredibly stupid moment, wondered why in the hell she was so sore.

In the next instant, though, the night before came rolling back through her mind with the force and strength of a runaway freight train. "Oh God."

Slowly, hesitantly, she looked over her shoulder at the man in her bed as he stirred, mumbled, and rolled over to look at her.

And just like that, her head exploded.

"Oh God!" She jumped off the bed, realized she was standing there stark naked, and made a mad grab for the afghan at the foot of her bed. Well, actually twisted around the foot post of the bed, but close enough.

"Are you always this noisy when you wake up?" Paul complained, and opened one eye to glare at her.

"Only when I'm horrified."

"Gee, thanks."

She clutched the afghan tightly and drew it around her like some half-assed robe. "For God's sake, Paul. What were we thinking?"

"There wasn't a lot of thinking going on as I remember it."

"That's obvious." She paced back and forth across the room, just at the end of the bed. Seven steps to the marble-topped dresser, sharp "U-ie," then seven steps back to the window. She kicked at the tail of the granny square afghan, as if it were the train of an elegant gown. Pushing one hand through her hair, she tried to gather her thoughts, but all that came back to her was the night in Paul's arms. The things he'd done to her. The things *they'd* done to each other.

She looked at him, propped up on one elbow, the

sheet draped low over his belly and his . . . Stevie looked away. "Oh God. . . ."

"Are you praying or what?"

"Would it help?" She shot him another look that said she wanted him to say yes.

"No."

"That's what I thought."

"Why are we awake so damn early?" He glanced at the window. "The sun's not even up yet."

"Baking. I have to start the baking downstairs before my morning regulars show up and—" She broke off, raced to the window, and tripped on the stupid blanket and nearly pitched herself right through the glass. Maybe that would have been better. She swept the lacy curtains aside. "The storm's over. And your car is right outside."

"That's where I parked it."

"And it's been there all night."

"Well, yeah," Paul said, and sat up, letting the sheet drop to his waist. "It's pretty much trained to stay in one place."

"That's funny," she said, and heard her voice lift higher and higher. Deliberately she tried to get a grip. She pulled in one long breath after another, telling herself to remain calm. This wasn't a tragedy.

Hell.

Who was she kidding?

She turned around to face him. "You've gotta get out of here."

"Good morning to you, too."

"No shit, Paul." She turned and walked out of the bedroom.

He heard her moving around the living room, muttering to herself. Easing himself up and out of bed, he walked after her. This was too much. No one should expect a man to be able to think without caffeine in his bloodstream. Although, he thought as he caught a glimpse of Stevie's smooth, tanned bottom through the holey afghan, there were other ways to wake a man up.

"What are you looking at?" she demanded when she turned around, the blanket clutched to her bosom as if she were some Victorian maiden.

He nodded at her. "There's a lot of holes in that thing, Stevie. I can still see your—"

"Well, don't look."

"Trust me, even if I don't look now, I looked last night and I remember."

"You just have to forget," she said with a wild shake of her head. Then she seemed to notice that he was standing there naked, leaning against the doorjamb, arms folded across his chest. She slapped a hand across her eyes. "Oh God."

"You know, He's probably getting tired of you calling Him."

"Then why doesn't He answer?" she demanded, defiantly shifting her gaze from him to—heck, anywhere.

"And do what?" Paul wanted to know.

"Hell." She threw her hands wide, felt the afghan slip, and made a desperate grab for it. "Smite me down! Send frogs, pestilence . . . frogs. Something."

"You said frogs twice."

"They're icky. Worth more than one mention as a plague."

"Overreacting a little, aren't you?"

She pushed her hair back from her face again and Paul noticed the flash of panic in her eyes.

"Overreacting?" she repeated. "If word gets out that your car was here all night . . ."

The thought of that impacted in his mind and Paul at last saw her point. Chandler was like any other small town. Always on the hunt for a good piece of gossip. And the old biddies in town would chew on this one for a good long while. He and Stevie would be the topic of conversation for months.

But that wasn't what finally got him moving. He had problems of his own to deal with at the moment. He hadn't expected to sleep with Stevie last night. But now that he had, all he could think about was that he wanted to throw her back onto her bed and make love to her again.

Hell, if this kept up, he'd never get over Stevie and get on with his life.

CHAPTER FOUR

NICK CANDELLANO WOKE UP with a crick in his neck and the sun beating against his eyelids like the fires of hell on Judgment Day.

"Oh, man," he muttered thickly. "Too many years of Catholic school." Cautiously he opened one eye, then snapped it closed again. *Way* too bright out there. Reaching up, he rubbed the back of his neck in a futile attempt to ease the aching knot there. And when it didn't help, he gave it up, forced himself to open both eyes, and tried to remember how he'd ended up spending the night in his car.

"Carla's wedding," he said aloud, prompting what felt like an especially fuzzy memory. His gaze wandered over his surroundings. Idly he noted the twisted strands of lights dangling from the trees like tinsel. Baskets of once-beautiful flowers had been spilled and beaten into the now-muddy field. Tables and chairs lay haphazardly where they'd fallen during the sudden storm last night, and that's when he remembered.

He'd tried to leave when the rain hit. But he hadn't been able to start his car. Blinking, forcing his eyes open wide, as if that would get rid of the blurry sensation in his brain, Nick reached for the ignition and turned the key. Instantly the radio, tuned to a rock station, blasted into the stillness with a wail of guitars and a pounding drum—not to mention a screeching singer—that set off minor explosions in Nick's already-aching head.

"Jesus." He punched the button, blew out a breath, and took a moment to enjoy the blessed silence. Finally, when he thought he could move without shattering, he turned the key harder.

The engine turned over and cranked. And cranked. And cranked. But it didn't catch.

"Damn it." He flicked the key off again and slammed one hand down on the steering wheel. What the hell good was a shiny new Vette if it wouldn't start?

There'd been nothing wrong with the car yesterday, though. He was sure of that much, at least. So the only explanation for this was . . . *Tony.*

Scrubbing one hand across his face, Nick fought down the rising swell of nausea churning his guts and the insistent throbbing in his skull. His older brother, Tony. Town sheriff and professional asshole. Always sticking his nose in where it wasn't wanted.

"Goddamnit, Tony!" It came out as a shout and he instantly regretted it. The grandfather of all hangovers was *not* something to toy with. Keeping one hand clapped to his forehead in case what was left of his brain tried to fall through the hole in his head, Nick

opened the car door and stepped out. His Gucci-clad foot instantly sank into thick black mud.

The stuff oozed over the soft leather and swamped his foot completely. "Damn it." Sliding unsteadily, he held onto the car door and pulled himself the rest of way out of the Vette. No point in worrying about the mud now. Ankle-deep in the slop, Nick turned a bleary gaze on the surrounding area. The storm had kicked in wild and fierce, then whooshed out again just as quickly. What was left of his sister's wedding reception lay scattered across the empty meadow.

"The place looks like I feel." Nick shook his head and regretted it. Carefully tipping his head back, he squinted into a clear, brassy sky and snarled at the sun. It didn't help.

He felt like cold shit, no doubt looked like the back end of hell, and his mouth tasted like he'd been grazing on a toxic waste dump. Yeah, the hometown hero was looking real good. His right foot slipped farther into the mud and the cold, wet sludge filled his shoe.

Great.

Slamming the car door shut, he started for town, fighting to pull his feet free of the swamp with every step. The first thing he needed, besides a kick in his own ass, was a jumbo cup of coffee. Or a dozen. Then he'd have to face his older brother and get him to put the Vette back together.

Nick'd worry about putting himself back together later.

"I'm serious; you've gotta get out of here." Now that she was dressed and feeling just a touch more in

control, Stevie practically ran down the stairs from her loft to the shop and kitchen below. But it didn't matter how fast she ran; her memory kept pace with her. And it seemed determined to keep flashing images of the night before across her still-dazed mind. As if her brain were flipping through a stack of still photos, she saw Paul, naked. Paul, on top of her. Paul, kissing her. Paul. Paul.

Oh God, Paul.

His footsteps sounded out right behind her. But she didn't need to hear him to know he was there. Heck, she *felt* him.

"We didn't do anything illegal, Stevie."

"Barely," she murmured, softly enough that she didn't think he'd hear her. His chuckle told her differently. "This isn't funny."

"Right. It's ridiculous."

She flicked him a glance over her shoulder as she stepped into the store, made a sharp left, and headed through a swinging door into the kitchen. She pushed it shut behind her and let it slap into Paul as he followed her.

"Ow. That hurt."

"Then my work here is done." She ignored him. That was the ticket. The way to sanity. Last night hadn't happened. Nothing was different between them. He was still Pocket Protector. Paul, computer genius. Mr. Safe. Mr. Responsible.

Mr. Slow Hands.

Stevie stopped just inside the kitchen and slapped her forehead against the closest cupboard.

He chuckled again and she slanted her gaze to one

side to look at him. His dark hair was rumpled, his tuxedo jacket was slung over one shoulder, and that stiff white shirt—with no buttons—hung wide, exposing his impressive abs and dark tan.

Her mouth watered.

"Please go away," she said.

He shoved one hand into his pocket and gave her a slow, lingering look. "And if I do, that makes last night disappear?"

"No, but it makes it easier not to think about it."

"And I want to make that easier, why?"

"Paul, we both know that last night was a—"

"-mazing?"

"Mistake," she corrected.

"Probably," he said, and his gaze swept over her again, igniting her skin, sending bubbles of awareness tripping through her bloodstream. "But I want you again anyway."

Her stomach dived for her feet and Stevie swallowed hard. "Don't say that." She mentally gathered up the unraveling threads of her self-control and tied them into a knot to keep from leaping onto the cold marble pastry counter and inviting him to join her. "This can't happen," she said, and wasn't really sure if she was telling him or reminding herself.

"Yeah, I know."

"You do?"

Hell, yes, he knew it. Just standing here looking at her, though, was almost enough to change his mind. Color filled her cheeks, her eyes flashed with emotion, and nerves hummed through her body, making her seem as if she were drawn tight enough to snap. Paul

dropped one hand to the counter's edge and curled his fingers around it just to keep from reaching out and grabbing her. Squeezing it tightly, he channeled his frustrations into his grip and allowed his features to remain a hell of a lot more composed than he felt.

Spending the night with Stevie was just not something he'd planned on. Oh, he'd thought about it a couple hundred thousand times over the years, but hadn't really expected it to happen. Now that it had, he damn well wished he had a plan for what to do next.

Paul Candellano was a big believer in plans. He liked knowing the odds. He enjoyed a good spreadsheet, and it was in his nature to have a reason for everything. He was, first and foremost, a scientist. Give him a puzzle to solve, a riddle to untangle, an equation to work out, and he was a happy man.

Ask him to understand Stevie Ryan and his response to her . . . and he was lost. Hell, only yesterday, at his sister's wedding, Paul had finally come to the conclusion that the only thing he could do was get over these lingering feelings for Stevie. And today there was a whole new wrinkle in their relationship. If you could call it that.

They'd had a friendship—built in part by her closeness to his family. But there'd always been something else between them, too. Just what that was . . . he'd never been able to figure out.

But whatever it was, it had just gotten a hell of a lot more complicated.

"So you'll leave?"

Paul pushed away from the counter and flexed his hand, tight now from that death grip on the cold,

smooth marble. "Yeah, I'm going." Like he should have gone last night. Swinging his tuxedo jacket off his shoulder, Paul shoved his arms through the sleeves and shrugged into the fabric.

He noted her gaze shift to his chest and back up to his eyes again and he enjoyed knowing that this wasn't any easier on her than it was on him. After all, she'd been driving him insane for years. Seemed only fair that she start feeling her share of the heat.

"Good, that's good." Stevie nodded, bent down, yanked open a drawer, and snatched one of the clean, fresh aprons folded there. Slipping the neck over her head, she kept her gaze averted from his while she reached behind to tie the apron strings into a bow at the small of her back.

Paul's gaze dropped to the curve of her behind and he'd barely had time to enjoy the view before he was lifting his gaze again and telling himself to get a grip. "Right." He adjusted the fall of his jacket, pushed one hand through his hair, then headed for the nearest way out. Slapping one hand onto the swinging door that led into the shop, he paused and looked back at her.

She was watching him leave and he felt the power of her gaze punch into his midsection with the solid blow of a well-aimed fist. "Stevie," he said and waited for a response.

"Yeah?"

"Last night?"

"Yes?"

His back teeth ground together and he forced himself to stand still instead of stalking across the distance

separating them. That wouldn't do any damn good at all. Better to just say this and call it a day.

"Last night . . ." he repeated, "it didn't happen."

She sucked in a breath, held it, then released it again in a slow rush of air that seemed to sigh into him from across the room. Folding her hands in front of her waist, her fingers clenched together until her knuckles whitened. "That's probably a good idea."

"Yeah."

"So okay then." She paused. "We're . . . okay?"

He gave her a smile, and judging by her expression, it wasn't much of one. "Why wouldn't we be?"

"Right." She nodded. "Why wouldn't we be?"

He pushed through the door and walked across the shining wooden floors of the Leaf and Bean. His footsteps echoed in the silence and every instinct he had was clamoring for him to turn around and go back into that damn kitchen. He wanted to grab her, toss her over his shoulder, and cart her right back up the stairs to her bedroom. Paul stopped at the front door and flipped the latch, unlocking it. When it was open, he stepped outside into the early-morning chill.

Tendrils of fog still lay across Chandler like a blanket made of tattered gray silk. Dampness settled against his skin, but it didn't come close to cooling off the fire still lingering in his bloodstream. He had a feeling nothing short of a blizzard would.

His gaze swept over the still-sleeping town. Antique street lamps lined wide Main Street where tidy shops sat behind neatly swept sidewalks. A few trees dotted the length of the street, their roots pushing up through the sidewalks until the cement squares looked like

rolling hills. The city fathers had tried a few years ago to pull the trees and repair the cement. But old Mrs. Henderson and her Friends of the Trees group had tied themselves to the endangered elms and vowed to stay there until the mayor changed his mind. The mayor, a man dedicated to remaining in office, had finally surrendered and now made do with slapping cement patches on the sidewalks from time to time.

Paul wondered if he'd surrendered to his feelings for Stevie last night or if he was just patching up the empty places inside with a temporary fix. Great. He was equating his hunger for Stevie with sidewalks. Oh, yeah. He was in good shape.

He glanced at the morning sky and noted the streaks of rose and lavender bleeding into the horizon, announcing the coming sun. Within the hour, Chandler would start sputtering to life. Stevie would be first of course, with the other early-morning types staggering to her place for coffee.

But by eight, the town would be awake and bustling. Just like it was every day. Chandler, the town where he'd grown up, was as comfortable and dependable and predictable as an old movie you'd seen hundreds of times. Nothing ever changed here, and that was part of its charm.

But for Paul, something had changed last night. Pretending nothing had happened wasn't going to put enough of a spin on it, either. Reaching into his pockets for his car keys, Paul walked toward the gray 4Runner parked outside the Leaf and Bean. He hit the alarm button, the car beeped at him, and he opened the door. Climbing in, he slammed it closed behind him,

jammed the key in the ignition, snapped on his seat-belt, and shoved the car into reverse. Steering it down the silent street, he tried to tell himself that there was still a way out of this mess.

All he had to do was find it.

By the time the morning crowd arrived, Stevie was ex-hausted. She'd been baking like crazy all morning and still hadn't managed to work off the frenzied energy jumping through her.

Amazing, really, she thought, feeling the cells in her body actually skipping. Being with Paul had been a real eye-opener. Nothing she'd ever experienced—not that she was all *that* experienced—could compare to what she'd felt in Paul's arms. Which meant . . . what?

"Zip, that's what." Honestly, why couldn't she just let it go? Why couldn't she simply be grateful for the orgasm—make that *plural*—and move on? What had she told Carla not so long ago? *Use a man, then dump him.* But this was different, she told herself firmly. This was Paul. It wasn't as if she could cross his name out of her little address book and never see him again. He'd been a part of her life since she was twelve—and that wasn't going to change.

God, Stevie, stop analyzing everything.

She forced a smile she didn't quite feel as she leaned across Ben Zion's table to refill his coffee cup.

"Ah, Stevie," he said, inhaling the scent of the rich Jamaican brew, "run away with me and be my Coffee Queen."

She grinned at him and patted his lined, weathered cheek. Ben Zion hadn't seen the sunny side of seventy

in more than five years. But as he was willing to tell anyone who'd listen, *Snow on the roof don't mean there's not a fire in the house.* "Ben, if we run off together, what'll Erma do?"

At the mention of his wife, Ben winked, took a long sip of coffee, and sighed before saying, "She'd hunt us both down like dogs."

"My kind of woman." Stevie laughed and kept moving, telling herself to concentrate on her customers rather than the twisted mess her life had become. Nodding to her regulars, stopping to chat with the sprinkling of tourists, she wandered the room while Grace Boyd manned the counter.

Stevie'd been doing this for years now and it was second nature to her. She loved her shop. Loved getting up before dawn to bake the scones and muffins and cookies that her customers wolfed down during the long day. Loved seeing the same faces every day, being a part of Chandler, belonging to the simple, uneventful chain of life that continued to unfold in this small town.

Stevie had come to Chandler, her father's hometown, when she was twelve, and it had been an awakening. She'd never known a regular routine. Or had friends for longer than a school semester. But here in Chandler, life was different from anything she'd known before. Thanks to her father.

Her parents, the original odd couple, had met in college, when Stevie's father, Mike, was ambitious and driven. When he made his first million, he married Joanna, and the two of them traveled and partied and played until bad investments cost Mike most of his

money—and his wife and child. Mike had moved back to Chandler and taken over the family hardware business, and Joanna took Stevie off to Europe and married her next rich future ex-husband.

But at twelve, Stevie had gone from being a weary, world-traveling kid to carrying her lunch to school. And she'd thrived on it. Chandler became everything she'd always wanted. It still was today. Stevie loved knowing that she'd made herself a place here. A place where she had friends. A connection. And even a sort of adopted family.

The Candellanos.

Frowning slightly, she weaved her way through the cluster of small round tables and tuned the snatches of conversation around her into the background. The Candellanos.

They'd been her touchstone most of her life.

And she couldn't . . . *wouldn't* lose them.

Although sleeping with *two* of them could put a chink in the relationship. Oh Lord, could brains actually dissolve?

"For the love of God, give me coffee."

Stevie half-turned at the sound of the familiar voice. Looking up, she stared into Nick Candellano's bloodshot brown eyes and felt her stomach give a lurch.

Nick.

Her ex-boyfriend.

And twin brother of the man she'd just slept with.

Oh, good Lord. This was starting to sound like an episode of the *Jerry Springer Show*.

"Do I have to beg?" Nick asked.

"Could be entertaining," she admitted, and let her

gaze sweep over him. Still wearing his tux from the night before, Nick had mud halfway up his pant legs, and his feet were completely covered by a layer of dried mud that made him look like he was wearing cement shoes. His jaws were covered by whisker stubble and his hair was practically standing on end.

He looked like a poster boy for an antidrinking campaign.

"You look hideous," she said.

"Probably look better than I feel."

She gave him the once-over again. "Don't count on it. But clearly, coffee is needed." She walked around him to the end of the counter, then slipped behind it to snatch up a large bright red earthenware mug. Filling it to the brim with the strong Jamaican coffee, she slid it across the counter at him and waited while he took a seat.

Nick's hands curled around the mug as if he were trying to absorb the heat soaking through the ceramic finish. Then slowly, reverently, he lifted the cup to his mouth and took a long drink. He hissed in a breath as the steaming liquid slid down his throat, then expelled it in a rush. "I may live."

"Now where've I heard that before?" she wondered aloud. She'd poured coffee for her ex on many a "morning after."

"Yeah, I know," he muttered thickly, and lifted one hand to stop the lecture he was obviously expecting.

Stevie kept her mouth shut. For the moment. Though she was grateful that at least she'd stopped thinking about Paul. But she had to wonder what the hell was going on with Nick. He'd never been a big

drinker before. Oh, he was more than willing to party hard with his friends. But the last few weeks, he'd been drunk or hungover most of the time. And that just wasn't like him.

Still, it wasn't her business. Not anymore. For years, she'd loved him. Secretly planned a future with him that included the proverbial white picket fence, two-point-five children, and the family dog. She'd nourished those dreams and counted on them more than even she'd realized. Until the night her dreams shattered and lay in jagged shards at her feet.

Until the night two years ago when she'd gone to Nick's apartment unexpectedly and found him doing the horizontal tango with an NFL cheerleader. She'd picked up a lamp, tossed it at his head—and missed, unfortunately—and walked out. Then, just like that, she was alone again. At least, in her heart. Her mind. Surrounded by people she loved, yet alone because the one man she'd believed loved her had ripped her heart out of her chest and stomped on it.

She'd lost her dreams. She'd lost her pride. And she'd lost the man she'd thought Nick was.

Her stomach fisted just at the memory of that particular humiliation. For a while she'd hated him, but then that had passed, too. Finally. She could actually look at Nick these days without wanting to either hug him or hit him. She still cared, of course. She didn't want him to go out and get run over by an 18-wheeler or anything. But she didn't *care* care.

Which was a good thing, considering she'd just had the best sex of her life with the man's brother. Oh God, no comparisons. Please.

Jerry Springer reared his ugly head again.

"Have you seen Tony?"

"Many times."

"Please," Nick said in a near whisper, "no jokes. In a battle of wits, today I am unarmed."

Stevie set the coffeepot back onto its burner, then turned and leaned against the counter, folding her arms in front of her. "Okay, then no. I haven't seen Tony this morning."

"Damn it." He took another drink of coffee and seemed to sit up just a bit straighter. The gift of caffeine once again to the rescue. "I checked at his office before coming here. He must still be at home."

"Probably."

His gaze met hers. "Have you seen Paul?"

"Why would I see Paul?" Jesus! She leaped up and away from the counter as if she'd been burned. Was it stamped on her forehead? Did she have the words *Paul Was Here* branded on her chest? "Paul hasn't been here. Why would he be? I mean, he doesn't live anywhere near here and—"

"Okay," Nick interrupted, raising his voice enough to make him groan. "Christ. I was just wondering if you'd seen him. Thought maybe he could figure out what the hell Tony did to my car."

"Tony. So all you really need is to talk to Tony."

"What I need is three hundred aspirin and a Bloody Mary in a blender."

Suddenly irritated—both with Nick and with herself for coming so unglued at the mention of Paul's name—Stevie leaned in close to him. Then checking to make sure none of the local gossips could overhear her,

she snapped, "What you *need* is to work out whatever's turning you into the town drunk. It ain't pretty."

"Thanks for kicking me while I'm down."

"Hey, you want flattery, call a cheerleader."

"Please," Nick said, groaning, "I beg you to shut up. If I ever meant anything to you, please stuff a sock in it."

He had meant something to her once. In fact, he'd meant everything. At least, she'd thought he had. So she did back up and leave him alone. For old times' sake. And because after last night . . . she couldn't be Nick's life preserver anymore.

CHAPTER
FIVE

TWO DAYS CRAWLED BY and Stevie was getting crankier by the minute.

Which didn't make the least amount of sense. For God's sake, it's not like she was sitting around waiting for Paul to call. She didn't *want* him to call. She only wanted him to come over and——

Okay, back up.

She didn't want that, either—in her more rational moments. But when her brain went to sleep and her body started screaming, Stevie wanted him bad. Any way she could get him.

Which was *so* not a good thing.

Carrying another box of muffins, cookies, and scones out to where her car was parked behind the shop, she went over all of the reasons why she should never see Paul Candellano naked again.

"One," she muttered, hefting the box into the trunk and shoving two others out of her way, "he's a Candellano, God help me." The cellophane wrap covering the

top of the box fluttered at a corner and Stevie straightened it. "The Candellanos are your only *family*, Stevie," she went on, and made her voice stern so she would listen to herself. "You think they'll be happy about you going from Nick to Paul? You can't bounce from brother to brother, for the love of God. Hell, Beth'll lock Tony in a closet for safekeeping."

She groaned and straightened up. Scooping her hair back from her face, she took an extra second to slap her forehead with the heel of her hand. This was all just so . . . *tacky.*

True, she hadn't been involved with Nick in more than two years. But once upon a time, they'd been an item. She'd been so sure that Nick was the one man in the world for her. She'd imagined them married, with kids, living in Chandler, having dinner every Sunday at Nick's mom's—only then Stevie would have been an *official* member of the family.

And it had all been so real. So clear to her that she'd never noticed that the Nick she was dreaming about and the *actual* Nick were two completely different guys.

How many times over the years had she cried on Paul's shoulder about something Nick had done or said? And now she'd gone from crying on that shoulder to *biting* that shoulder and—she closed her eyes. "Okay, hyperventilating probably won't help."

She slapped one hand to her chest and took several long, deep breaths. Her heart rate slowed down and her breathing evened out, but nothing else had changed. Stevie was still sitting in the middle of a potential catastrophe.

What if Mama and the others found out about her

and Paul? Stevie swallowed back the knot of anxiety lodged in her throat and held on to the raised trunk lid to keep from swaying unsteadily.

Mama Candellano had always welcomed her, and the woman had been delighted when Nick and Stevie had become a couple. Eventually, Mama, too, had dreamed about Stevie and Nick getting married and making some beautiful grandchildren for her. And when it had ended between her and Nick, Mama had still made sure that Stevie remained a part of the family. Stevie thumped her forehead against the raised trunk and closed her eyes.

Just last year, Mama had hinted that she thought Stevie was Nick's one chance at stability. At making a U-turn on his fast-living road. Mama'd counted on Stevie's loyalty and her long-standing affection to save Nick from himself. But it hadn't worked out that way.

Stevie couldn't save him. Nobody could. That would have to come from Nick. Instead, she'd chosen to save herself, by leaving Nick and standing on her own two feet. Mama had said she understood—but Stevie had the feeling that the older woman was still waiting patiently for Stevie and Nick to get back together.

What would Mama say if she knew that not only was that *not* going to happen . . . but Stevie was now with Paul? Would Mama think her some kind of tramp for skipping from one brother to the next?

"Yes. Of course she would." God, Mama would give her "the look." That look that left a burning ache in Stevie's chest and an emptiness in her heart. The look that said Mama was disappointed in her.

They'd all hate her. They'd have to. What family

wouldn't? Heck, if she didn't know herself better, *she'd* hate her, too. This was all so . . . sleazy somehow. Stevie rolled her shoulders and winced. She'd never thought of herself as sleazy, and yet . . . if the Scarlet Letter fit . . .

Plus, she knew darn well, if it came down to choosing sides and picking either Stevie or Nick and Paul . . . she'd be on the outside looking in. The Candellanos would close ranks and she'd lose the only family she'd ever known.

She'd be alone again.

Every cold, lonely corner of her heart suddenly ached fiercely.

"Are you going to lose it all because of an attack of hormones?" she muttered, and slammed the trunk shut. Metal crashed against metal and she absentmindedly patted her car in silent apology. "No. No, I'm not."

She never should have let that night with Paul get so out of control. Heck, she still wasn't exactly sure how it had all happened. All she knew for certain was that she'd like to have it happen again. *If* there were no consequences. If no one would be hurt. If beggars could ride. If wishes came true.

No chance of that.

So no chance of reliving that sense of magic.

And knowing that was enough to make her nuts. Especially in the middle of the night, when there was only her heartbeat in her house. When the only sounds of life were the voices coming from the television that she routinely left on for company. When she lay there in her bed, feeling more alone than anyone should have

to be. When the thought of Paul touching her was enough to light backfires in her bloodstream.

That was her only problem.

If she could just avoid nighttime, she'd be good.

Except of course for times like now . . . when it was broad daylight and all she could think of was Paul.

"Damn it." Disgusted, she walked to the driver's-side door, opened it, and climbed in. Firing up the engine of her trusty red Blazer, Stevie pushed thoughts of naked Paul out of her mind and concentrated on getting to the local shelter in one piece.

He was doing the right thing.

That was important.

It was, in fact, one of the main rules Paul lived by. Do the right thing. Maybe that made him some kind of Boy Scout or something, but it had always seemed like the smart thing to do. Not to mention the easiest.

When you started lying and creating all kinds of diversions to get you out of whatever you should have been doing in the first place, it became a real time waster.

"So why," he asked himself, staring out the second-story window of his office, "isn't it easier?"

For two days he'd buried himself in work. Shutting himself up in the office, he'd had his secretary hold all calls and he'd simply dived into the new program design project he'd been working on for months. Work had always been his great escape. His brother Nick had the football field and Paul had computers. Algorithms. Numbers. What bored most people to tears fascinated Paul. Always had.

He'd discovered a long time ago that he was good at design. Good at finding new and better ways to do things. He held the copyright on several programs, everything from games to radar-tracking software.

But for the first time in his life, the work wasn't holding his interest. Not even his latest baby, the program he was developing for the government to help them track satellite movements with more accuracy. Ordinarily, he'd be hip-deep in facts and figures and projections.

But right now, he couldn't care less.

Bracing both hands on the wide windowsill, Paul stared out at the parklike view stretching out below him. But he barely saw the cypress trees, the oaks, or the rolling greenbelt, the function of which was to disguise the fact that the office building was in an industrial park. The pastoral view was supposed to ease stress, to make the surroundings more conducive to creativity.

But it couldn't help when the man staring at it wasn't seeing the greenery here, but was instead staring at a spot more than fifteen miles away. In his mind's eye, he saw a tiny shop squatting on the Main Street of Chandler.

His fingers curled tight around the painted sill and squeezed the wood as if he were trying to snap it in two. Ever since he had made the decision to get Stevie out of his mind and life, she'd been in it deeper than ever.

Hell, she'd even invaded his sanctuary—the office.

He *had* to get over her. There was no happily ever after here. She was his twin brother's ex-girlfriend. And despite the fact that Stevie and Nick hadn't been

together in more than two years, Paul knew there was a bond there. Something strong and sweet. Something he'd never be able to touch. And he was pretty sure Stevie was still half in love with Nick. That kind of feeling didn't just disappear. It went into a coma, maybe. But one of these days, Paul's dick-head brother would come to his senses, realize what a beautiful, sexy, smart woman Stevie was, and want her back— she'd go running.

She always had before. Why wouldn't she this time, too? And there Paul would be . . . left holding what was left of his heart.

"No thanks," he muttered, and pushed the dark image from his mind. Besides . . . not even counting the Nick connection, Stevie was practically a member of his family. There were rules about this kind of thing, and damn it, Paul followed the rules. Without rules, there was chaos. And he wasn't about to invite chaos into his family—or his life.

But it was only temporary, he told himself. It had to be. He could get over her. Shouldn't be any more difficult than learning how to live without breathing.

When his phone rang, he practically lunged for it— eager for a chance to get out of his own thoughts. Dropping into the chair behind his desk, he said, "Hello?"

"Well, hi. . . ."

He smiled. Only one woman in the world could put that many syllables into the word *hi*. "Hi yourself, Anna."

"I'm touched. You recognized my voice."

Hard not to, he thought. Up until a few months ago, he'd spent most of his spare time listening to that soft,

incredibly sexy South Carolina drawl. A writer, Anna James was beautiful, intelligent, and the latest darling of the entertainment media. Hollywood was filming her newest book and she was being splashed across the pages of *People* and *Us* magazines.

"Anna," he said, smiling, "how could any living, breathing male forget you?"

"Hmm . . . if that's true, why is it you're up there working while I'm in Hollywood pining away for you?"

"Pining?" Oh, he doubted that. A tall, sleek redhead with a body built for sin and a mind that could think circles around most people, Anna wasn't a woman to be ignored.

There was a long pause. "Not going to buy that, are you?"

"Not quite. I caught the latest issue of *People,*" he said. "You look good."

"Thank you, sir, and on that lovely compliment, I have a favor to ask you."

"Ask away."

"Are you busy tomorrow night? I could use an escort to this tedious party in the hills and . . ."

She kept talking, but Paul had stopped listening. He liked Anna. Really did. If they were still together, life would be a hell of a lot more peaceful than it was at the moment. But when she left for Hollywood three months ago, they'd ended what they had, and there was just no point going backward. Especially now.

"I can't," he said softly, interrupting the flow of musical speech. "Work."

"Darlin'," she said on a sigh of disappointment, "you work way too hard."

"It's a curse."

"Uh-huh. But if you get tired of 'work,' you give me a call, okay?"

"You'll be the first," Paul said, leaning back in his chair. "Now why don't you tell me all about what a splash you're making in Hollywood?"

Behind him, the door opened and a soft hush of noise slipped into his office. Fingers danced on keyboards, filtered music sighed from speakers, and the smell of coffee burning on a hot plate stained the air.

"Paul?"

"Hold on," he said into the phone, then spoke to the woman standing in the doorway. "Max, I told you I don't want to be disturbed."

"Well, pardon the hell out of me, Your Majesty."

Paul sighed, dropped his chin to his chest briefly, then looked up again at his secretary. Maxine Devlin. Iron gray hair, narrowed blue eyes, bright red business suit, a ramrod up her spine, and a defiant tilt to both of her chins. Happily married to a Marine for the last thirty-five years, Max took no crap from her colonel husband *or* the Corps, so she sure wasn't intimidated by a man she considered young enough to be her son.

If she wasn't so damn good at running his world, he'd have fired her. With her permission, of course.

"What is it?"

She glanced at the notepad in her hand, though Paul knew it was just for show. The woman had a memory like a steel trap. Nothing escaped her. Nothing went unnoticed. Nothing was ever forgotten.

"General Halliwell called this morning to set up a phone conference for two this afternoon. He needs

more information on the program you're working on for the DOD."

The satellite-tracking program. When it was finished, it would be the best thing he'd ever done. And doing something for his country made him proud. But he was in no mood to talk to the general about it today. He shook his head. "Cancel it."

"I will not."

There she stood, in the office doorway, a pillar of bright color in an otherwise drab room. She faced him down with a steely gaze he imagined could have sent entire Marine battalions running for cover.

"Who's the boss here?" he asked, tightening his grip on the phone receiver.

She gave him a brief smile. "You're the boss. But I'm in charge."

He'd argue with her, but what was the point? She was right. His office—hell, the company—would crumble into dust without Maxine and they both knew it.

"Fine," he said, surrendering to the inevitable. "Tell me when it's time."

She glanced at her watch, then back up at him again. "Time."

"Shit." Then, uncovering the mouthpiece of the receiver, he said, "Anna, I've got to go." He hardly heard her say good-bye as he hung up and scraped one hand through his hair. He didn't even notice when it fell back across his forehead an instant later. "Max, why didn't you tell me?"

One gray eyebrow lifted and the toe of her right shoe tapped against the battleship gray carpet.

"Right," he said. "I told you no interruptions." Then

it dawned on him. "Why'd you let Anna's call through?"

The older woman shrugged. "You looked like you needed a distraction or two."

She had no idea.

The phone on his desk rang.

Max checked her watch again. "That'll be the general."

Dutifully Paul swiveled around in his chair, without sparing a glance at the dozen or more framed awards and certificates hanging on the wall behind the desk. Pushing thoughts of Stevie to one side, at least temporarily, he reached for the phone.

By the time Stevie got back from the homeless shelter, it was late and she was thankful she'd told Sarah to close up the place for her. She was beat. Tired enough that she had actual hope of really sleeping that night. Minus the dreams that had been flitting through her mind the last few days.

At least until she pulled into her parking space behind the shop and saw Paul standing beside his car, waiting for her.

All of her good intentions flew out the window. That stern lecture she'd given herself earlier was forgotten in the flash of pure, undiluted 100 proof desire that swept through her with just a glimpse of him.

What was happening here? Just a week ago, she'd have grinned at her "pal" and been glad to see him, but she certainly wouldn't have been quivering in her boots.

Tonight it was a different story. The tux was gone,

but that didn't seem to make a difference. The antique street lamps glowed with a dim yellow fog light and cast a golden haze around him that looked damn near magical. It winked off the lenses in his glasses and made his eyes seem to sparkle. He leaned against the front fender of his gigantic, *it's all about size* car with his arms folded across his chest. One foot was crossed over the other, and to anyone else he would have appeared casual. Relaxed.

But to Stevie's hormone-driven vision he looked just as tightly strung as she felt.

Uh-oh.

She threw the car into PARK, cut the engine, and took a minute to absorb the silence, hoping it would fill her with some sort of inner peace. Hell, she'd have chanted if she'd thought it would do any good.

Eventually, though, she had to open the door and step out. He obviously wasn't going anywhere and she wasn't about to hide out in her car.

"What're you doing here?" Well, that was a warm welcome, she thought as she closed the door again and set the alarm.

"Freezing my ass off."

The night air was cold and damp, coming in off the ocean with icy fingers. Stevie should have been cold, too. But suddenly her blood was red-hot and she felt a flush of heat that rushed from her head to her toes and back again—with a pit stop in one particularly sensitive spot.

Oh, she was in serious trouble here.

She glanced around furtively, half-expecting one of the Terrible Three, the town gossips, to be lurking

behind a bush or tree, just waiting for something juicy to happen. No one was there, of course. But facts didn't get in the way of her feeling as if she were doing something subversive by meeting with Paul in a dimly lit alley. God, it was James Bond–like, but without the cars and guns and babes. Still, the tension in the air felt thick enough to chew.

She slung her purse over her left shoulder and took a few steps until she was just out of arm's reach of him. Not that she didn't trust herself or anything, but why take unnecessary chances?

"I meant," she said, "what are you doing *here*?"

"Waiting for you. Shelter day, right?"

Stevie bristled a little. "Yeah, so?"

He straightened up slowly, almost lazily, and every move seemed calculated to raise her blood pressure. In the pale light his hair looked the same shade as his sweater and his worn jeans looked soft and too darn good. "Why so defensive?"

She inhaled sharply and told herself it was the scent of sea air she smelled, not his spicy aftershave. Paul. It's just Paul. Nope. Didn't work. Because Paul was no longer just Paul. And now she was babbling even in her own head, and that couldn't be a good sign.

"Because," she said, moving for the door, "everyone's always telling me that I'm nuts to give away so many baked goods to the shelter. And I'm not in the mood for a lecture."

She unlocked the door and pushed it open. Quickly she ran a practiced eye across the kitchen. As always, Sarah Boyd had done an excellent job. Everything was neat and tidy. Counters clean and awaiting the next

day's work, the scent of blueberry muffins still hung in the still air.

When Stevie stepped inside, Paul followed her and closed the door after him. She almost gulped.

"I've never given you that speech, have I?" he asked.

No, he hadn't. In fact, he'd never said anything about her tendencies to give away food or coffee or take in strays. But that didn't mean he wasn't thinking it, just like everyone else, up to and including her mother. "No, but—"

"That's just who you are, Stevie."

She laughed shortly. "Crazy?"

"Kind," he corrected.

Her heart hiccuped. She looked at him. "It's not kindness," she said. "It's just—"

"What's the matter?" One corner of his mouth lifted into a half-smile that tugged at something deep inside her. "Compliments make you uneasy?"

No, she thought, *Paul* made her uneasy. Which was crazy. He was her friend. Had been her friend for years. And that was something she didn't want to lose any more than she wanted to lose her closeness with his family. Still, the way things were going, she was bound to lose one or the other.

Setting her purse down onto the closest counter, Stevie sighed. "Paul, why did you come here tonight?"

"I had to."

"Why?"

"To tell you that us . . . seeing each other is a bad idea."

"I figured that out already. You remember? The last

time we talked about this?" In fact, she'd spent the last couple of days thinking about little else. But somehow hearing Paul say it again really fried her. "Look. We can't change what happened, but we can stop it from happening again."

"Right." His voice was a caress that dripped along her spine and rolled along her nerve endings, igniting sparks of pleasure that dazzled and spun her head.

Her breath caught in her throat and darn near strangled her. The light from outside speared through the kitchen windows in wide golden wedges. The only sound in the room was the pounding of her own heart. He took a step closer in the darkness and Stevie could have sworn she actually *felt* waves of heat rippling off his body.

Nope. Things were way too cozy in here. All of the darkness and pretty, romantic lighting. If they weren't careful, they might—Stevie walked around him, drew the blinds to shut out the soft lamps, and hit the light switch, flooding the room with safe, bright, unflattering fluorescent light.

Of course, that only meant that she could see him more clearly. And what she saw in the depths of his brown eyes was enough to make her shiver in raw expectation.

Paul took his glasses off and hooked them at the neck of his sweater. He probably shouldn't have come here. He could have done this over the phone.

But he'd had to see her.

His gaze moved over her slowly, thoroughly, not missing a thing. Her blond hair was wind-ruffled, but then, he knew she liked to drive with the windows down

so she could feel the air rushing past her. Her eyes looked dark and stormy and . . . haunted somehow. That hit him hard. He'd never meant to push her into a place that created those kinds of shadows in her eyes.

He hadn't meant for any of this to happen. Now that it had, though, they had to deal with it.

"Stevie," he said her name softly, and it whispered into the room with a hidden plea he hadn't known would be there. Reaching out, he smoothed her hair back from her face and felt her tremble at his touch. Something inside him turned over.

She sighed. "You shouldn't have come tonight."

"I know."

She sucked in a gulp of air and blew it out again in a rush. Turning her face into his palm, she closed her eyes. "I'm glad you came."

"Yeah," he said. "I know."

"You should go now." Her eyes opened and her gaze pinned him with a direct hit.

"I know that, too."

"Don't go."

"Not a chance."

Threading his fingers through her hair, he cupped the back of her head in his palm and pulled her close. She came willingly, eagerly, and his mouth came down on hers like a starving man turned loose on a banquet.

His left arm wrapped around her waist and held her to him, slamming her body tight against his, until her heartbeat pounded in time with his and shook them both to their bones.

He parted her lips with his tongue, demanding, taking, offering. He tasted her, sweeping into the warmth

he needed so desperately. At the first taste of her, alarm bells went off inside his mind, and his body went on red alert. Blood pumped, heart raced, and every nerve, every cell, came stunningly, shockingly alive with want. Need.

She moaned, a small whisper of sound that slipped from the back of her throat straight into his soul. She reached up, wrapped her arms around his neck, and clung to him as if he were the one thing in the world that would hold her upright in the suddenly tilting universe.

Leaning one hip against the stainless-steel counter beside him for balance, Paul poured himself into the kiss. Tongues darted together, twisting, twining, in a dance of heat that promised even more to come. His body tightened until he was pretty sure he'd spring free of his jeans—and he almost hoped he would. It'd save time.

He had to have her.

There was no style. No slow build of warmth and desire. There was only frantic need pumping inside him. It was the same every time he touched her. And a part of his brain shouted at him to go slow. To savor. To experience. But that voice was silenced by the roaring in his ears and the driving need to claim her.

Shifting his grip on her, he let his hands drive over her body, lifting the hem of her pale green shirt, skimming up over her rib cage to her breasts, hidden beneath a swatch of lace. Deft fingers unhooked the front clasp of her bra and then his hands were filled with her breasts. His thumbs and forefingers tweaked and pulled at her nipples until she arched into him, offering him another muffled groan of pleasure that darted inside him like a lancing blow.

She tore her mouth from his. "Now, Paul. Now."

"Now," he agreed, and dropped his hands to her waistband. Quickly he unzipped her pants and tugged them down, pushing her panties along with them. She kicked them free of her legs and, gasping for air, began tugging at the button-front closure of his jeans. Her fingers moved against his skin, brushed his erection, and drove him to distraction. Finally, when he couldn't stand it another minute, he pushed her hands aside. "I'll do it."

While he tore his jeans off, Stevie yanked at his sweater. She plucked his glasses free and tossed them onto the counter, then pushed her hands beneath the hem of his sweater. Her palms skimmed along his chest and he sucked in air through gritted teeth as her fingernails scraped across his flat nipples.

At last, he grabbed her waist, picked her up, and slammed her bottom down onto the stainless-steel counter.

"*Cold*," she gasped.

"Not for long," he promised. Then he parted her thighs and pushed himself into her depths.

Stevie inhaled sharply, deeply, and shifted on the counter, to move closer to him. She wrapped her legs around his middle and hooked her ankles at the small of his back, pulling him closer, deeper.

With their bodies locked together, Paul paused long enough to tear his sweater off, then yank at her shirt, tugging until the tiny pearl buttons went zinging around the room like small white bullets.

She laughed, throwing her head back and offering him her breasts. "My turn to lose a shirt, huh?"

His mouth moved over first one nipple, then the

other, teasing, toying, drawing, suckling. He paused only long enough to say, "Don't think of it as losing a shirt. Think of it as gaining sex."

"Right," Stevie murmured, and clutched at him, her fingernails digging into his shoulders as he straightened up and rocked his hips, claiming her again and again. Branding her from the inside out with his hard, driving need. With his touch, his heat, his desire that rocketed through her as surely as it did through him.

Over and over he moved, taking her, driving her higher and higher. She held on to him and drew his mouth close for a kiss she needed as desperately as she usually did air. His hands slid over her body. She arched into him and rode the waves of sensation coursing through her. His body slammed into hers and it wasn't enough. She wanted him deeper, harder, stronger. She wanted to feel him slide all the way into her soul. She wanted, needed, all of him.

"Paul . . . Paul. . . ." Words, gasped out on short puffs of air. It was all she had. All she could offer him as he drove her on, his body a driving force that couldn't be denied.

"Let go, Stevie." His voice came in a groan near her ear. "Come now and let me watch you. Let me see you go over."

He drew his head back and she stared up into his dark, stormy gaze, losing herself in his eyes. He reached down between their bodies and slid his fingers over one particular spot until skyrockets exploded behind her eyes and, on his next sure thrust, the world followed, dissolving into a shudder of sparks and

splinters of light that dazzled her vision and melted her bones.

She barely heard him call her name before everything went black and she tumbled gratefully into the abyss.

CHAPTER
SIX

"IF WE KEEP THIS up, we'll kill each other."

"Not a bad way to go," Paul said.

"How did we get upstairs?"

"Hell if I know."

Stevie groaned and rolled off the bed, coming to her feet and snatching up the afghan to wrap around her like some sort of crocheted, holey shield. Déjà vu, she thought, remembering the last time Paul had been here. Still, it didn't matter if he could see through the darn thing or not. Her need for it was more emotional than physical anyway. She scooped her hair back from her face, then wished she'd left it hanging down in front of her eyes. At least then she wouldn't have been able to see naked Paul, leaning back against her headboard like some self-satisfied king.

Of course, why wouldn't he be satisfied? For the last two hours they'd done little more than crawl all over each other. She gave herself a mental forehead

slap. Maybe the road to hell really *was* paved with good intentions.

A cool sea breeze slipped beneath the partially opened window to scatter goose bumps across her skin. Moonlight spilled in through the yawning gap in the plain white curtains, stretching across the bed like some wide silver welcome mat, enticing her back to Paul's side. As if she needed more encouragement.

"What're we doing?" she blurted, mostly to keep her mind from wandering right back to where it wanted most to go.

"Taking a break?" He gave her a slow, crooked smile and Stevie had to wonder why that grin hadn't been driving her insane for years.

"So not funny." Stevie wrapped that afghan tighter around her and tossed one end of it over her shoulder as if it were an elegant stole.

"You want witty," Paul told her, "let me get my breath back and I'll see what I can do."

"I don't want witty conversation, Paul. I don't know what I want. No, wait. Yes, I do. I want to know what's happening here. With us. Between us." Babble, Stevie. Thatta girl. She pulled in a long, deep breath, and when that didn't help, she started pacing, kicking that afghan out of her way as she moved. "This is just so . . . weird."

"Thanks."

She paid no attention to the insulted tone of his voice. Whether he liked it or not, what was happening between them was *way* out of character.

"It is. Look at us." She spun around, caught her foot

in the blanket, and staggered before catching her balance again. "We're *friends*. At least, we were."

He sat up straighter and she refused to glance down to where her flowered sheet pooled on his lap. "We still are."

"Really?" She moved closer to the end of the bed. Poking one hand out of the folds of the afghan, she waved it at the mattress. "I don't do this with my *friends*, y'know."

"First time for everything."

"God!" Angrily she pushed her hair back out of her eyes again. "Are you really so . . . unbothered by this? Is it really no big deal to you?"

He tossed the sheet aside, swung his legs off the bed, and stood up. "Is that what you think?"

"I don't know what to think. Isn't that what I'm saying here?"

"And you figure I've got the answers?" He bent down to snatch up the jeans he must have carried upstairs. He tugged them on, not bothering with underwear while Stevie watched his every move.

A part of her still couldn't believe Paul Candellano was here. In her bedroom. Climbing out of her bed. But there he stood, in a shaft of pale moonlight that stretched across his broad, well-muscled chest like a stamp of approval.

He didn't bother buttoning the jeans up. He just folded his arms across that impressive chest, planted his feet wide apart in what could only be called a fighting stance, and gave her a look that was so hot, Stevie felt her hair singeing.

"You think I have some plan, is that it?" he asked, his voice growling out into the darkness.

"I don't know," she said, throwing her hands up, then quickly grabbing at the edges of the afghan again. "I was hoping *somebody* did."

"Yeah, well, I guess you're SOL."

"Apparently." Shaking her head, Stevie shuffled around and plopped down onto the foot of the bed. She didn't budge when Paul came around and took a seat just beside her.

Here she sat, bemoaning the state of her life at the moment, and even sitting beside the man who was making her life bemoanable, if that was a word, was enough to stir things up inside her again. What kind of a sicko did that make her?

He leaned forward, braced his elbows on his knees, and asked, "Why do we have to analyze this, Stevie?"

"Why?" She shifted him a look and tried not to notice how amazing his profile looked in the moonlight. Okay, *that's* why. "Because we're friends."

"You said that before."

"And you're Nick's twin."

"Actually," he said, straightening up and meeting her gaze, "I prefer to think of Nick as *my* twin."

She gaped at him. "Like that's a distinction?"

"Depends on your point of view." He slanted her a look. "Besides, this doesn't have anything to do with Nick."

"Doesn't it?" she argued, then kept talking when his features tightened. "I mean not just Nick specifically, but your family."

He turned his head from side to side, then shifted his gaze back to hers. "I don't see anyone here but us."

"Then you're not looking close enough."

"What the hell are you talking about?"

"This. This . . . *thing* we have or don't have, or might have, I'm not sure really, but whatever it is—if anyone finds out—"

"They rarely stone people in Chandler anymore," Paul said dryly. "And since my brother's the sheriff, I do have a little pull that might save us from a firing squad."

"You're making jokes?"

"Makes more sense than what you're doing."

He didn't see it, Stevie told herself. Maybe he didn't want to, but she saw it all so plainly. As if it were playing out in front of her, she saw the Candellano family choosing up sides. Nick or Paul. A family split. Divided. All because of her.

Well, she wouldn't do it. She wouldn't throw a train wreck at the only family she'd ever known. "You should go," she said, and stood up, deliberately keeping a little distance between them.

"Just like that."

"Paul, I don't want to lose our friendship. I don't want your family to hate me. I don't want—" Stevie broke off, held up one hand, and shook her head. Though her body was still humming from his touch, misery clouded her mind as she said, "I don't want to do this anymore. I *can't* do this anymore."

Paul looked up at her and recognized the frustration and confusion he saw written on her features. Hell,

those same sensations were pouring through him, too. He hadn't expected any of this to happen, and now that it had, he damn sure didn't know what to do about it.

He'd actually thought that sleeping with her one more time would "get it out of his system." Help him get over the feelings he'd carried around for her for years. But that hope had gone down the toilet. Now not only did he have to conquer his old, familiar "crush", he also had to get past the very real memory of being inside her. Being surrounded by her eager heat. By the taste of her. The scent of her. The look in her eyes when she went over the edge with a gentle push from him.

Oh, yeah. This was working out great.

"You're right. It'd just be too big a mess. For everybody." Paul stood up and looked around the moonlit bedroom for the sweater he'd been wearing when he got here. He didn't remember coming upstairs. Didn't remember them leaving the kitchen or dragging their clothes along with them. But the evidence was there, hooked over the arm of an overstuffed chair that crouched beside a well-stocked bookcase. Taking a few long strides, he grabbed it, yanked it over his head, and shoved his arms through the sleeves.

"I am?"

She sounded surprised. Hell, he was, too.

"Yeah. You are. But you're also making way too much out of this, Stevie. It's lust, pure and simple."

She blinked.

He picked up his glasses off the top of the bookcase and slipped them on. As soon as they were in place, he felt the emotional distance they'd always given him

slide into place as well. The only problem was, he could see her even more clearly now. He saw the flash of hurt in her eyes and he knew he'd put it there.

But there was no backing out now.

"Really."

"Yeah, really." He pushed one hand through his hair, then buttoned up his jeans and started scouting for his Nikes. When he spotted them on the floor where he'd tossed them a couple hours ago, he scooped them up and clutched them in one tight fist as he turned back to look at her again. "We've known each other too long to be fooled, Stevie. There's no hearts and flowers here. Just a mutual itch getting scratched."

Her eyes widened briefly, but a moment later she nodded stiffly. "Right. And now that it's been scratched, we can—"

"—go back to the way things were between us," he finished for her.

"Good," she said, nodding again, and he wasn't sure if she was trying to convince him or herself. "That's good. Better."

"Yeah. Better."

"So," Stevie said, "it'd probably be a good idea if you didn't come around for a while, huh?"

"Yeah. That's probably a good idea."

Silence dropped into the space separating them and slowly, inexorably, built a wall, brick by brick, as the seconds moved past. He felt it going up and didn't know how to smash it down. Or even if he should. Hell, he didn't want to love Stevie.

He wanted to get the hell over her so he could have a life.

If that meant a wall, then he'd just have to live with it. "I'd better go."

"That's probably a good idea," she said, and took a step back so there was no chance of him brushing up against her when he left the room.

Paul paused in the open doorway and looked back at her. Moonlight danced on the edges of her hair and pooled in the depths of her blue eyes until they almost seemed to glow with some sort of inner light. And Paul had to force himself to keep from reaching for her. To reclaim the warmth he'd found so briefly in her arms.

But if they were going to be just friends again . . . then he didn't have the right.

Paul spotted his brother's Vette the minute he pulled into his driveway. A quick flash of something that felt a lot like guilt shot through him. Paul squeezed the steering wheel, flexing his hands as if trying to wring that guilt out of his mind. It almost worked. Until he parked the car and saw Nick, sprawled on the front steps looking like a man who'd lost his last friend.

"Shit." He still had the taste of Stevie on his mouth and now he had to look his twin in the eye and pretend that nothing had happened. Hell. He should have taken acting classes rather than concentrating on all those useless science courses.

Unsnapping the seatbelt, he turned off the engine and climbed out. A cold, fresh wind swept across him, ruffling through his hair and chasing away the last of the warmth he'd taken home with him from Stevie's place.

"Hey, brother." Nick leaned his back against the

stair rail, one leg drawn up so he could rest his elbow on his knee and prop his head on his hand.

"What're you doing here?" Paul started forward, flipping his keys in his right hand.

"Thanks for the welcome. Good to see you, too."

Paul stopped, took a breath, and tipped his head back to stare at the night sky. Counting to ten had never worked for him, but staring at the stars was a pretty good stall tactic. Tonight, wide, thick clouds raced across the stars and the wind quickened as if signaling another coming storm.

But then he could have guessed at that without the hints from Mother Nature.

Bracing himself, he turned to look at his brother. "It's late, Nick."

His twin unfolded himself from the stairs, stood up, then unsteadily leaned one hip against the railing. "Yeah, I know. Getting later all the damn time."

"You drunk again?" Paul's eyes narrowed as he watched the other man. In the last few weeks he had gone from sometime party animal to dedicated drinker. And the change hadn't exactly been a plus for his personality.

Nick reached up and shoved both hands along the sides of his head. "Fair question, and no. I'm not. Stone-cold sober and not really loving it."

"You used to be pretty good at it," Paul said with just a touch of sympathy. "It'll come back to you."

"I guess." Nick avoided his brother's eyes, shifting his gaze around the yard, squinting into the darkness, staring blankly at the trees dancing in the wind. "I need to talk to you."

After his little heart-to-heart with Stevie, Paul was in no mood for more conversation. All he wanted now was a shower and a bed. But watching his minutes-older twin, he knew that wasn't going to happen.

Family.

If there was one thing the Candellano children had been brought up to believe it was their parents' favorite saying, *Family Comes First.* No matter what, you stand for your family. Friends will come and go, but your family would always be there. To which Carla usually added, "Whether you wanted them to be there or not."

Paul smiled to himself at the thought, but he knew his relationship with Nick went even deeper than his feelings for the rest of his family. They were twins. They'd shared a womb. Growing up, they'd shared a bedroom and more than one plan for world domination. They'd teased Carla as a unit, driven Tony crazy, and together they'd formed a united front against Mama and Papa when punishments were handed down.

Twins. As close as any two people could be. Despite their differences, they shared a bond that no one else could ever touch. A connection that couldn't be broken—though Christ knew it had been bent often enough over the years.

"Come on in," Paul said, surrendering to the inevitable. He started up the six redwood steps that led to the narrow deck running across the front of his house.

Nick's steps sounded out slowly behind him, and Paul braced himself for a long night. Whatever had crawled into Nick's guts to fester had apparently picked tonight to show itself.

Paul shoved the key in the lock and turned it, opening

the door and hitting the switch on the wall at his left as he entered.

Instantly, soft, muted light spilled into the darkness, dissolving shadows, creating warmth. His gaze shot around the familiar room. Floor-to-ceiling bookshelves were aligned on each side of a river rock fireplace. Hardwood floors gleamed in the overhead light, and the four overstuffed chairs crowded in front of the fireplace practically screamed at a person to sit down and relax.

Paul tossed his keys on the high bench by the door and kept walking, passing through the living room and turning left into the large, efficient kitchen. Light wood cabinets lined the walls, and a butcher-block table for two sat before a bay window that overlooked the wide front yard.

Nick kept pace with him, and when Paul offered to make coffee, Nick just nodded and plopped down onto one of the two chairs drawn up to the narrow table.

Nick watched his brother and wondered why his twin was so much more together than he was. How in the hell had his life gotten so far out of control? He felt like he was spinning and the world kept rushing past at such amazing speeds he could barely make out the colors in the swirl of motion.

But then, he and Paul had always been vastly different people, twins or not. Even their homes were complete contrasts. Nick's place was chrome and glass and . . . *cold.* He'd paid a decorator to come in and do the place and he'd never felt at ease in it. Hell, he spent as little time there as possible. It was just an apartment, after all.

But Paul had a damn nest here. He'd bought the land and had a custom home built. Cost a damn fortune, no doubt, but it was worth it. Richly wood-paneled walls, hardwood floors, and enough books to stock a library. Yet the . . . feeling in the house was . . . inviting. Welcoming. Good thing, since Nick really needed to feel welcome tonight.

"So where were you tonight anyway?" Nick asked, wanting to avoid thinking as much as possible. He leaned back in the chair. "I was waiting outside forever."

Paul slapped coffee into a filter, dropped it into place, and flicked the ON switch. "You should've come in. You've got a key."

Nick scraped one hand across his jaw, fingering the two days' growth of whiskers. "Your key's at my place. Haven't been there in a couple of days."

"Where've you been?" Paul glanced at the coffeepot while it bubbled and hissed, as if mentally hurrying it along.

"I asked you first," Nick said with a forced smile, not really wanting to talk about the last couple of days yet. "So who were you with tonight? Judging by the way you're dressed, you weren't out with that writer. Was it the astronaut?"

"No," Paul said tightly. He didn't want to talk about his old girlfriends. Didn't want to stroll down memory lane with Nick. "It was . . . nobody."

Nobody. Hell, Nick thought, he'd been stocking his life with nobodies for two years. At least Paul's nobodies had class. Women with brains as well as bodies.

Someone you could actually talk to without being bored into a stupor. "Been there, done that."

"Right." Paul changed the subject abruptly while he poured out coffee for each of them. "So what're you doing here anyway?"

"That's the million-dollar question."

"What's the answer?" Paul asked, carrying two cups of coffee to the table. "Still black?"

"Yeah." Nick took the cup from his brother and curled his fingers through the wide handle. He stared at the steam lifting from the cup and twisting into the air as if he could see his future in the swirling mists. "I haven't changed that much."

Paul shook his head and took the seat opposite Nick, stretching his legs out and crossing his feet at the ankles. "The last month or so, Nick, you've changed plenty."

"That's 'cause I'm screwed."

"Yeah, I've noticed. So has everyone else in the family."

Nick winced at the direct hit.

"Just say it, will ya?"

"That's the trouble. Haven't been able to say it. Not to you. Or Mama. Hell," he muttered thickly, "not even to myself." Nick lifted the cup and noted with some small amount of pleasure that his hands weren't shaking anymore. One good thing, anyway. Taking a sip, he let the hot liquid slide down his throat and hit his empty stomach like a blessing. Warmth spread through his system, chasing away the cold he'd been carrying with him since that last day at his orthopedist's office. "I'm through."

"With what?"

Nick lifted his gaze to Paul's and forced himself to say the words he'd been trying to forget for weeks. "I'm finished with football. My career's over." He took a breath and said the rest of it. "My knee's fucked. The doctor said one more good hit and if I'm lucky, I'm looking at a cane for the rest of my life. Not lucky, and I'm popping wheelies in hospital hallways."

God. The words were hanging in the air like some black banner of death. He could practically see them. Feel them, wrapping around him like a shroud or something. Everything he'd worked for. Everything he'd been shooting for since high school was now done. Taken from him because he'd gone one way and his knee'd gone the other.

Paul winced. "Jesus, Nick."

"Yeah, I know." Nick stared into his cup again as if trying to see beyond the surface of the coffee and into his own murky life.

Paul slammed his coffee cup down onto the table hard enough to slosh some of the dark brew onto the wooden surface. "That's why you've been drinking half the state dry for the last month?"

"Seemed like a plan at the time," he muttered, noticing that he wasn't really getting the sympathy he'd expected from his own damn twin.

"Bullshit."

Nick's gaze snapped up to his brother's. "What?"

"I said bullshit. That wasn't a plan; it was a retreat."

"That's great." Anger surged through him. "Thanks for the support."

"You don't need support. You need a kick in the ass."

Nick's eyes narrowed and his blood pumped hot and ready through his veins. Hell, it'd be good to pop somebody. A little pain to the body might be enough to ease the pain in his mind. "You want to give it a shot?"

Paul shoved one hand through his hair and damn near snatched out a handful just as a distraction. "Tonight . . . don't tempt me."

"Damn it, where's my sympathy?" Nick stared at his brother. Despite the subtle competition between them over the years, he'd always been able to count on Paul. Until now . . . when he really needed him. Had Paul gotten so damn successful now that his brother's problems didn't matter a damn? "I thought you'd understand."

"Yeah. I understand that you're acting like a damn fool. So you lost football. So what?"

"So what?" Nick jumped up from the chair with enough speed to flip it over and it clattered on the floor, sounding like the snap of bones. "You can say that to me? What if this was you, huh? What if some doctor behind a mile-wide desk looked at you and said you could never touch a damn computer again? What then, brother?"

Paul jumped up, too, and faced him down. For a computer geek, Paul had always been plenty fit. They even used to work out together until Nick turned pro and started working with a trainer. Watching him now, Nick almost hoped his twin would throw a punch. It'd feel good to work off some of this . . . crap running through his system.

"If I couldn't touch a computer, I'd find something else to do."

"Just like that?" Nick snapped his fingers and glared at his twin. "You could give up what you've been working for your whole damn life with no problem?"

Paul's hands were bunched at his sides as if he were as ready for a good brawl as Nick was. "It wouldn't be easy, but I'd do it. Just like you will."

"Do what?" Nick demanded. "What the hell am I supposed to do now?"

"Did you expect to play ball forever?" Paul argued.

"No. But damn it, *I* say when it's over. Not some damn doctor."

Paul swallowed back the anger crouching at the base of his throat. He stared at his brother and felt the old instinctive urge to protect rise up inside him. No matter what else went on between them, he and Nick had always watched each other's backs. They'd stood up for each other against bullies in school and covered each other's asses when their parents went on the warpath. Now was no different.

"What do you do?" he asked quietly, watching the tension slowly seep out of his brother's stance. "Any damn thing you want, Nick. That's the point."

"I *want* to play football."

"You can't."

"I never wanted to do anything else."

"Yeah," Paul said, reaching out to slap one hand on his brother's shoulder and squeeze. "I know."

"I don't know how to do anything else, man."

"You can learn."

"Yeah?" He snorted. "You want to hire me at your fancy-ass think tank company?"

"Not particularly," Paul admitted.

Nick laughed shortly. "See?"

"There are plenty of places that would jump at the chance to hire Nick Candellano. Things change," Paul said. "You'll adapt."

A long minute ticked past while the simple truth dropped into Nick's consciousness. He didn't want to let it in. Wanted to keep ignoring reality and fight for the life he was meant to live. The life he'd worked hard to get. But there was no saving it. It was done. His dreams were over and Paul's were riding high. Where was the fair in that? Finally, though, he looked at Paul. "We're not gonna fight, are we?"

Paul released a breath. "Doesn't look like it."

"Almost a shame. It's been a while."

"Yeah, it has," Paul agreed, taking a seat again and reaching for his coffee.

Nick sat down, too, grabbed his cup, and took another long drink to steady himself again. "You remember the last one?"

"Not likely to forget it," Paul said, smiling now in memory. "Three years ago. At the Fourth of July picnic. You cheated at the softball game."

"I was safe," Nick said automatically.

"Out by a mile and you know it."

"Hey, the day hasn't come when you could beat me on a playing field."

"I did that day," Paul countered.

They sat there in the kitchen, each of them comfortable enough to lapse into a thoughtful silence that ticked past with a gentle, steady beat.

And after a few minutes, Nick picked up his coffee, took a long, deep drink, and set the cup back down

again. Looking at his brother, he said simply, "Change really sucks."

Paul thought about all of the other changes that had happened in the last few days and wondered what his brother would have to say about any of them if he knew. But Nick wasn't going to know. The guy was low enough already. Hearing about his twin and Stevie would topple him over the emotional razor's edge he was busy balancing on. Besides, it was over. Yet another change. So Paul kept his mouth shut. No point in opening up that can of worms now. So instead, he just agreed. "Damn right it does."

CHAPTER SEVEN

"I'M TELLING YOU, STEVIE, those kids from the karate class are about to knock my fence down."

"It can't be that bad, Mrs. Frances."

The older woman blew at a lock of dyed red hair as it dangled like a fishhook over her forehead. Then she picked up her cookie, took a savage bite, and chewed. Waving her arms, she chopped and slashed an invisible enemy as a demonstration. "Those little thugs come out of that class with way too much energy to spare and they're chopping at my picket fence and screaming like they're about to attack."

Stevie set the coffeepot down onto its burner, then turned back to face one of her best customers. "They're not thugs; they're just kids."

"Thuglets," the woman said. Using what was left of her cookie as a pointer, she jabbed it toward Stevie. "You mark my words. Those little brats need their bottoms warmed, or pretty soon they'll be knocking over liquor stores."

Stevie's lips twitched. "Don't look now, but you're starting to sound like Virginia."

The other woman's eyes bugged open, then narrowed. "Well now, you're just being mean."

Laughing, Stevie shifted a look at Virginia, one-third of Chandler's Terrible Three. The older women had snagged a table in the only splotch of sunlight in the shop. They huddled together, like the old crones in that play of Shakespeare's—which one was that? Didn't matter. All they needed was a bubbling cauldron. They had the nasty dispositions already.

Virginia—always on the lookout for "gangsters"—wore two red circles of what she still called *rouge* on what used to be her cheeks. Just like her mentor, Abigail. But her skin had faded and sunk so much, she was pretty much just drawing with crayon on her bones. Abigail, the leader of the little coven, was at least fifteen years older than Virginia's seventy-five, but what she lacked in age she made up in mean. Abigail's rouge was even darker. And Rachel, the last member of the Three, was only in her sixties, but her spirit was as wizened as the other two's faces put together.

Scary bunch. They were always the first to leap on whatever piece of gossip came their way, and they had a network of cronies who could distribute that news fast enough to make Federal Express look like a wagon train.

Stevie looked away from the women and back to Mrs. Frances. "Did you talk to Tony about the kids?"

"Yes, for all the good that'll do," the woman complained. "When he was a kid, the sheriff used to hit my fence with his baseball bat like he was Babe Ruth in Yankee Stadium."

The phone rang, an ear-splitting shriek, designed to be heard above the everyday noise in the shop. Laughing at the woman's disgusted expression, Stevie took a step back, grabbed the receiver, and said, "Leaf and Bean, how can I—"

"Stevie!"

The voice sounded a million miles away, but she'd have known it anywhere. "Carla!" Stevie waved a frantic hand toward her counter girl, Sarah, to take over for her as she rounded a corner, taking the phone with her into her cubicle of an office.

Sitting down in the chair behind her tiny cluttered desk, Stevie leaned back, propped her feet on the edge, and ignored the papers sliding off to land on the floor.

"How are you? How's Chandler?"

"Good and the same," Stevie said, her fingers curled tight around the receiver. "How're things there?" she asked, and hoped to hell Carla's first trek back into the search-and-rescue business was going well. After all, she'd delayed her honeymoon to be able to go and help people through a disaster.

"They're great," her best friend said. "Tough. Disappointing and frustrating sometimes, but great."

"Good. That's good." Just two years ago, Carla'd given up what she did best because of a tragedy she held herself responsible for. Good to know that she'd finally managed to put it behind her.

"Hey, have you seen my husband?" Carla was saying. "And how weird is it that I have a husband?"

Stevie grinned. "No, he hasn't been around. I hear, though, that he's got some Mafia guys helping him set up his new office."

Carla laughed and the sound bubbled over the distance and filled up a lonely spot in Stevie's heart. "Good to know Virginia's still in fine form."

While Carla talked, Stevie's gaze shifted around the small office, sliding across a framed photo of her dad and a poster of the Caribbean she'd tacked to the far wall as a reminder of her last vacation. And right now that white beach and clear, green water looked like paradise. The fact that she was imagining Paul surfacing from the waves, water sluicing down his tanned, sculpted chest as he reached up to push his wet hair off his face, had nothing to do with it.

"Anything new?"

"Huh?" Stevie snapped out of it and told herself to concentrate. "What? . . . Uh, nothing. Nothing's new." Just old friends finding new ways to connect. And connect. And connect some more.

"No new guy?"

"No." Old guy, Stevie thought with a silent groan.

Oh God. She sat up, propped her elbows on her desktop, and stared down at the papers scattered across the surface as if looking for the secrets to the universe in a shipping order for sugar.

"Have you seen Nick lately?"

This just kept getting better. "Yeah, he's fine, too."

Nick. Stevie and Nick. Nick and Stevie. Even Carla thought of the two of them as a pair. Though they hadn't been together in more than two years, the Candellanos still thought of them as linked. And if they found out about her and Paul?

She pressed her fingertips against her temple, hoping to ease the throbbing ache that had just leaped into

life. Pounding in time with her heartbeat, pain pulsed inside her, bright and hot.

But Carla was talking again and she forced herself to pay attention.

"Mama okay? I tried to call her"—Carla's voice faded, crackled, then came back again—"wasn't there."

"I'm losing you, Carla," Stevie said, raising her voice to be heard over what sounded like locusts chewing at the phone wires.

"Storm coming—" The crackling got louder. "Gotta go—you soon."

"Bye!" Stevie shouted, and when the dial tone buzzed in her ear, she lowered the receiver and stared at it as if she could see her best friend's face. Best friend. That meant a lot. Heck, it had meant everything to the twelve-year-old girl Stevie had been when she'd first moved to Chandler.

Finding Carla, having a friend like her, had been, for Stevie, like finding a pot of gold at the end of a rainbow. Living out of suitcases, wandering the world in the wake of her mother, an elegant gypsy, Stevie had hungered for the kind of friendship Carla had offered her.

Someone to talk to on the phone. Someone to giggle with and cry with and get in trouble with. Someone who liked you no matter what.

Carla, being raised in a normal, loving family, had more self-confidence than anyone Stevie had ever known. And over the years, that bravado had rubbed off on Stevie and taken the edge off the shy little girl who had never really felt wanted.

Hanging up the phone, Stevie leaned back in her chair and let her memory take her back to those early years with Joanna. She had taken Stevie with her when she left Chandler, not because of any great maternal instinct—the woman had all the nurturing skills of a praying mantis—but because people would have talked had she abandoned the infant she'd never really wanted in the first place.

For years, Stevie had followed in her mother's wake, always aware that she was just a steerage passenger who'd somehow slipped past the gate to first class. Her mother's boyfriends either spoiled her or ignored her, and her long succession of stepfathers signed the checks that sent her to boarding schools. Until she turned twelve.

That was the year Stevie finally found the courage to tell her mother that she wanted to live with her father. Mike Ryan. The man who welcomed her every summer for three glorious weeks. The man who took her fishing and allowed her to wear cutoff jeans and get dirty. The man who tucked her into bed at night and kissed her forehead. The one person in the world who loved her.

Joanna had agreed, more than willing to get rid of a child who was living proof that Joanna was getting older. But it hadn't mattered. All that was important was that Stevie'd finally found a home. A place to belong. She smiled as she remembered how good it had been to go to school every day with the same kids. To make friends. To walk down the street and have people call her by name.

And soon after moving to Chandler, she'd also found

Carla. Her first, and last, best friend. The huge Candellano family was overpowering and overwhelming. They opened their arms to her and pulled her inside, and between her own father and Carla's family, Stevie's soul had soaked up all the love she'd missed out on in her first twelve years.

Stevie stood up, letting her fingers trail across the phone receiver. Family. That's what it was all about.

Now that her own father was gone, Stevie was alone again except for the Candellanos. She couldn't lose them. Couldn't lose that last connection.

"Hey, Stevie!" Sarah opened the office door and stuck her head inside. Her bright red hair looked frazzled and she was out of breath. "You coming back out here or what? A whole soccer team just dropped in and I'm drowning."

"Right." Stevie started for the door, deliberately putting her thoughts of the Candellanos, Carla and most especially Paul, out of her head.

At least for now.

Sunday night dinner at Mama Candellano's was required. No matter where you were, how you felt, what else was going on in the world, Mama expected her family sitting around her table, eating. If there was a nuclear blast, Mama would wait for the toxic clouds to disappear, then start ladling sauce onto fresh pasta. But tonight was special. Carla was home from her first search-and-rescue mission in more than two years, and she and her new husband were honeymoon-bound.

Paul opened the back door of the old Victorian, stepped into the kitchen of his childhood, and inhaled

deeply. Years rolled back and he was a kid again, racing in to beat the others to the dinner table. Man, there was just nothing else in the world like the smell of his mother's kitchen. Whatever else you could say about Mama—and there was plenty, he thought wryly—the woman was a magician in the kitchen.

"Wipe your feet." The "magician" didn't even turn from the stove to see which of her children had entered.

The familiar command brought a smile to Paul's face. Some things in his life, at least, remained unchanged. His mother. This house.

The Candellanos had come to California a few generations back. They'd settled in and around Monterey, following the jobs to be found with the fishing fleets, the vineyards, and the canning factories. Italian immigrants settled in Northern California and brought their traditions with them. Then Paul's father had met Angela, seventeen, beautiful, and fresh off the boat from Italy. She'd come to California to visit relatives and hardly spoke English. But she'd taken one look at Anthony Candellano and had never gone back to her village in Sicily. They'd married and moved to the tiny town of Chandler, to give their children a home outside the city—where they would all look for work outside the factories and the fishing boats.

Paul smiled at his mother's back. She and his father had given their children everything. A home, unconditional love, understanding, and the occasional slap to the head when necessary. And he wouldn't trade a single memory of life in this house for any amount of money.

"I already wiped my feet," he said. "I know the drill."

Mama turned from the stove to look at him, delight sparkling in her dark brown eyes. "Paul! You're early."

Angela Candellano's smile deepened the creases in her face and lit sparks of pleasure in her dark brown eyes. Her black hair, liberally streaked with gray, was drawn to the top of her head in a style she'd been wearing since he was a kid. She was a little wider than she used to be, but she hadn't slowed down any.

"Hello, gorgeous," Paul said, and crossed the room to her, sweeping her up into a tight, fierce hug. She laughed in his ear and slapped at his shoulders.

"Let me go," she said, giving him a quick kiss on the cheek.

"Only if you feed me," he teased, and gave her one last squeeze before releasing her. Still a beauty, he thought. And since his father's death she'd taken over as head of the family, running her house and her life and her children's lives as she saw fit.

"Ravioli," she said, turning back to the stove to give the pot of sauce another stir. She was as much a scientist as any he'd ever seen at work in a lab. His mother never worked from a recipe. She used a little of this, a little of that, and regularly produced heaven.

"Sounds great." Paul stepped to one side of her, leaned one hip against the edge of the countertop, and watched his mom while she worked. Steam lifted from a stainless-steel pot and the scent of his mother's sauce was almost enough to make him drop to his knees, weeping with gratitude.

"You've seen Nicky lately?" she asked, flicking a glance at him, then concentrating on the swirl of the wooden spoon as she stirred tirelessly.

"Yeah," Paul said. "Saw him a couple nights ago."

"Something is wrong there." She shook her head slowly, and when her lips kept moving, though she wasn't making a sound, Paul knew she was rushing through one of her quick, heartfelt demands on heaven.

Mama didn't just pray for her family. She pelted heaven with demands, requests, and indignant reproaches when she felt they were due. Paul had always had the distinct feeling that if God were paying attention, He'd do well to make sure Angela Candellano stayed happy.

But she wasn't happy now. Nick might think he was real slick at hiding what was bothering him. But obviously, their mother was on to him. Hell, they'd never been able to put one over on Mama when they were kids. Why would Nick think he could get away with it now? The woman made the CIA look like incompetent gossips. Her network of spies had kept all of her children on their toes growing up.

But at least in this one case, Mama could relax. Yeah, there had been something wrong, but Paul was pretty sure Nick was through the worst of it now. At least he hoped so. "He'll work it out."

"You should help," Mama told him, reaching for the dish towel slung over her left shoulder. "He's your brother."

Paul sighed and let his gaze wander the familiar room. The same green-flecked linoleum. The battered old green Naugahyde bench-seat breakfast nook. Worn counters, herbs potted on the windowsill, pictures of kids on the refrigerator—only now those photos were of her grandchildren, Reese and Tina. Coming here

was like stepping into a time warp, once a week. And inevitably he walked into this room and felt twelve years old again.

But a man had to take a stand sometime. Even against so formidable an opponent as Mama.

"Nick has to help himself." Besides, he wasn't sure that Nick would want his help at the moment. After all, things were going great for Paul right now, while Nick seemed to be neck-deep and sinking fast.

"Family helps family," she said, inclining her head so she could give him a good long stare.

"Some things you just have to do yourself."

She pulled the spoon from the pot and smacked it hard against the edge before setting it down on the spoon rest in the middle of the stove top. Reaching up, she wiped her hands on the dish towel slung across her left shoulder, then gave Paul a quick pat on the cheek. "You were always the one with the patience. Most like your papa. Nicky . . ." She sighed and shook her head. "Impatient. Too much of your grandpa in him. He wants what he wants and he wants it now. Is not good."

That about summed up the difference in the twins, Paul thought. He'd always been the one to think a problem through, work at it in stages until finally he'd worked it to its logical conclusion. Nick, on the other hand, was more likely to pick up a hammer to slam away at something in his way. And to give him his due, it had always worked for him. Until lately.

"Yeah," Paul said, reaching into his pants pocket and pulling out an envelope. He turned it in his hands, staring at it, but seeing Nick's face the other night.

Desperation was never easy to watch. And seeing it in his twin was especially hard.

"Maybe Stevie is the answer."

"Huh?" Pay attention, Paul. "What about Stevie?"

His mother brushed nonexistent wrinkles out of the front of the spotless apron tied around her thick waist. Then, never noticing Paul's reaction to her suggestion, she walked to the loaf of fresh bread waiting for her on the counter opposite. She talked as she picked up a serrated knife and started slicing. "Stevie. She was good for Nicky. Maybe she could be again, eh?"

A cold, tight fist closed around his heart. Jesus. Mama matchmaking? With Stevie? "Stevie and Nick broke up a long time ago, Mama."

"I know, I know, but maybe not forever. Stevie is a good girl. Nicky needs a good girl. He should settle down. Have a family."

With Stevie?

She shot Paul a look over her shoulder. "You could maybe talk to her. Tell her that Nicky needs help."

If Mama pulled this off, it wouldn't be Nick needing the help, but Paul. For God's sake. He scraped one hand across his face and shook his head. Wouldn't happen. Stevie was over Nick. Right? She didn't still care. Did she?

But he'd be damned if he'd help.

"So, you'll talk to Stevie."

"I don't think so."

"There's a problem?"

"Hell, yes—"

Her eyes narrowed.

He backtracked. "Sorry. Yes, it's a problem. Stevie's

not interested in Nick anymore. That's over." At least he was pretty sure it was over. That's what he'd been telling himself. But what if it wasn't? What if she was still carrying a torch for Paul's twin? What if she was just making do with him, Paul—the consolation prize—until Nick wised up and came running back to her?

Would she go back to Nick?

No.

Bullshit.

Christ. He didn't say that out loud, did he? No. If he had, his mother would be slapping a dish towel at him and yelling in half-intelligible Italian. She always reverted to Italian when on a rampage. And cursing in Mama's house would bring down the wrath of Angela faster than anything.

But he was safe. His mother was concentrating on the bread and whatever plan she was hatching. "Over isn't always over. Love is something you can't plan, Paul. Is something that just happens. And when it's right . . . nothing will stand in the way of it." She looked at him and waved the knife for emphasis. "Nicky was happy with Stevie."

"Yeah, but was Stevie happy with Nick?" Okay, that he *had* said out loud. And his mother was looking at him like he'd grown another head. Which he could have used.

"What's that mean—"

"Look, Mama," he said, changing the subject, a little late, but better than never, "before everyone else gets here . . ." He held out the envelope and wasn't surprised when she didn't take it. They went through this every month.

Mama was still under the impression that Paul was a struggling underpaid scientist. But the plain truth was, he wouldn't have to work another day in his life if he didn't want to. Licensing the rights to the advanced programs he'd designed had seen to that. But he couldn't imagine *not* working. *Not* coming up with new and improved computer programs.

He loved a challenge.

Which, he thought, might explain why he was so drawn to Stevie.

Scowling at him, his mother said, "I don't need your money, Paul. You should save it."

"I save plenty."

"Save more. Your papa always said to save and—"

"I know what Papa said, and this is for you."

She huffed out a breath and shook her head. "Is not right. I don't take money from my children."

"If you don't take it," he said, leaning in and bending low enough to drop a kiss on her forehead, "I'll just hide it in the house somewhere."

Her mouth worked as though she wanted to argue with him a little more, but he knew he'd won again when she just sighed. "Is silly, though," she said, taking the envelope and sliding it into the front pocket of her apron. "I don't even spend it. I'm just keeping it for the girls."

He grinned. "Do whatever you want to with it. It's yours. Hell—heck," he corrected quickly. "Spend it on fast cars and handsome men."

She pretended outrage, then crossed herself as she said, "Your papa heard that."

"Papa agrees with me."

Her eyes narrowed to dangerous slits. "So stubborn."

"Just like Mama," he said, and grinned wickedly when she whipped the dish towel off her shoulder and gave him a playful smack in the arm with it.

Then the back door opened and Mama shouted, "Wipe your feet!"

A moment later, Stevie walked into the room and Paul's grin slowly faded. It had been two days since he'd seen her. Two days since he'd held her and tried to convince himself that whatever it was between them had burned itself out.

And now just one look into those deep blue eyes of hers—and he knew he was a pitiful liar.

Dinner was delicious. And loud. And just a little weird.

Sitting around the dinner table with the Candellanos was nothing new. But sitting next to Paul feeling his thigh pressed along hers was. Not easy to keep her mind on chewing when she was busy counting the tiny lightning strikes flashing along her leg to ricochet around her insides. She scooted farther toward the edge of her chair, trying to put a little distance between them, but Paul only shifted position, too. Stevie inhaled slowly, deeply, counted to ten, then twenty, then—

"Hello? Earth to Stevie . . ."

"Huh? What?" She came up out of her thoughts like a drowning woman breaching the surface of the water. Her gaze flicked around the table quickly and landed on Carla's perplexed face.

"Where were you?" she asked.

"Sorry. Daydreaming."

"Must've been good."

Good? Oh, man. Beneath the table, Paul's fingertips trailed along her upper thigh, and Stevie hissed in a breath. What was he doing? They'd agreed. It was over. And even if it weren't, why was he doing this *here*? At his mother's table? She dropped her napkin, swatted at his hand, and gulped when he caught her hand and held it beneath the table. Delicately, like the touch of a feather, his fingertips traced patterns across her palm. She shifted in her seat, trying to deal with the distraction of Paul's sudden attention. But it was no use. Her brain short-circuited, but unfortunately, Carla was still expecting an answer.

"Good? Uh-huh. Sure. Whatever."

"You okay?" Concern glittered in Carla's brown eyes, and Stevie immediately felt even guiltier than she had a minute ago. For heaven's sake, she was sitting at the family table having sex fantasies.

Good thing she wasn't Catholic, because she was pretty sure this would be considered a fairly big sin.

"I'm fine," she lied, and crossed her legs, inching them farther away from Paul. For all the good it would do her, since he still held her hand in a firm grip that told her he wasn't letting go anytime soon. *Concentrate, Stevie.* "So, you're finally getting to leave on your honeymoon."

"Day after tomorrow," Carla practically cooed as she pulled at a slice of bread and popped the tiny piece into her mouth. "Mama's going to watch Reese and Abbey and we're outta here."

"Paris . . . sounds fabulous." Actually, all she remembered of Paris was one very elegant hotel and a lot

of cranky French people. But who was she to rain on Carla's honeymoon parade?

"I can't wait."

"I can tell." And damn it, she was happy for Carla. The woman was so in love she damn near glowed. Which was wonderful and lovely and . . . okay, Stevie could privately admit to a little envy.

She didn't have *love*.

She had . . . patty-fingers under the table.

She had amazing sex she couldn't tell anyone about.

She had . . . Stevie frowned to herself. Just what exactly *did* she have?

"You guys?" Nick spoke up, pitching his voice to carry over the babble at the table.

It took a minute or two, but everyone quieted and turned to look at him. There were shadows under his eyes and he lacked the usual flash of confidence that he generally wore as easily as most men did a suit and tie.

Stevie felt a pang of sympathy for the man she'd once cared so desperately for. But she noticed that as Nick began talking, Paul released her hand.

She missed that singing warmth.

"I'm through with football," Nick said, and instantly voices rose up in question. But he waved one hand at them all, quirked a half-smile, and said, "It's my knee. Doc says I can't take another hit, so that's that."

"Ah, Nicky. . . ." Angela pushed up from her chair and walked around the table to her son. Dropping one arm around his shoulder, she gave him a hug, then smacked the back of his head.

"Hey!" He grabbed at the spot. "What was that for?"

"You don't tell your family what's happening in your life?" Mama's hands dropped to her hips. Never a good sign.

"I just did."

"Too late. This is what was wrong. I felt it. I knew it."

"The Great Mama," Carla murmured, earning a chuckle from Tony and a frown from their mother.

"Make jokes." Mama threw her hands high and let them slap against her sides again.

Stevie glanced at the man beside her and noted the tension in Paul's expression. Whatever he was thinking, though, was a mystery. And Stevie wasn't sure she wanted that particular mystery solved.

"It's no big deal," Nick was saying. "I had a couple of rough weeks, but I'm over it."

Paul snorted, but no one paid attention.

"So that's why all the booze?" Tony asked, his dark gaze coldly furious.

"Yeah." Nick gave his older brother a sheepish grin. The same smile that had always been his key to escaping punishment of any kind. The smile that could coax or seduce or tempt. The smile Nick used as faultlessly as a trained soldier used his M-16.

Stevie knew that smile too well. In their time together, he'd pulled it on her time and again, getting her to forgive him for one thing or another. Until the cheerleader, she reminded herself. Then, finally, she'd had the courage to say "no more" and walk away.

"Stupid, Nick." Tony leaned forward and folded his arms on the table. "Really stupid."

Everyone talked at once then and Stevie sat back in her chair, trying to become just a little bit invisible. She

didn't have a part in this. She wasn't in Nick's world anymore. And that's how she wanted it.

She slanted a sideways glance at Paul, though, and saw him silently drumming his fingers on the lace tablecloth. The longer Nick talked, the further Paul seemed to drift into the background. And for the first time, Stevie realized that it had always been like that. Nick was the movie star and Paul was just an extra.

Stevie looked from person to person at the table, noticing how everyone was focused on the Golden Boy. She sat forward, riding the spurt of indignation jumping in her belly. For God's sake. Was Nick really all *that* fabulous?

Stevie shot him a look and was surprised to find him staring at her. He gave her his patented *ain't I great?* smile and waited for the impact. How was he to know it didn't happen?

Then he said, "Stevie used to tell me there was life outside football. Guess it's time I listened to her advice."

Uh-oh.

Stevie stiffened, Mama smiled indulgently, and Paul pulled even farther away.

CHAPTER EIGHT

SHE HEARD THE CRY first.

After parking her car behind the Leaf and Bean, Stevie stepped out, set the alarm, and turned for the shop.

But that pitiful whimper stopped her in her tracks.

Cocking her head, she held her breath and listened. A brisk sea wind whistled down the alley, rustling bits of paper as they were carried off into the darkness. Stevie tugged the collar of her sweater up higher around her neck and pushed her hair back out of her eyes.

Where?

Then it came again. Fainter, more . . . helpless, somehow. Just the slightest sigh of sound that seemed to carry somehow over the sweeping wind. The pitiful cries came again, faint, weak, and drew Stevie to them like metal shavings to a magnet. Rubbing her upper arms against the chill of the early-evening damp, Stevie followed the sound that was tugging at her heart.

Stevie walked quickly, carefully, out of the halo of lamplight and into the shadows.

Here only the moonlight dappled gently, and in a tiny patch of silvery light she saw the cardboard box and the tiny scruffy head that poked up from within.

"Oh," Stevie cooed, and dropped to one knee on the asphalt. She paid no attention to the loose gravel digging into her skin right through the fabric of her pale yellow linen slacks. Carefully, cautiously, she reached one hand forward to hold her fingers out for the little dog to sniff.

But the animal ducked its head, clearly trying to avoid being smacked. It couldn't weigh more than five or six pounds, and probably two or three of *that* was dirt. A spurt of anger shot through Stevie, then dissolved into the well of pity rising inside her. Poor little thing. So used to abuse, it apologized for existing with its every move.

At least the dog was free of whoever had hurt it, Stevie told herself. It wasn't much of a silver lining, but it was something. She wasn't surprised to find a dog abandoned behind her shop. Most people around Chandler knew that she took in strays, no questions asked. There'd been many mornings she'd stumbled across a box full of kittens or puppies or . . . like now, a poor abused creature too afraid to recognize good fortune when it finally happened.

"It's all right now, sweetie," she crooned, letting her voice take on a singsong quality. "No one's going to hurt you now."

Just as she reached into the box for the dog, though, headlights sliced through the darkness like bright white swords. Momentarily blinded, Stevie blinked and ducked her head, waiting for the spots in front of

her eyes to dim. The car came to a stop behind hers. Its powerful engine roared like some barely contained beast, straining at a threadbare leash—then, a moment later, it was suddenly silenced. Stevie straightened up, her insides jumping. Paul? She'd left him at his mother's house, still talking to his family. She hadn't expected to see him again tonight. Didn't know if she *wanted* to see him again tonight. For all of his touchy-feely tricks under the table, the minute Nick had started talking, Paul had withdrawn from both the conversation *and* Stevie. The skitter of nerves in the pit of her stomach settled into a cold, hard knot. Nope. Paul shouldn't have come here tonight. And she was just about to tell him that when the driver's-side door opened and Nick stepped out.

Stevie battled the blast of disappointment that shot through her at first sight of Nick. Completely illogical. Made absolutely no sense. She hadn't wanted to see Paul. He wasn't here. So why was she mad?

Never mind.

"Go away, Nick."

He laughed, clearly convinced she couldn't possibly be serious. "Oh, nice welcome."

"When I actually *invite* someone over, they're welcome."

"Damn, Stevie." He winced and shivered dramatically, as though someone had dropped a snowball down the back of his shirt. "That ice in your voice'll turn a man to stone."

"You seem lively enough."

"I'm used to you."

Stevie sighed. "Lucky me."

"Jesus." He drew his head back and stared at her. "What's up with you, anyway?"

Good question. Too bad she didn't have an answer. Or at least not a simple one. So rather than trying to come up with something believable, Stevie turned her back on Nick and stooped beside the box again. She smoothed her hand across the little dog's head and felt it quiver. "Shh. It's okay." She scooped her hands beneath the frail body and wanted to cry. Poor thing felt like a small furry bag of sticks. Its rib cage stood out and she felt its heartbeat fluttering against her palm. Cradling the dog close to her chest, she stood up just as Nick walked up beside her.

He instantly took a step back and grimaced. "Christ, what is it?"

She shot him a dark look. "A dog."

"Don't bet on it."

The animal melted into Stevie's body and slipped into her heart in the same moment.

"Jesus," Nick said, distaste plain on his face. "I can actually *see* fleas jumping off that thing and onto you."

Stevie was just so not in the mood for this. "Nick, why are you here?"

He shoved his hands into his pants pockets, rocked back on his heels, and gave her his best smile. The one that used to curl her toes and warm her skin. Funny. Tonight it just irritated her.

"Just thought I'd come by for a cup of coffee."

Stevie shook her head and watched him. Amazing. But what was more amazing was that she'd been nuts about this man for years and never really noticed just how self-centered he could be. All he could think of

was how he was feeling at any given moment. The rest
of the world could be imploding, but if Nick Candell-
lano was A-OK, then how bad could things be?

"You know what?" she said, stepping around Nick
to head for the back door. "Shop's closed."

Nick kept pace with her. "Come on, no cup of coffee? Not even for an old friend?"

"Nick, it's late, I'm tired, and I have to take care of
this little guy."

He couldn't believe it. Stevie'd always been there
for him. Back in the old days, he had been able to de-
pend on her as the one constant in his life. No matter
what else was happening, Stevie Ryan loved Nick
Candellano. Okay, sure, he'd been an asshole. He'd
fucked up more than once. But Stevie had never given
up on him. She'd always been his ace in the hole. Well,
except for not bailing him out of jail that time. But
now, when he needed her most, she didn't even have
time for a cup of coffee?

Man. What the hell was wrong with the world?

First Paul giving him grief and now Stevie?

She stuck her key in the lock and turned it. But Nick
had never been one to give up easy. This was still Stevie. *His* Stevie. She'd come around. She always had.
He slapped one hand on the doorjamb beside her head
and leaned down. "Stevie honey, take pity. A little coffee. A little conversation. I'm having a rough time right
now and—"

Still cuddling that flea motel close to her breasts,
she shot him a look he'd never seen from her before.
Stevie Ryan looked completely disgusted with him.
And he wasn't real sure what to do about that. Slowly

Nick straightened up and, suddenly uncomfortable, jammed his hand into his pocket.

"You know what, Nick?" she said. "As fascinating as your problems seem to you . . . and as hard as this may be for you to believe . . . I'm just not interested."

Then she walked into the shop and closed the door on him. The quiet *snick* of the lock being turned from the inside sounded like a gunshot—and hit him every bit as hard. Nick blinked and stood there like a moron, staring at the damn door, waiting for her to open it again and smile and say, "Just kidding."

But that didn't happen.

Seconds ticked past and stretched into minutes. Overhead, clouds obscured the moon, and the alley, but for the old streetlights, went dark. Shadows reached out for him and a cold wind slipped down the collar of his shirt and still Nick stood there, stunned.

She'd shut him out.

Left him in the dark.

Alone.

What was he supposed to do now?

Paul went for an early-morning jog, hoping to push the memory of dinner at his mother's house clean out of his mind. Instead, the solitude seemed to sear every separate image into his brain as though it had been carved in by a laser. Of course, if he'd really been trying to take his mind off Stevie, then he wouldn't have driven to Chandler to do his morning run, now would he? Doesn't mean anything, he thought. He often used the wide bike and running path that wound along the cliff's edge above the ocean and then cut across town

to meander through the patch of woods just to the east. True, he hadn't been over here in a couple of months, but what did that matter?

He ran the familiar path because he didn't even have to think about it. He could have run this path blindfolded. Which he might as well have been for all the attention he paid his surroundings. Trees, rocks—hell, even the ocean could have been wiped from the earth and he wouldn't have noticed. All he could see was his mother, smiling at Stevie and Nick as if they were some stupid little couple sitting on top of a wedding cake. And Nick taking it all in, like his just due. Sure, screw around on Stevie—treat this amazing woman like shit—then, when you're good and ready, smile and say, "Sorry," and everything was forgiven. Perfect.

And so Nick. Like everything else in his life, crap turned to gold. And while the world applauded Nick, Paul slipped into the background and became wallpaper. Until recently, that is. Now, Paul was doing great and Nick's life was in turmoil. Guilt tugged at Paul, despite the fact that he knew Nick's problems could be solved by Nick growing up and taking control of his own damn life.

But he'd never really had to before, had he? It had all come so easily to Nick that now he wasn't prepared for a battle. While Paul had quietly been going about realizing his dreams. Working so low under the radar that no one had noticed him. No one knew just how well his company was doing. No one knew that in his own sphere he was pretty much considered a damn genius. No one knew that he had more money than he knew what to do with.

"Well, whose fault is that?" he grumbled as he stopped running long enough to stretch his legs against the trunk of an old, scarred oak and take a breather. Muscles pulled, his breathing evened out, and his heartbeat slowed to a steady rhythm. Finally, he dropped to the ground, stretched out in the still-damp grass, and stared up at the cloud-tossed sky. It was his own damn fault. He'd done it to himself.

He'd kept his career so separate from family, how could they know what was going on with him? Hell, Nick was on television playing football while Paul was tucked away in an industrial park twenty miles away. He'd hidden his life, his feelings, from everyone, figuring that no one would be interested anyway.

Even now, he'd managed to screw up. Instead of putting Stevie out of his mind, forcing himself to get over her, as he'd planned, he'd let her drop even deeper into his life. And this time, when she took Nick back— as he didn't doubt for a moment that she eventually would—it'd kill him to watch the two of them together.

Because now it wouldn't be fantasies driving him insane. He'd have the very real memories of being with her. Inside her.

"Idiot."

He flung one arm across his eyes. Computer genius. Scientific wonder. The Department of Defense came to him to solve their strategy problems. Leaders of industry called on Paul Candellano when things looked grim. Hollywood tapped him for special effects. Hell, even his most recent computer *game* was back-ordered. He had more awards for clear, analytical

thinking and troubleshooting than there was room on his office wall to hang them all.

But when it came to Stevie Ryan, he was just another idiot.

Shaking his head, he sat up, wrapped his arms around his knees, and stared off into the thick patch of woods just across from him. Dappled sunlight fractured through the tree limbs and scattered on the ground like golden coins. Silence settled over him like a blanket until more runners went past, breathing heavy, their footsteps drumming on the dirt path. A soft wind ruffled his sweat-soaked hair, making him remember the feel of Stevie's fingers, spearing through his hair as she dragged his mouth to hers. And with that memory came dozens of others. More potent. More tangible. More haunting.

Instant frustration roared through him with all the subtlety of a runaway train. Grinding his back teeth together, he scraped one hand across his face and told himself to get it together. "It's not like you're in love with her," he reasoned aloud, as he always did when faced with some kind of problem. "You're just . . . fascinated. A little attached, maybe. But this is nothing you can't get over."

Nodding, he stood up and yanked off his sweaty T-shirt, crumpling it in one tight fist. The air against his skin cooled him off a little, but not much. "Think of her as a cold," he muttered, already beginning his run again. His footsteps pounded out a rhythm that jarred his bones. "A virus. You can beat a virus. Sure, it gets into your blood, heats you up a little . . . but it's not

fatal." See? He smiled to himself. Now that made sense. Scientific. Rational. Logical.

He picked up the pace, and in a few minutes he was passing the runners ahead of him. Anyone watching him would think he was trying to outrun a pack of demons, hot on his heels.

And he was.

The trouble was, Paul's demons were running with him.

Under all that dirt lay a pretty cute dog.

Sort of.

Stevie glanced at the tiny thing and felt a pang of sympathy. In the morning sunlight, there was no hiding the fact that the little animal had led a less than blessed life so far. Even clean, Scruffy, as she'd been appropriately named, looked a little rough around the edges. Her brown hair stood up on end at the crown of her head, and one of her ears was bent over at a weird angle. But she had a sweet nature and big brown eyes that still shone with trust despite whatever she'd been through.

"Is that a dog?"

Stevie shifted a look at Joe, her longtime mailman, as he skirted wide around Scruffy.

"Of course it's a dog."

"Couldn't be sure, but it pays to be cautious." He kept a wary eye on the animal as she inched over to cower behind Stevie. Quickly Joe thumbed through the stack of mail in his hand, then thrust a bundle at Stevie.

"Another stray, huh?"

"Yep," she said. "Who could resist such a face?"

"When are you going to stop trying to save the world anyway?" he asked.

"I'm not trying to save the whole world," she told him, hardly paying attention to the familiar conversation. "Just my little corner of it."

"You ought to keep fish. Neat. Clean. In a bowl." His bushy gray eyebrows drew together as he scowled at Scruffy. "Don't bite."

"You're prejudiced against dogs."

"My scars give me the right."

Stevie smiled at him. "Maybe it's the uniform, Joe."

"Nah." He shook his head until his graying ponytail swung like a pendulum. "Dogs don't need to see a postal uniform. They can spot a mailman at fifty yards. Even when I'm off duty, they growl at me. Hell, my *own* dog doesn't like me." He backed away, not trusting the newest addition to the Leaf and Bean. Dogs didn't have to be big to bite.

Stevie chuckled and dropped her gaze to the stack of mail in her hand. Bill, bill, bill, ooh, new catalog. Damn. A letter from her mother. Well, she'd worry about that later. It was way too early in the morning to have to deal with Joanna. Shuffling that long white envelope with the British stamp on it to the back of the stack, she lifted her gaze back to the mailman. "You ever consider therapy, Joe?"

He wagged one finger at her. "You know what they say . . . you're not paranoid if they really *are* after you."

Joe left whistling, and alone again, Stevie forgot about the mail and just enjoyed her view. Gazing up and down Main Street, she watched the early-morning types shake up Chandler. The usual assortment of jog-

gers were winding their way into town after running along the beach or through the patch of woods just to the east. Several women were already inspecting the fruit in front of the small grocery store on the corner, and Sheriff Tony Candellano was making his first walk down the street. Knowing Chandler, Stevie had no doubt that Tony's ears would be ringing with complaints or questions or demands.

Now that summer was over, the citizens of Chandler could turn their full attention to the business of getting ready for the Autumn Festival. In a town that depended on tourists for survival, you had to come up with lots of different celebrations that could take you through the year. Summer—hell, it was summer. But still, there was the big Fourth of July blowout. The end of September meant Fall Festival, when local artisans set up shop in the meadow for the arts and crafts fair. And soon tour buses would be rolling through, taking people on day trips to see the foliage that would be dotting the countryside with brilliant splashes of scarlet and gold.

Winter meant Victorian Christmas—with street stalls selling everything from hot apple cider to meat pies and roasted chestnuts. Then in spring there would be Flower Fantasy, when the farmers for miles around ran the flower market, selling cut flowers, plants, seeds, and bulbs.

Stevie smiled to herself. True, things around Chandler were pretty predictable . . . but ruts weren't always a bad thing. There was comfort in knowing that her roots ran deep here. That she had friends. And a family . . . of sorts.

Her brain flashed to the Candellanos, which brought up thoughts of last night's dinner—and Nick, showing up at her door. Irritation raced through her like a bad fever. Nick. Assuming she'd be waiting for him with open arms . . . despite the fact that they hadn't been together in more than two years.

And Paul. What was he up to? Had he encouraged Nick to come by? Did he know about it? Was he just going to step aside and say, "Go for it, Nick. I've had her, now I give her back to you"?

The seeds of irritation blossomed into a brilliant ball of rage that settled in the pit of her stomach. Was she some sort of prize, to be handed off to whichever Candellano brother was interested at the time? Oh, she knew damn well that she'd been Nick's "fallback" girl. If things got rough, go see Stevie. She'd make you feel better. And in all honesty, she had to admit that that was her fault as much as Nick's. She probably should have broken up with him years before she finally did. For both their sakes.

But Paul. What was she to him? Up until recently, she'd known exactly where she stood with Paul. He'd been her friend. The one person besides Carla whom she could talk to about . . . *anything*. But now, all of that had changed. They weren't just friends anymore. And they weren't lovers—not when they were both making promises to never do *that* again.

So what did that leave? What exactly was she to him? A quick roll in a rumpled bed? Was he living out a little fantasy? Or was she a chance for Paul to finally get one-up on Nick?

Scruffy leaned into the backs of her legs, and even

through the red mist of anger coloring her vision, Stevie felt the little dog shivering in the cold, damp wind. Instantly Stevie pushed thoughts of the Candellano twins out of her mind and stooped down to pick the dog up. "Aw, it's okay, sweetie," she whispered. "Never mind about those guys. We'll go in now, okay?"

Fall was in the air and the wind had enough bite to it that she knew her shop would soon be bustling. Lifting her gaze, Stevie watched as storm clouds gathered out over the ocean. Black and dangerous-looking, the clouds hunched together, roiling in a wind too high for her to feel. And she knew the storm was parked out there, over the water, waiting to gather strength before lurching toward shore to slash thunder, lightning, and rain at Chandler and the cliffs below.

It seemed, she thought as she turned for the shop, that she was being besieged by storms . . . physical and emotional.

And she was getting a little sick of it.

CHAPTER NINE

STEVIE KEPT THOUGHTS OF the Candellanos from crowding her mind by concentrating instead on business as usual. She determinedly lost herself in the daily rituals that she'd always enjoyed. Until recently, at least. Until thoughts of Paul's eyes had replaced thoughts of ordering a new blend of tea. Until remembering the exact touch of Paul's hands on her skin had swept away any interest in refining that lemon/raspberry scone she'd been working on.

This really wasn't fair. She wasn't even enjoying her business anymore.

Leaving the unopened mail in her office, she forgot about the bills and postponed reading whatever it was her mother had to say. She'd learned long ago that Joanna's letters to her only daughter were prompted solely by whatever her own needs were at the time. There'd never been any mother-daughter bond there. Of course, how could there be? Joanna had always been more interested in finding her next former husband

than she was in paying attention to a daughter who was a living testament to the passing of the years. Every time Joanna looked at her daughter, she saw herself getting older. And it wasn't easy pretending to be thirty-nine when faced with a twenty-seven-year-old "little girl."

Sighing to herself, Stevie pushed thoughts of her mother to one side. Actually, into the tiny dark corner of her heart where wishes still lived. Where she sometimes indulged in a fantasy of what it might have been like to have a *real* mother. The kind who noticed your existence. The kind who made cookies. And went to PTA meetings. And took you shopping for your first bra—instead of sending you out with a maid who didn't speak English and insisted on measuring you in front of God and everybody.

Okay, enough. Slamming a mental door against any more memories, Stevie focused on wiping down the shop's highly polished oak countertop. "'Morning, Jessie," she said, and smiled as the other woman merely grunted in response. The new kindergarten teacher, Jessie was a fanatic jogger and never missed a morning's run—rain or shine—or the steaming cup of coffee that followed it. The woman didn't talk much; like most of the early-morning crowd, she preferred silence. Which today, suited Stevie perfectly.

She had company, but no reason to be chatty on a day when she wasn't even good company for herself. Shifting a look at the others in the room, she picked up a coffeepot and headed out on her rounds. Cups needed to be refilled, whether she was in a good mood or not.

"'Morning, Harry," she said, and poured just a half-cup into the mug on the table.

"C'mon, Stevie," Harry whined. "Top me off, will ya?"

She smiled and shook her head. "Sorry, Harry. Ellen told me to cut back on your caffeine."

"Aw, what the wife don't know . . ."

Stevie winked at him. At sixty-five, Harry was fighting his wife's new health food kick with everything he had. "The wife *always* knows."

He grumbled, but picked up his mug to at least savor the scent of the rich brew.

Stevie kept walking, pausing as she made her rounds to smile or chat as the customers wanted. Her early-morning people usually liked to keep to themselves. But a few were always more than willing to talk. People like Hannah Jefferson, sitting in the corner, hunched over her morning cup of tea. The lonely ones. The ones without families.

Like her.

Thoughts of Paul and that unopened letter from her mother had naturally opened up old avenues of regrets. Stevie liked to think of the Candellanos as her family, but the plain truth was . . . she didn't have *anyone* she really belonged to.

There were no cousins or aunts or grandmothers. And since her father's death a few years ago, she'd felt that loss even more than she had as a kid. Carla might complain about her brothers or whine that her mother was interfering . . . but at least Carla had people to whine *about*.

What did *she* have?

Stevie half-turned to glance through the partially opened office door behind her. Scruffy's raggedy little face looked back at her. Stoic. Silent. She sighed again. She had a tiny dog that no one else wanted. She had strays. Animals and people who had no one and nowhere else to go.

And just what did that say about her? No husband. No kids. No boyfriend—Paul's face flashed across her brain, but that was just a knee-jerk reaction. He was no more hers than Nick was. Not that she wanted Nick anymore. Heck, did she even want Paul? Outside the bedroom, that is.

"Stevie?" a voice called out. "Cinnamon muffin and save my life?"

She shot a glance at Dave Jenkins, the football coach at Chandler High School. Smiling, she said, "Coming up, Coach."

She reached into the display case, pulled out a cinnamon muffin, and slipped it onto a paper-doily-covered blue ceramic plate. As she carried it across the room she thought about Paul again. Stupid, she told herself as anger flicked at the corners of her mind. Paul. She still couldn't believe how he'd pulled away from her last night. For all of his teasing fingers under the table, he sure as heck disappeared fast. And then Nick shows up at the shop. Had Paul *known* Nick was coming over? Had he graciously stepped aside, giving his twin a free road to Stevie? And if he had, who the hell had told him he could do that? What made him think he had any say at all in what happened in her life?

"Sugar-free?" the coach asked as a matter of course.

"Natch," Stevie assured him. Despite the fact that she was firmly convinced of sugar's health benefits, she always kept a sugar-free stash around for customers such as the coach. Leaving him to it, she headed back to the counter and noticed that one of the coffeepots was nearly empty. On automatic pilot, she made a fresh pot while her brain kept on truckin'.

Despite Mama's so obvious hints, Stevie wouldn't be swayed. She didn't want a husband. Not really. Not even when faced with the lonely silences that closed in on her when she was alone in her apartment. Hell, she'd watched her mother—whose picture should be in Webster's dictionary under the word *flighty*—go through five perfectly good husbands. Joanna was on her sixth marriage now, and only God knew how long that one would last. So Stevie'd seen firsthand just how "eternal" wedding vows could be. And though a part of her longed for what Mama and Papa Candellano had had . . . the realist in her knew that the chances of that happening were about as good as—well, getting struck by lightning while she stood inside the Leaf and Bean.

She tensed briefly, half-expecting a thunderbolt to blast through the roof and roast her to a crisp—Fate's little way of reminding her just who was in charge around here. When it didn't happen, she shook her head, pushed the coffeepot under the filter, and slapped the button. In seconds, the machine hissed and burped and steam lifted from the top, twisting and dancing in the moving air as yet another early-morning type pushed open the front door.

Bells jangled in welcome, and Stevie turned with a smile to greet the newbie.

The smile slipped the minute her gaze collided with Paul's.

The impact of his level stare slammed into her hard, and Stevie almost swayed with it. His hair was sweat-dampened; his running shorts showed off his tanned, muscular legs. Stevie's mouth went dry. His T-shirt, with the phrase *Scientists Do It With Knowledge,* fit him like a sweaty second skin. Plus, she had reason to know that his T-shirt wasn't false advertising.

Back that thought up, she ordered silently. No sense in torturing herself. Besides, she wasn't horny at the moment.

She was mad.

He could get coffee anywhere.

But the only place he could get a look at *her* and find out what had happened the night before between her and Nick was here. At the Leaf and Bean.

The bells on the door clanged again as the door closed behind him. He continued to study Stevie. Her wide blue eyes suddenly looked as deep and stormy as the ocean, pounding relentlessly against the shore just a few hundred feet away. He wondered what she was thinking. Wondered why her smile had disappeared the moment she saw him. And wondered what the hell he was doing here.

He shouldn't have come.

Hell, he was a damn genius. He *knew* he shouldn't be here. He should have gone home, showered, changed, and gone to work. He should be putting thoughts of Stevie out of his head completely. Hadn't that been the plan all along? To get over whatever feelings he was still carrying around for her?

Yeah, right. That had worked out real well.

Well, he had two choices here. He could turn around and bolt. Pretend he'd never stepped into the Leaf and Bean. Or . . . he could brave the less than welcoming glare she was giving him and find out the answers to his questions.

It was humiliating to admit——even to himself—that he much preferred the idea of not facing Stevie's anger. But because the temptation to leave was so strong, he forced himself to walk farther into the shop. He lifted a hand to the coach, smiled at Harry, and continued on. His long legs carried him across the floor in a few easy strides. Stevie's eyes didn't look any warmer close up.

"Hi." Good. Clever, he told himself. Real smooth. *This* from a man who thought nothing of giving speeches in front of hundreds of colleagues?

"Why are you here?"

"Ouch." He drew his head back and looked down at her. Her eyes seemed to ice over while she was looking at him. Not a good sign. "Nice greeting for a paying customer."

One blond eyebrow lifted. "Customer? That's it? You're here for coffee?"

He shifted position, a little uneasy with her tight smile and clipped voice. "Isn't that why most people come in here?"

"Fine." She nodded, whirled around, poured him a cup so quickly, the hot liquid sloshed over the rim and splashed onto her hand. If she even felt the stinging heat, she gave no sign of it. Slapping the cup down in front of him, she ignored the small lake of coffee staining

her counter, held out one hand, and said, "That'll be two-fifty."

"Christ," he muttered. "What crawled up your ass and died?"

"Oh, that was charming." She set the coffeepot down before glaring at him again. Lowering her voice, she whispered, "Did you learn that lovely phrase in rocket scientist school?"

"All right," Paul said, wiping spilled coffee off the counter with a wadded-up napkin. "I can see this wasn't a very good idea."

"That's what I like about you," she said, snatching the soggy mess from him and wiping the counter with a clean dishcloth. "You're a real quick study."

His back teeth ground together. "Look, Stevie, I only came by to—"

"To what?" she interrupted quietly with a quick glance at Jessie, just a few feet away, to remind him that people were close enough to hear them. "Find out how it went between me and Nick last night?"

He actually winced. Either she was psychic or he was way more transparent than he'd always thought. And if it was the latter, he could only be grateful he'd turned down a college offer to join the CIA.

She read his expression and her own features went thunderous. "So you *did* know Nick was going to stop by here last night." Stevie hissed in a breath and shook her head even as she leaned in close enough for him to catch a soul-shattering whiff of her perfume. "Why didn't you warn me? Why didn't you tell me?"

"There wasn't time," he grumbled, glancing around to reassure himself that no one was paying attention.

Nope. They were safe. The morning crowd were all sitting huddled over steaming cups of coffee or hidden behind opened newspapers. Small consolation.

"Right," she said. "No time to call and say, 'Look out, here comes Nick'?"

"He left Mama's right after you did."

"Uh-huh. But not you. No, not good ol' Paul. What? Did you stay behind to help Mama plan the wedding?"

"What wedding?" Christ, he was just not awake enough to do battle with Stevie. When a man went to war with this particular woman, he needed all thrusters firing.

Stevie pushed away from the counter, clearly disgusted. "You're unbelievable. I thought you—never mind." Then she spoke up louder, so everyone could hear her. "I'll be in the office, so if you need refills, just help yourselves."

No one answered and Stevie turned around sharply, stepped into her tiny cubicle of an office, and closed the door firmly behind her.

Paul stared at the door for a long minute and felt his own temper snapping at his insides. For chrissakes. He hadn't done a damn thing and he was the one being roasted. And suddenly he had plenty of sympathy for the people who'd faced Stevie's temper in the past. In all the time they'd been friends, he'd never experienced the full frontal assault of Stevie's anger. But then, they'd never really been involved deeply enough to stir up that kind of passion, had they? Until now, that is.

Passion. Desire. Rage.

This was turning out to be a real thrill ride.

"Do an end run," the coach offered.

"What?" Paul turned to look at the man who'd been Nick's high school mentor.

"Son," the man said slowly, "when a woman has her defensive line holding tight . . . you've got to do an end run. Outflank her."

Great. Now he was getting romantic advice from a man who thought stadium lights made for atmosphere.

"She wants you to follow her," Jessie pointed out quietly.

"Yeah?" Paul shot her a look.

"What've you got to lose?"

"Good point." He'd worry later about the fact that too many people were paying attention to what was happening between him and Stevie. Right now, there were other considerations.

Thoughts of leaving and heading off to work were completely dismissed as he stepped around the edge of the counter and grabbed that doorknob. Hell. If she wanted a battle, then she could damn sure have one.

He opened the door, stepped inside, and closed the door behind him again. He didn't mind a fight, but he didn't want an audience.

Stevie didn't even look up. "Get out."

"No." Paul folded his arms over his chest, planted his feet wide apart, and waited for her to look at him. It didn't take long.

She shot him a dangerous glare from under her lashes, but Paul wasn't about to be chased off. Not until he'd had his say. Sitting behind her incredibly small desk, she stared at her computer screen and did a great job of deliberately ignoring him. But Paul

wasn't fooled. He could almost feel tension radiating off her body.

"You want to tell me what this is all about?" he demanded.

"Nope."

"Fine. I'll tell you."

She snorted, but kept her gaze on that damn computer screen, and suddenly Paul knew how he must look when someone was trying to get his attention. Damn it.

"You're pissed off at Nick and taking it out on me."

"Sure. Whatever."

"Tell me I'm wrong."

Slowly Stevie's icy blue gaze lifted to his. "You're wrong."

Paul ignored his self-preservation instincts and walked around the edge of her desk. Stopping right in front of her, he bent down, grabbed her upper arms, and dragged her to her feet. She yanked free of his grasp, but since there was nowhere to go in the tiny office, they still stood just a breath apart.

A low, fierce growl sounded out just before Paul felt a stabbing pain in his ankle. "Hey!"

"Scruffy, no!" Stevie said it quickly, instinctively, even though she probably regretted stopping the little mutt from chewing on Paul's foot.

"What is that?" he asked when the bag of fur let go of him and scooted under Stevie's desk.

"It's a dog. Why do people keep asking me that?"

"The latest?"

She nodded. "I found her last night." She turned her

gaze back up to his. "Just before I sent your brother packing."

Relief pushed its way through Paul's heart. She hadn't let Nick inside. Hadn't talked to him. Kissed him. Hadn't . . . He should have known. But he'd been so sure that Stevie would once again take Nick back into her life the minute he turned on the charm.

"So you're not pissed at Nick. You're pissed at me," he said.

One corner of her mouth quirked, but there was no humor in the half-smile. "Ah, we have a winner, folks! You've won a year's supply of Turtle Wax. Thank you for playing."

"Knock it off, Stevie." He glanced down to make sure the little mutt wouldn't attack again in Stevie's defense. But the wild-haired thing had crawled back under her desk. So he felt free to give his attention to the furious woman in his arms.

She swung her hair back from her face. "Why?"

"Because I want to know why the hell I'm getting frostbite just by looking into your eyes."

"You know," she said, "for a smart guy, you're pretty stupid."

"Enlighten me."

"Fine." She planted both hands on his chest and shoved. He didn't budge an inch. Huffing out a breath, she gave that up and snapped, "You want to know why I'm mad? Think about it, Paul. Last night? At your mother's?"

"Yeah?"

She actually growled, which Paul considered a real

hint of danger. Hell, she sounded meaner than the little dog had.

"You practically had your hand up my crotch at the dinner table."

He remembered. Hell, he could almost feel her damp heat now. He hadn't been able to keep from touching her. Feeling her warmth. Even the threat of his mother sitting at the head of the table hadn't been enough to make him keep his hands to himself.

"Then Nick started talking and you pulled away so far, you might as well have been in New York."

He scrubbed one hand across the back of his neck. True. "Yeah, well, everyone started talking and—"

"Not everyone," she interrupted. "Just Nick. Then your mother starts in on the happy couple routine and you pull even further away. What's the deal here, Paul?"

"You're pissed because I stopped touching you even though we both agreed that we should stop?" Hell. Wasn't the best defense a good offense?

"I'm pissed because of *why* you stopped." She shoved at him again, and this time he moved enough to let her scrape through, brushing her body against his, just enough to set it on fire. "Nick talks, you pull back. Mama gives me that orange blossom/June wedding look and you practically disappear."

"It's complicated."

"No, it's not," she said hotly, shooting him a look that should have killed him. "It's simple. I figured it all out just a while ago."

"Is that right?"

"Oh, yeah. You don't really want me. You just wanted to know that you could get Nick's old girl-friend in the sack."

A red haze colored the edges of his vision and Paul had to squint just to keep her in focus. His blood boiled and a temper like she'd never seen before bubbled in his guts, churning until he wanted to shout, just to let some of it out.

But Stevie was still talking. Still going on, her voice rattling in the tiny office, her words bulleting into his body like a shotgun blast, peppering his skin. Thunder roared in his ears and he had to struggle to hear her. But damn it, he wasn't going to miss a single word of it.

"Congratulations, stud," she said with a sneer. "You finally managed to one-up your brother. Feel better now? Feel good? You managed to screw me *and* Nick at the same time. Good for you. Now get out."

She turned her back on him and pretended to stare out the tiny window at the small square of blue sky overhead. But Paul wasn't fooled. Her shoulders were so tight, her body was practically humming. Her words still echoed in the room, slamming into him again and again and feeding the rage that swam through his bloodstream at such a pace he could hardly breathe.

"You finished?" he asked.

She nodded sharply.

"Good." He grabbed her, spun her around in his grasp, and then pulled her tight against him. Her head fell back, her hair spilling loosely, brushing across his hands as he held her shoulders in a grip that she'd never get out of. "My turn."

"You don't get a turn."

"Wrong." His gaze locked on hers for one long minute, then slipped past her eyes to slide across her cheeks, her nose, her mouth. Every damn thing about her fascinated him. Even her vicious temper and ridiculous ideas. Damn it, if he had any sense at all, he'd be rushing out of this tiny room and letting her think whatever the hell she wanted to think. At least then, it would be over. He could stop thinking about her. Stop dreaming about her. But he couldn't do it. Couldn't walk away like this.

"You're an idiot, Stevie."

She tried to jerk free, but he held her fast.

"Forget it. You had your say, now I'm going to."

"I don't want to hear it."

"Tough shit."

She inhaled sharply, as if preparing to blast him again with another hot earful, but then she changed her mind, clamped her mouth shut, and glared at him. Probably figured the best way to get rid of him was to humor him.

"You think I *liked* knowing Nick was coming over here?" he demanded. "You think I got any sleep last night, wondering if you two were doing a fast bounce on the mattress?"

"Thanks so much—"

"*My* turn," he reminded her with a steely voice and a tightening of his grip on her arms. "What was I supposed to do? Say, 'Don't go to Stevie's. I'm sleeping with her now'? We both already decided we didn't want anyone knowing what happened between us."

"Yeah, but—"

"And you've known me most of my life. You *really* think this is about me one-upping Nick?"

Her bottom lip quivered, and for one horrifying moment, Paul thought she was going to cry. And if she did, it'd kill him. Damn it, how had this gotten so far out of hand? He'd only wanted to find his own life. To move on. To leave boyhood crushes behind him. Now he was in deeper than ever and wasn't sure how to get out. Or even if he wanted out.

"I can't believe this," she muttered. "This is just *so* not how I saw my life. Sleeping with both brothers. Well, only one. But everyone thinks I'm sleeping with the other one and no one knows about you and then even you think I'm sleeping with Nick, and if this gets any weirder they won't even let us on *Jerry Springer*."

He smiled in spite of everything. Stevie babbling was just something that would always make him smile. "At last. A bright spot."

"This isn't funny."

"Yeah, I know. But it's not a crisis, either. As for Mama . . . she's got plans to marry off Tina and the kid's two years old. Mama's plans mean *nothing*."

"You pulled away last night," she accused. "The minute Nick started talking, you pulled away from me."

He let his hands slip from her shoulders down her arms to the sides of her breasts. So close to heaven, he could almost feel the sweep of sensation pouring through him. She shivered and it rippled along his spine like a slow, teasing touch. "Yeah. Yeah, I did."

"No excuses?"

"None that make any sense."

"Swell."

"I want you," he said tightly, his voice a low rumble

of sound that echoed in the small room. "That's honest, too."

She took a breath, then let it slide from her lungs in a soft sigh. "Yes, but it doesn't solve anything. Doesn't change anything."

Paul reached up and brushed her hair back from her face, his fingers smoothing across her skin with a gentle light touch that sizzled between them. "Maybe it doesn't have to. Maybe it's enough all by itself."

"For how long?" Stevie trembled inside as her body turned to liquid fire with the simple touch of his hand. Her knees wobbled, and when he eased her back onto the edge of her desk, she went willingly. Hey, it was better than falling over.

"How long do you need?" he asked, and dropped one hand to the damp, hot heart of her.

Stevie gasped and arched into his touch. He bent and took her mouth with his as he caressed her right through the fabric of her jeans. Why? How? How could he do this to her so easily? How could she keep allowing herself to wander down this amazing path? Where was all her self-control?

Then thought died under the onslaught of too many sensations. She moved against him, arching, rocking, moaning. Papers scattered, pushed off the edge of the desk to fall in a silent snowstorm to the floor.

He cradled her in the crook of one arm and parted her lips with his tongue. He tasted her, explored her mouth, giving and taking with a need that built and swarmed inside him like a summer storm pounding at a tin roof. His hand worked her body, kneading the

denim and the tender flesh beneath. He rubbed her core and tasted her sighs as she gave herself to him silently, completely.

He felt the rush of satisfaction as the first tremors crashed through her body.

Stevie's hips rocked wildly and she clutched at his shoulders, hanging on for dear life as he pushed her higher and higher and finally over the precipice, only to catch her and hold her tightly as she fell.

CHAPTER TEN

BUT WHEN THE TINGLING tide of satisfaction settled into a low hum, Stevie came back to her senses and sat up, pushing Paul away. Shaking her head, she scooted off the edge of her desk, bent down to pick up the scattered papers, then stacked them neatly on the desktop.

Turning, she faced him. "This didn't solve anything."

"Didn't know it was supposed to."

"Paul. . . ." His name came out on a sigh. There was so much. In her heart. In her mind. And none of it made sense. And trying to talk to Paul about it didn't help. Lately it seemed as though anytime they were in a room together, they started out talking and ended up breathing heavy. Hell, nothing about her life made sense anymore.

When she and Nick broke up, Stevie'd thought her heart was irreparably broken. She'd put all of her hopes and dreams into that relationship and losing them had about crushed her right back into the lonely little girl she'd been when she'd first arrived in Chandler. But

she'd lived through the pain of his betrayal. She'd taught herself to ignore the flash of sexual heat she'd always felt around him until now there was nothing left. But Paul was different.

In so many ways.

He was her friend, first. For too many years, he'd always been there—a shoulder to cry on, an understanding ear to whine to. And damn it, she missed that. She missed being able to call him and just talk. To rag him about the latest succession of women strolling through his life. To tease him about how he spent too much time at work and not enough time just enjoying his life.

Damn it.

She missed *him*.

She missed her *friend*.

Oh, the sex was great. Fabulous. First-class. Better than anything she'd ever experienced before. But was that all it was? Was she just a passing blip on his radar screen? Okay, fine. Even she didn't really believe that he was simply using her as a means of finally trumping his twin. That so wasn't Paul.

But at the same time, she had to wonder if she wasn't just making the same mistake she had before. Was finding something in Paul another way to hang on to the Candellano family? And how could she trust her own judgment? She'd been miserably wrong about Nick. What if she reached out and made a grab for Paul only to discover she'd made another mistake?

No. She couldn't risk it. Because this time, if it all fell apart in her hands, her heart wouldn't survive the pain.

"I thought you were going to be using the new software I brought you last month."

"Huh?" Stevie blinked at the shift in conversation, then looked at Paul, bent over, tapping at her keyboard and studying the computer screen.

"The new bookkeeping system I got for you," he said, sparing her a quick glance as his fingers flew over the keys with a sure, steady stroke that reminded her just how talented those fingers were. "You said you were installing it."

Well. From the sublime to the boring. "I was, I just didn't have time to—"

"It only takes a few minutes."

"Sure, if you're Wonder Boy."

He shot her a quick grin that melted her teeth. "Aren't you lucky that Wonder Boy happens to be here?" He pulled out her chair, plopped down into it, and leaned closer to the screen, squinting just enough to look sexy as all get-out.

"Paul, you don't have to do this now."

"No problem."

Stevie shook her head. He'd never leave now. He was on the hunt. Like some ancient warrior going after the prize buck in the forest, Paul wouldn't stop until he'd hunted down every last whatsis and whosis in the computer program. "Where're your glasses?"

He patted his T-shirt, then shrugged. "Didn't think I'd need 'em this morning."

"So come back when you've got 'em."

"Nah. I can do it. You'll be up and running in a few minutes."

"Great," she said, perching on the edge of the desk to watch him work. "Then it shouldn't take me more than a month or two to decipher the book that explains how to use the darn thing."

He didn't tear his gaze from the screen, so Stevie studied him while he talked and worked.

"You don't need to know the whole book. Just the parts that you'll be using. I can show you in no time."

He shoved his right hand through his hair impatiently and Stevie smiled. He was so busy concentrating, his chair could catch fire and he wouldn't notice. Focused. That's the word she'd use to describe Paul. Whatever he happened to be doing at the time held his complete attention. Whether it was installing a new computer program or stroking her body into a frenzied state that only he could ease.

Oh boy.

Stevie shifted a little on the desk, suddenly warm and liquid again. Amazing how he could do that to her without even trying. He'd just blasted her senses with the quickest, sexiest hand job she'd ever known and now here she sat, eager and primed for more.

Was this what her life would be like from now on? Her gaze locked on Paul. Her friend, fixing her computer—and her lover, torturing her body.

"You really need a new computer, Stevie," he muttered as figures flashed across the screen. "I mean, you're driving a tractor and the rest of the world has Ferraris."

Typical. That computer was almost brand-new. But unless it was the biggest and the fastest and the flashiest, it was just secondhand scrap metal to Paul.

She smiled to herself as she listened to Paul's muttering get thicker and faster. This is the Paul she knew. The man she'd missed so much. The man she was comfortable around. Now all she had to do was figure out how to mesh this Paul and the new Paul into her life—without messing everything up.

Too bad she didn't have a book telling her how to do that.

Rosie's café was packed.

Not all that surprising, Stevie thought, considering Rosie Halloran made the best chicken salad in Central California. Although, with the fall weather turning downright nippy, Rosie's homemade soups would be a draw, too.

A small place, Rosie's had all the charm of a welcoming home. Lace curtains hung in the windows, wide oak beams crisscrossed the walls and ceiling, and what looked like candlelit chandeliers hung from the rafters on draping black chains. The twenty or so tables sprinkled around the room were mismatched and no two chairs were alike. Each of them had an upholstered seat in wildly clashing fabric, and together they somehow seemed to meld into a country kitchen sort of feel. Fresh daisies in tiny cobalt blue vases sat on every table, and heavy silverware lay across thick linen napkins.

The view of the ocean was spectacular from any of the wide windows—though the ones up front also boasted a front row seat for the smacking of waves against the rocks. Salt spray dusted the pristine glass, droplets shining like gold dust as the afternoon sun danced across the panes.

Rosie did a huge tourist business, but her mainstays were the locals, who were always crowding the place, looking for a break from cooking themselves. Stevie glanced around at the crowd and smiled warily at Virginia, sitting alone at a table for three. The older woman gave Stevie a regal nod, then returned her attention to her surroundings. Wouldn't want to miss a chance at any gossip.

A knot of tension tightened in the pit of Stevie's stomach. Great. The Terrible Three would be within eavesdropping distance from her and Mama.

Mama.

What could she want? Stevie reached for her glass of iced tea and absently stirred it with a straw. Ice cubes tinkled against the glass and played gentle music to accompany the conversations swirling around her.

She checked her wristwatch. Twelve-fifteen. Mama was late. Good sign? Bad sign? Oh, man. Stevie groaned and told herself to stop looking for trouble. Sometimes a cigar was just a cigar.

Still. Angela Candellano had called just after Paul left the Leaf and Bean and told Stevie when and where to meet her for lunch. Told. Not asked. A command performance—sort of like the Sunday family dinners. Except that these lunches were one-on-one—with no help in sight.

Since Stevie'd moved to Chandler when she was a kid, there had been only two other times when Mama had pulled the *come to lunch* thing with her.

The first time, she'd been fourteen and Mama had taken her to the ice-cream parlor at the corner of Main Street. There she'd given Stevie a stern lecture about

boys. With Joanna way too busy to take care of such minor details herself—not to mention the fact that she was living in Portugal at the time—Mama Candellano had decided that it was up to *her* to deliver "the Talk." She'd tackled Carla first, then taken Stevie on. With no escape, Stevie had stared unblinking at her ice cream while Mama told her everything she'd ever wanted to know . . . and more.

She could still remember the sting of embarrassment—and the sweet, secret pleasure of knowing that Mama had treated her like her own daughter.

The second time she and Mama had done the bondy thing, it was right after Stevie had found Nick with the cheerleader. Pain still clawing at her, she'd sat across this very table from Mama and listened as the other woman had offered to beat her own son senseless on Stevie's behalf.

Hard not to love a woman like that, Stevie told herself.

But the question now was, what could be so important that Mama would call another meeting? Unease unwound through Stevie like a spool of ribbon uncurling into a pile on the floor. Could she have found out about Stevie and Paul?

She was about to find out.

"Ah," Mama said as she hurried to the table and slipped into the chair opposite Stevie. "You're here. I'm late. Tina was sleeping and Beth had to work. Tony came home early, so he's watching the baby." She smiled and Stevie's heart warmed at the wide familiar grin. "This is good. We have a chance to talk a little."

"Is everything all right, Mama?" She studied the other woman, from her graying black hair, tugged into a topknot on the crown of her head, to her dark eyes, snapping and crackling with an energy most thirty-year-olds would envy, to the dress she wore. Mama's favorite, green cotton with small yellow flowers dotting the fabric, it had been around for years and yet somehow always managed to look starched and fresh.

Mama drew her head back and clucked her tongue. "What's not all right? We can't have lunch?" She glanced at the menu, but only for the ceremony of it. She would order what she always ordered and everyone knew it.

It was good to have a constant in your life. One person who wouldn't change on you or do a 180 when you least expected it.

The waitress appeared as if by magic, took out her notepad, and looked at Mama first. "Hi, Mrs. C. What'll it be? Your usual?"

Mama shrugged and smiled. "That's good, Donna. How's your mother?"

"Oh," the blond girl said as she picked up the menus, "she's fine. Dad's a little worried, I think, but Mom's happy."

Intrigued, Stevie looked at the girl she'd known for years. "What's your mom up to?"

Hot red color swept up Donna's cheeks, but the smile tugging at her mouth couldn't be ignored. "She's pregnant again."

"A gift," Mama said solemnly.

"That's what Mom says," Donna told her. "But I think five 'gifts' are enough already. Besides, it's a little

embarrassing." The girl leaned over and lowered her voice. "I mean, everyone at school's gonna know that my parents—"

One of Mama's black eyebrows lifted as she reached over to pat Donna's hand. "What are they going to know? That your parents love each other? Such a crime."

"Yeah, I guess you're right," Donna said, but she still didn't look convinced. "How about you, Stevie? What'll it be?"

"Chicken salad," she said promptly, and ignored Mama's tongue clucking.

"Got it. One chicken salad, one chicken parmigiana." Donna turned so fast, her long ponytail swung out in a wide arc. "Be back in a jif."

"You don't eat enough," Mama was saying. "You're too skinny already."

"I'm fine," Stevie said, thinking about Donna and her parents. Five kids in that family already and now there would be a sixth. And it would be welcomed and loved and cherished just like all of its brothers and sisters. A pang of something sharp and sweet echoed inside Stevie before she let it go. Envy was pointless. Besides, she didn't want a husband, remember?

"So," Mama said, sliding a quick glance to Virginia before lowering her voice. "Nicky's through with football."

A sinking sensation opened up in the pit of Stevie's stomach. She should have known. Should have expected this. Hadn't Mama given her and Nick that "happy couple" look just the other night?

Step carefully, she told herself. Don't say too much.

Don't say the wrong thing. Heck, why not just don't say *anything*? With any luck, Mama would do all the talking and wouldn't even require input from Stevie.

"Is better, I think. A grown man running around playing catch." She shook her head firmly, picked up her napkin, and flicked it open with a snap before settling it across her lap. "Is not a good way to live."

Uh-oh. Mama's accent was getting thicker. Not a good sign. Carla always swore that Mama kept her accent because she enjoyed being "colorful." And the more upset she got, the thicker the accent.

"Nicky is so unhappy," Mama was saying.

Where was that food? Stevie shot a look toward the kitchen door, hoping, unreasonably, that Donna would come striding toward them carrying food it had only taken thirty seconds to prepare. Okay, that wasn't going to happen. She'd have to talk.

"Nick loved football."

Mama's eyes actually *gleamed*. "Nicky loved *you*."

Oh God.

"*Loved* being the operative word there, Mama," she said, keeping her voice low, even. "Past tense. It's been over between us for a long time."

Mama waved one hand at her. "Ah. Is love ever over? No. Is changed. Is different, maybe. But over?" She shook her head again, absolutely refusing to give in on that point.

Swell.

"Mama," Stevie said, trying again, though she knew she had to go at this carefully. Nick was a Candellano. The Golden Boy. The light of Mama's eye. Oh, no pressure. "Mama, you remember why we broke up."

Angela Candellano's lips tightened and thinned into a grim slash across her wide, usually smiling face. "He was an idiot. All men do stupid things, Stevie. They learn, though."

"Yes, but—"

Hallelujah! Donna came bustling back, carrying their lunches. It took a couple of minutes to get everything set up, and when the girl turned and headed off again, Stevie jumped into the conversation before Mama could get her train back on the tracks.

"Nick and I are just friends now."

"Friends is not a bad place to start," Mama said with another shrug.

Yeah, but she'd already started with a different friend. Oh God. What would Angela have to say if she only knew that while she was scheming to get Nick and Stevie back together, *Paul* and Stevie were doing the horizontal limbo?

Oh God again. She knew what would happen. She'd get tossed out of the Candellano circle. Out into the cold. The dark. Alone. Oh God.

Stevie forked a bite of salad into her mouth, but the food clogged on the way down her throat. Not a good thing. Desperate, she grabbed for her iced tea and took a long swallow. Great. With any luck, she'd choke to death on a lettuce leaf and her problems would be over.

Although what a stupid epitaph would *that* be?

"You were always good for Nicky, Stevie," Mama was saying as she pushed her lunch around her plate with the tip of her fork. "With you, he didn't drink so much. Wasn't so sad."

Why would he have been sad? Stevie wondered silently. He was sleeping with half of San Jose.

"Mama—"

"I only ask that you think about it maybe. You could remember how good it used to be. How you used to love him."

She'd spent way too much time trying to forget how she'd felt about Nick. And now that those feelings were truly gone, sometimes Stevie wondered if she'd ever really loved him. Or if he'd been more of a habit for her. She'd always cared for him, so she simply expected to care for him. It was instinctive. Like breathing. Eating. Stevie loves Nick. Simple. Uncomplicated.

But was it really?

Had she honestly been that crazy about Nick? Or was it just that she'd wanted so much to really belong to someone—to his family—that she'd convinced herself she loved him in order to get what she thought she wanted?

Crap.

That was a hell of a thing to realize about yourself.

"Nicky is having a bad time," Mama was saying. "He needs you."

Man. Nobody played the guilt card better than Mama. Stevie stared at the woman across from her and knew, deep in her bones, that she would be willing to do almost *anything* for her. At a time in Stevie's life when she'd felt lost and alone, Mama and her family had taken Stevie into their hearts. Given her a sense of belonging when nothing else had.

And just thinking about losing that was enough to

make Stevie want to cry. Naturally his mother would try to do whatever she could to ensure Nick's happiness. But Stevie simply couldn't give Mama what she wanted. That ship had sailed.

A part of Stevie wondered what it must be like to be loved so fiercely—even as she admitted that she would probably never know.

"No, Mama," Stevie said softly, her gaze locking with Angela's, "Nick doesn't need me. The only one who can save Nick now is *Nick*."

Mama blinked back a sudden terrifying sheen of tears, but then she nodded and straightened up in her chair. "Is true. He has to find his way himself."

Stevie drew a long, deep breath of relief. Then blew it out in exasperation when Mama finished her speech.

"But when he does . . . he'll need someone. That could be you, Stevie."

Frustration bubbled inside her, but she kept quiet, preferring to let the subject end as Mama went into grandmother mode, telling her all about Reese and Tina. Stevie concentrated on her salad, forced herself to chew and swallow, and tried to listen to Mama, all the while sifting through the thoughts racing through her brain.

Mama loved her, true. But the bottom line was, Stevie wasn't a Candellano and Nick was.

She felt as though she were on the outside of life, looking in, and someone had just dropped another pane of glass onto the stack separating her from the party.

Paul stared out his office window at the greenbelt. He had no idea what time it was, but judging by the sun, it

was sliding into late afternoon, and he hadn't done a damn thing all day. There was a stack of messages on his desk and a meeting he was supposed to be attending . . . whenever. But he couldn't seem to think about anything but Stevie.

Big surprise.

He shoved both hands through his hair, then pushed them into his pants pockets. His gaze locked on the window glass, but instead of seeing his own reflection staring back at him, he saw Stevie. The way she'd glared at him that morning. The way she'd snapped and snarled at him. The way she'd melted in his arms when he touched her.

Oh, yeah. This forgetting-all-about-her thing was really moving along.

A knock on the door and then it was opened. Paul didn't even turn around to look. "Go away, Max."

"Love to," his assistant snapped. "Unfortunately, I just missed the last flight to Bermuda."

Surrendering to the inevitable, Paul shifted her a look. He knew damn well Max wouldn't leave until she was good and ready. It'd happen faster if he helped her out a little. "Fine. What is it?"

"Your meeting with the design team is in"—she checked her trim silver watch—"fifteen minutes."

"Great. Buzz me when it's time."

"I live to serve." Sarcasm dripped from every word, but she didn't move. Didn't leave.

"Something else?"

"As a matter of fact, yes. Your mother's here."

"My *mother*?"

What might have been a smile flitted across Max's

stern face and disappeared a second later. "That's what she claims. Since we've never met, I can't be sure, but—"

"Okay, okay." He threw both hands up. "Send her in." Fear rocketed through him. Was somebody dead? Mama had never been to his office. Not in the three years he'd been here. Up until ten seconds ago, he would have been willing to bet she didn't know where his office *was*. So it had to be something big to get her down here.

Mama stepped through the doorway and Paul asked, "Is everything all right?"

She looked at him as if he were crazy. "Everything is fine. I can't come to see you at work?"

"You never have before," he pointed out, but bent his head to plant a kiss on top of her head. The scent of rosewater greeted him and instantly took him back to his childhood.

Max actually smiled before she left the room, closing the door quietly behind her.

"There has to be a first time," Mama said, absently patting his arm as she walked past him to drop her black leather purse on his desktop. "Is a nice place," she said as she did a slow turn. Her gaze swept the room, taking in the view from the window, the deep, cushioned couch and matching chair. She noted the ficus tree in the corner, the television and stereo set on the far wall, and then her gaze stopped on the wall of awards behind his desk.

"Mama—"

"Shh." She waved a hand at him and walked closer, her gaze never leaving the framed citations and

plaques, glinting in the spray of sunlight dancing through the windows. Leaning in closely, she read one, then another, and then another.

Paul shifted uncomfortably as she continued, and tried to dismiss the small tug of pleasure he felt, watching his mother look at the proof of his successes. He wouldn't have gone out of his way to show her these awards, but he could admit, at least to himself, that he was glad she was finally seeing them.

Then she turned to face her son. "What is this?"

"What?"

"This." She pointed at the awards. "When did you get all of these?"

Paul shrugged and stuffed his hands into his pockets again. He'd never been much on tooting his own horn. Hell, the awards wouldn't even be hanging here if it were up to him. Every damn award he won, Max framed and hung on his wall. For a while there, he'd tried to play "hide the award," but eventually he'd given up in the face of Max's determination. "The last couple of years. It's no big deal, Mama."

"Uh-huh." She planted her hands on her hips and glared at him. He wasn't really worried until he noticed the toe of her shoe tapping violently against the carpet. "No big deal it is to be called Man of the Year?"

He tried a laugh. It didn't work. Fire snapped in her eyes. Plus, he'd noticed that her accent was getting thicker. "There's a new one every year."

"Funny. You have one for being a funny man, too?"

"Mama, it's just a couple of awards."

"Your papa would be ashamed."

He felt that blow hard. "Why? What'd I do?"

"You don't tell your *family* what happens in your life?"

"It's not my life. It's just about my work, Mama. Nobody cares."

She was across the room in a flash. He'd forgotten she could move that fast when really pissed. He'd also forgotten just how hard she could hit. The slap on the side of his head reminded him.

"*I* care. Your brothers care. Your sister cares." She crossed herself quickly. "And your papa, God rest his soul, *cares.*"

He rubbed the spot on his head and winced. "If you cared any more, I'd be unconscious."

"Funny again." Shaking her head, she reached up and laid her palm against his cheek. "You would shut your family out of your life?"

"I'm not," he argued, even while a corner of his brain reminded him that he was doing just that as far as it concerned Stevie. But that was different. Right?

"You are my son, Paul. I love you."

He smiled. "I know you're proud of me, Mama," he said softly. "I didn't need to show you the awards to make you tell me."

"Always so quiet," his mother murmured. "Like your papa."

"Mama," he said softly, grateful the storm appeared to be over, "why'd you come down here anyway?"

Angela blew out a breath that ruffled the one stray hair that had drifted free of her topknot. Glancing back at the wall of awards her son had won, she thought about his question for a long minute. She'd come here

to try to get Paul's help in bringing Stevie and Nick together again. Worry for Paul's twin kept her prodding, interfering. She only wanted her children to be happy. Was that so wrong?

But now . . . seeing what Paul had accomplished had given her second thoughts. Oh, she'd always known that Paul was her quiet achiever. He'd never needed the applause that Nick had always craved. Paul could do what needed to be done whether there was an admiring audience there or not. Nick needed people to see him. He needed approval. Paul found his own approval.

And maybe, she thought, looking up into her son's steady gaze, maybe it was time that Nick found his own way. Just as Paul had. As Tony had.

Frustration bubbled inside her, but she fought it back. Sometimes the best thing a mother could do was stay out of things. Nodding to herself, she said, "Nothing. Is nothing. I just wanted to see your work. Your mother can't visit?"

"Anytime," he said, pulling her into his arms for a long, tight hug.

Another brisk knock on the door announced Max. "Sorry, boss," she said, poking her head in the partially open door. "But the meeting—"

"You go," Mama said, pulling away to walk over and pick up her purse. "Go to work. Win more prizes." She wagged a finger at him. "And tell me about them."

He grinned and she saw pride in his eyes. "I promise."

Paul's mother left in a rush of green flower-sprigged cotton. There was something else going on; he was damn sure of it. His mother never did anything without a reason. But he didn't have time to worry about it

now. The scent of rosewater seemed to follow him as he marched off to the meeting.

The heavy cream-colored stationery crinkled as Stevie's fingers tightened on it. Her mother's handwriting—large, flamboyant letters, scrawled in brilliant peacock blue ink—filled the page.

> *Stephanie*
> *My husband the Barrister insisted on my making a will and sending you a copy. As I continue to enjoy excellent health, this is simply a legal precaution. Joanna*

"Touchingly personal, as always." *Stephanie.* Her mother was the only person to ever have called her by her actual name. Her father had christened her Stevie when she was still a baby. But Joanna insisted that "nicknames are common." And maybe, Stevie thought, that's why she liked them so much. Still, the nagging little twinge of pain she always associated with her mother zinged her heart, but it would pass. It always did.

Stevie sighed and unfolded the sheaf of legal papers. Her gaze sliding over the legalspeak, Stevie read it quickly, more out of curiosity than anything else. There were the usual bequests ... usual for her mother, anyway. Ten thousand dollars left to the maid who'd been with her for twenty years—as opposed to the hundred-thousand-dollar gift to the medical facility that handled Joanna's biannual eye lift.

Fifty thousand left to a tarot card institute and five thousand to her chauffeur.

Yep, Stevie thought. That was fairly typical. There were plenty more along the same lines, and Stevie couldn't help wondering what the "barrister husband" had thought of his wife's peculiarities.

Then the word *trust* caught her eye.

Stevie read that passage once.

She straightened up.

And read it again.

Her mouth went dry.

One more time.

Sister?

She had a *sister?*

CHAPTER
ELEVEN

"OH MY GOD."

Stevie jumped to her feet and her chair toppled over, clattering loudly against the plank wood floor. She didn't care. Hardly heard it. Her own heartbeat was pounding so loudly, it deafened her to everything else.

Her hands closed over the edges of the will, crumpling it in a tight two-fisted grip. The room spun wildly around her, like one of those strange special effects shots in a horror movie.

A sister.

"I have a sister." Saying the words aloud felt . . . well, okay, weird. But wonderful. Amazing.

When the world stopped spinning, her gaze dropped to the will again. She focused on the few lines that interested her most:

> *A trust fund has been arranged for my men-*
> *tally deficient daughter, Debbie Harris. This*
> *trust will remain in place for Debbie's lifetime.*

> *On Debbie's death, the trust fund will then be*
> *dissolved and any and all remaining monies*
> *are to be donated to Reach for the Stars, the*
> *organization which has provided Debbie's*
> *home.*

Mentally *deficient*?

Jesus, what an ugly word.

A well of empathy for a sister she'd never known existed rose up inside Stevie. And matching it came a fountain of anger for her mother. "For God's sake, Joanna," she muttered thickly, past the knot of emotion in her throat. "This is low even for you."

But was it, really?

Stevie had plenty of less than pleasant memories from her childhood. Not that she'd ever been physically abused in any way. After all, you had to be noticed to be smacked around. But she'd learned early on that she was little more than an annoyance to her mother. And if Joanna, whose mothering skills ranked right up there with those of a praying mantis, ignored a so-called normal child, what kind of life would Debbie have lived? Images of a locked attic on the top floor of a Gothic manor rose up in Stevie's brain, and it disgusted her to know that she probably wasn't far off.

"But how could she not at least *tell* me about my own sister?" Yet even as she ground out the question, she already knew the answer.

Joanna had dumped her child in a home and then never given her another thought. A chill raced along Stevie's spine. Jesus. She came from that woman. It

was almost enough to make a person run out and get her tubes tied—just to end the line of rotten mothering.

But she was wasting too much time thinking about Joanna. This wasn't about her. Not now, anyway. There'd be time later for phone calls and recriminations. Right now, Stevie had to figure out where her sister was.

She had a sister. Family.

Harris. Her last name was Harris. That made her the daughter of Joanna's—quickly Stevie mentally ticked off her mother's husbands in chronological order. First on the list was Stevie's own dad. But he'd been followed by Miguel Santos, then Rory Hudson and Michael Harris and *someone* Franco and now the unfortunate barrister Henry Whiting-Smythe.

Okay, Michael Harris. Stevie had vague recollections of a short man with a kind smile. But she'd only been ten years old then and had spent most of her mother's marriage to Michael in a boarding school in Sussex, so she didn't recall much else.

It didn't matter so much, though. Because now she knew that Michael Harris had given her the best gift ever. He'd given her *family*.

And in the space of a few mind-numbing seconds she indulged in all sorts of fantasies. She and Debbie, living together. She and Debbie going to lunch, shopping, laughing. Spending Christmases together. Thanksgiving. All of those family-centered holidays would now seem new and more important than ever.

She'd have someone to spend them with.

She'd have someone to love.

Stevie sucked in a huge gulp of air in a futile attempt to calm down the swarms of butterflies dancing around in her stomach. She had to find her. Had to find Debbie. She should call London. Talk to Joanna.

Glancing at the clock on the wall above the television, she noted the time and did a quick calculation to British time. Four A.M. over there. Not a good time to catch Joanna at her best. Stevie grimaced tightly. Besides, she had a few things she wanted to say to dear old Mom and wanted Joanna perfectly awake and coherent when she said them.

So what could she do?

Her skin felt too tight. Nerves hummed and she actually *felt* electricity buzzing in the still air.

This was *big*.

Too important to keep to herself. Heart pounding, blood racing, excitement jangled in her nervous system. She had to tell *somebody*. Racing to the phone, she jumped over Scruffy as she poked her little head out from under the coffee table.

"Sorry, Scruff, gotta call—" Phone receiver in her hand, Stevie stopped and stared down at it as if waiting for it to speak to her.

Call *who*?

Her instincts shouted, Carla! But Carla was on her honeymoon. Fingers sliding across the numbered buttons, Stevie's mind moved at lightning speed. Yes, ordinarily, she would call Carla. But tonight, there was really only one person she wanted to talk to. One person she *needed* to talk to about this.

Chewing at her bottom lip, Stevie punched in the

right numbers, slapped the receiver to her ear, and listened as the phone on the other end of the line rang.

On the fourth ring, Paul answered, and he sounded winded. "Hello?"

His voice was husky and breathless and Stevie instantly imagined him wrapped around some brilliant scientist or astronaut. Her brain painted an exceptionally clear picture of a tall redhead leaning into Paul and biting his ear and running her fingers up and down his naked back and—

"Yo! Stevie!" Paul practically shouted into the phone, and Stevie pulled the receiver from her ear in self-defense.

"You don't have to shout."

"Well, you weren't answering me, so I figured you were dead or something."

"And shouting would bring me back?"

"It was worth a shot."

Stevie smiled. If there was a redhead there, he was ignoring her, which was okay by Stevie.

"Okay, you're zoning out again." Now he sounded patient, interested.

"Sorry. My brain's busy." Understatement of the century.

His tone changed instantly. "Everything all right?"

"No, not all right," she said, glancing down at the will she still held tight in her right fist. "Everything is . . . different."

"What is it?" His voice dropped another notch, hitting that low rumble of sound she associated with darkness and wrinkled sheets and slow hands and fast breathing.

She didn't want to say this over the phone. She wanted to see his face. Watch his reaction. "Can I come over?" she asked.

"Now?"

"Yeah. Is it a problem?" *Please say no.*

"Come. I'll make coffee."

"God, no, don't do that," she laughed, loving the rush of expectation rushing through her at the thought of seeing Paul. At the thought of how her life was about to change. At . . . *everything.* Probably she shouldn't be going to Paul's. Not with how things were between them right now. But she'd worry about consequences later. Right now, she needed her friend. "Get the pot ready. *I'll* make the coffee."

"Deal."

The sound of her tires on the drive pulled Paul to the front porch. Damn it, he shouldn't be so happy to see her. Shouldn't have gotten such a charge out of hearing her voice on the phone or knowing that she wanted to come to him. But he couldn't seem to stop himself. Just thinking about her gave him the kind of rush he used to get after solving some intricate calculation. At meetings, he caught himself drifting into thoughts of Stevie when he should be taking notes. He wasn't getting much sleep anymore, either, since every time he closed his eyes, he saw her. Hell, they couldn't be together for more than five minutes without groping each other like a couple of teenagers in the backseat of Dad's minivan.

Stevie'd slipped deeper and deeper into his life. She

was more than his friend. She was his lover. His . . . *what,* exactly?

Hell, he didn't know.

Paul Candellano, boy genius, didn't have a damn clue what was happening to him.

And at the moment, he didn't give a rat's ass. All that was important was that Stevie was here. Now.

He stepped out onto the porch, feeling the cold, damp wood planks pressing against the soles of his bare feet. A chill ocean-scented wind slapped his face and stung his lungs as he dragged in a deep breath and waited while she climbed out of her car.

In the moonlight, her blond hair shone like silver and her fair skin damn near glowed like porcelain, lit from within. Wearing worn, faded blue jeans and a bright red sweatshirt with the Leaf and Bean logo across the front, she looked impossibly young and fresh and . . . Christ, face it. Breathtaking.

Shoving his hands into the back pockets of his jeans, Paul kept his gaze locked on Stevie as she walked across the yard, carrying a small paper sack. The wind tossed her hair across her eyes and she reached up to pluck it free, shaking her head, swinging her hair into the wind, and laughing like a loon.

He grinned in response. "What's so funny?"

"Not funny!" she called back, and ran the last few steps separating them. She took the stairs two at a time and threw herself at him, wrapping her arms around his neck. "It's amazing, Paul. Absolutely amazing."

Yanking his hands free of his pockets, Paul slid his arms around her waist and squeezed, loving the feel of

her body pressed along his. When she pulled her head back to smile up at him, he stared down at her. In the pale glow of the porch light, her blue eyes sparkled.

"You won't believe it."

"So tell me."

"I have a family."

She said the word like it was holy. And to her, Paul knew it was. All she'd ever wanted, for as long as he could remember, was to belong . . . *somewhere*. Someone like him, who'd grown up surrounded by loud brothers and a sister—fighting for any small square of privacy you could carve out for yourself—could sometimes forget just how precious family was. It was sometimes easy to take for granted something that others would give anything for. Stevie's whole body trembled with excitement—he felt it rippling through her. And he hoped to hell that whatever had happened to make her so damn happy wasn't going to eventually blow up in her face.

"What do you mean, family?"

She kissed him. Quickly, fiercely, hungrily, and every cell in his body woke up and shouted, Hot damn!

"I've got a sister," she said, effectively ending his little sexual side trip. "Her name's Debbie and she lives in Monterey."

Paul just stared at her. Happiness radiated from her like heat from white-hot coals. The desire raging inside him settled into a low simmer that warmed him without the fire.

"How?" he asked. "Who? What?"

Stevie grinned and kissed him again. "All excellent questions. Let's make some coffee."

"Right." He let her go and she rushed past him into the house. Paul followed after, listening to the sound of the heels of her sandals clicking against the wood floor as she walked straight into the kitchen. She knew her way around his place as well as she did her own. Over the years, they'd spent a lot of time together here. Of course, most of the time, she'd been complaining about Nick, but Paul hadn't cared. He'd liked spending time with her even though a part of him had wanted her to look at him as something more than a friend. Though now that she had, there was a whole new world of problems.

"So," she was saying, and he made himself pay attention, "Joanna's new husband, the lawyer, remember? He had her make out her will and then told her to send me a copy."

"And . . ." He stopped at the doorway to the kitchen and leaned one shoulder against the doorjamb. Crossing one bare foot over the other, he folded his arms across his chest and studied her. She moved quickly, as Stevie always did, as though she had this perpetual motion machine locked inside her body, constantly propelling her along. His gaze dropped to the curve of her behind as she moved confidently around the room. She pulled the bag of ground coffee from the refrigerator and set up the coffeepot. Once she'd hit the POWER button, she turned around, braced her hands on the counter's edge, and smiled again.

"*And . . .*" she said, that smile fading a bit as shadows crept into her eyes. "Forgetting about all of Joanna's bizarre bequests, there was a mention in there

about a trust set up for her—and I quote—'mentally deficient daughter, Debbie.'"

"Whoa."

"Yeah." Disgust flashed across her features. She wrapped her arms around her middle and held on as if trying to keep a tight grip on the emotions obviously charging through her.

The coffeepot hissed and sizzled, and steam lifted from the top, like the lonely mist that drifted in off the ocean. Neither of them said anything for a long minute or two.

Paul waited for her to go on. He couldn't imagine what she was feeling, thinking, but he watched as her expression shifted with heartbreaking speed. Her world had been turned upside down. And now she had to figure out what it would do to her life. How much she *wanted* it to do to her life.

"What do you think it means?" she asked, her voice so low, the hissing coffeepot almost completely engulfed it. "Mentally deficient." She pushed away from the counter and paced up and down the length of the kitchen, talking more to herself than to him. "I mean, of course I know what it means, but does it mean a mild disability or does it mean—"

"I don't know, Stevie. It could mean anything."

She looked at him and her eyes were wide and vulnerable and so full of confusion and misery, Paul's heart ached. He straightened up and walked toward her. Dropping both hands on her shoulders, he said, "You'll find out. *We'll* find out."

Sucking in a sharp breath, Stevie slipped out from under Paul's hands, as if she didn't trust herself to stay,

and stepped back. "I have to know if she's okay, Paul. I have to know. I mean, Joanna just brushed Debbie out of her life. What if she's living in a terrible place?" Her hands shoved through her hair. "What if they're mean to her? What if she's wondering where her mom is? What if—"

He walked a wide circle around her, wanting to get closer, but unwilling to trust himself at the moment. Besides, she hadn't come here to be held. She came here to talk. To have him listen to the fears rushing through her.

"Joanna wouldn't put your sister—"

Stevie stopped him with a cold, hard look.

"Okay, fine," he conceded. "Maybe Joanna wouldn't care much where her child was. But what about Debbie's father? What was he like?"

Stevie paced again, keeping her distance from him even as she talked. She was just too . . . vulnerable right now. It would be too easy to lean on him—that's all she really wanted to do at the moment. She wanted him to put his arms around her and tell her it would be all right. "He was . . . nice. I don't remember much about him, really. I was only ten and they weren't married long." A harsh, strained laugh shot from her throat. "No surprise there." She scooped her hair back from her face and squeezed her skull as if trying to hold her brain in place. "I just can't believe this, Paul. I can't believe Joanna never told me. I never knew that Debbie was out there. What if she needed me? What if all her life, she's been wondering why she's so alone? What if—"

"Stevie, stop." He came closer and dropped his

hands onto her shoulders again, and this time she didn't move away. This time she stood still and let the warmth of him slide down deep inside, to where cold, dark shadows curled in the bottom of her heart.

"I have to see her."

"Sure you do."

"She has to come and live with me."

He sighed and shook his head. "Stevie, don't make plans until you've met her. Until you get the answers to some of your questions." He gave her a reassuring smile to take the sting out of his words, but said them anyway. "She has a life. A life you don't know anything about. She might even be happy."

She nodded, inhaled sharply, and blew the air out in a long sigh. "I know, I know. But what if she's not? It's just that I have so *many* questions. And it feels like I'm wasting time—"

"It's already been—" He broke off. "How old is she?"

"I don't know, I tried to figure that out by remembering when Joanna was married to Michael, but it's kind of blurry, dates and stuff, but I was ten when Joanna was pregnant—or when she was married to Michael Harris anyway. So that would make Debbie about seventeen."

"Uh-huh." When she looked up at him, he shifted one hand to smooth her hair back from her face, then scraped the pad of his thumb along her tear-dampened cheekbone. "It's already been seventeen years, Stevie. One more night won't hurt anything."

"Yeah, I guess I know that. It's just . . ." Words dried up, but her eyes didn't. She took a breath again, let it

go, and fought to control the quiver in her bottom lip before she said, "She's my *family*, you know?"

"I know. I know, Stevie." He bent his head to kiss her, tasting tears and hope along with the sweet taste that was pure Stevie. She touched him. In ways he hadn't even completely realized yet. Her tears wept into his heart and ached gently as he pulled her close and tried to give her the comfort she so obviously needed.

"Paul," she said, breaking the kiss and staring up into his deep brown eyes. "I didn't come here for this. I didn't want—"

"I know, Stevie." He rested his forehead against hers. "Damn, I know that."

"I should go."

"Probably," he conceded.

Their gazes locked, her arms came around his neck, and when she leaned into him he felt her surrender. He picked her up, cradling her close to his chest as he turned and left the kitchen. Walking soundlessly across the rug-strewn wood floor, he went to the wide staircase leading to the loft bedroom above. With her head on his shoulder, he carried her up the stairs and walked to his bed.

The massive pine four-poster was wide and soft and inviting.

"Paul, what're we doing?"

"What we do best," he said, and set her on her feet long enough to bend down and toss the quilt to the foot of the bed. When he turned back to her, she was watching him, her eyes filled with too many emotions to read

and understand. She pulled in a breath, then let it shudder from her, and Paul reached for her instinctively.

His arms closed around her and locked her tightly to him. She nestled her head on his chest briefly before pulling just far enough back to look up at him. "This isn't why I came here."

"I know," he said, his gaze drifting over her features, etching the very feel of her into his memory.

"But I don't want to leave."

"I know that, too." And then he kissed her, bending his head to claim her mouth with a tenderness that rocked them both.

Achingly slowly, sweetly, he stripped her out of her clothes, his fingertips brushing across her skin, sending shivers coursing through her body. Paul wanted, *needed,* to comfort, to reassure, to caress her body and ease her wounded heart.

He devoured her, his mouth taking hers in a lazy, determined assault on her senses that threatened to overwhelm him as well. Her hands moved to the hem of his shirt and she yanked it up, breaking his kiss long enough to pull the shirt over his head and toss it to the floor. Then their mouths met again and tasted, explored, each other while hands wrestled clothing, working buttons, zippers, teasing flesh.

In a few hasty seconds, they were naked and Paul tumbled her onto the fresh white sheets. Her hair spilled out around her head looking like a wild, careless halo. She reached for him and he moved into her embrace, loving the feel of her hands sliding down his back, her short, neat fingernails scraping lightly at his skin.

She was all. She was everything. In her arms, nothing

else mattered, and as that thought registered, a part of his brain told him to be worried. But his brain wasn't in charge now, so he disregarded the mental flashing red lights and gave himself over to the wonder of Stevie.

Stevie stared up into his dark eyes and saw flashes of emotion dazzling their depths, and a part of her wondered what he was feeling, thinking. But those questions and others were quickly lost in the sweet rush of sensation spiraling through her. His hands were everywhere, and wherever he touched her, heat erupted. Her body burned for him, her soul hungered for him, and somewhere in the midst of the turmoil racing through her brain, she realized that she was in far deeper than she'd imagined. Than she'd been willing to admit.

There was so much here, in his arms. More than she'd ever known before. There was tenderness and strength and a frenzied burning that exploded between them with the slightest touch.

As he shifted, to trail hot, damp kisses along her chest and to her breasts, she stared up at the beamed ceiling overhead. From above, moonlight poured through the skylight, washing the oak planks until they glowed with a nearly golden sheen. Shadows danced and moved and kept time with her as she writhed beneath him.

His mouth closed over her nipple and she arched into him, demanding more, needing more. He gave it to her, his tongue flicking at the sensitive flesh until she was gasping for air and not caring if it didn't come. All that mattered was Paul. His mouth. His hands. His

breath on her body, dusting across her flesh like a blessing.

And then he moved again, parting her thighs and slipping inside her. She welcomed the hard, solid length of him and felt at peace. He withdrew and entered her again, spiraling her higher, faster. His touch gentle, his kisses madness, he relentlessly drove her as she moved with him, her hips rocking to the rhythm he set.

She watched his face and knew he was feeling everything she did. Knew that this time, things were different. There was a tenderness here that surprised them both and fed the flames already engulfing them.

Stevie wrapped her arms around his neck, threaded her fingers through his hair, and whispered, "I need you, Paul."

He stilled briefly, bent his head to give her a too-brief kiss, and then pushed himself deeper inside her. "Come for me, Stevie. Let me watch you go over."

His hips swiveled and a dazzling sense of expectation lit up her insides. Tingling nerves shot arrows of sensation to every corner of her body. She wrapped her legs around his waist and held him to her, moving her hips, feeding those tingles.

He moved again and she gasped, spreading her legs wider, more open, giving herself to him, freeing her body to take its pleasure. Surrendering to the magic she'd only found with Paul.

"That's it, baby," he whispered. "Let go. Let me have you."

With her surrender came the first small explosion. She felt it cascading through her. Her fingernails dug into his back. Her hips lifted and she rode the wave of

completion with a soft gasp and a shudder that rippled through her and entered him. And only then did she feel him give himself up to the wonder—as he buried his face in the curve of her neck, murmured her name, and joined her in the clouds.

A few minutes later, the phone rang and Paul groaned. Reluctantly rolling off of Stevie, he pulled her up close to his side as he reached for the cordless on the bedside table. She snuggled into him, pillowing her head on his shoulder.

That insistent ringing came again and the shrill tone invaded Paul's brain. He jabbed the TALK button. "What?"

"Hey, that's friendly."

Nick.

Paul tensed and wrapped his free arm even tighter around Stevie's naked shoulders, as if somehow defending her from prying eyes. "What's up?"

"Just something amazing, that's all," Nick was saying, and now that the head rush Paul had experienced in Stevie's embrace was fading, he heard the excitement in his twin's voice. "I had to tell you."

"I'm listening." He glanced down at Stevie, but she wasn't paying attention to him. Good.

"I've got an interview," Nick said, practically crowing into the phone. "CBS. I'd do color commentary for their football coverage."

"That's great," Paul said, and meant it. Though he damn sure wished Nick had found another time to call.

"Yeah, I know. I'd be perfect for this, Paul."

"Uh-huh."

"You sound weird," Nick said, suspicion coming across the phone line clearly. Then a second or two later, he chuckled. "Oops. Called at a bad time, did I?"

"You could say that." Paul winced as Stevie moved her head to look up at him.

"Who is she? Anyone I know?"

Damn it. He couldn't answer. Instead, he dodged and weaved, as if he were running a combat-training course, trying to avoid live weapons fire. "I've really gotta go," Paul said, even as Stevie's eyes narrowed and she pulled as far away as she could get, considering Paul's tight grip on her.

"Right, right," Nick said, but didn't hang up. "Before you do . . . you know where Stevie is? I've been calling her place and she's not home. I gotta tell her about this. She'll be so jazzed."

Stevie elbow-jabbed Paul in the side and he let her go with a whoosh of air shooting from his lungs. Naked and furious, she sat straight up in his bed and glared at him.

Shit.

"No, Nick, I don't know where Stevie is." The lie tripped off his tongue and he watched it slam into Stevie.

"Okay then, sorry to interrupt. I'll just hunt her down myself." Nick laughed again and added, "Give my apologies to your ladyfriend, okay?"

"Right." Paul heard the dial tone humming in his ear and he knew Nick had hung up. But the damage was already done.

His gaze locked with Stevie's. Her eyes darkened

with fury. He almost couldn't blame her. He'd lied to Nick about her while she was lying right there in his arms. And he knew the minute he hung up, this pleasant little afterglow was going to explode in his face.

CHAPTER
TWELVE

NICK PUSHED THE END button on the cordless black phone, but he didn't set it back into its cradle. Instead, he held on to it as if it were still a link to his brother. His family. To someone outside this chrome-and-mirrored nightmare that was his home.

He glanced around the room, his gaze drifting across the black leather couch, the glass coffee table, and the bizarre alienlike artificial flower arrangement the decorator had picked out. There wasn't a rounded corner or a soft spot in the whole place. Even his bed was a futuristic slab surrounded by tall silver spires.

And he hated it all.

Instantly a memory of Paul's comfortable home leaped into his mind. Funny, how he'd never noticed before just how well Paul had done. Before, Nick had always been too busy enjoying his own life to think about his twin's. Now that he didn't have a damn thing to think about, he had more than enough time to realize that Paul was doing way better than he was.

And this god-awful apartment just defined their differences.

Nick couldn't remember ever actually liking the place. But then, until recently, he hadn't spent much time here. And in the last few weeks he'd spent entirely too *much* time here.

Jumping to his feet, he tossed the phone onto the couch as he passed it on the way to the terrace. He stepped through the French doors and instantly squinted into the rising wind.

Three floors below his condo, cars streamed along the street; people strolled and talked and laughed. Restaurants shone brightly in the darkness, lamplight lying like scattered gold pebbles on the ground. The sounds of traffic were muffled three floors up, and the silence was empty.

What he missed was the sound of the ocean. The steady, rhythmic slap of waves on the shore, sounding like a heartbeat. Here in San Jose, the night sounds were so different from Chandler. Here the streets were lit up and people were out on the town half the night. In Chandler, there was . . . quiet. There was time to think—even when you didn't really want to be doing any thinking. And at home there was the ocean. Wild, untamed by docks and jetties and tourists on their Ski-Doos.

But he hadn't lived in Chandler in years. Why was it suddenly sounding so damn great again? Nick bent down, leaned his forearms on the iron railing, and told himself he was really slipping.

"What is wrong with this picture?" he asked himself, his own voice sounding way too loud in the stillness.

"Paul's in bed with some babe, Stevie's out on the town, and Nick Candellano is sitting home alone."

Shaking his head, he straightened up, curled his fingers around the cold, damp iron, and tightened his grip. Stevie. Who was she seeing? Why did he care? It wasn't any of his business what Stevie did. Hell, she'd made it plain enough that they were in the past. He knew it as well as she did. But even after two years without her, he couldn't help wondering what his life would have been like if he hadn't fucked it up so badly.

And he wondered if whoever she was with realized what a lucky bastard he was.

"Okay," Paul said, pushing himself up into a sitting position. "Before you say anything . . ."

She swung her hair back out of her eyes, sat straight up, and folded her arms beneath her breasts. Blue eyes narrowed on him, she said, "This sucks."

He just looked at her. Hell, he'd been expecting a wild fury, judging by the daggers still shining in the depths of her eyes. "Huh?"

"This." She unlocked her arms and held them out wide, encompassing his bedroom and them. "This whole thing just sucks."

"Look, it was a little awkward when Nick called," he said, knowing that didn't nearly cover it. Christ, he'd almost felt like the "other" man, hiding from a jealous husband. Which was ridiculous, since Stevie and Nick hadn't been an item in more than two years.

But old habits died hard. Paul had been looking out for Nick most of his life. And he couldn't just suddenly turn on a dime and say something he knew damn well

would puncture Nick's pride at a time when the man didn't have much pride left. Nick's whole life had tumbled down around him. He didn't have football anymore. He didn't have Stevie. He didn't have focus or a challenge or . . . *anything,* really. So now sure as hell wasn't the time for his twin brother to tell him that he'd been sleeping with Nick's ex-girlfriend.

"It's not just that," she said, scooting to the edge of the mattress and swinging her legs to the floor.

"Then what?" Paul asked. "I mean, if you're pissed off because I didn't tell Nick you were here . . . I thought we agreed not to tell anybody what was going on."

"Oh, we did." She nodded at him as she paced, her bare feet smacking hard against the wood floor. "And that's part of the problem."

His gaze followed her and he told himself to pay attention to what she was saying—not what she looked like. But hey, he was only human. Moonlight streamed in through the skylight over his bed and lit her up like a pale neon sign. Her lightly tanned skin shone with a golden light and her blond hair looked damn near silver.

Arguing with a naked woman took focus, damn it.

He tucked the sheet down over his lap, drew one knee up, and rested his forearm on top of it. "Okay, what's the whole problem, then?"

She stopped dead and stared at him. Planting her hands on her nicely rounded hips, she tilted her head to one side and said, "Jeez, where should I start?"

"Pick a spot."

"Fine. How about this?" She took a step closer to the end of the bed. "I don't want to feel like I'm some

high school kid, hiding her sex life from Mommy and Daddy. I'm too old to play this game, Paul."

"Who's playing?"

"We are. It's nuts." She threw her hands wide and let them slap back down against her thighs. "We keep saying this has got to stop. But it doesn't. It just keeps happening. We're like two sets of hormones on overdrive, for God's sake."

She waved one hand at him and the rumpled bedclothes. "Like tonight. I didn't come over here to get 'lucky.' I came over here to see my friend." She pulled in a deep breath. "I needed to talk to you about something huge in my life."

"We talked."

"Yeah. Then we came up here and—"

He pushed one hand through his hair. Guilt roared up and bit him hard. "Yeah, I know." Hell, he hadn't planned on this, either. But it seemed that whenever he was in the same room as Stevie, nature took over and to hell with everything else.

"Look," she said after a long minute of silence had ticked past. "I know this is going to sound a little less than credible, considering that I'm saying it while naked, but I'm not going to do this with you anymore. I can't. I won't."

"Why the hell not?" Jesus. Did he just say that? Where had that come from? Scrambling off the bed, he faced her on his own two feet and tried not to look below her eyes. It was hard enough to concentrate as it was.

"Are you serious?" she demanded.

"Yeah. . . ." Hell, that sounded real decisive. But it was as good as he could come up with at the moment.

All he knew was, he didn't want this—whatever it was they had—to end.

"There's lots of reasons why not and you know them as well as I do."

"Name one."

"Well . . ." She groped for it, waving both hands in the air, and Paul realized that she'd spent so much time with his very Italian family, she even *thought* with her hands, like the rest of them.

"We don't even have a relationship," she blurted.

"Sure we do," he countered. "We're friends and we have great sex."

"And that's enough? That's good for you?"

He snorted a laugh. "Are you really asking if it's good for me?"

"Very funny." She acknowledged that jab with a nod. "I know it's good *for* you. I'm not an idiot. I want to know if it's good *enough* for you."

"Why do we have to analyze it?" Man, even he couldn't believe what he was saying. He was the *king* of analyzing. Give him any problem at all and he would take it down to the very smallest possible denominator. And now here he stood, arguing to *not* think? What the hell was going on?

He reached for her before his brain exploded, and the instant his hands came down on her arms, he knew damn well he didn't want to stop touching her. Didn't want to stop sleeping with her. Didn't even want to think about never making love to her again.

So there went his whole "Get over Stevie" plan, up in smoke.

"Don't you get it?" she demanded. "I'm risking too much here. I can't do it."

"What's being risked, Stevie? What's so damn sacred?"

"Your family," she countered, and impatiently swiped one stray tear from her cheek. "Your mother."

"What the hell are you talking about?" His insides twisted, and worry crowded the pit of his stomach.

"About the fact that your mother is important to me."

"What's my mother got to do with what's between us?"

"I was with Nick, remember?"

"Not likely to forget."

"When Nick and I broke up, things got weird."

His gaze narrowed on her. "How?"

"Mama was . . . *different.* Less warm. Less—just *less,* okay?" God, it was hard even thinking of those first tenuous weeks after her breakup with Nick. Stevie hadn't felt comfortable going to the Candellano house. She'd stopped attending the Sunday dinners—and hadn't gone back until Carla had dragged her. She couldn't go through that again. Because this time, she knew that another breakup with one of Mama's boys would be the proverbial straw to Mama's camel.

"You're crazy," Paul said with a snort of derision. "You're a part of the family. Always have been."

"Yeah, but it's different. I'm adopted into the family. I can be cut off."

"Are you nuts?"

"Maybe. Sure feels like it sometimes."

"Mama *loves* you."

Stevie sighed and felt a heaviness settle in her heart. "I know. And that's what I can't risk."

Before he could say anything, she tried to shrug out from beneath his hands. "If you touch me, I can't think," she muttered.

"Me, neither," he admitted, then added, "Thinking: bad. Feeling: good."

His thumbs moved on her skin and Stevie felt the flash fire erupt inside her and start to spread. Another second or two and she'd be on her back in the middle of that bed and every notion of leaving would have evaporated.

"Damn it, Paul, cut it out."

Instantly he let her go and the sudden lack of warmth pooled into a hard knot of ice in the pit of her stomach.

He inhaled sharply and blew it out in a rush of frustration that she felt as well as heard. "My family has nothing to do with what's going on between us."

"Don't they?" she retorted. "When Nick called, you turned into a stone statue. If it didn't matter, why didn't you just tell him I was here?"

"He's having a hard time right now and—"

"See?" she whispered. "Not so easy after all, is it?"

"Guess not," he conceded, after a long tension-filled minute. "But we don't have to let them matter here. All I'm saying is, why don't we just enjoy what we have together?"

"And what is that, exactly?"

He shoved one hand through his hair and Stevie saw his frustration mount in the unconscious motion.

"Something more than we had a couple weeks ago."

"And less than we should have."

"There are rules, then?" he asked. "Things we *should* have before going any further? Like two hundred dollars for passing Go?"

"So clever. An answer for everything." Stevie stepped around him and stomped to the other side of the bed. It wasn't easy to stomp when barefoot, but she made the extra effort. Snatching up her clothes, she threw him a furious glance before tugging her jeans on. "I don't know about the astronauts and the scientists you usually sleep with . . . but this simple little coffee shop owner needs to know what's going on in her own life."

"Simple? Yeah," he muttered. "You're as simple as quantum physics."

"That's not the point."

"What is the point?" he demanded, grabbing the sheet off the bed and wrapping it around his waist like a half-assed toga. "What's missing here? Flowers? June weddings? Eternal love?"

"Ha!" She zipped her jeans, grabbed her bra, and put it on. As she pulled her sweatshirt over her head, she kept talking, her voice sounding muffled. "Right. With a mother like mine, I'm looking for eternal love. In my family, eternal lasts as long as it takes to find a decent divorce lawyer."

"Bullshit."

"What?" she asked as her head popped free of the sweatshirt.

"You heard me. That's bullshit, comparing yourself to Joanna. You're nothing like her and you damn well know it."

"Maybe," she admitted, feeling a swell of relief that at least Paul didn't see her as being the same kind of woman as her mother. "But we don't know that for sure. Maybe if I were to get married, it'd turn out to be the same kind of roller-coaster ride Joanna's always on."

"I don't believe it."

"I don't want to, either. But the threat's always there. In the back of my mind."

"You would never have forgotten about Debbie. You don't dismiss people from your life, Stevie."

She pushed her hair back from her face and stared at him. This had all gotten so confusing. It had spiraled into a world of its own, and she didn't know the laws, the rules, here. What she felt for Paul had changed. Shifted. Into something that she couldn't—or wouldn't—admit even to herself. Because once she did, there would be no going back. There would be no friendship. No nothing.

And she didn't think she'd be able to bear that.

This was driving her insane. She didn't have a clue what she wanted from Paul. All she was completely sure of was, she didn't want to do anything that would risk her connection to the Candellano family. Stevie's relationship with Mama had survived her breakup with Nick. But if she and Paul were to try making something together and *it* was to fail, too . . . what were the odds that she'd still be welcome at Mama's house?

Then she'd have lost everything.

No. Couldn't do it. Couldn't risk it.

And really couldn't stand here talking about it anymore. She headed for the staircase.

"I gotta go."

"Just like that?" He sounded amazed. "In the middle of an argument?"

Stevie sighed and paused, one hand on the richly carved banister. Her thumb smoothed over the intricate design work etched into the oak. "The argument's over, Paul. And so are we."

"Over?" he shouted as she started down the stairs, her footsteps thumping loudly. "We're over? When did we start?"

Stevie winced at that direct hit, then stopped at the foot of the stairs and looked back up at him. In the moonlight pouring through the glass in the roof, Paul looked . . . amazing. In that sheet, he could have been some ancient Greek prince or a Roman warrior or any number of women's fantasies. With his hair all mussed and his bare chest still gleaming with sweat from their latest romp in the sheets, he was enough to weaken stronger women than her.

Which probably explained why she spent nearly every moment with him *naked*.

God. Her heart twisted painfully in her chest. There was something here. Something that could have been . . . might have been . . .

Shaking her head, she said softly, "That's the whole point, Paul. We never really started anything. So let's walk away before ending it ends our friendship, too."

The next morning, Stevie spent two hours on the phone. She called everyone from her mother—who didn't answer, big surprise—to her lawyer, to finally, the people who ran the Reach for the Stars foundation. When they wouldn't budge on refusing to give out

information on Debbie Harris, Stevie called her lawyer again and sicced him on them.

It hadn't taken long for them to cave.

And now here she was, sitting in her car outside a small, well-tended Spanish-style house just off Van Buren. The street was tree-lined and quiet. Sunlight dappled the street as it poured through the trees from a clear sky overhead. A soft wind sighed in off the ocean, carrying the scent of the sea along with that of a nearby fireplace.

"Well, you were worried about nothing," she muttered as her gaze slid back to the house where her sister lived. There was nothing Charles Dickensy about the place. Tidy, the front of the house was lined with neatly clipped hedges and two bright yellow chrysanthemum plants that looked ready to take over the world. A U.S. flag flew from the flagmount on the long, deep porch, and potted flowers sat on the edges of the steps leading to the front door.

It looked . . . nice.

Stevie climbed out of the car, swallowed back the ball of nerves crowding the base of her throat, and started for the door. A group of kids on skateboards whizzed past and Stevie stepped quickly, getting out of the line of fire. When one of the boys yelled back, "Watch out for the retards," though, Stevie wanted to chase the little bastard down. But in heels, she'd never catch him.

Heels. She shouldn't have dressed up. She wasn't going to meet the queen. She should have been casual. Friendly.

Retards.

She threw another furious look at the receding kids and bit down hard on her bottom lip to keep from shouting after them. Fine. So Debbie lived in a nice house on a nice street in a nice part of town.

But the *people* weren't nice.

At least, not that little bunch of shits. Nerves battled with outrage in the pit of her stomach, and righteous indignation came out the winner. Her instinct to protect a sister she'd never met was damn near overwhelming. How dare they pick on Debbie? Was there anything in the world meaner than a kid?

Her heart ached for how much Debbie must be hurt by thoughtless people and cruel children. How many times over the years had she cried and had no one to share the pain with? Had Debbie ever longed for family, as Stevie had? Had she ever wished she had someone standing beside her to defend her?

Still grumbling and staring after those kids, Stevie told herself she should have brought Paul with her. He would have been able to catch that damn—no. She turned off that line of thought, fast. Paul wasn't a part of this. Paul was her friend. And that's all. That's it.

If regret stung a little with that admission, it was just something she'd have to learn to live with.

Her fingers curled around her purse's leather strap as she slung it over her left shoulder. She walked carefully up the brick walkway, her confident steps slowing just a little the nearer she got to the house.

What was she doing?

What if Debbie didn't want to see her?

What if she blamed Stevie for never coming before?

Stevie stopped dead. What if she only made things worse by coming here?

The front door flew open before she had time to obsess on any more questions. A middle-aged woman with kind eyes and a wide smile stepped onto the porch. Her graying blond hair was pulled into a ponytail and she wore blue jeans and a red long-sleeved shirt. "Hi," she said, coming down the steps quickly in her Keds. She held out her right hand and said, "I'm Margaret—call me Margie. You must be Stevie. Am I right?"

"Yeah," she said, feeling more foolish than ever for wearing her black skirt and deep lavender silk blouse. But she supposed some lessons from Mother were too deeply ingrained to ever completely get rid of. And the one thing Joanna had *always* insisted on was a good first impression.

Yeah. Joanna. Queen of etiquette. The woman who'd dumped her less than normal child in a home and never looked back. There's one to emulate.

"Hi, it's nice to meet you."

"I'm so glad you could come," the woman said, already drawing Stevie up the steps. "Debbie will be so excited to meet you when she gets home."

Disappointment rang out inside her. "She's not here?"

Margaret must have been able to read the expression on her face. "Don't worry; she won't be much longer. She's at work."

"She works?" Oh God. Had she said something stupid?

"Sure," Margaret, "call me Margie," said, leading

her into a lovely living room. "All of my girls work. They're fiercely independent, which I admire."

"Oh," Stevie assured her, "me, too. Independence gets my vote."

"Good." Margie studied her for a long minute. "I see a resemblance between you and your sister."

Stevie's heartbeat quickened. It was the first time anyone had said that phrase to her. *You and your sister.* Funny how much impact a few little words could make when strung together. "You do?"

"Oh, yeah. In the eyes. Color of your hair."

"Debbie's a blonde?"

"*California* blonde, she'll tell you," Margie said as she sat down in an overstuffed chair and waved Stevie into another one. "Sit. Would you like some coffee? Tea?"

"No, thanks." Stevie was too nervous to sit. All kinds of pent-up energy kept her walking around the room, looking at knickknacks, studying framed, childishly done artwork. "I'm good."

Crossing her legs, Margie steepled her fingers together and said, "I didn't have a chance to warn Debbie about your visit. She'd already left for work when I got the call from your lawyer."

"Warn her?"

Margie smiled and gave her a little shrug. "Probably not the right word, but close enough. You know, the kids get really emotional sometimes, so you might want to prepare for that. Debbie may be almost eighteen, but emotionally, she's much younger."

"It's okay," Stevie said, suddenly feeling the need to defend her sister again. This time to the woman who

knew Debbie far better than Stevie did. "I'm pretty emotional myself."

The woman gave her an understanding smile as she said, "Good. Then how about I give you a tour of the house while we wait?"

"I'd like that."

It was a lot bigger than it looked from the street. The house was built on a shotgun pattern. Straight back with rooms jutting out from a main hall every few feet. It was old, but in excellent condition, and every square inch had been lovingly decorated.

There were four girls living here with their house-mother. Two of them were home, and the other girl, like Debbie, was off at her job.

But meeting Marybeth and Stacy in the kitchen helped Stevie relax and prepare for meeting her sister.

"I'm making lunch," Marybeth announced as she stirred a pot of macaroni and cheese.

"Smells good," Stevie told her.

"And I'm gonna eat it," Stacy said from her spot at the kitchen table. The youngest of the four girls, Stacy couldn't have been more than fifteen. Her wide brown eyes sparkled and she leaned into Margie for a hug as the woman passed behind her chair.

Stevie felt that lump in her throat again. They were a unit, the people here. Margie and the girls had created a home. And made themselves into a family. She couldn't help wondering if Debbie would have room for her in her life. Here . . . there was love and laughter and, once again, Stevie felt as though she was on the outside, looking in.

The front door slammed open and echoed down the

long hallway, followed by a girl shouting, "Margie, I'm ho-ome!" in a singsong note children had probably been using for centuries.

Stevie's glance shot to Margie. The woman smiled and nodded and Stevie turned back to look at the kitchen door. Nerves jumped. Her mouth went dry. She could actually *hear* her own heartbeat thundering in her ears.

Then she was there.

In the doorway.

No taller than Stevie, Debbie stopped dead on the threshold, to stare openly at the stranger in her kitchen. Debbie's blond hair was pulled back from her wide face into a ponytail. Her big, heavy-lidded blue eyes were filled with curiosity and her mouth curved in a hesitant smile. She wore a blue T-shirt with the aquarium's logo across the front and a name tag that read: DEBBIE.

"Hi," Stevie said.

"Hi," the girl answered, her grin spreading. "Who are you?"

"My name's Stevie."

Debbie lifted one hand to her mouth, laughed, and shook her head. "That's a boy name."

Laughing herself, Stevie said, "Yeah, I guess it is. My real name is Stephanie, but I don't like it much."

"Oh. Like my name is Deb-o-rah, but I don't like that, either?"

"Yeah. Like that."

"Debbie," Margie said as the two other girls in the room turned to watch. "Stevie came to see you to give you a surprise."

"Really?" Debbie practically hummed in expectation. "I like surprises."

"I'm glad," Stevie said. "Because the surprise is, I'm your sister."

A brief spark of disbelief lit Debbie's eyes, then was gone again in a heartbeat. And in its place was pure, unmistakable *joy*. As simply as that, she'd accepted Stevie's presence as she would a beautifully wrapped Christmas present. "My sister?"

"Uh-huh," Stevie said, because she couldn't talk around the knot in her throat that simply refused to dissolve.

"But I didn't used to have a sister."

"I know," Stevie managed to say. "I didn't find out about you until yesterday. I came as soon as I could."

Debbie ran up, threw her arms around Stevie's waist, and hugged her tight. Stevie held on to the younger, stronger girl and swayed with the surge of emotion pouring from Debbie straight into her heart.

"I always wanted a sister," Debbie said, her voice coming muffled against Stevie's chest.

"Me, too, sweetie," Stevie assured her, and ran one hand down the soft blond hair, so much like her own. "Oh, me, too."

CHAPTER THIRTEEN

AFTER A SHARED LUNCH of macaroni and cheese, Debbie took Stevie to her room.

"I made this," the girl announced, picking up a clumsily painted vase.

"It's very pretty."

"Yes." Debbie nodded and carefully set her ceramic vase down on top of a small dresser. "I'm good at painting, Margie says, so maybe I'm gonna be a artist."

"Why not?" Stevie watched the girl move around the room, pausing every now and then to hold up a treasure to be admired. Everything was going so much better than she'd dared to hope. Debbie was wonderful. Trusting, sweet, and yet fiercely independent. They seemed to get along so well already—as if Fate had planned for them to meet like this all along. Her heart singing, Stevie mentally started making plans.

The house was great, the people who lived here were very nice, but Debbie was her *sister.* And families belonged together. She could almost see the two of

them, working side by side at the Leaf and Bean. She would introduce Debbie to Chandler, and everyone in town would love her. There wouldn't be any name-calling there. Stevie would make sure of it.

A Down's syndrome child had enough to put up with without having to deal with other people's ignorance. In Chandler, Debbie would be protected. Loved.

"And we're gonna go to her concert next time they come here," Debbie was saying, and Stevie listened up.

"A concert?"

"Uh-huh." Debbie stared up at a poster of Britney Spears and Stevie almost chuckled. Down's syndrome or not, some teenage things remained a constant.

"You like Britney, huh?"

"Yeah," Debbie said, throwing her a fast smile. "She's pretty and she sings really nice. I can almost dance like her, too. Me an' Marybeth practice sometimes and Margie says we're really good."

"I bet you are," Stevie said, and sat down on the edge of Debbie's single bed. The room looked like it could have belonged to *any* teenage girl. It was a little small, but the fact that it was crowded with *stuff* probably added to the illusion. Clothes were strewn on the floor, posters of not only Britney but also 'N Sync and Han Solo decorated the walls. Stuffed animals crowded bookshelves already overflowing with papers and books of every size. There was a small stereo sitting atop an oak chest of drawers, with a scattered pile of CDs lying beside it and a closet that looked packed to the rafters.

For the first time since stepping into the house, Stevie felt a moment's worry. Debbie was settled. Happy.

She'd led a full life that Stevie knew nothing about. Maybe she wouldn't want to move to Chandler. But the moment that thought hit, Stevie discounted it. Of course she would. She'd want to be with her family, too. Hadn't the girl been as excited as Stevie to discover a sister? Debbie could be just as settled, just as happy, in Chandler. With her sister.

Besides, realizing how much time they'd missed together only made Stevie more determined than ever to not miss any more.

"Do we have more sisters?"

Stevie looked at Debbie as the girl took a seat beside her. "Nope. It's just us." Well, as far as she knew. But up until a day ago, she would have sworn she was an only child. So until Stevie had a chance to talk to Mommy Dearest, she wouldn't put money on anything.

"That's okay. I like us."

"Me, too," Stevie said, chuckling.

"I hafta do chores soon," Debbie said. "Then we get to go to the movies tonight."

"That sounds like fun."

"We go all the time," the girl said, grinning. "Margie really likes movies and we do, too. So we go and then we get pizza and that's really good, too. And sometimes when we walk home, we sing songs."

Pleasure shone in Debbie's eyes and Stevie tried very hard to be pleased for her. Clearly, her little sister was more than well taken care of. She was happy. She was loved. She didn't *need* Stevie.

And that stung.

Heck, *no one* needed her. She'd hoped—well, not that Debbie had been suffering in any way, but that

somehow she would need Stevie as much as Stevie needed to be needed.

Oh, good God, she was beginning to confuse *herself*.

But the point was, Debbie hadn't needed her because the girl hadn't even been aware of Stevie's existence until an hour ago. Now that she did know, things would be different.

"You can come if you wanna." Debbie's offer came hesitantly, as if she half-expected to be turned down.

But with the Leaf and Bean officially closed for the day, Stevie didn't have to rush back. And truthfully, she wouldn't have rushed back to her empty apartment anyway. Not while she had the chance to discover even more about this sister . . . this piece of her heart she'd only just found.

"I'd love to."

Paul wandered through his house and told himself he should have gone to work. At least then, even if he didn't accomplish something, he would have felt as though he'd tried. As it was, he'd taken the day off only to move through his own house like some sort of displaced spirit, looking for a new place to haunt.

But with his brain racing at top speed, he couldn't sit still. Ever since the night before, when Stevie had stormed out of his house filled with righteous indignation, he'd been thinking. And thinking. And thinking.

He hadn't come up with a damn thing.

Plopping down at his desk in the corner of the main room, Paul lifted the lid of his laptop and waited what felt like an eternity for the screen to disengage from standby.

Bracing one elbow on the desktop, he scrubbed his face, scratching at the whiskers he hadn't bothered to shave that morning. His eyes felt gritty, like they'd been rolling in sand. "No sleep'll do that to you," he grumbled as the screen flickered to life in starts and sputters.

When it cleared, he stared at the document he'd been looking at off and on all night. He'd made it a couple of weeks ago . . . back when he could still think straight.

The List.

Very scientific.

Very logical.

Everything spelled out in black and white.

Scowling at the screen, Paul stared at the spreadsheet he'd prepared on the pros and cons of loving Stevie. Each side boasted a few points. He read them again now, though he didn't need to. After these last couple of weeks, he knew them by heart in no particular order.

"'She might still be half in love with Nick.'" He winced. "Okay, that's a big one—however unlikely." Remembering her in his arms, her eagerness, her touch, her warmth, he couldn't bring himself to believe she was still in love with his brother—even partly. But he had to consider everything if he was going to do this logically.

"'Stubborn.'" He snorted a laugh. "Now there's an understatement." Continuing, he read off, 'Always trying to save everyone and everything.'" There were a couple more, but nothing really important.

He ticked off the points from the Pro side just as

quickly. " 'Stubborn.' " He liked a woman with a mind of her own who wasn't afraid to take a stand. " 'Always trying to save everyone and everything.' " Who wouldn't admire a woman so dedicated to rounding up the hurt ones, the lost ones? And then there was the last point. The one reason that outweighed all the rest on either side.

Paul leaned back in his chair and pushed one hand through his hair, scooping it back from his face as he stared at that one last point.

" 'Pro: She's Stevie.' "

And that pretty much said it all.

"Well, that was a waste of time," he muttered. "Like it or not, this problem is *not* going to be solved logically, or scientifically." Disgusted with himself, he slammed the lid down again, putting the computer back on standby. Standing up, he stalked across the room, pulling his white T-shirt off and shoving it into a back pocket of his jeans as he went. He hit the back door, threw it open, and stomped outside. Taking the back porch steps two at a time, he stepped down barefoot onto the sun-warmed grass and kept walking.

The stand of trees behind his house rustled in the ocean wind that dusted through his hair and eased the heat of the afternoon sun pouring down against his back. Paul glanced around, barely noticing the familiar landscape, then moved toward the chopping block at the back of the house.

Thoughts of Stevie stayed with him, and the tension coiled in the pit of his stomach seemed to snap, sending vicious jabs of regret and anger and confusion to every cell in his body. Gritting his teeth, he walked

straight to the gnarled old stump of a lightning-struck tree, his gaze locked on the ax jutting up from it. He grabbed the smooth wooden stock of the ax and worked it up and down until the sharp blade came free.

Paul tested the blade with his thumb and nodded to himself as he picked up a small log and set it on end atop the stump. He liked coming out here. Chopping wood gave him a chance to work off whatever frustrations were chasing him and, at the same time, build a store of firewood for winter.

Swinging the ax high, he brought it down with a crash, and the sharp blade sliced that log neatly in two. He propped one of the halves on end again and split it into quarters. Then he did the same, over and over again. His shoulders ached, his arms stung, every time the hum of contact sang along the ax blade and up the stock. Sweat ran down his back and chest, streamed into his eyes, but he kept going, slamming that ax into the logs.

His mind blanked and that's just what he'd been aiming for. The steady thunk of the ax blade digging into wood sounded out like a bass drum in the afternoon quiet.

Stevie.

Risking her. Risking their friendship.

Getting over her.

"Ha!" He picked up another log. "Not happening," he told himself. Then he tried to push her out of his mind again, but she kept creeping back in. Her eyes. Her smile. Her sighs. She was there. Everywhere. Surrounding him and there was no escape.

And truthfully, he didn't want one.

Somewhere along the line, things had changed. He wasn't so much interested in getting *over* her as he was in getting her *under* him.

So if he wasn't trying to forget about her, what was he aiming for? He wanted her in his life. But did that mean love? And if it did, what if she wasn't interested? That'd be a just punishment, wouldn't it? He finally decides that yes, he loves her, only to be told, *No thanks*? Yeah, that'd be perfect.

He slammed the blade down hard into the stump, grabbed his T-shirt out of his back pocket, and wiped the sweat from his face. Tossing the T-shirt aside, he grabbed the ax handle again.

"Hey."

Turning, Paul watched as Nick crossed the grass toward him. Guilt reared up inside him, but he pushed it down. What the hell did he have to feel guilty about? That his life *wasn't* in the toilet? Well, Nick's wasn't exactly *in* it, anyway. Circling the rim, maybe. "Hi."

Nick pushed his Oakleys up until they were sitting at the top of his head. He glanced at the growing pile of kindling and fire-ready logs, then back at his brother. "Working something out, are you?"

"Thought I was," Paul said, shoving his hands into the back pockets of his jeans. Nothing had been solved. He hadn't come up with a solution to the circus his life had become. All he'd gotten for his trouble were blisters on his palms. "Turns out, all I was doing was making kindling."

"At least you accomplished something," Nick said, and started walking around the yard. Kicking stray

pieces of wood back toward the pile, he shook his head. "You know, I don't have a damn thing to do?"

"Find something," Paul said, and tried to keep the impatience out of his voice. Hell, it wasn't Nick's fault that Paul felt like tearing something in two.

"I don't know what to do."

"You've got that interview."

"That's not a sure thing," Nick argued. "That's the problem."

"Yeah, that's a real problem, all right."

"What's that supposed to mean?"

Paul sighed. "It *means,* there are tons of people who'd kill to have your problems. Poor you. Too much money and nothing to occupy your time."

"Thanks for your support."

Shaking his head, Paul said, "No way are you pulling that on me. I've backed you. Always. Now it's time for you to do it yourself."

"Easy enough for you to say. You haven't lost anything that's important to you."

Hadn't he? With the way Stevie had rushed out of his house the night before, Paul had the distinct feeling he'd lost something there was no replacing.

"Damn it, Nick, there's more to life than football." He felt bad for his twin. Couldn't be easy going from being a star to a nobody. Plus there was the fact that Paul's own career was climbing even as Nick's was fading. That had to be hard for Nick to swallow, too. He'd always been on top. Coming in second was not something he was used to.

"I know that." He scowled, braced his feet wide apart, and folded his arms across his chest. "But without

football, I've got nothing. You don't know what it's like, Paul. Applause, women, endorsement offers." He sliced his hand through the air. "Then nothing. It's all gone."

"You knew it would end at some point."

"Yeah, but it was going to end when *I* said so. Not some damn doctor."

"It happened. Deal with it. Get over it."

Nick just stared at him. "That easy, huh? Just 'Get over it'? What the hell do you know? You're the man on the way up, right? Everything coming up roses? While I'm on a downhill slide into a pile of shit."

"Am I supposed to apologize for working hard?"

"No, but you could try to sound a little less sanctimonious, Saint Paul."

"You're an idiot."

Nick snorted. "Wow, you're a counselor, too. Thanks for the insight."

"Christ, you're a pain in the ass."

Nick inhaled sharply, scrubbed his hands over his face, and grumbled, "I think Stevie's seeing somebody."

Paul snapped a look at his brother and hoped to hell Nick couldn't see the neon sign on his forehead that was flashing out IT'S ME. Judging by what Nick said next, though, he hadn't noticed anything.

"Can you find out who it is?"

"Why the hell would I do that?"

"For me," he said, as if that was all the reason needed. "'Cause we're brothers. 'Cause my life is crap."

"So I should spy on your ex-girlfriend for you?" Paul shook his head. "No way."

"All I'm asking you to do is talk to her. Find out what you can."

Paul's hands fisted at his sides. Anger and resentment bubbled inside him as he stared at his twin. So much for feeling bad for him. For feeling guilty for doing well while he was in a downward spiral. Damn it, Nick's sense of entitlement had Paul ready to punch him. "Since when do you give a good damn about Stevie?" he managed to ask through clenched teeth.

Nick shrugged, blissfully unaware of his brother's boiling anger. "She was always so good for me," he said fondly, staring off into space as if looking at a private home movie playing in his brain. "When she was with me, things clicked. My life clicked."

Unbelievable. Paul just glared at him. Nick looked backward and saw only what he wanted to see. Only the touchdowns, not the fumbles. So typical. "You're fucking amazing."

Snapped out of his pleasant memories, Nick looked at him. "What?"

" '*She was good for me,*' " Paul recited, spitting the words out. " '*My life clicked.*' It's always about you, isn't it, Nick?"

His twin matched his glare. "What the hell's with you?"

Paul reached up and shoved both hands through his hair, scraping his fingers across his skull almost hard enough to draw blood. All of his life, he'd stood up for Nick. He'd joined the crowds cheering for him from the sidelines. He'd been on his side. Twins. Against the world. Blood thicker than water. He knew his twin's good points and bad points and loved him anyway.

But right now—at this moment—Paul wanted to plow his fist into Nick's face. "It's you, man. Jesus. All you can think about is what Stevie can do for *you*. But when were you any good for *her*?"

"Huh?" Surprised, Nick looked at him.

"Christ, you didn't even consider that, did you?" Paul took a step toward his brother, then stopped. If he was within arm's reach, he just might give in to his urges and slug him. And what would be the point? He *still* wouldn't get it. "You cheated on her. You made her cry. You broke her heart."

"We broke up," Nick said. "Shit happens."

"You were screwing every cheerleader within reach."

Nick shifted position, clearly uneasy with having his sins laid out in front of him. "Stevie and I weren't in an exclusive relationship."

"It was exclusive as far as she was concerned," Paul told him. "And when you broke her heart, it was *my* shoulder she cried on." God, it had killed him. Wanting to hold her and kiss her tears away and being unable to say or do anything about his own feelings because she'd been too damn unhappy. "Why would I want to help you do that to her again?"

Nick stiffened, finally picking up on the strain between them. He took a step closer and almost looked ready to throw a few punches himself. "Who're you? Her nanny?"

"I'm her *friend*," Paul said, and realized that no matter what else he might be to Stevie, he would always be her friend. Despite her worries. Despite what was going on at the moment, nothing would ever change that. He would always care about her. "And I'm damn

well not going to set up my *friend* to get shafted again. Not even for you, Nick."

Reaching up, Nick pushed his Oakleys down until they shaded his eyes again, keeping Paul from reading the emotions in his twin's face. "You won't help me?"

"No."

"Guess I know where I stand, then." Nick stalked toward the corner of the house, headed for the front.

Paul watched him go, then reached for the ax handle again. He felt the need to smash more wood into splinters. "At least *one* of us knows."

After pizza, and an action movie that had left Stevie damn near deaf, she and Debbie and the others walked back to the house. Streetlights puddled the sidewalks with golden light, and their little group moved from one to the other of them as if following the yellow brick road.

While the other girls and Margie walked a few feet ahead of them, enthusiastically murdering one of Britney's latest hits, Stevie slowed her pace. As she'd hoped, Debbie slowed down, too, until the two of them were really walking alone.

"Did you like the pizza?"

"It was terrific," Stevie said, smiling.

"And the movie, too?"

"Uh-huh." But truthfully, she wouldn't have been able to tell anyone what the movie had been about. She'd spent most of her time in the darkened theater watching her sister's shifting expressions. Everything Debbie felt was written on her face. She held nothing back, laughing or crying as she felt it. Smiling, Stevie

remembered the girl's shriek of surprise during the movie and how she'd grabbed at her big sister's arm.

In that one instant, Stevie had been swamped by love for the girl she hadn't even known existed until the day before. There was a ... *connection* between them. Shared blood, if not shared lives. Her heart ached for all the time lost. All the years when they'd been apart, neither of them knowing about the other. Each of them assuming they were alone.

But no more.

Taking a deep breath, Stevie said, "Debbie, I was thinking—"

"'Bout what?"

"We're sisters and—"

"I know." She laughed and shook her head slowly.

"Don't you think sisters should live together? Be a family?"

Debbie stopped dead and looked at her. A huge delighted grin spread across her wide face. "You wanna come and live with me?" She reached out and briefly squeezed Stevie hard. "You could work at the aquarium with me and stay in my room and we could—"

"No," Stevie said, interrupting the excited flow of words before Debbie had her packed and moved. Though she'd gotten it wrong, the girl's reaction sent pleasure darting through Stevie. At least she knew Debbie *liked* her. "No, honey, I meant I'd like you to come and live with me. In Chandler."

Debbie stared at her. In the lamplight, her eyes glistened and she looked suddenly worried. Unsure. "But I have a house."

"I know, but—"

"And I have a room and you saw it." Debbie's chest heaved with the frantic pounding of her heart and the quick, gasping gulps of air whooshing in and out of her lungs. "You said you liked it," Debbie accused.

"I do, honey, it's just that—"

Debbie rubbed her mouth and chewed at one finger. "And I have friends and a job and—"

Her voice cracked as it hit a high note she couldn't quite contain. She reached up and jerked at her ponytail, tugging at it nervously, as if she needed to be doing *something,* but she couldn't quite figure out what.

"I don't wanna leave," she said, her voice hiccuping out of her and trembling as it hit the air. "I like it *here.* You can't make me go," she said. "You can't. 'Cause I can't. I can't go and leave Margie. . . ."

Worried, Stevie stepped in closer and wanted to cry when Debbie moved back—away from her. Pain twisted Stevie's heart and she wondered where this had all gone so wrong. She hadn't meant to upset her sister. She'd only wanted to help. To bring Debbie home. To give them both the family they'd never known.

"Ah, honey, don't be upset—"

"I don't wanna move. I like it here. I *know* it here." She shot an anxious look up ahead to where Margie and the other girls had stopped beneath a streetlight. The three of them were watching and Stevie felt like she'd kicked a puppy in front of the ASPCA.

"This is my place. I live here. And . . . and . . ."

"It's okay, Debbie. Honest. It's okay," Stevie said quickly, letting the words flow, hoping they'd get through. Hoping she could somehow fix what she'd unthinkingly broken.

"I don't have to—"

"No, honey. You don't have to do anything you don't want to do. Honest."

Debbie still looked worried, but at least she wasn't breathing quite as hard and the frantic gleam in her eyes had dimmed a little. "Okay, 'cause I don't wanna go. I wanna stay here."

Then she hurriedly walked ahead to join Margie and her friends, keeping a safe distance between her and Stevie.

Stevie had to fight back her own tears, now. The sting of them had her blinking. Her sister didn't want her. Debbie had a life that didn't include Stevie.

All of the dreams Stevie'd been entertaining since yesterday splintered into tiny jagged shards that tore at her heart.

CHAPTER FOURTEEN

STEVIE DROVE DOWN THE short alleyway and parked behind the Leaf and Bean. Shadows crouched at the corners of the building, and when she flicked off her headlights the darkness reached out for her. She shut the engine off and the silence surrounded her, pulsing as if it had a life of its own.

"Better get used to it," she whispered, and her own voice was quickly swallowed up by the quiet. Heart aching, she leaned forward and rested her forehead on the steering wheel. Her hands fisted around the cold black wheel and she squeezed it tightly. With her eyes closed, she could still see Debbie's shocked, scared expression.

"You went too fast," she said on a groan. "Too far, too fast. You pushed her and she ran." Now she'd be lucky if her younger sister wanted to see her again at all.

Oh, Margie had assured her that Debbie would be fine. That she'd settle down and by Stevie's next visit would have forgotten all about how upset she'd been.

But Stevie couldn't help thinking that she'd blown it. She'd had a chance for a family of her own, and in her rush to claim it, she'd ruined her own chances.

She should have given the girl time. Time to get to know her. Time to get used to having a sister. Time to visit Chandler, see the shop, see what kind of life they could have together.

In short, she thought, disgusted with herself, she should have listened to Paul. Damn it. He'd warned her not to make plans so quickly. Encouraged her to go slowly. But how could she have been expected to be patient when she'd finally been handed the one thing she'd hungered for her whole life?

A family of her own.

"Stevie?"

"Jesus!" She jumped a foot off the car seat, swung her head to the left, and saw Nick's face nearly pressed against the rolled-up window. As her heart slid down from her throat and back into her chest, Stevie narrowed her gaze on him and counted to ten. *Then* she'd kill him.

Flinging open the car door, she watched with satisfaction as he back-stepped to avoid getting hit. Clutching her purse, she climbed out, keeping her gaze locked on him. "What the hell are you trying to do? Scare me to death?"

"Didn't mean to scare you," he said, giving her that million-watt smile that used to turn her knees to liquid.

"Well, you did," she said tightly, and headed for the back door of the shop. Walking a wide circle around him, she sighed to herself as he fell into step behind her. Oh, yeah. The fates had a great sense of humor.

After the day she'd had, to now be faced with the mistakes of her past was just too much.

"Look, Stevie," he said, and leaned against the wall as she jammed the key into the dead bolt. "I'm sorry I scared you, but I had to wait for you. Had to tell you my great news."

She turned the lock but didn't open the door. The fastest way to get rid of him would be to let him say what he'd come here to say and be done with it. In the yellow glow of the fog lamps, Nick looked excited and pleased with himself.

"Okay," she said, emotional fatigue coloring her words, "what is it?"

He reached out to push her hair behind her ears and only let his hand drop when she pulled back from his touch. Nick frowned slightly but didn't let her recoil spoil his moment. "I've got an interview. With CBS Sports. I'd be doing color commentary for their football coverage."

There was a gleam in his eyes that Stevie remembered. And even emotionally drained as she was, she realized that a few years ago, she would have been delighted for him. She would have praised him and offered support. She would have wrapped her arms around him and taken him off to bed to celebrate.

Now?

There was nothing.

Strange, she thought. How so much could change in a person's life in so little time.

"That's great, Nick," she said, and turned the doorknob, ready to be alone with her misery. "Good luck."

He reached for her, grabbing her forearm just tight

enough to keep her from slipping away from him. "Hey, wait; that's not all," he said, and she could tell from his expression that her reaction had disappointed him. Well, it was a good day for disappointment, wasn't it?

"Nick," she said, "I'm tired. I've had a long, miserable day and I want to go to bed."

"Yeah, but I'm not finished," he said quickly.

If she'd had the strength, she might have laughed. How like Nick. *He* wasn't finished; therefore, no one else was, either. He hadn't noticed the weary sadness in her eyes. He hadn't picked up on the fact that she'd been crying all the way home—and the light in the alley was bright enough to show off her smudged mascara, she knew. He hadn't heard the distress in her voice or noticed the slump in her shoulders.

Had he ever? She wondered now. Had Nick ever once looked beyond his own needs, his own feelings, to be concerned with hers? Nope. Not even when it came to sex. Man. What did that say about her? That she'd been so hungry for love that she'd been willing to take whatever cast-off affection Nick had offered?

Good God.

She didn't know which of them she disliked most at the moment. Herself? Or Nick?

"The interview's in San Francisco," he was saying, talking faster now, as if he finally understood that she'd already stopped listening. "I was thinking that you and I could go. Stay at that B and B on the Bay you liked so much?" He ran his fingertips up her forearm until she jerked back from him like she'd been burned.

"For God's sake, Nick," she blurted, far too tired

and unhappy to care how she sounded. "What does it take to get through to you? We are *not* together. I'm not interested in going to San Francisco with you. Going *anywhere* with you."

"Stevie. . . ." He winced at her tone but apparently couldn't bring himself to believe she was serious. "We were good together once, and—"

"No, Nick," she said quietly, anger gone now, replaced by a deep well of loneliness that threatened to swallow her whole. "We weren't good *for* each other. And it's been over for a long time."

"It doesn't have to be."

"Yeah, it does."

He stared at her and she could see the disbelief shining in his dark eyes. And a part of her realized just how hard it was for Nick to accept that there was something—or someone—he couldn't have. She just didn't have the patience to listen to him anymore.

"There's somebody else, isn't there?" he snapped.

"What?" Stevie reached up and rubbed at a spot between her eyes. Pain pounded there, in time with her heartbeat, and Nick wasn't helping.

"You've got some new guy." He pushed away from the wall and threw his hands wide. "I knew it. I knew that's what was going on. That's why you don't want to see me."

Again anger fluttered to life in the pit of her stomach. Honestly. Nick never had been able to just let something lie.

"Who is he?"

She shook her head. "Go away."

"Tell me, damn it."

She considered it for a second. And for that one brief moment in time, she wondered just what his reaction would be if she told him that she'd been sleeping with his twin. But in the next instant, Stevie realized that that would only keep her standing here in the dark listening to Nick, and open a can of worms she wanted kept sealed shut. Besides, all she really wanted now was to go lay her head down on a pillow.

"This is none of your business, Nick."

"The hell it's not."

Apparently, it was going to take an anvil on the head to get through to him. And she was in just the right mood to do it. "We're *over*. Have been for two years. Who I'm seeing or not seeing is none of your business. Do you get it yet? Do you understand that I don't want to see you anymore?"

Nick snorted a choked-off laugh and took a step back, away from her, shaking his head as he went. "I knew it. Some guy outflanked me."

"Jesus, will you just go home?"

"I told Paul," he said. "I told him just today that there was some other guy—"

She stopped, one foot into the kitchen of the shop. Though a part of her was urging her inside, to ignore what Nick had just said, she couldn't do it. Call her a masochist, but she had to know. Looking back at him, Stevie asked, "And what did Paul say?"

"Said he didn't know anything and if he did, he wouldn't tell me."

"Well, that's perfect." Of course, what had she expected? That Paul would tell his twin that it was *him* she'd been seeing? That they'd been hopping in and

out of each other's beds? That Nick was out and Paul was in? No. But somehow, no matter how irrational it sounded, she wished he had. Even though she didn't want Mama to find out, she wished that Paul had cared enough to tell his twin the truth. Didn't make any sense at all, she thought. But then, what had, lately?

Stevie nodded slowly, gave Nick a grim smile, and walked into her shop. "Thanks a bunch for stopping by."

Then she closed the door and locked it.

Paul scowled at the knock on his front door. As he shot a quick glance at the clock on the far wall, his frown deepened. Eleven o'clock. Nobody delivered *good* news that late at night. But then, it had been a crappy day—why not have a lousy end to it, too?

"If it's Nick again, though," he said through clenched teeth, "he's not getting out of here again without a punch in the mouth."

He stalked across the room, grabbed the brass knob, and threw the door wide. Whatever he'd been expecting, it hadn't been, "Stevie?"

She lifted her gaze to his and he was lost. Those deep blue eyes were swimming in tears, and evidence of still more shone in the lamplight like silver on her cheeks.

Paul grabbed her and pulled her inside. He didn't care why she was here. It was enough that she was. But there was something going on here. She'd come to him in tears and he'd do whatever he could to help. He pushed the door shut with a quick kick and held on to her shoulders with both hands. "What is it? What happened?"

She drew a long, shaky breath and blew it out through trembling lips. "I didn't want to come here," she said with a sniffle. "I mean, it's too hard to come here. And then after Nick—"

Everything in him tensed. "What about Nick?"

"I don't want to talk about Nick," she said, and took another gulping breath. "He's not important. This is, and . . . I just had to talk to someone . . . to *you*."

Her bottom lip quivered and Paul's heart twisted for her. Whatever was going on, it had cost her a lot. She looked . . . broken.

"Tell me," he whispered, his hands on her shoulders gentling.

"Oh God, Paul," she said, leaning close until she could rest her forehead against his chest, "I blew it big-time."

"What, baby?" he asked, wrapping one arm around her and using his free hand to soothe up and down her spine.

"Debbie," she said, leaning more heavily into him. "I *so* screwed it up."

Paul winced and felt her pain like a lance to his own heart.

"I went too fast. I asked her to move here with me and I shouldn't have. I scared her and I didn't mean to, but now it's too late and she'll never want to see me again and I finally found a family and now it's gone again."

"Shhh. . . ." Paul wound both arms around her and held her tight while she cried, while she let go of her dreams and tried to find hope in the rubble.

"It's a mess; it's all a mess," she whispered.

"No, it's not." He smiled and shook his head. "It'll be okay."

"How?"

He shifted one hand to her face and tipped her chin up until he could look into her eyes. Smoothing her hair back from her face, he said softly, "You'll *make* it be okay."

"You think?"

"I *know*," he assured her, and held her gaze until he finally caught a glimmer of a smile teasing the edges of her mouth. "Now come on in, I'll make coffee, and you can tell me the whole story."

She sniffed again, reached up, and brushed the tears from her cheeks. Giving him a watery smile, she managed a weak laugh. "I'm not *that* upset. *I'll* make the coffee."

"Okay." He waved her ahead of him, toward the kitchen.

She stopped just in the doorway and looked up at him. "You should know, though . . . I didn't come here for—"

Paul cut her off with a finger on her lips. "Believe it or not, Stevie," he said, "I'm not actually thinking about tossing you onto a bed right at the moment."

"No warning necessary, I guess." She scooped her hair back from her eyes. "I don't cry pretty. I get all puffy and red-eyed and—"

"And beautiful," he interrupted, then gave her behind a nudge. "Now make some coffee already."

Three days later, it was Tina's third birthday and there was no getting out of the party.

Stevie clutched a can of soda and leaned against the white picket fence that circled Tony and Beth's backyard. In the center of things, at an extravagantly decorated picnic table, sat Tina, a dark-eyed toddler with all of the Candellano charm and her mother's smile. Reese, Carla's stepdaughter, hovered close to the tiny girl, supervising the opening of presents.

Any other time, Stevie would have enjoyed the party. But she was still so miserable, so sick at heart over how things had gone with Debbie, she wasn't in much of a mood to be around people. She hadn't even been able to contact her mother, since, as Joanna's butler had assured Stevie time and time again, "Madam is unavailable." Whatever the hell that meant.

A cold, damp wind tugged at the hem of Stevie's ankle-length aqua skirt and she pulled the edges of her black cardigan closed over her cream-colored cotton blouse. She shook her head, swinging her wind-tossed hair out of her eyes, but instantly wished she hadn't bothered. Because now she could see everyone way too clearly.

Tony was making like the paparazzi, snapping picture after picture of his little girl. Mama was slicing her prized strawberry cake into thick wedges. Beth was just coming out of the kitchen carrying yet another tray of sandwiches.

But it was Nick and mostly Paul who held Stevie's attention. Nick hovered on the edges of the gathering. His face a storm cloud, he so clearly didn't want to be there. He made a point of tossing disgusted glances Stevie's way every few minutes.

Paul was directly opposite her. She could feel him

watching her, yet any time she glanced at him, his gaze was somewhere else. He hadn't tried to talk to her. Had actually spent most of the party deliberately keeping a distance between them. And maybe it was for the best.

Since her impulsive stop at his place the other night, she hadn't talked to Paul at all. But damn it, he'd been there for her when she'd needed him most. He hadn't tried to seduce her. Hadn't tried to do anything more than comfort her on a night when she'd needed it so desperately. And in that couple of short hours with him, Stevie'd found new reason to mourn the loss of his friendship. She'd missed their easiness with each other. Missed listening to him, missed his calm presence and rational thinking.

She'd missed her friend.

Just what she'd been afraid would happen, *had*. In the furnace blast of passion, they'd lost each other's friendship. Not so very long ago, Stevie would have felt free to call Paul, day or night, just to talk. Now she couldn't. Because they didn't just talk anymore. They kissed; they made love; they argued. But the old ease between them was gone.

And the last three days without him had been so hard. She'd wanted . . . *needed* to talk to him some more about the mess she'd made of things. But since she'd arrived at the party, he'd avoided her like he was a vampire and she was wearing a garlic necklace. Grimacing tightly, she told herself she wasn't being logical. Or fair. But that just didn't seem to matter.

"Man, you look serious."

Stevie came up out of her thoughts slowly, like a

woman waking from a coma. She blinked, looked at Beth, and forced a smile. "Just thinking, I guess."

Beth dropped one arm around Stevie's shoulder. "No thinking allowed at a Candellano party. You know that."

She smiled and this time it was a real one. "You're right. How could I have forgotten?"

"Beats me." Beth pointed with her can of Coke. "Did you see that dress Carla FedExed to Tina?"

"Gorgeous." Stevie took a sip of Coke and said, "Not even a honeymoon can keep Carla from birthday shopping, apparently."

"You gotta love it. A Candellano never forgets family." Then Beth leaned in and asked, "What's up with Nick? Have you noticed? He looks like hell."

"Who knows?" Stevie said, unwilling to be drawn into *that* conversation. Yet it irritated her, too. Even after two years, the family still tended to look at her and Nick as a couple. So she wouldn't feed that train of thought. Instead, she changed the subject. "I can't believe Tina's three already."

"I know." Beth shook her head and sighed. "It went so fast. And now I'm getting baby fever again."

"Really?" Okay, here was a surprise. "But you just started back to work and I thought you were all focused on that."

Sheepishly Beth shrugged, let go of Stevie, and leaned back against the fence. "Yeah, I know. Stupid, huh? But I guess what was *really* important to me was the fact that I *could* work if I wanted to."

"Ah. . . ."

Beth laughed and shoved Stevie. "Oh, don't give me

that sage sound like you understand what I'm saying. Even I don't understand me half the time."

"Okay, fine. I think you're nuts. Happy?"

"Delirious." She shifted her gaze to her husband, and Stevie watched the woman practically salivate.

What must it be like to have that? To love and be loved and be so secure in it that you could undress your man with your eyes and not give a damn who saw you? A pang of envy whispered through her, but she let it go again. Heck, if she couldn't have that kind of happiness, she was at least glad her friends did.

"Yeah," Stevie said. "Tony's a cutie."

"Hmm?" Beth turned, looked at her, then grinned. "Sorry, was I daydreaming again?"

"Looked like it was a good one."

"Oh," the woman said, "it's *always* a good one." Then her smile faded a little when she looked back at Tony. "Although this week's been a little slow, what with Mrs. Zenovsky and everything—"

"What?" Stevie straightened up a little at the mention of the town gripe. Ada Zenovsky would complain to God about the color of the sunset if she could just find a telephone that would dial heaven. Everything irritated the old bat, and she made sure she irritated as many people as possible in return. The woman had to be a hundred and ten years old—and mean went straight from her wrinkled face right into her bones. "What's she been up to now?"

Beth sighed. "She complained to the city council that Tony wasn't patrolling her part of town enough." As Beth shot a sidelong glance at Stevie, a smile quirked her lips and she added, "It seems the local kids

have taken to moving her mailbox and hiding it every night. She found it in the bushes, on the roof, in her garden . . . somewhere different every night."

"And she blames Tony?" Incredulous, Stevie just looked at her. "That's been going on for years. I remember when we—"

Beth's eyebrows lifted and wiggled. "Yeah, I remember, too. My favorite place to put it was under her car. You remember that old Cadillac she used to drive?"

"Remember it?" Stevie shuddered. "I swear she used to aim it at me." The only thing saving the kids of Chandler these days was the fact that the mean old woman had shrunk so much she couldn't see over the steering wheel anymore.

"You and every other kid in town." Beth sighed again. "Anyway, now she's decided to make a complaint every time it happens and she blames Tony for not stopping it."

"Is it going to hurt him—I mean, his job?"

"Nah." Beth shook her head and then reached up to pluck a long strand of auburn hair out of her eyes. "The council loves him. Besides, if they tried to get rid of Tony, they'd have to hire somebody else and he'd probably demand more money."

"True. But still . . . the old bat."

"Yeah, I know. And Mama is really pissed."

"Really?"

"You know Mama," Beth said with a resigned sigh. "She wants to go after Ada and rip the old biddy's lips off. Hurt one of her kids and Mama'll hunt you to the ends of the earth, just to make you pay."

"That's Mama," Stevie said, and shifted her gaze to

the older woman. Mama took Reese's face between her hands and gave her a loud, smacking kiss to the forehead, then spent the next few minutes rubbing a dark red lipstick print off the child's skin. As Stevie watched, Mama walked over to Nick, whispered something to him, then smacked him on the back of the head.

Whether it was the smack or the words, Stevie didn't know, but Nick got up and joined the party. Then Mama headed for Paul, and when she reached his side, she wrapped her thick arms around his waist and squeezed.

Stevie shivered. Family was everything to Mama. Her kids and her grandkids were her world. And just like Beth had said, there was nothing Mama wouldn't do to protect them. Just as she would never forgive someone who hurt one of those she loved.

A sinking sensation opened up inside Stevie and a draft of cold shot through the resulting darkness within. The thought of being on Mama's hit list was enough to make her cringe inwardly. Her gaze shifted slightly, locking with Paul's.

Even from across the yard, she felt the power of his stare slam into her. Her body lit up with that steady regard from those warm brown eyes. Yet even as her blood thickened and heartbeat accelerated, Mama straightened up and away from Paul and gave Stevie a wide smile.

And in that instant, Stevie realized anew just how precious that woman was to her. The thought of losing her was unimaginable.

CHAPTER FIFTEEN

"You stare at her any harder and you're gonna burn your eyeballs out."

Nick, sprawled in a lawn chair, tipped his head back to look up at his older brother. "Butt out, Tony."

"Happy to," he said, and followed Nick's gaze to Stevie, standing on the opposite side of the lawn, talking to Beth.

Stevie looked tired, sad, and, despite the smile on her face, just a little detached from what was going on around her. Tony didn't know what was going on with her, but he didn't have to know specifics to know that she was going through a hard time right now. So she sure as hell didn't need her old boyfriend giving her grief.

And as not only Nick's big brother, but also the town sheriff, Tony figured it was time to put in his two cents' worth. "I'll butt out as soon as you stop making a damn fool of yourself."

Nick pushed himself to his feet. "What's that supposed to mean?"

Tony gave a quick glance around to make sure the family was far enough away that he could talk. He moved, putting himself between Nick and the others. Then keeping his voice low, he said, "You know exactly what I mean. Back off Stevie."

"Since when do you tell me what to do?"

"Since you've been acting like you *need* it."

"Well, I don't."

Nick started past him, but Tony wasn't going to be put off. He'd been watching his brother for weeks now. Watching him slide into an alcoholic stupor, then climb out of the bottle only to throw himself the longest-running pity party this town had ever seen. But it was time that party ended.

His grip on Nick's upper arm tightened when the other man tried to pull away. "You keep this up and you're gonna move from pitiful ex-boyfriend into the stalker zone."

Nick's eyes bugged out. "Stalker? I'm not stalking anybody."

One black eyebrow arched. "I notice you didn't argue the 'pitiful' part."

Nick's mouth tightened, and beneath his hand, Tony felt his brother's muscles bunch, then slowly relax again.

"I just want her back. Is that so bad?"

Sympathy for his brother warred with impatience, and this time, impatience won. "Depends on *why,*" Tony said, bringing his nose to within an inch of Nick's. "If you're only looking for her to pull you out of trouble like she used to . . . then yeah. That's bad. If you really *love* her, that's something else." He paused

and watched Nick's eyes as he asked, "So. Do you love her, Nick?"

Nick's gaze dropped. The fight slumped out of him and Tony let him go. Nick shoved both hands into his pockets, looked past his brother to the woman across the yard, and admitted, "I don't know."

Shaking his head, Tony pointed out, "See, that should tell you something. If you loved her, you'd *know.*"

Nick scraped one hand across his face. "Hell, I don't know anything anymore."

"That's a start," Tony told him, and turned around to watch his family. His daughter, so beautiful it terrified him to think of her growing up and dating. His new niece, laughing and chattering away as if she hadn't been frozen in silence only a short month ago. Mama, in her element, bustling around the yard, force-feeding everyone. Beth. Tony smiled. The love of his life looked at him and gave him a slow wink that told him once everyone left, she was going to make him an even happier man than he was at the moment.

And Paul and Stevie. Tony frowned to himself as he realized that the two friends were studiously avoiding being anywhere near each other. When Paul went one way, Stevie went the other. It was as if they couldn't stand to be close. Or, he thought, as he noted the expression on Paul's face . . . maybe they just didn't trust each other to be close.

Tony shot Nick a quick look. The other man hadn't noticed a thing. Not surprising, since lately, all of Nick's time was devoted to himself. But maybe, Tony thought, as interest hummed inside him, that was a

good thing. If Nick actually did come out of his own narcissistic existence long enough to notice that his twin was moving in on Stevie . . . well, it wouldn't be pretty.

But it just might be the best thing for everyone all around.

Slapping Nick on the back hard enough to make the other man stagger, Tony moved off toward his wife. He needed to get the female reaction to what he thought he might have maybe noticed.

But his plan dissolved a minute later when a familiar voice shouted, "Hi, everybody, we're back!"

Carla stood on the back porch, her new husband right behind her and the two of them grinning like idiots. Reese and Abbey, Carla's golden retriever, took off like shots. Racing across the yard, her pigtails flying, Reese threw herself at Carla while Abbey jumped up and planted her front paws on Jackson's chest.

Grabbing her stepdaughter up into a fierce hug, Carla looked over the child's head toward Mama and asked a silent question. Mama smiled, letting her know that everything was fine. And just like that, the family was complete again and the celebration kicked up a notch.

After gifts had been unwrapped and lunch eaten and dessert served, Stevie finally managed to get a minute alone with her best friend.

"You look fabulous," she said, giving Carla a fierce, tight hug.

"I *feel* fabulous," Carla told her, and shook back her thick mane of dark curls. "Let me tell you, when you

do it right, marriage is definitely worth the price of the ticket."

Not something she'd be finding out, Stevie thought, but she grinned anyway as she led the way to a pair of lawn chairs set up a ways from the rest of the family. "So, is Jackson even better now that you're all legal?"

They sat down and Carla shot a glance at her husband, holding on to their six-year-old daughter, Reese. He laughed at his little girl's mile-a-minute chatter and Carla sighed. Abbey settled on the ground beside her and plopped her chin on Carla's foot.

"Oh, yeah." Carla shifted her gaze back to Stevie, leaned back in her lawn chair, and sighed, "Stevie, Paris was *awesome*." She smiled and her eyes lit up as if there were twin candles behind them. "Flower stalls everywhere, and the scent of those flowers makes even the air seem thicker, richer." She took a breath and raced on. "We went on this dinner cruise down the Seine and it was so romantic. Lights from the city dazzled on the water and there were strolling violinists on the boat and the music just drifted along with us, as if it were floating on the air." She sighed again, closed her eyes, and said, "We had the cutest little hotel, too. The guy who owned it was so excited. He'd just renovated the place and kept insisting that we lean out our window to see our view of 'zee tower.'" Carla laughed and opened her eyes. "But to see zee tower, you had to lean out so far, you would have plopped onto zee ground."

"Sounds wonderful," Stevie said, though it didn't resemble in the slightest the Paris she'd seen as a child.

But then, she'd spent most of her time in a hotel room with a baby-sitter who didn't speak English. Oh, yeah, Joanna had been a terrific mother from the word go.

Another sigh came from Carla as if she was savoring her memories. "We did the museum thing the first day or two, and after that it was just long walks along the river, midnight suppers at sidewalk cafés, and long, sweaty bouts of good old-fashioned sex. God, it was great. The whole trip. Just . . . great."

Stevie watched Carla's face, the emotions flickering over her features in a wild dance of happiness and contentment. She damn near vibrated with pleasure, and despite the problems in Stevie's life, she was so glad *somebody* was having a good time. "Well then, guess it's a good thing you didn't use him, then lose him."

"Yeah," Carla said, shifting her sparkling gaze back to Stevie. Her lips twitched. "And it's a good thing you didn't actually scoop his heart out of his chest with a garden rake, too."

Stevie winced, remembering the threat she'd made when she was worried that Jackson Wyatt was going to hurt her best friend. "He told you about that, huh?"

"Yep." Chuckling, Carla added, "He said, and I quote, 'Stevie's scary,' end quote."

Scary? Not anymore. Scared, maybe. No, not really scared. Just worried and confused and sad and . . . okay, horny. *God.* She dropped her head into her hands and groaned.

"Jesus, Stevie," Carla said, the teasing note in her voice gone instantly as she scooted in closer to her

friend. Abbey whined and moved with her, not willing to let Carla get away from her again. "What's wrong?"

A muffled, only slightly hysterical chuckle shot from her throat. "How much time do you have?"

"How much do you need?"

Lifting her head, Stevie looked at the other woman and felt her soul get just a little bit lighter. What a gift it was to have someone you could count on like that. No questions asked. Just "How much do you need?"

"God, I've missed you."

"Ditto," Carla said, then dropped one arm across Stevie's shoulder. "But I'm back now. So, spill."

She wished she could spill the whole thing. But she just couldn't bring herself to look into Carla's dark brown eyes and say, *Oh, I've moved on from one of your brothers to the next one; think it'll be a problem?* She just couldn't do it. Couldn't risk having Carla pull away from her.

Thankfully, though, there was plenty else to whine about. And she started out with the biggest part.

"I have a sister," she blurted.

Carla's eyes nearly popped out of her head. "No way! The Wicked Witch of the West had a baby?"

"Yeah," Stevie said, chuckling at the idea of Joanna pregnant now. "Seventeen years ago."

An amazed yet delighted grin curved Carla's mouth. "No kidding?"

"No kidding," Stevie said, nodding. "A sister. And she's terrific."

"That's fan—" Carla's words ended abruptly the moment she noticed the misery in Stevie's eyes. She

winced in sympathy, and though it must have cost her, since no Candellano was genetically capable of being quiet for too long, she clamped her lips shut and waited for the rest.

Paul walked up and plopped down on the ground in front of their chairs. Reaching out, he slapped Carla's knee and said, "Hi, gorgeous. Glad to have you back."

"Thanks," she said, smiling, then threw a glance at Stevie.

"Private conversation?" he asked, catching that hesitant look.

Stevie shifted her gaze to him and thought about asking him to go away. But it would be hard to explain that to Carla. They'd been friends too long. Carla would think it weird, and she didn't need to make anyone suspicious.

Oh, man, she was starting to think like a James Bond movie or something. Suspicion. Spies. Sexy. Seduction.

She pulled in a breath and exhaled sharply. "No," she said, meeting Paul's gaze squarely. "It's okay. Stay. You know most of this anyway." But she looked at Carla as she said, "I blew it." A single tear rolled along her cheek until she impatiently brushed it away with the back of her hand.

Paul frowned but didn't say anything.

"Tell me," Carla said, and while Stevie talked, her best friend held her tight and listened.

When she finally finished, Carla gave her a hug, then said, "Call her, Stevie."

"And say what?" she asked. "Sorry about worrying you? Sorry about pushing too hard, too soon, too fast?" Okay fine, Debbie hadn't been terrified. But she had

been anxious. Confused. And her big sister had been the one to shake her happy little world.

Nice job, Stevie.

"No." Shaking her head, Carla shrugged. "Just tell her you love her. You want to come see her. Spend some time with her."

"Exactly," Paul piped up, and Stevie's gaze shot to him. She read support in his eyes, encouragement, and her heart lifted a little.

Through her tears, he looked blurry, so Stevie blinked in a futile attempt to clear her vision. "You think she'll want to see me?"

"Of course she will," Carla said.

"Why wouldn't she?" Paul demanded.

"You sound so sure."

"I am," Carla said, and, grinning, slapped one hand across Paul's mouth so she could have her say. "You're family. Sisters. There's a bond there that can't be broken. That's blood, Stevie," Carla said, dipping her head so she could look her friend in the eye. "There's nothing stronger than family. Nothing I wouldn't do for my brothers. Or for you."

He peeled her fingers off his mouth. "Then how about letting me talk?" Before she could say anything, he reached out and took Stevie's hand in his and rubbed his thumb across her knuckles. "Like Carla said, it's family. You're Debbie's only family, too, you know."

"I know," Stevie said, and wanted to fall into Paul's arms, feel him hold her, feel his strength surround her. But she couldn't. Not here. Not now.

Maybe never again.

She felt the brush of his thumb all the way to her bones.

Damn it, this just wasn't fair.

Here she was, surrounded by a loving family—a part, yet *not* a part of the people she loved the most. Once again, she was on the outside looking in.

Paul's gaze fixed on her and she read the question in his eyes. *Are you okay?*

She nodded, resisting the nearly overwhelming urge to throw herself into his arms. Resisted bursting into tears because she wanted, *needed,* his arms around her. Here. Now. In front of God, Mama, and the rest of the family.

Instead, she oh-so-casually withdrew her hand from his grasp. She felt the loss of his warmth as she would have a sudden loss of oxygen.

She couldn't have Paul. And there was now a rift between her and Carla that her friend wasn't even aware of. She couldn't, wouldn't, talk to her best friend about any of this.

If she opened her mouth about Paul, then her friend would have to choose sides. And Carla's love for her brothers would eventually mean that Stevie would be the one left out. No. She wouldn't risk another friendship. She had too few left.

"And speaking of family," Carla said thoughtfully, letting her gaze slide to where one of her brothers sat sulking in the shade of the oak tree. "What's going on with Nick?"

Paul stiffened, but only Stevie seemed to notice and she groaned. "Why does everyone ask me that? I don't know." Of course she *did* know. He'd been acting like a

selfish, self-indulgent child. Just as he always had. But she was pretty sure Carla wouldn't want to hear that, no matter how true it was.

Her gaze shifting back to her friend, Carla said tentatively, "I know he was a jerk, Stevie, but you loved him once."

"A long time ago."

"Maybe it's just the romantic haze of a honeymoon talking," Carla said, "but are you sure it's over? Sure you're not interested in giving him another chance?"

"Christ, Carla," Paul snapped, letting go of Stevie's hand as if he'd been burned. "When they were together, he slept with half the cheerleaders in the NFL."

"Gee, thanks for the stroll down humiliation lane," Stevie said tightly. Surreptitiously she rubbed the spot on her hand where his fingers had touched. She could still feel the warmth.

"Yeah, that was real sweet of you, Paul."

He snorted and leaned back. "You're the one who thinks she should get back together with Captain Grabass."

"You know, Paul," Carla snapped, giving her brother the "evil eye" look she'd picked up from their mother, "you could be a little more understanding."

"Understanding?" he said, straightening up and glaring at his sister. "I understand him perfectly. You're the one who keeps looking for a silver lining in the dark cloud that is Nick, for God's sake."

"All I'm saying is—"

"Forget it," Stevie said, making her voice loud enough to be heard over Carla and Paul, but not loud enough to carry to the rest of the party. Man, talking to

the Candellanos was almost an Olympic event. Both of them turned to look at her. But she met Carla's gaze for the simple reason that she didn't trust herself to look into Paul's dark brown eyes. "Carla, trust me when I say it's over."

Nodding, she sat back in her chair. "Yeah, I guess I knew that. And honestly, I don't think you *should* take him back." She paused to stick her tongue out at Paul. "But I've gotta say, there's a part of me that's disappointed. For some weird reason, I always sort of thought you two would patch it up and end up together."

While Carla talked, Stevie's gaze eventually shifted to Paul. It was inevitable. Like moths to flames. Like kids to peanut butter. Like chocolate sauce to sundaes.

He glanced at Carla, as if making sure the coast was clear, and when he was sure she wasn't watching him, he gave Stevie a smile that curled her toes and warmed places inside her that had been lonely *way* too long.

Something inside Stevie turned over. Her heart ached and her eyes filled again, but this time not over Debbie. Over what-might-have-beens that had gotten lost in the mist of what was.

"So what do you think?" Tony asked Beth as she cuddled in close to him. Now that the party was over, mess cleaned up, and Tina asleep down the hall, he'd finally had the chance to tell his wife what he'd noticed that afternoon.

"Hmm?" She trailed her fingertips across her husband's bare chest.

Tony sucked in a gulp of air and tried to ignore the

flicker of heat that sizzled through him. "About Paul," he said. "Paul and Stevie?"

Man. Even saying those two names together sounded a little weird. It had always been Nick and Stevie. Even when he hadn't deserved her, they'd been a couple. Hell, even after they broke up, the family still said their names as if they were one word . . . NickandStevie.

Beth rose up on one elbow and levered herself over him. Her shoulder-length auburn hair swung down in a red velvet curtain that dusted his skin and made him wonder why in the hell he was bothering with his brothers' problems at the moment.

"I don't know," she said, and this time slid the flat of her palm across his chest, threading her fingers through the dusting of dark curls. "It might not be the best thing for Nick."

"Maybe it's time something happened that wasn't best for Nick," he grumbled, despite the fact that she'd dropped her head to kiss the base of his throat.

Her breath dusted across his skin. "He's pretty fragile right now, Tony."

"Then he'd better toughen up." Family loyalty was one thing. But he wasn't going to help Nick be an ass.

She raised her head and looked down at him. "And you'll toughen him up by having his ex-girlfriend be with his twin? That's cold."

"I'm not saying that's what's happening," Tony back-stepped just a little, since Beth's eyes were starting to heat up. "All I said was, Paul and Stevie were acting a little strange today."

"And from this you build a romance."

He wiggled his eyebrows at her. "Hey, I'm a romantic guy."

Beth rolled on top of him, straddled him, and sat straight up. Pulling her long turquoise nightgown off over her head, she arched her back. When his hands covered her breasts, she smiled down at him and said, "Romantic, huh? Prove it."

"Are you okay?" Paul asked when Stevie answered her phone.

"Not great," she said, "but better."

"Good." Damn it, this shouldn't be so hard. He should be able to talk to her easily. He'd known her most of his life. And yet, today at the party, he'd avoided her like the plague. Except for those few minutes when he'd intruded on her and Carla. Hell. It was a wonder she was willing to talk to him at all.

"Look, Stevie," he said, gripping the phone receiver so tightly, he was half-surprised it didn't snap in two. "About today—"

"Don't, Paul."

"Don't what?"

"Apologize."

He sighed and shook his head. Saying he was sorry was all he had left. Hell, at the party, it had about killed him to keep from holding her when she'd poured her heart out over Debbie. He'd wanted to hug her, soothe her, assure her that everything would work out.

Because if he'd held her, he wouldn't have been able to stop. He'd have had to kiss her, taste her, rediscover the wonder that was Stevie. And that would have set

off a chain reaction throughout his family that he didn't think either of them was ready for.

"Fine. I won't. But I think you're the first woman I've ever known who told a man *not* to apologize."

"I'm unique." This time there was a trace of a smile in her voice, and it helped him to hear it.

"You are that," he agreed. Hell, he'd known for years that there was nobody like Stevie. No other person he'd ever met had the heart she had. "You looked beautiful today," he whispered, and walked to the wide front window, where he could stare out into the darkness and pretend he was looking at her.

"Don't say that, either."

"Stevie—"

She sighed heavily and he swore he could *feel* her misery. "Paul, let's just leave it where it is."

"And where's that?"

She laughed, but he didn't hear even the slightest tinge of humor. He slapped one hand on the wall beside the window and leaned in, unconsciously doing one-armed push-ups to get rid of some of the wild energy pulsing inside him.

"Where?" she repeated, fatigue in her voice. "Halfway between heaven and hell. It could go either way."

Paul closed his eyes briefly and fisted his hand against the wall. "Damn it, Stevie—"

" 'Bye, Paul."

A dial tone hummed in his ear until he punched the END button.

Outside, the wind off the ocean whipped the trees into a frenzied dance, limbs bobbing, leaves tearing

free to twist in the swirling air. Clouds rushed across the sky, obliterating the stars, darkening the whole world as if in sympathy with the shadows inside him.

He felt her absence like an open wound. How could she have become such a part of him so quickly? How had she gone from friend to the sound of his own heartbeat in a few short weeks?

And what the hell was he going to do about it?

Carla was right, Stevie thought two days later as she ran along behind Debbie. The younger girl's grip on Stevie's hand was warm and tight, and Debbie's laughter floated back to her on a brisk, cold wind.

It felt as though they'd been running for hours. They'd already been to the park, up and down Cannery Row, and for a long walk along the shore. Debbie had more energy than three people. And she wanted to show her big sister all over Monterey. No way was Stevie going to spoil the fun by telling her that she'd been to Monterey hundreds of times.

Besides, seeing everything with Debbie made it all seem new anyway.

"Come on," Debbie said, tugging hard again. "Over here is the jellyfish place and it's really pretty."

"Run ahead," Stevie told her, laughing. "I'll catch up."

"'Kay!" With that, she dropped Stevie's hand, turned into the wind, and ran toward the next exhibit at the Monterey Aquarium.

The fall weather had thinned out the tourist crowds quite a bit, but the locals were still strolling around the area. The touch pool, the penguins, and the octopus were big crowd pleasers. The otters, Mae and Goldie,

all sleek brown fur and silly smiles, were cute enough to keep visitors there forever. The little guys stared up at the people looking at them, and just for a second, Stevie had to wonder just who was watching whom.

But Debbie didn't let Stevie stay in any one place long enough to really look at it. The younger girl was so excited to show Stevie the place where she worked, she could hardly stand still.

A cold wind rushed in off the ocean, fluttering colorful flags atop the buildings and balloons tied to the wrists of laughing children. Stevie zipped up her sweatshirt and tugged the collar up higher around her neck.

"Stevie!"

She picked up her speed and smiled to herself at Debbie's excited shout. Her little sister had forgotten all about the tears and near hysterics that had ended Stevie's last visit. And Stevie was grateful. If she couldn't have Debbie living with her, then she at least wanted this closeness.

"See?" Debbie shouted as she came closer. "See? See? This is the jellyfishes. There's lots of 'em and they're all floating and swimming. And everybody likes 'em best, but my favorite's the otter and sometimes I get to feed 'em, too, if I'm careful."

Stevie grinned at the flow of information. Her heart swelled with love for this girl, for the charm and the warmth and the pure joy of her. Then Stevie noticed the woman just behind Debbie and how she was staring at the girl with pity in her eyes.

And just like that, a small curl of shadows crept into the day. Stevie had to fight the urge to snap at the woman. Her protective instincts were on overdrive. It

wasn't the first time it had happened. Stevie'd caught the sympathetic glances from adults and the snickering from children. But Debbie never seemed to notice. Or if she did, she didn't care. She was simply oblivious to anything that distracted her from her own happiness.

So maybe, Stevie thought, she could learn something from her little sister.

"Look," Debbie was saying, demanding her sister's attention as she pulled her into the exhibition. "See? Isn't it pretty?"

Stevie stepped inside, stopped dead, and looked at the wall of glass in front of her. Inside the tank, hundreds, maybe thousands of jellyfish danced in the clear blue water, looking like ghosts streaming across a summer sky. They moved with a slow, undulating rhythm that was nearly hypnotic.

"Pretty." Debbie rested her head on Stevie's shoulder.

"Beautiful," Stevie said, reaching up to stroke her sister's cheek.

Alone again in her hotel room, flushed with love for the sister who'd been hidden from her for years, Stevie tried one more time to contact her mother. She'd dialed the number so many times over the last week, she knew it by heart. Punching the buttons with one stabbing finger, she waited for the connection to go through, then drummed her fingernails on the hotel tabletop while she listened to the phone ring.

This time, when the snooty butler answered, he put her through immediately to her mother.

"Stephanie?" Joanna's smooth, silky voice carried

over the phone line, and Stevie noticed her mother had picked up a British accent.

"Mother, why didn't you tell me about Debbie?"

"Debbie who?"

A tight groan slid from her throat. "Debbie your daughter. My *sister.*"

"Oh, bloody hell. Deborah."

"How could you do it, Mother? How could you just throw her away?"

"Don't be so dramatic, Stephanie. For heaven's sake, there's no reason for melodrama." Impatience came through the line, loud and clear.

But Stevie wouldn't be put off or calmed down. She'd just spent the day with a wonderful kid. A kid whose own mother had handed her off to strangers. Pacing around the generically decorated hotel room, Stevie started talking again, pushing words past clenched teeth.

"Why didn't you tell me about her?"

"What would be the point?"

"Because she's my family."

"Really, Stephanie. The child is retarded."

"And that makes her what?" Stevie damn near shouted. "Expendable? Useless? Less than acceptable?"

"Really, Stephanie, there's no reason to be insulting."

"*You're* insulted? Oh my God."

"You're being melodramatic again."

"Mother, the 'child' is all grown-up now. Have you ever once even visited her?"

"Why would I?" Joanna asked. "The child's father arranged for a trust fund. She's been well taken care of and will be for the rest of her life."

"And that's all?" Stevie stopped in front of the window looking out over the bay. Fishing boats squatted out on the dark ocean and lamplight shimmered around them, making golden silhouettes on the black surface of the water. On Fisherman's Wharf, lights twinkled, and along the beach walk, couples strolled under the street lamps.

Everywhere else in the world, normalcy ruled.

Here on the phone with her mother, Stevie was in the Twilight Zone.

"What else is there?"

"Haven't you ever visited her?"

"Why would I? I pay people to look after her."

"That's it?" Stevie went on. "No concern? No curiosity about your own child?"

"If you're going to wallow in hysterics, this conversation is at an end."

"Hysterics?" Stevie pulled the phone away from her ear and stuck her tongue out at it. Slapping it back into place, she said, "You think *this* is hysterics?"

"Good night, Stephanie," Joanna said just before the quiet click and soft dial tone told Stevie she was now talking to herself.

"Good night, *Mom*." She hung up the phone and tried to ignore the cold settling over her. Jesus. Tarantulas made better parents. And she'd *come* from that woman. Stevie rubbed her hands up and down her arms, trying desperately to rub away the chills snaking through her body. She felt so damn . . . *alone*.

Tears stung her eyes, but Stevie deliberately blinked them back. She wouldn't cry over Joanna. Not again.

She'd wasted enough tears in her childhood. There weren't any left.

She'd planned on staying overnight and going home in the morning. But being in the empty hotel room wasn't what she needed at the moment. What she needed was to be surrounded by the familiar.

To be home.

To talk to someone who knew something about love. About parenting.

She needed Mama.

CHAPTER
SIXTEEN

MAMA'S KITCHEN SMELLED LIKE childhood.

Stevie stopped on the threshold of the open back door. Sunlight spilled into the room, and just for a second, she enjoyed all of the memories that came rushing to greet her. *She and Carla, sitting at the breakfast booth, shelling peas. Mama, teaching the two girls how to make lasagna. Paul and Nick, crashing through the kitchen, snatching still-hot cookies from the cooling trays. Cold drinks and warm hugs and always, always, Mama.*

"Come in! Come in!" Mama shouted, waving a dish towel at Stevie to get her attention. "You're in time to help make sandwiches for tonight."

"Tonight?" Stevie repeated, walking into the kitchen and dropping her purse on the green Naugahyde breakfast booth seat.

Mama shook her head. "You forgot? End-of-summer picnic on the beach?"

"That's tonight?" How had she forgotten? It was a

tradition. On the last Saturday in September, the Candellanos trooped to the beach, took over a couple of the fire pits, and gave summer a good send-off.

She looked forward to the late-night picnic every year. Until now. This year, though, she hadn't even given it a thought. Not surprising really, considering her brain was just one or two thoughts away from exploding.

"Is tonight," Mama said, and finally looked up from the mountain of cold cuts she was tossing onto loaves of Italian bread with the panache of a Vegas blackjack dealer. One look at Stevie, though, and she dropped what she was doing. "What is wrong?"

Now that she was here, standing in front of the woman she'd been waiting to talk to since last night, Stevie couldn't think of a good way to start. Thoughts jumbled in her mind, each of them fighting for recognition. There was so much she wanted to say. And so much she couldn't. So she settled for saying simply, "My mother."

"Ah. . . ." Mama nodded, came around the center island, and took Stevie's elbow in a hard grip. Steering her toward the breakfast booth, she gave her a little nudge, and once she was seated, Mama sat down opposite her. "So," she said patiently, folding her hands atop the scarred tabletop, "tell me."

And just like that, she did. Like a balloon losing its air, Stevie talked, telling Mama all about Debbie and how great she was and how she'd only just found out about her. She talked about Joanna and shivered as she recounted last night's conversation with the woman.

"Stevie," Mama said when she finally ran out of steam, "you shouldn't do this anymore."

"Do what? Talk to my mother?" Stevie reached for a napkin and began to systematically shred it.

"No." Mama reached across the table and snatched the napkin. Clucking her tongue, she muttered, "You and Carla. So much alike." Then she took a breath and blew it out again, ruffling one stray lock of steel gray hair. "You must stop waiting for your mother to be who you want her to be."

Rationally she knew that was good advice. Emotionally was a different story. No matter how often she told herself that Joanna was no *Leave It to Beaver* mom, there was a small corner of Stevie's heart that just never stopped hoping. Of course, that was the same corner of her heart that never stopped bleeding, too. Shaking her head, Stevie said, "I keep thinking that one day, she'll change. Maybe when she's older. She'll realize she wants to be a mother."

Exasperated, Mama snorted. "She wanted to be a mother or she would have found a way to *not* be."

"Trust me, Mama," Stevie said, "she was no mother."

"Not the one you wanted, yes," Mama agreed. "But your mother anyway."

"Great. Born of Spiderwoman. What does that make me?"

Mama chuckled. "Makes you Stevie."

She smiled in spite of everything. Fine. Having Joanna for a mother had made her the woman she was today. But let's look at that woman for a minute, she thought but didn't say, since she didn't want Mama jumping up to slap *her* on the back of the head.

Yes, Stevie was independent and, generally speaking,

pretty happy. But she was also alone. She'd never wanted to be married because she was so damn afraid of starting up another marital merry-go-round—just like the one she'd seen growing up. She was damn near *terrified* to have kids, for fear mothering instincts were inherited.

Oh, yeah. Joanna had done a helluva job on her older child. Heck, Debbie, if you thought about it, had really gotten the sunshine end of the deal.

"You're a good girl, Stevie."

"Thanks, Mama." She smiled and swallowed the sigh crouched at the base of her throat.

"But a foolish one."

Stevie blinked. "Huh?"

Mama scooted out of her seat, walked to Stevie, and bent down to kiss the top of her head. Then came the loving little slap, just to make sure Stevie knew she belonged.

"Stop trying to make your mother something she is not."

"But—"

"And stop thinking you're like her." She wagged a finger in Stevie's face to make her point. "Who loves every stray like a new baby? Who is sitting here in my kitchen not helping me make sandwiches and worried about her sister? Be thankful for your sister—don't waste time thinking about lost years." She used her fingertips to tilt Stevie's chin up until they were looking at each other. "Enjoy now."

The icy, hard shell around Stevie's heart cracked and the break was almost painful. Tears stung her eyes again and she tried desperately to fight them back. She

was willing to bet she'd cried more in the last few weeks than she had in her whole life.

"No tears, Stevie," Mama said, patting her cheek. "You must learn to trust yourself—and those who love you."

Trust.

If she could do that, she could tell Mama the whole truth. About how she was pretty sure she was dangerously close to being in love with another one of Mama's sons. And that she didn't have a clue what to do about it.

Oh, no.

Couldn't be love.

If it was, then what would she do?

"Oh God." She dropped her head into her hands and prayed for a stroke.

"No time to bother God now," Mama announced, tugging Stevie to her feet. "Now time to make sandwiches."

Paul cleaned his glasses on the hem of his dark blue sweatshirt and turned his face into the howling wind. Standing on the cliffs above the beach, he had a bird's-eye view of the sand and the ocean. Moonlight shone down from a starry sky and touched the edge of far-flung whitecaps, making the sea foam glow with a weird green phosphorescence that looked almost ghostly in the darkness. It was low tide and the small rippling waves seemed to sneak toward shore, sending out cold, wet fingers, reaching for the people already gathered around the fire pits.

Sliding his glasses back on, he let his gaze drift across the family, smiling as he saw little Tina and

Reese chasing Carla's dog Abbey along the water's edge. Then he saw Stevie. She and Carla were standing together, keeping an eye on the kids. Paul's gaze locked on Stevie and he let himself enjoy the moment of being able to watch her without being seen.

A tight knot formed in his guts and his heart thudded painfully in his chest. She threw her head back and laughed at something Carla was saying. Stevie's blond hair flew wild and free in the wind, and in the moonlight it looked almost silver. Her long legs looked great in faded denim jeans, and the oversize sweatshirt she wore did nothing to hide the figure he knew was beneath. As she bent down to scoop up Tina and throw her high in the air, his niece's giggles bubbled in the air.

And Paul's hands fisted at his sides.

Stevie looked perfect like that. With a laughing child in her arms and the wind in her hair. He etched the picture she made into his brain so that even fifty years from now he'd be able to look at this one snapshot in time and see her as she was now.

As he would always see her.

Scowling to himself, he started down the rocky slope toward the beach. His running shoes skidded on the loose gravel and sand, but he could have made the walk blindfolded. He knew every step, every niche in the ground. He and Nick used to take this same trail down to the beach when they were kids. They'd played pirate in the coves and later, they'd tried their hand at surfing, until the board cut loose one day and banged into the back of Nick's head.

Paul frowned again as he reached the bottom. If he hadn't been with Nick that long-ago day, his twin

would have drowned. And realizing that had him looking for Nick in the crowd. Standing beside one of the
fire pits, he was talking to Tony and, for the first time in
days, actually looked happy.

Good sign? Bad sign?

Hell, who knew?

"Paul!" Mama shouted. "You're almost late."

He grinned and kissed her as soon as he was close
enough. " 'Almost late' actually means 'on time' in most
cultures, Mama."

"Funny. Everybody's funny." She handed him a can
of lighter fluid. "You make the other fire; Tony made
this one."

Paul tore his gaze from Stevie to take the can being
thrust at him. "We don't really need two, do we?"

Mama sniffed. "Always have two."

"Fine. Tradition must be upheld."

They had too many damn traditions. Like the tradition that said "Nick and Stevie" forever. Like the tradition of him looking out for his twin no matter what.
Like Nick expecting life to *keep* handing him gifts, despite the fact that he clearly didn't appreciate them.

Mind racing, Paul set off for the second cement ring,
not twenty yards from where the family had already set
up camp. He only half-listened to the sounds of his family, rushing toward him and receding like the waves,
sliding toward shore before easing back out to sea.

He shoved twists of newspaper between the stacked
logs, then squirted the mess with the lighter fluid.
Striking a match, he cupped it in his palm to protect it
from the wind, then touched the wavering flame to the
edges of the papers. The fire caught quickly, snatching

at the fuel, feeding on itself with quickening snaps and crackles, dancing along the logs, flickering in the wind.

"Nice job, Boy Scout," Nick said, coming up behind him.

"I wasn't a Boy Scout," Paul reminded him. "You were."

"Oh. Right." He laughed shortly and took a long sip of beer. "Damn, that was a long time ago."

"Yeah." Paul eyed the beer bottle, then looked at his twin. "How you doin'?"

"Fine, *Mom*. This is my first beer."

"Good. When's the interview?" Paul asked, shoving his hands into his jeans pockets.

"Tomorrow." He stared off at the ocean, squinting into the wind, and said, more to himself than his brother, "I've gotta get this. It'd be perfect."

Old loyalties rose up inside Paul as he watched his brother and, for the first time in weeks, didn't feel that stab of irritation that had become such a familiar thing. He and Nick shared something that very few people would ever understand. That twin thing—scientists could call it what they wanted—was so bone-deep, so ingrained in nearly every damn cell, it was a hard thing to hold out against for very long.

He slapped Nick on the back and waited for his brother to look at him. "You'll get it," he said. "It's your turn, right?"

Nick met his gaze and held it for a long minute. Then shrugging, he tried to brush it all off with a smile. "Right. My turn. Why shouldn't I get it?"

"Exactly."

"Come on, you guys," Carla said, coming up behind

them and threading her arms through theirs. "Food's on, and you know how cranky Mama gets when people aren't eating."

And as they had been as kids, the three youngest Candellanos walked, locked together. An indivisible wall against outsiders.

"You don't tell ghost stories?" Jackson asked, surprise in his voice. "What the hell kind of campfire is this?"

Carla grinned and leaned into him. "It's not a 'camp' fire at all, dummy. It's an end-of-summer fire. Completely different."

Stevie and Paul sat opposite the newlyweds, and between the heat of the fire and the desire humming in the cold, damp air, she felt like she was sitting on a stove top. She cast a sidelong glance at Paul, leaning forward to jab a long stick at the burning logs. Wavering shadows danced across his face, and a reflection of the fire sparkled in his dark brown eyes, giving them an almost hypnotic magic. But then, that wasn't surprising, was it? She'd been mesmerized by him for three weeks now.

He scowled at the flames as red-hot cinders lifted into the air, dazzled in the wind, then winked out of existence. Stevie thought she saw tension etched into his features. But maybe that was just wishful thinking.

It had been days since they were together. Days since he'd held her. Long, lonely nights since the last time he'd touched her. And the fires inside her were burning a hell of a lot hotter than these little bitty bonfires.

"Okay," Jackson said, laughing, "an explanation is required for non-Candellanos." He cradled his new wife against his chest and looked at Paul.

One corner of his amazing mouth quirked in a half-smile. "End of summer is a celebration," Paul said. "And I'm pretty sure it started with our folks celebrating the fact that we'd all be going back to school and getting out of their hair."

Carla laughed. "Probably."

Paul smiled at her, then turned his head so he could see Stevie, too. She was a part of his memories. She'd always been there. From the time they were kids. She'd had a piece of his heart for years. "But however it started, it ended up being just a big excuse for the family to get together and eat outside."

"As opposed to all the eating you usually do *inside*," Jackson said, laughing.

"Exactly." Paul looked at his brother-in-law. "And then of course, Papa liked the idea of making fires. Which is why it's 'tradition' to have two rings." He chuckled and glanced to the other fire, where the rest of the family sat in a wide circle, toasting marshmallows on straightened-out wire hangers. "I think Papa was a closet pyromaniac."

Stevie laughed shortly and gave him a shove. "He was not!"

Paul grinned at her. "Okay, maybe not. But I *do* know one thing for sure," he said, and looked deep into Stevie's eyes. "With two fires, Mama and Papa could let us kids toast marshmallows at one fire while they did a little snuggling at the other."

Something in her eyes flashed and he knew she was feeling the same damn thing that had a grip on him. And knowing that didn't make him feel any better.

"Well," Jackson said, splintering the tension-filled

moment, "snuggling sounds pretty good to me." He stood up and then reached down to pull Carla to her feet. "But I think we'll take a little walk, first."

Carla smiled up at him, and the pleasure on her face would have been evident to a blind man. Paul's back teeth ground together. Though he was happy for his little sister, he couldn't help resenting the fact that while she was free to hold her husband, if he so much as hugged Stevie, it'd set off a Candellano civil war.

Carla and her new husband, arms wrapped around each other, moved out of the circle of firelight and into the deeper shadows closer to the water's edge.

Stevie sighed as she watched them. "They're good together, aren't they?"

"Yeah," he said, but he wasn't watching his sister as she moved farther into the shadows. Instead, his gaze was locked on Stevie. In the firelight, she looked almost impossibly beautiful. Dancing shadows played on her features. Flames danced in her eyes.

Then slowly, as if she sensed his gaze on her, she swiveled her head to look at him. And the fire he saw in her eyes had nothing to do with the reflection of the flames shimmering in those wide blue depths.

"God, I miss you," he whispered, and his voice was nearly swallowed by the rush of the ocean and the hiss of the fire.

"I miss you, too." Stevie wrapped her arms around her up-drawn knees, then rested her chin atop them. "It would be so much easier—*better*—if I didn't."

An icy wind shot in off the ocean and breathed into the fire, sweeping brightly lit cinders and sparks along with it as it raced off again into the darkness.

Stevie shivered.

"Cold?" Paul asked, then gave a self-conscious laugh. "Stupid question." He shifted, moving close to her.

"What're you doing?" Stevie leaned away as he draped one arm around her shoulders and pulled her in tight to his side.

"Keeping my 'pal' from freezing to death," he muttered darkly, and sent a quick look at the others, none of whom were paying any attention to them. "Relax, Stevie. No one's going to think anything."

He felt the tension in her drain away as she melted against him. It was all he could do to keep from drawing her onto his lap, wrapping both arms around her, and kissing her until neither of them could breathe.

But *that*, someone would notice.

A flicker of irritation snapped to life inside Paul and he tossed another glance at his family. Would it really matter so much? he wondered. Would they really come unglued if they found out that he was in love with Stevie?

Love?

Shit.

Everything in him stopped dead. He would have sworn even his heartbeat stuttered to a halt.

Love?

Something he hadn't counted on. Something he hadn't really expected. Sure, he'd had a crush on her for most of his life. But who would have thought that trying to get over that crush would be the impetus to making him fall so in love with her?

Stevie rested her head on his shoulder, and when her breath dusted against the base of his throat, he felt that soft sigh right down to his soul.

The thing to do here was look at the problem from a scientific standpoint. Rationally. Logically.

A. He was in love with her.

B. He wasn't at all sure he *should* be.

C. He didn't have a clue what to do about it.

Carla laughed, low and throaty, as she turned into Jackson's arms. Her new husband—God, she loved the word *husband*—swept her into a fierce hug and buried his face in the bend of her neck. Over his shoulder, she saw Stevie and Paul, huddled close together, Paul's arm around her, Stevie's head on his shoulder.

And there was something so . . . *intimate* about the scene, she almost looked away. Until she realized what she was thinking and told herself she must be wrong.

But as the firelight played on her brother's features, she noticed the tension, the hunger, drawn there and a small kernel of worry took root deep inside her.

"It's okay, Scruffy," Stevie said as she stepped into the too-quiet loft apartment. Strange how empty her house had been feeling lately. And up until recently, she'd been so content here. Not completely satisfied with her life of course, but she at least hadn't been desperately lonely. Like now. "I'm home, Scruff!" she called out, ignoring the ache in her throat.

The tiny dog scuttled out from under the coffee table and hurried toward her, claws ticking out a quick rhythm against the wood floor. Smiling, Stevie dropped her purse and went down onto her knees to welcome the little cutie. In just a week or so of regular meals and baths and lots of love, Scruffy had undergone a

transformation. Her coat was sleek and shiny and her ribs were no longer standing out against her skin like the brass rings on a barrel. That one ear was still crooked, but now she looked like a well-loved pet.

Oh, she'd never be a blue ribbon winner, but then, heart was so much more important than beauty. Stevie scooped the dog into her arms and cuddled her against her chest. Scruffy wriggled like a puppy, licking, whining, and doing everything she could in doggyspeak to say, I'm so glad to see you!

"Let's get you some dinner, okay?" Stevie walked into the kitchen, still carrying Scruffy, then set her down when she picked up the stainless-steel dog bowl. For company, Stevie talked to the dog while she worked. "You're such a cutie now, I bet we could find you a new home with no problem."

Scruffy sat on her haunches and cocked her head as if listening intently.

"Do you like kids?" Stevie asked. "I bet you do. I could find you a place with kids. . . ."

Scruffy barked once.

"Is that a yes or a no?" Stevie laughed, shook her head, and carried the bowl of food to the placemat against the wall. Setting it down, she plopped down, too, bracing her back against the wall. She stroked Scruffy gently while the dog ate.

Poor little thing still took tiny bites of food, then backed away, as if trying to protect what little she could take in one bite. Stevie sighed, shook her head, and smiled softly. Of all the dogs and cats she'd taken in over the years, this one tiny animal had crept into her heart and taken root. There was something so lost

and yet so trusting about her. It didn't seem to matter what her previous owners had done to her. Scruffy's nature was to forgive.

To love.

She, too, wanted to belong. And Stevie could identify with that. So maybe the answer to Scruffy's housing problem was a simple one. Two lonely hearts deserved each other, right?

"You're not going anywhere, are you, Scruff?" she whispered, stroking the dog's head with her fingertips. "You're going to stay right here with me, huh?"

For the first time in her life, she had her *own* dog. That was sort of like family. Right?

The phone rang and Stevie groaned as she looked at the clock. Ten-thirty. "Who the hell . . . ?" She pushed herself to her feet and headed for the living room. "This better not be you, Nick." She grabbed the phone. "Hello?"

"Stevie?" A woman's voice, anxious. Strained. "Thank God you're finally home."

Frowning, she asked, "Who is this?"

"It's Margie. Debbie's housemother?"

Instantly fear caught at the base of her throat and damn near strangled her. "What is it? What's wrong?"

"I've been calling you all night," Margie said, words hurtling through the phone line, tumbling one after the other.

Stevie glanced at the answering machine. The red light blinked frantically, silently, admonishing her for not being at home when she was needed.

"What's happened, Margie?"

"Debbie's gone."

"Gone? *Gone?*" Stevie's fingers tightened on the receiver. "Gone where?"

"That's the thing. She left a note. I just found it two hours ago. Says she's coming to see you."

"To see me?" Fear rattled through her. How would Debbie get here? And if she'd left more than two hours ago, she should have been here by now. "Oh God."

Margie sighed and Stevie heard the relief in it. It was much easier to be worried *with* someone than to have to do it alone. "I've called the police," she was saying, and Stevie listened up, afraid to miss something vital. "Told them I think she went to the bus station. I don't know how many people they're putting on this, though. I'd go down there myself, but I don't want to leave the other girls alone and—"

"I'm on my way." Stevie slammed the phone down, her hand lingering on the receiver briefly, before she snatched it back up again and punched in a familiar phone number.

When he answered, she simply said, "Paul? I need your help."

CHAPTER SEVENTEEN

PAUL HIT THE GAS and didn't let up once. With Stevie beside him in the passenger's seat, he kept his gaze on the road as he steered his car in and out of traffic. He passed a slow-moving white van, then squeaked between an 18-wheeler and an SUV, and he would have sworn the only thing separating them was a coat of paint. But this was no time for timid driving.

He spared Stevie a quick glance and almost wished he hadn't. Light flashed in and out of the car as headlights of other vehicles speared into the darkness, then zoomed off again. Stevie's features were tight, she had a death grip on the armrest, and her eyes were filled with a misery so deep, he ached for her.

"This is not your fault," he said, though he almost didn't expect her to hear him—and certainly not to believe him.

"Really." She didn't look at him. She kept her gaze locked on the road ahead of them as if just by staring she could hurry them along. Make them reach their

destination that much faster. "Who else, then? I should have been home. Should have been there to get Margie's call."

"What are you, psychic?" he demanded. "You were supposed to *know* that you'd be needed tonight?"

"No, but—"

He glanced over his left shoulder, then changed lanes again as the driver behind him honked in futile fury. "Ah. Then what? You're supposed to stay at home from now on? Just in case there *might* be an emergency?"

"You don't have to make it sound stupid."

"I'm not making it sound stupid. It *is* stupid."

Then he told himself to shut up. He wasn't helping. Wasn't making the situation any better. He was only giving her more grief. And that she didn't need.

From the moment he'd picked up the phone and heard the tight, thin thread of fear in her voice, Paul had been hers. Whatever she needed, he'd do. Whatever she had to have, he'd get. If that meant giving her quiet time to panic, then so be it.

He kept his mouth shut for the rest of the drive, only nodding as she gave him muttered directions. When he pulled up in front of the neat Spanish-style house, Stevie bailed from the car before he'd even had time to turn off the engine.

The porch light was on, a pale yellow beacon, guiding them in. The front door opened when she was halfway up the walk and an older woman, clearly near the end of her rope, came down the steps to meet her.

"Any word?" Stevie asked.

"Nothing." The woman shot Paul a glance, then

focused on Stevie again. "I've been trying to think, though. And I think I know where she went. It's really the only place that makes sense."

"Where's that?" Paul spoke up, and the woman's gaze snapped to him again. In the moonlight, she was all cool suspicion and frayed nerves.

"Who're you?"

"A friend," Stevie said, drawing the woman's attention back to her. "Where do you think Debbie went?"

"The bus station," Margie answered immediately. "The girls all love the bus. Love the idea of getting on-board and going places. They've never really ridden alone before, though, and I could be wrong. But if Debbie was really trying to get to your house, I figure that's how she planned to get there."

"How would she know where the station is?" Stevie heard the fear in her own voice and snapped her mouth shut rather than listen to more of it.

Margie rubbed one hand across her mouth, shot an uneasy glance over her shoulder at the front door, where the other girls were silhouetted against the light from the living room. "I've taken them all down there to watch people getting on the bus. They like to pretend they're planning trips. And then we have lunch and come home—" She broke off and looked at Stevie again. "Is this really important at the moment? Can't you just go and check?"

"Sounds like a good place to start," Paul said, then asked, "Did you call the police?"

"Yes." Disappointment rang in her tone. "They said they'd get to it as soon as possible."

"We can't wait for them," Stevie said, looking to Paul.

"We're not about to. Let's go." He grabbed her elbow, turned her around, and headed for the car, his long legs practically sprinting down the sidewalk.

Stevie looked back over her shoulder. "I'll call the minute we know anything."

Whatever Stevie'd been expecting, this wasn't it. The Greyhound station in Monterey was basically a ticket counter in a minimart.

Coolers filled with soft drinks lined one wall and there were shelves full of snacks and books and magazines. The place was nearly empty. Apparently most people in Monterey were more interested in driving fifty-thousand-dollar cars as opposed to riding in a hundred-thousand-dollar bus.

Stevie's anxious gaze scanned the faces of the small crowd of people gathered in the minimart waiting for the next bus. But Debbie wasn't there.

While a weary mother rocked and her hungry baby wailed, Stevie hurried to the ticket counter, where a bored-looking woman sat beneath the Greyhound sign, flipping through a magazine. Stevie stared through the Plexiglas, clenched her fingers over the counter's edge, and leaned in. "Have you seen a young woman here tonight, buying a ticket?"

"You'll need to give me a better description than that," the woman, about thirty, with a tired smile, said, barely looking up from the glossy pages she seemed fascinated by.

Paul was suddenly right behind Stevie. She felt the warmth of him pressing into her and she clung to the

strength she drew from his presence as he leaned in and said, "The girl's seventeen. Blond hair, blue eyes. Name of Debbie Harris. Oh. And she has Down's syndrome."

That got her attention. The woman looked up and nodded. "Yeah. She was here. Cute kid. Seemed a little nervous, though. Sort of scared."

"*Was* here?" The fractional burst of relief that had shot through Stevie disappeared again in a fresh flash-flood of worry. "Where'd she go?"

"Took a bus. To San Francisco." The woman shot a quick look at the huge round clock behind her. "Left nearly an hour ago."

"San Francisco?" Stevie's heart sank. She actually felt her heart slide from her chest to the soles of her feet. Oh God, Debbie. Alone. In a city the size of San Francisco. She'd be terrified. Lost. She wouldn't know where to go or who to talk to.

And what if she talked to the *wrong* person? Stevie's stomach twisted around a ball of nerves that seemed to send tentacles of icy apprehension to every square inch of her body.

Paul stepped back from the counter and pulled Stevie along with him.

"We missed her," she whispered, her voice thready, her breath hitching in her chest. "I can't believe it. Somehow, I thought we'd catch her before she got on the bus. I told myself that maybe she wouldn't actually board one. Or that the police would get here before us and stop her or—"

"Enough already," Paul said, taking her face in his hands. His thumbs moved over her cheekbones,

stroking, caressing, soothing. "Don't worry. We'll be moving faster than the bus. We'll get there either before her or right after."

She looked up at him and read his concern, his determination to succeed, in the depths of his eyes, and in that instant, he was Han Solo and Albert Schweitzer and Superman all rolled into one. No matter what else was going on between them, he'd answered her call for help with no questions asked. He'd listened to her rant and shouted back when he thought he could get through. He'd driven to Monterey like a crazy man on a moment's notice and now he was ready to race a bus to San Francisco. He was her hero—her hero with wire-framed glasses, a cool smile, and dangerous brown eyes.

And just like that, Stevie *knew* it would be all right. She knew he'd do everything he could to make sure of that. And the jangle of nerves that had been tied into fretful knots inside her suddenly and unexpectedly dissolved. Her heart lifted again and she was pretty sure she'd survive the night after all.

She reached up and covered his hands with hers. Giving them a squeeze, she nodded. "You're right. We *will* find her. It *will* be all right."

"Atta girl," he muttered with a quick, fierce grin. "Now let's get the hell outta Dodge."

"Right behind you, Obi Wan."

That actually got a chuckle out of him. Then he grabbed her hand, pushed the door of the minimart open, and drew her outside into the star-filled night.

While Stevie stared out the side window at the scenery whizzing past, Paul kept his eyes on the road ahead as

he hit the speed dial button on his cell phone. He stared at the twin slashes of brilliance pouring from his head-lights as he listened to the phone ring and ring and ring and—"Tony?"

"Yeah." Tony grunted, snorted, then demanded, "Shit. Do you know what time it is?"

"Too damn late and getting later with every second you waste," Paul snapped. He knew he'd woken Tony from a deep sleep, but that was the least of his worries at the moment. He'd calmed Stevie down, but he wasn't fooled. He could damn near *feel* the tension rip-pling off of her in waves.

"What's wrong? What're you talking about?"

Tony sounded crabby as hell but more awake. One thing he had to give Tony, it didn't take him long to catch on to a situation.

"Stevie's sister," he started, then launched into a de-tailed but brief sketch of just what was going on. He finished by saying, "We need you to call the San Fran-cisco P.D.—get somebody over to the bus station to head Debbie off just in case she beats us there."

"Done," Tony said, and this time his voice was all cop. Wide awake and in charge. "I'll call in a favor with a friend of mine. He's a detective in the city."

"Thanks, Tony." Paul shot Stevie a quick look and saw her mouth thin into a tight, narrow line.

"No problem. And, Paul?"

"Yeah?"

"Be careful, huh?" He paused. "You crash your car and wind up in a hospital bed, Mama'll make your life a living hell."

Paul laughed shortly, appreciating the release of

tension, however briefly. "I'll watch it. You take care of your end."

He disconnected, tossed the phone onto the console between the front seats, and reached over to squeeze Stevie's left hand. "Tony'll take care of things."

"I heard."

Light flickered over her features and was gone again, leaving her in shadows. He wished he could see her eyes. See whether she was believing him or if she'd resorted to self-torture again.

"We'll probably beat her there, Stevie. And Debbie's perfectly safe as long as she's on the bus."

"Maybe."

"Maybe?"

She turned to face him, and in a split-second flash of light that illuminated her features, he saw that whatever relief she'd been feeling was gone again.

"I do believe we'll find her. But she's alone, Paul. She has nobody. What if she gets nervous? Or scared? Or worried? Then what?"

"And what if she's enjoying the drive? Enjoying being on a trip?"

Stevie sucked in a long, deep breath and let it out in a slow slide of frustration. "I hope she is. But the point of all this is, it's my fault."

"Bullshit."

"It is, Paul." She pulled her hand free of his and clenched her own together until her knuckles whitened and her fingers cramped. "If I'd just stayed out of her life entirely, then she'd be safe at home with her friends. But no. I had to go running in. Didn't stop to question. Wonder if it was the right thing to do. No."

She shook her head, unclenched her hands, and scooped them through her hair, scraping it back tight across her scalp. "I didn't even bother to wonder if she'd want or need a sister. I was only thinking about myself. I wanted to . . ." she took another breath and the last word shuddered from her, *"help."*

"Well, yeah," Paul growled, clearly disgusted, "there's an act worthy of a firing squad. Good call."

"She was *happy*, Paul." Stevie'd been thinking of little else for the last half hour. As the signposts flashed by with bright bursts of light, only to fade into darkness as Paul's car hurtled past, she'd finally realized that Debbie's situation could only be blamed on *her*, Stevie. "Like you said the first time I told you about her. She had a nice life, a good home, a job she loved. And what did *I* do?" she asked, not really wanting an answer. "I rushed in like the Tooth Fairy or something and threw her whole life into turmoil. Hell, I made her *cry* the first time we met."

"Jesus, Stevie," Paul interrupted when she slowed down for breath, "climb down off your own back."

"I can't. It's because of me that Debbie's lost and we're running around in the dark, chasing Death on the freeway."

"Thanks for your confidence in my driving," he noted as he darted in between two slow-moving cars to gain another car length.

She hissed in a breath at the maneuver. "And what if the police in San Francisco miss her? What if she slips past them without being noticed?"

"She won't."

"But what if?"

He reached for his phone and tossed it to her, never taking his gaze from the iridescent lane markers. "Call Carla. Put her on alert. If Debbie gets past the police, we may need her and Abbey to do their search thing."

"A search? In San Francisco? Can you say 'needle in a haystack'?"

His jaw tightened. "If the needle's there, we'll find it."

"Oh God."

"For chrissakes, Stevie, stop rushing out to meet Trouble. Wait for it to find you, huh?" He punched the accelerator and zipped around a slow-moving SUV. "We're gonna make it. We'll beat her there and everything'll be good."

She wanted to believe. She really did. Only the thought of Debbie alone in a big city absolutely terrified her. But her hero was driving. Moving in and out of traffic with the aplomb of a guy working his way through a crowded dance floor. Maybe it would be all right. Maybe they *would* beat the bus in. Maybe she should do like he said and just relax—"Brake lights!"

She shouted the words the instant her brain picked up on the fact that ahead of them, cars were stopped dead.

Seconds stretched into lifetimes.

Paul slammed on the brakes and a high-pitched scream rose up from the tires as they grabbed at the asphalt. The back end of the 4Runner swung to the left, but Paul fought the steering wheel to correct the slide. The car shuddered to a stop behind a white Toyota with inches to spare. Paul's gaze shot to the rearview mirror and his viselike grip on the steering wheel relaxed a bit as he saw the guy behind him slow to a safe stop.

A sea of red brake lights swam in front of them. The freeway was backed up and everyone on it looked like they were in a parking lot, fighting to get out.

"Must be an accident up ahead," he muttered, and slapped his hand against the leather-wrapped wheel. "We're gonna be here awhile."

So much for beating the bus into the city. Stevie shivered, took a deep breath, blew it out again, then said, "What was that about waiting for Trouble to find me?"

He slanted her a look, scowled, and said, "Call Carla. Put her on alert."

Stevie's fingers curled around the phone. She stared down at the softly glowing buttons for a long minute, then stabbed out Carla's phone number. And while the phone rang, she sent up a silent prayer, asking any angels currently not doing anything special to fly over that bus to guard it.

And Debbie.

They were more than an hour late. The bus had arrived, disgorged its passengers, and left again on another run. Dozens of people walked in and out of the terminal, all of them in a hurry and none of them Debbie.

Stevie jumped off the escalator on the third floor and scanned what she could see of the place. The walls were gray on the bottom, white at the top, and crisp, clean navy blue trim finished it off. The station itself was neat and clean and not very big, considering the size of the city it served.

She and Paul turned right, checked out the few people crowded around the snack bar, then continued on into the main lobby area. At least sixty scrolled metal

chairs—the kind that looked lovely but were uncomfortable to sit in for very long—were sprinkled across the floor and a few vending machines lined against the far wall.

Dozens of people milled around, dragging suitcases and cocking their heads in an effort to understand the disembodied voice coming across the loudspeaker system.

Stevie's gaze swept the room and noted with dismay that there were five exit doors leading from the lobby and Debbie might have taken any of them.

"Now what?" She said it out loud, though she hadn't really meant to. Stevie knew darn well what was next. Turn the place upside down until they found her sister.

Paul's thoughts were right on the same track. "Let's talk to one of the ticket clerks, see what we can find out."

There were five ticket windows lining the counter. They picked one and Stevie smiled at the friendly-looking blonde behind the glass. "Can you help me?" she said.

"I can try," the woman answered, flicking a glance at Paul. "What do you need?"

"My name is Stevie Ryan. I'm here looking for my sister, Debbie Harris. She's eighteen, she has Down's syndrome, and she came in on the bus from Monterey. Do you know—"

"It's okay." The blonde smiled as she interrupted. "She's safe. We got word from the San Francisco P.D. and we intercepted her when she got off the bus."

"Oh, thank God," Stevie muttered, and collapsed against the counter.

"She's okay?" Paul asked.

"She's fine," the woman assured him, with a worried look at Stevie. "When someone needs help, we usually bring them back here, behind the counter. And we keep them here until we either find their people or get word from the police. My supervisor alerted security and they came up to get her. She's there now."

"Where?" Stevie asked.

The kind blonde pointed. "Take the elevator down to the first floor and follow the signs."

"Thanks," Paul said as they headed off again.

Downstairs, their identification was checked out and then they were following a security officer to a small office. The man accompanying them was talking, but Stevie barely heard him.

"San Francisco P.D. said we were to hold the girl here until you arrived. She's been in the security office since Greyhound alerted us of her arrival. Tried to get her something to eat, but she won't talk to anybody. All she'll do is cry."

"It's okay," Paul said. "We appreciate the help."

"We do," Stevie added, but all she could think was, Debbie's crying. She was probably terrified by now at how her little adventure had ended up. But Stevie was so relieved, it was hard to stay upright. Her legs seemed to move anyway, though, despite the jelly in her knees.

"She's in there," the big man beside them said, nodding to a closed door.

"Thanks." Paul opened the door and the first thing Stevie heard was her sister. Crying.

Debbie's eyes were red-rimmed and her features

were twisted in a miserable scowl as she hugged herself and wailed like . . . well, like a lost child.

"Debbie." She said it like a grateful prayer, but her whisper was heard.

"Stevie!" The girl lifted tear-rimmed, miserable eyes to her and instantly, happiness washed across her broad features. Then she shot out of her chair and hurtled toward her big sister.

Stevie caught her and only swayed slightly at the impact of her sister's body against hers. Relief staggered her. Debbie was safe. And healthy. Oh, good. Very good. *Thank you, thank you,* she prayed silently. How was it possible? she wondered wildly while she soothed Debbie's heartfelt sobs. She'd known her sister such a short time and already the girl was a huge part of her heart. How did that happen so quickly? So completely?

Was it just blood calling to blood? She'd had so little real experience with *family,* she couldn't be sure. But the Candellanos had this . . . connection with one another. Something she'd always envied. Now that she'd found it, too, there wasn't anything she wouldn't do to keep it. Pulling back, she looked at her sister's red-rimmed eyes and felt her heart turn over.

Sniffing, Debbie huffed in a breath. "I came to see you, but the bus went to the wrong place."

"I know, sweetie, it's okay now."

"And then a p'liceman came, but he didn't take me to jail."

"Good. I'm glad."

"And the lady upstairs gave me candy."

Smiling, Stevie listened as Debbie rattled on for a

few more minutes, recounting her adventures but never letting go of her sister.

"I wasn't supposed to talk to anybody 'cause they're strangers, but they kept talking to me and then a p'liceman told me that you were coming, but you didn't come and now I'm really tired, Stevie, and I wanna go home, 'kay?" She frowned and looked over Stevie's shoulder. "Who's that man?"

Without even turning around to look, she knew it was Paul. She could have sensed him there even if she'd been blindfolded.

"That's Paul," she said. "He's my . . . *friend*. And he came to help me take you home, all right?"

Debbie grinned, then turned her gaze back to Stevie. "Now? 'Cause I wanna go home now. I wanna tell Margie I'm okay and then I wanna sleep in my bed and go to work and then I don't wanna be here anymore and can we go now?"

Words jumbled together into one long, drawn-out sentence filled with longing and misery and relief, and rather than try to sort them all out, Stevie just nodded. When Debbie hugged her again, burying her wet face in the curve of her sister's neck, Stevie looked over her shoulder to Paul, smiling at her. His gaze slammed into hers and Stevie knew that though this little episode had had a happy ending, Trouble had found her again already.

She was in love.

CHAPTER EIGHTEEN

IT WAS A QUIET ride home.

Stevie phoned Carla and then Tony to thank them and let them both know everything was fine. Debbie called Margie to let her know she was safe and on the way back. Then satisfied and completely relaxed, the girl settled into the backseat and fell asleep. And in the quiet dark of the car, Stevie was too overwhelmed with her new realization to even talk to the man beside her.

What could she say?

Thanks for saving my sister, and by the way, I love you?

No. God, it sounded like a badly written play.

Besides, she couldn't *love* Paul.

That way led to disaster.

The Candellanos rose up in her mind. One after the other, their faces swam before her tired eyes, and each of them looked disapproving.

Big surprise.

God, what had she gotten herself into? How had this

happened? How had she allowed herself to fall in love with her best friend? And how in the hell was she going to get out of this unscathed?

Answer: She wasn't.

No matter what she did, how she handled this, there was going to be pain. If she stopped seeing him altogether, there would be the misery of losing not only her best friend, but also the man she loved. If she continued to see him, there would be the misery of being with her best friend and being unable to tell him that she loved him—because if she *did* tell him how she felt, then she would lose the rest of his family. Not to mention the fact that he might not *care* if she loved him.

Her head pounded in time with the thump of the car tires riding across the stand-up lane markers on the freeway. The hum of the wheels on the asphalt seemed to be just the right frequency to drive nails through her brain.

"Tired?" Paul asked. "Exhausted," she said.

"Try to sleep. It's another hour or so to home."

"Right." She swallowed hard, turned her head on the seat rest until she was looking at him, and then, through slitted eyes, studied his profile in the darkness. Strong, quiet, responsible Paul. The man she loved. The man she couldn't have. The man who—No. Try to sleep, she told herself.

If she was lucky, her brain would shut off and she wouldn't even dream.

After dropping Debbie off with promises of e-mail and a nice long visit in a week or so, Paul and Stevie were back on the freeway headed for Chandler.

With Stevie asleep in the seat beside him, Paul blinked, rubbed his aching eyes, then shook his head to wake himself up. It had been a long night and he was ready to sleep for a day or two. Hell, the freeway was starting to blur and that wasn't good. He took the exit for his place. Stevie didn't wake up until he'd parked the car in his driveway.

"What?" She sat up straight as he opened her door and unhooked her seatbelt.

"Too tired to drive anymore," he said, reaching for her to draw her out of the car.

"Paul . . ."

"*Sleep,* Stevie. We're going to *sleep.*" He yawned and started pulling her toward the house. "Trust me when I say your virtue is perfectly safe."

She stumbled, and he stopped long enough to pick her up. Cradling her against his chest, he kept walking, on automatic pilot now. Her hands went around his neck, and even through the fatigue dragging at him, Paul's blood stirred. Didn't even surprise him. Stevie was enough to get to him through a coma.

He took the steps, shoved the key into the lock, opened the door, and carried her inside. Kicking the door closed behind them, he didn't stop. If he did, he was half-afraid he wouldn't get going again.

A few minutes later, he was standing beside the unmade bed and laying Stevie out on the mattress. She hardly moved as he undressed her, then drew a quilt up to cover her. In another second or two, he was undressed and lying beside her. Sound asleep, she turned toward him, cuddling against his side.

For one brief, beautiful moment, he enjoyed the feel

of her body aligned along his. But exhaustion ran too deep for his brain to function for long. Wrapping his arms around her, he closed his eyes and joined her in dreams.

Hours later, he woke to the silken glide of her fingertips stroking his skin. Paul opened his eyes and stared up into Stevie's steady gaze. Levered up on one elbow, she smiled down at him and let her fingers trail across his chest. His breath caught.

"Good morning," she said, smiling.

"It is now," Paul assured her, and caught her hand in his. Sunlight poured in through the skylight overhead, spilling gold across her shoulders and shining in her hair.

"What are you up to?"

One corner of her mouth lifted as her gaze drifted down his body. When she looked into his eyes again, she said softly, "I'd say you're the one who's *up* to something."

True enough. Paul moved quickly, tipping her over onto her back and moving to pin her to the bed. He bent, kissed her briefly, and still with the taste of her on his mouth, said, "Last night, I promised you your virtue would be safe."

"My virtue is long gone, Paul," she said, reaching up to cup his cheek in the palm of her hand. "And I want you."

His heartbeat thundered in his ears and blood pumped in a fury throughout his body. He gave her a slow smile. "Then that works out well. Because I *always* want you. Always have. Always will."

He kissed her again, and this time, it was a slow, leisurely kiss as he savored the taste, the texture, of her lips. She gave and he took, devouring her, consuming her, taking her into his blood, under his skin. She breathed in, he breathed out. They were one, and he felt the connection right down to his bones.

This was magic. Her touch. Her sighs. She was everything he'd ever wanted and more. He'd found his heart in her and he didn't think he'd ever be completely whole again without her.

Stevie shivered as his hands explored her body. She sighed into his mouth and arched her back as his fingertips closed on her nipples, tugging, pulling at the sensitive tips. Electricity hummed through her body, setting small fires sizzling through her bloodstream and lighting up every nerve ending like neon signs.

He was everywhere at once, moving over her body with feather-light strokes, teasing, tormenting, driving her higher and higher. He promised heaven and then stopped just short of taking her there. His breath dusted her skin. His murmured words drifted into the sun-kissed air and settled over her like a sigh.

She moved against him, with him, following his lead, then shifting and leading him. He matched her, touch for touch, kiss for kiss, and when he moved to cover her with his body, she opened to him, welcoming him home. He entered her on a sigh of satisfaction and she felt him fill her, become a part of her, and she wanted to keep him locked within her body forever. Great.

"Come with me," he whispered, and she looked up into dark brown eyes and lost herself in their depths.

Love sang inside her, making each moment with him more precious than before.

"Take me with you," she said, and reached up to draw his head down to hers for a kiss. Their lips met, briefly, fiercely, and the first tremor rattled through her. "Oh God, Paul."

She gasped, tensed, held her breath, and rode the wave of pleasure cresting inside her. And watching his eyes glaze over, she held him as he followed her into the heaven he'd promised.

Love.

Who knew love could hit a person so hard, so fast?

But now that Stevie's body had stopped buzzing, her brain was on red alert. She'd damn near blurted out the truth while he was still inside her, and wouldn't that have been perfect? She could have had an up close and personal shot of his features going slack with shock.

No one had ever said anything about love.

And now that it was here, she didn't have a clue what to do about it.

From behind the closed door of the bathroom she heard the shower come on, and smiled to herself at the thought of Paul, all wet and soapy and naked and—she slapped herself on the forehead with the heel of her hand. For God's sake, think about something else.

An idea presented itself, and desperate, she went with it. Pushing herself up out of the rumpled bed, she walked naked across the floor, grabbed Paul's robe from a nearby chair, and pulled it on. Scooping her hair out from under the collar, she walked to the bathroom door.

"Paul?"

"Yeah?"

"Okay if I use your computer to e-mail Debbie?"

"Sure, go ahead. Be out in a minute."

"Take your time," she said, then added in a whisper, "A year or two wouldn't be out of line." But, she thought as she headed for the staircase, a couple of years wouldn't matter anyway. She had the distinct feeling that she could go thirty years without seeing him and then the moment she did, she'd be flat on her back, yelling, *Take me, sailor!*

Stevie went downstairs and straight to Paul's desk. Naturally, everything was in perfect order. His closed laptop sat square in the center of the desktop. A system of cubbyholes, all neatly closed of course, housed stamps and pens and envelopes. She knew his desk drawers were just as painfully neat, and she had to wonder—how could he be such a picture-perfect computer geek and a love god at the same time?

"Just one of Fate's little jokes," she told herself. "Like falling in love with your friend." *Real funny.*

Shaking her head, she lifted the lid of the computer and waited while the standby light flickered to life. In a few seconds, the screen lit up, went black, and then came on again—a document already open.

Paul turned away from the rush of water and reached for the shampoo. God, he loved knowing Stevie would be waiting for him when he emerged from the shower. Loved knowing she was in his house. Hell, had been in his bed. A part of him hoped that maybe this was the real start of what lay between them. Maybe she'd be

able to see that they could build a life together. If he could just get past her defenses. Get past her need to save his family and the whole damn world. His heart squeezed painfully in his chest and he wondered if he was being an idiot. Everything with her sister had turned out well. Crisis over. Debbie safe. Stevie had stopped ranting and ragging on herself.

But even as he thought about letting it all go, he knew he had to say something. On that long drive to San Francisco, when her fear and anxiety had pumped words from her mouth in a flood of self-recrimination, he'd mostly kept quiet. Thinking she needed to talk. To say everything that was stoppered up inside her. But now that it was all over, he couldn't just pretend he hadn't heard her. Couldn't gloss over the things she'd said. Like how all of this was her fault. And she should have been waiting at home just to receive a phone call that might never come. She had to let go of this stuff.

He just didn't know where the hell to sta— "Oh, shit!"

Stevie was down there. In his office. On his computer.

"Hell. Shit. Damn!" Shampoo dribbling down his face and neck, he made a dive for the bottom half of his sweats and raced for the stairs.

"Don't open it. Do . . . not . . . open it—"

Stevie blinked and read the words on the screen again. What was left of the deliciously languorous sensation in her body dissolved like sugar dropped into boiling water. But she wasn't hot. She was suddenly, completely, bone-deep *cold*.

"Stevie, no!" Paul's voice came from upstairs,

shouting, though it sounded more like a frantic whisper in a hurricane to her. Must be all of the blood pounding in her ears.

Breathing heavily, her hands clenched around the edge of the desk, Stevie looked at Paul's neatly done Pro and Con list and read it slowly, for the third time.

" *'The Pros and Cons of Loving Stevie.'*"

"Con. Number one. 'Stubborn.' Since when is stubborn a bad thing?" Her blood pressure rose.

"Two. 'Always trying to save everyone and everything.'" Her eyeballs started to throb.

"Thr—"

As if from a great distance, she heard him running, his footsteps pounding down the stairs. She stood up and turned to face the door and glare at him. He skidded, wet and naked, to a stop just a few feet from her.

"Jesus, Stevie. You didn't see—" The computer. Open. Paul. Dead man. He'd forgotten all about the damn thing the last few days. Which said a lot for just how wrapped up in Stevie he'd become.

"You son of a bitch."

"You did." *Damn it.* Paul reached up and wiped dripping shampoo out of his eyes with the leg of the sweatpants clutched in his fist.

"Three," she reiterated, her voice hard. " *'She might still be in love with Nick'*? Oh my God."

"Stevie—"

"You can't possibly believe that. Not when we—I— *you.*"

"You were never supposed to see that."

"Oh well," she said, grinding the words out through clenched teeth. "That changes everything, doesn't it?"

Shampoo ran down into his eyes and he swept it away. Stevie hoped he'd been blinded.

"You've got to listen to me."

"No, I don't. I can't *believe* you did this," she snapped, fury dancing in her eyes and jittering out around her in a wild aura of doom.

"I can explain—"

"No thanks!" she shouted, and reached for the brass lamp at the corner of his desk. Snatching it up, she threw it at him.

She'd always had a good arm. Paul ducked as it sailed past, then winced as it clattered against the wall behind him. Better the wall than him, though.

"Just calm down for a second—"

She glared at him.

"—and let me explain."

"There is absolutely *no* explanation that is going to make this sound any better."

"Just listen for a minute and—"

"You're unbelievable." She tugged the belt of his robe tighter and actually managed to look dignified in navy blue terrycloth. "You made a *list* of the reasons why you shouldn't have anything to do with me?"

Sounded even worse when she said it. It had seemed like such a good idea at the time, though.

"I don't know whether to be angry that you even thought of me like one of your defense department reports, or hurt that you needed to do that and were still making love to me." She slapped both hands to her forehead as if she could push this new knowledge right out of her brain.

"Damn it, this isn't a conversation I want to have

naked," he muttered, and jerked the sweatpants on over his damp skin.

"This isn't a conversation *I* want to have at all," she said, and stalked past him.

But he grabbed her arm and dragged her to a stop. Looking down into her stormy blue eyes, Paul could hardly believe that just a few minutes ago they'd been hazy with spent passion. Now she looked as though she wouldn't have a bit of trouble killing him.

"Listen to me, Stevie—"

"Why should I?" she cut him off, and tugged free of his grip. "I already read the list. What was number four again? Oh, yes. 'Cranky before her period.' Jesus, Paul! Trust me, you've said enough."

"I never meant for you to see that." He threw his hands wide, then slapped soap out of his eyes again. "I forgot all about the damn thing. I did it when I was—"

"Being a jerk?"

"Thanks." He smirked at her. "Okay, yeah. Maybe I was a jerk for making the list. But that's who I am. I write things down. I think logically. Rationally."

"Right. And I'm the idiot who gets written *about* like a statistical report. Now that's sensitive, Paul. Gee, I'm all warm and fuzzy here. Can't you tell?" She shook her head and started for the front door.

He stopped her after a few steps. Grabbing her upper arm, he pulled her around to face him. When she tried to fight free of his grip this time, he just held on tighter.

"Damn it, Stevie, you've been making me nuts for years."

"Thanks a lot."

"That's not what I meant."

"Well," she said, cocking her head to give him a small unamused smile, "lists come pretty easy to you. Why don't you write down what you *really* meant and then I can read *that,* when I have time?"

"You think this is easy?" he demanded. "You think being around you and pretending nothing is happening is *easy?*"

"It hasn't exactly been a walk in the park for me, either, you know." Stevie planted both hands on his chest and shoved. Like trying to shove a mountain. He just stood there, glowering at her. "But *I* didn't make up lists on why to stay away from you."

"It wasn't like that."

"Sure seemed that way to me. What do *you* call it?" She held up one hand to keep him quiet. "No. Never mind. I don't even want to know. God knows what you're thinking that you *didn't* write down. Besides, this isn't just about us, anyway. It's not even all about that stupid list. I mean, sex is all fine and dandy—"

"Fine and dandy?"

She ignored him. The list still stung, but there was more at stake here than a list that hit every last one of her insecurities. "We have to think about how this affects everyone else. There are more than just the two of us involved here, you know. What about Mama? What about Nick? And Carla and—hell. Everybody?"

He stared at her blankly. How had they gone from a spreadsheet to his family?

Then he got a bead on what she'd just said. "How about *Nick?*" he asked dangerously. "How . . . about . . . Nick?"

"Yes. Your brother. Your twin. That Nick."

"Why are we giving a damn about Nick right now?"

"We're giving a damn because he's family. That's why. Because he's . . . *family* and—*you're* the one who brought him up by putting his name on that list. Never mind." She shook her head, refusing to think about that again. "I'm just saying that we have to think about the family."

"And how about yours? How about little sister Debbie?"

"Her, too."

"Doesn't it get old, Stevie?"

"What?"

"Saving the whole goddamned world?" So much for keeping quiet. Frustration tugged at him, but he scraped one hand across his face and blurted, "Christ, Stevie, do you have to rescue the whole damn universe?"

"What?"

Stunned surprise shadowed her eyes, and he told himself to shut up and let her walk away. But he couldn't stop. Hell, he didn't *want* to stop. This had been coming for a long time. Might as well get it said. Maybe once it was out in the open . . .

"You heard me." He threw his hands wide, then let them fall to slap against his thighs. "Jesus. All you've done is take the 'blame' for everybody's troubles and problems."

"That's because some of them *were* my fault."

"How is that possible?" he demanded, staring into her blue eyes and watching as anger slowly overcame the misery he'd seen there before. "Just how do you get to be the damned center of the universe? How is

everything that ever goes wrong anywhere *your* fault? Your problem to solve? *You should have been home to answer a phone you didn't know was going to ring? You shouldn't have rushed into Debbie's life and thrown it into turmoil?*"

She didn't like having her own words thrown back at her and actually winced as he said them. "I didn't say that, exactly."

"You don't have to say it," he said, snorting a choked-off laugh. "You *live* it."

"Wow," she countered, folding her arms across her chest like a shield. "Ladies and gentlemen, the Amazing Paul, mind reader extraordinaire."

"Cute," he snapped. "But I don't see you denying it."

"Of course I deny trying to save the world. It's . . . dumb."

"That's what I've always thought."

"What's that supposed to mean?"

"Think about it, Stevie," he said, leaning toward her as he grabbed her shoulders in a tight grip. "You've spent most of your life waiting around for Joanna to love you the way you want her to."

"Shut up," she said, but the words came out soft, squeezed past a sudden cold, hard knot in her throat.

"And Nick," he went on, his brown eyes flashing in the dim lamplight. "You loved him despite how he acted. You kept trying to save him from himself so he'd see you and love you the way you wanted him to."

"I loved him, once."

Paul winced as if she'd landed a hard blow to his ribs. Even the past tense of the word *love* didn't take the sting out of it completely. "I know. But he didn't

love you, not the way you deserved to be loved, and you never saw it."

She gave him a long, slow look up and down, then said softly, "There's a lot of things I never really saw until just now."

He smiled tightly. "That's real good, how your eyes go all icy and your voice gets as snotty as Joanna on one of her best days."

Stevie sucked in a breath. "Good shot. If you're keeping score, that was a direct hit."

"I'm not trying to hurt you."

"Well, you're doing a hell of a job."

He hadn't meant to hurt her. But he was. He could tell by the look in her eyes, and it was killing him. Yet he knew that stupid list had pushed to the surface what he'd been trying to hide. And he was damn tired of walking on eggshells when it came to what he was feeling about this woman. They were finally standing on the edge of a cliff. It was either get across it or jump in the hole and forget about living.

Tears stung the backs of her eyes, but Stevie refused to give in to them. She wouldn't cry. She wouldn't let him know that he was hurting her. That he was getting to her more deeply than anyone ever had before.

He moved his hands, cupping her face between his palms, staring down into her eyes, forcing her to meet his gaze. To feel what he was feeling. To know what it was costing him to say these things.

"Even the animals, Stevie. The cats and dogs you bring home. You're saving them, too. Now you have a new cause. Debbie. Not that your sister isn't a worthy cause, but damn it—"

She pulled away from him, eyes blazing.

He raked his fingers through his wet, soapy hair. "You save everyone but yourself."

One tear defied her best efforts and rolled along her cheek. She rubbed it away with the back of her hand. Then she inhaled sharply and exhaled just as fast. "Why are you talking to me like this?"

"Because I'm tired of not being seen, Stevie. You know why you never noticed me in all these years?" He shook his head slowly. "Because I didn't need saving. You didn't have to rush in and rescue me, so you couldn't see me."

"That's not true."

"Yeah, it is." Scraping one hand across the back of his neck, he looked like he wanted to strangle something. "You keep saving the world, hoping it'll change to the way you want it. Well, instead of trying to save the damn world, why don't you try to save yourself?"

"And your way's better?" she asked, when she could think again. When the chill of his words had eased enough that her brain was able to work again.

"My way?"

"The good son," she said, daring him to disagree. "The responsible one. The one who never disappoints. Always in Nick's shadow. Content to stay there, then bitch because he doesn't get noticed."

"Score one for you," he said softly.

Stevie's heart ached. *This* was exactly what she'd been afraid of. Agony pooled in the pit of her stomach and sent long, reaching fingers out to every corner of her body. Her love for him had ripped apart a friendship she'd always held sacred.

Hurting him was the last thing she would ever want to do. Yet here she was, going for his soft spots, just like he'd done to her. Because they knew each other so damn well, they knew where the skin was the thinnest, the nerves closest to the surface.

But she wouldn't do it anymore.

"I'm not interested in playing this game—or *any* game with you, Paul." She wiped at her streaming eyes with impatient hands, then a harsh, throat-scraping laugh erupted from her. Turning around sharply, Stevie made a break for the front door. "I'm outta here."

"You're leaving? You lose an argument and leave? Just like that?"

"I didn't *lose,* Paul," she said, tears clogging her throat. "*We* did." She grabbed his car keys off the table in the foyer, yanked the front door open, ran outside, and crashed into Nick's chest.

"Hey . . ." He held her back and away from him, his smile slipping into a worried frown. "What's . . . ?"

"Oh, drop dead," Stevie muttered, and shot past him, taking the steps at a run, then racing across the yard to Paul's car.

"Stevie!" Paul was just a few steps behind her. He couldn't let it end like this. Damn it, they hadn't settled anything.

And he couldn't . . . wouldn't let it end this way. He'd halfway hoped that she could love him as much as he loved her. Now he might never know—just because of that Goddamn list.

No. To have it all trashed at his feet was something he refused to accept. Refused to give up on. If that meant taking on Nick and Mama and the whole

Candellano bunch, then so be it. And he wasn't going
to let her leave, half-naked and in *his* car, for God's sake.

Nick grabbed at him. "What'd you do to St—"

Without even slowing his pace, Paul slammed his
fist into Nick's jaw, then kept going. Barefoot, he ran
out into the yard, calling her name like a maniac, in
time to see Stevie steering his car down the drive, spinning gravel into a wild fantail behind her.

CHAPTER NINETEEN

STEVIE MADE THE DRIVE to her place in record time. Would have been even faster if Tony Candellano hadn't pulled her over for speeding.

"This just keeps getting better and better," she muttered. She could still see the shock on Tony's face when he'd noticed that she was driving Paul's car, wearing a man's robe and pretty much naked beneath it. Thank God she'd had the sense to put Paul's robe on—otherwise, every last Candellano man would have had the chance to see her naked. At least Tony had been so stunned, he hadn't remembered to give her a ticket. Oh, yeah.

The perfect end to the perfect morning.

Her sometime-lover and ex-friend had humiliated her and embarrassed her with that stupid list. She leaves without her clothes—in a stolen car—and gets caught by the cop brother of said ex-friend.

If she'd read this in a book, even she wouldn't believe it.

Wrapped in her own robe, she clutched Paul's to her chest and walked across the room to the window that overlooked the alley where she'd left his car. Afternoon sunlight glittered on the gray 4Runner sitting behind her own little car. They looked so cozy, side by side. And yet they didn't go together at all.

Sort of like her and Paul.

She lifted his robe to her face and breathed deeply, inhaling his scent from the soft, faded terrycloth. Tears burned in her eyes and she paid no attention at all as they rained down her face. She had no one to hide them from now. No reason to pretend her heart wasn't breaking. And just like that, a brief, fierce crying jag hit, leaving her weak and wobbly. A few minutes later, she wiped her tears on Paul's robe and muttered, "Love sucks."

Sniffing, she glanced across the room to Scruffy, curled up on the sofa. "Ironic, isn't it, Scruff?" she asked. "Just when I figure out I'm in love with him, I find out that I didn't even really know him." Her fingers dug into the robe, squeezing the thick fabric tightly. "He made a *spreadsheet*, Scruff," she said, as if she still couldn't believe it. "A list to help him keep from caring for me."

It still stung. She'd lost her lover. The man she loved. But more than that, she'd lost her friend. Because how could she ever look at him again? How could she ever talk to him, knowing that while he was smiling at her, touching her, loving her, he'd be jotting mental notes and adding to his "list" of her apparently numerous faults?

Anger sparked inside her, sputtering to life in the pit

of the dark, empty hole at the bottom of her heart. But the hurt was so much bigger than the anger, the pain was overwhelming. Still, her brain worked. Tugging at that last scene with Paul. Pulling at every thread to every conversation. Reworking it, analyzing it. But no matter how she looked at it, she kept coming back to that list.

She'd thought he was different. She'd thought that he at least *cared*. But he'd turned out to be just like Nick. Like her mother. Not only didn't he love her . . . he'd taken it to new levels. He'd actually gone at it scientifically and figured out just *why* he shouldn't love her.

Stevie'd known all along that this time with Paul would end. "But it could have ended better than this," she said tightly, fighting a new wave of tears as she threw the window open and leaned out. Tossing his robe high, Stevie watched it take flight, dancing through the air, catching the slight wind, spreading out as if it were a pair of wings attached to some giant mythic bird. It seemed to take forever for it to land, and when it did, it hooked on the raised antenna of the 4Runner and lay still and flat, like a flag on a windless day.

Like her heart.

"There you go, Paul," she said, and closed the window again, locking it tight against the outside world. "Now you don't even have to speak to me to get your robe."

Turning away from the window, she let her gaze slide across the room. Sunlight glanced through the shining glass panes, filtering into every corner of the room, banishing late-afternoon shadows. Yet it did absolutely nothing to the darkness within her.

She walked to the sofa and curled up in the corner. The TV was on—just for company—the strident tones of the talk show host breaking into the silence that seemed so oppressive. Scruffy scooted in close, cuddling up against her. Stevie idly ran her fingers through the little dog's soft fur and smiled to herself despite her inner misery when Scruffy flopped onto her back for a better rub. "At least you love me, huh?"

So that was it, she thought. She could see her future mapped out in front of her as clearly as if it were highlighted on an atlas. She'd live right here over the Leaf and Bean. In these few small rooms. With a succession of dogs and cats, she'd shuffle through her life, smiling at customers and crying herself to sleep. She'd dream every night of a love she'd known too briefly, and always, she'd wonder, what if?

The phone rang and Stevie stared at it. She thought about not answering. After all, it might be Paul, and just how much humiliation was she supposed to take in one day? But it could also be Debbie. Or Margie.

She grabbed the receiver. "Hello?"

"Stevie, come downstairs and let me in."

"Carla." A well of emotions opened up inside Stevie—most profoundly, a weird sort of disappointment that it wasn't Paul on the phone. She would have liked the chance to hang up on him. Her fingers curled around the receiver and squeezed. Ordinarily she'd be happy to see Carla. A nice long talk with her best friend had always been enough to cheer her up when she needed it. But now—

"Hello? I know you're there, Stevie."

"Carla, I just don't feel like—"

"Telling me why you were driving Paul's car while naked?"

Stevie groaned. Thanks, Tony. "Your brother's got a big mouth."

"That's why I love him." Carla's smile came across in her voice. "The man is genetically incapable of keeping a secret."

"I'll remember that."

"So? You coming down or do I have to break down the door?"

In spite of everything, Stevie smiled. "I'd actually like to see that."

"Well, just got my nails done, so if it's all the same to you . . ."

"Right." Surrendering to the inevitable, Stevie stood up. "I'm coming."

Inside fifteen minutes, they were both on the couch, clutching water glasses filled to the brim with icy margaritas.

Stevie took a long drink and leaned back into the cushions. "At least you bring booze when you demand entry."

"Thought maybe you might need to talk about something."

"Like?"

"Like," Carla said, then paused for a drink herself, "why you were wearing a man's robe and driving Paul's car?"

"That could take quite a while," Stevie said, and wished she'd had time to finish her drink before starting in on this.

Carla propped her feet up on the coffee table, leaned back, and shot her friend a long knowing glance. "Do I look busy?"

"I don't know where to start."

"Start with what's going on with you and Paul."

Stevie watched her friend, trying to decide what she was thinking. But like Paul, Carla only let people see what she wanted them to see. Sipping at her straw, she let the icy concoction slide down her throat and hoped the numbing sensation would spread to her heart.

"Nothing's going on," she said softly. "Not now. Not anymore."

Carla sat up, swinging her long dark curly hair behind her shoulders. "So there was something."

"It . . . didn't start out to be anything. It just sort of . . . happened." God, Carla's wedding seemed like a lifetime ago. But it had only been a few short weeks. So much had happened. So much had changed in her life. And yet, for all the changes, for all the heartache, she was right back where she'd started.

Alone.

Reaching out, Carla took Stevie's hand and waited for her to meet her gaze. Then she said simply, "Tell me."

Tell her? Well, why not? She didn't have anything left to lose now, did she? Paul was gone and whether or not she'd be welcome at the Candellano house, it would never be the same again. *She* wouldn't feel easy there anymore. *She* wouldn't be comfortable at the house where she'd found so much love over the years.

So it had started. Her biggest fear. She'd lost Paul already. How long would it take the rest of the family to close ranks and shut her outside? Pulling in a deep

breath and blowing it out again, Stevie slapped the final coat of paint on this masterpiece of misery.

She might as well go for broke and tell Carla *all* of it. The good, the bad, and the ugly. She hated that she was braced for a body blow as she started talking. What she was about to admit could mean the difference between having Carla as a friend or an enemy. With the Candellanos it was "one for all and all for one."

She might very well end this day with no friends at all.

"I'm in love with your brother."

"Nick?"

"Paul."

Carla blinked. She looked like a cartoon character who'd been handed an anvil just as she went off a cliff.

"You're pissed," Stevie said softly, and mentally said good-bye to the first of the Candellanos.

"Not pissed. Confused." Carla shook her head and leaned back on the sofa again. "The word *stunned* wouldn't be out of line, either. Jeez, Stevie. I don't know what to say."

"Me, neither." Shoving one hand through her hair, Stevie took another sip of her drink, swallowed, then said, "I never expected this to happen."

Carla laughed shortly. "I know how you feel."

Stevie set her glass down on the coffee table with a solid *thunk*. "Oh, I don't think you can."

"Christ, Stevie."

"It doesn't matter anymore. It's over now."

"Over? I'm just finding out it started and now it's over?" Carla stood up and started pacing. Her footsteps slapped against the wood floor and sounded to Stevie's

bruised mind like a clucking tongue. "These guys are my *brothers,* Stevie."

"I know," she said, and felt her friend's withdrawal. Just as she'd expected, a line had been drawn in the sand and she was on the wrong side of it.

"I mean," Carla stopped, looked at her, and shrugged, "I guess I knew deep down that you and Nick would never really make it."

"Huh?" She slapped her ear with the heel of her hand as if she couldn't possibly be hearing right.

"Oh," Carla went on, waving one hand to dismiss even the thought, "you guys were *way* too different. Mr. Party Hearty and Miss Home and Hearth? No way."

Stunned, Stevie just looked at her. Carla'd never said anything like this before and she wasn't sure what it was going to mean.

"But now you love Paul?" Carla's voice dropped to a whisper as she kept talking more to herself than to Stevie. "Paul's way better for you, but what's this gonna do to Nick? How'll *he* take it? Nick's life sucks right now and—wait a minute. Why am I so worried about Nick? He's a big boy. He made his own messes, right? Well, now he'll just have to get a grip." She smiled, then another thought hit home. "God, Mama." Carla slapped one hand to her forehead. "Man, what a mess."

"I know," Stevie said, misery flooding her voice.

"You know I love you, Stevie," Carla said on a sigh. "But they're my brothers."

"I know."

"And I don't want to choose sides." Then she planted both hands on her hips, tipped her head to one

side, and admitted, "Okay, I did choose your side when Nick was such an ass two years ago. But this is just getting weird."

"I don't want you to have to take sides." That's what she'd been trying to avoid by making like a secret agent lover. But she could see the writing on the wall. It would be just as she'd feared all along. The Candellanos would become a small civil war. Brother against brother. Sides would be taken, battle lines drawn, and no matter what else happened, Stevie would be on the outside looking in.

Despair welled up inside her.

"Still," Carla said, and came around to sit on the edge of the coffee table in front of Stevie, "thanks to Jackson, I also know what it's like to *really* love someone."

Stevie sniffed and blinked to clear her blurry vision as she watched her friend in stunned silence.

Carla smiled and thought about it for a minute or two before saying, "So if you do love Paul, then you have to go for it."

"What?" Stevie couldn't believe it. She'd been completely prepared for Carla to be seriously pissed and stomp off. She'd expected shouting. Anger. She'd expected to lose her friend. Instead, she was getting understanding. Sympathy. And Stevie almost didn't know what to do with it. After all this, after all the worry, Carla didn't hate her. Her aching heart eased a little, which was almost as painful as the tearing break had been. But despite what Carla said now, it was all too late.

"You're crazy if you let me or Nick or Mama get in the way, Stevie." Carla smiled at her. "Love's too big. It's too important."

Important? It was *everything*. But she hadn't really known that until the chance of it was gone. God. Stevie'd thought there couldn't be any more pain than what was still simmering inside her. Apparently, though, there was room for more.

Yippee!

"Come on," Carla said, and, standing, held out one hand to her.

"Come on where?"

"Home."

Paul had missed her.

Because Nick, pissed off about his sore jaw, hadn't given him a ride into town, Paul had missed his chance to follow her right away. Now, two hours later, she was gone.

She wasn't at the Leaf and Bean.

His car was, though.

Paul stared at his robe, hanging from the antenna, and felt his insides tighten. The afternoon sun slid behind a bank of gray clouds, and with the sudden darkness came a chill that seemed to seep into his bones.

"Damn it." He threw a glance at the window above and wanted to scream her name, even though he knew she wasn't there.

"That's very unusual, isn't it?" A small, interested voice came from somewhere close by.

Paul turned around to see Virginia, Town Crier, approaching. Great. The old biddy's nose was practically twitching.

"Now why would a robe be hanging on your car?" she wondered aloud, coming close enough that he was

pretty sure she was going to start sniffing at him like some damned bloodhound.

His back teeth ground together, but he refused to give her what she wanted . . . which was a nice, juicy piece of gossip to trot around town. "I don't know, Virginia."

"Seems strange," she said, as if he hadn't spoken at all, "your car parked behind Stevie's restaurant. She's not here, you know."

"I know." Hell, he'd pounded on her door until his knuckles were bloody. Anger had him fuming. He'd wanted Stevie and got Virginia.

He must have been a real bastard in a past life to earn this kind of karma.

"But your car is," the woman added thoughtfully, and reached up to smooth lacquered hair that probably hadn't been mussed since 1925. "With a robe on it. Is it *your* robe?"

Oh, for God's sake.

What the hell had his day come to? It had started out with lovemaking, gone into war, and now here he stood playing word games with a woman who'd terrified him as a kid. Irritation pumped through him with a fierceness Paul hadn't expected. He'd been pushed to the edge and Virginia was all it had taken to send him right over the abyss. "Yes, it's my robe, Virginia," he snapped. "And it's hanging on my car because Stevie wore it home from *my* house."

A quick horrified intake of breath was her only reply. He could actually *see* the wheels in her brain turning. Hell. She was practically drooling.

Cold wind rattled down the alley, slapped hard

against Paul, and swatted Virginia before swirling off into the distance. Her hair didn't move.

Paul stepped closer to the old woman and noted that she stepped back, pretty spryly, considering her age. She didn't trust him. Well, fine. She and Stevie could compare notes later. But for now . . . "And you know what else?" he demanded, then went on without giving her a chance to speak. "She was *naked* under the robe."

Glee flickered in her eyes and he could almost see her feet dancing in place, itching to be running to her cronies, spreading the story all over everywhere. Good. He was through hiding. He was through with playing these stupid games. He was through apologizing for loving someone. He was through pretending that he *didn't* love Stevie so as not to upset the family.

Screw the family.

"And while you're telling tales, you might as well have it all," he said, suddenly deciding to let everything hang out.

"Well, I *never*!" Insulted but intrigued, she leaned closer, licking her chops.

"I *love* her."

Virginia's mouth fell open.

"That's right," he said as a wild laugh skipped from his throat. Then he tipped his head back, spreading his arms wide. *"I love Stevie Ryan!"*

"You're crazy, that's what you are."

Crazy?

He stared at her and thought about it, and as he did, another laugh shot from him.

Cool, calm, rational, *logical* Paul Candellano *crazy?*

Well, if he was, it was about time. He'd been logical too long. Rational too long.

And what had it gotten him?

Exactly nothing.

"You know what? You're right. I *am* crazy. And it feels great." Giving in to an impossible urge, he leaned down, planted a hard, fast kiss on the old woman's fire engine red lips, then grinned at her like a loon. "Spread the word, Virginia. Paul's crazy and Stevie's *his.*"

Then he whirled around, snatched his robe off the antenna, and tossed it into the backseat. Firing up the engine, he backed up, waved to the stunned old woman, and tore off down the alley. Now all he had to do was find Stevie and make her believe he loved her and that nothing else mattered—and he had to do it all before Virginia had the whole town talking.

Home.

Mama Candellano's would always be home to Stevie. Even if she was never welcome there again, she would have the memories of warmth and love and acceptance. And maybe someday that would feel like enough.

"So what is wrong to bring you two here?" Mama demanded, hands at her hips. The clean white apron she wore tied around her thick middle twitched and danced against her blue flowered dress while she tapped her foot noisily on the linoleum.

Outside, the wind kicked up, battering at the windows, howling under the eaves. A storm was coming in off the ocean—but Stevie was willing to bet it would

be just a spring shower compared to what was brewing in this tidy kitchen.

Carla glanced at Stevie. Stevie shook her head. She couldn't say it. Couldn't do it. She'd survived telling Carla. But she couldn't do this. Couldn't be the one to cut her ties to Mama forever. If it had to happen, let someone else do the breaking.

Sighing, Carla got the message, looked up at her mother, and said, "Stevie's got a problem."

One gray eyebrow lifted as Mama stared first at her daughter, then at Stevie. "And this problem means you can't talk? To me?"

"No, Mama." Stevie managed to squeeze the words past the knot in her throat, but she didn't know if she could say much more.

But Angela Candellano knew her people too well. Giving her daughter a quick nod to send her off into the next room, the older woman took a seat beside Stevie at the breakfast booth.

"Oof," she muttered as she squeezed between the table and the back of the seat. "This is smaller space than it used to be."

Stevie smiled, but tears brimmed in her eyes.

"Tell me, what's so terrible to make you cry?"

Her bottom lip quivering, Stevie took shallow breaths, air hitching in and out of her chest. "Oh, Mama, everything's so messed up."

"Your sister?"

"No, Debbie's fine."

Mama's eyes narrowed and she slapped one hand onto the tabletop. "Is it Nicky? Is he making you cry some more?"

"No, it's not Nick, either."

"Is good thing. You cried enough over Nicky. Would not be good to do it again." Mama turned Stevie's face up to hers. "Tell me."

And staring into those deep brown eyes that she'd loved and trusted for most of her life, Stevie took the biggest risk she could imagine. She told her surrogate mother everything, and when she was finished, she waited for the ax to fall.

Mama sighed, shook her head, then clucked her tongue in disapproval.

Stevie cringed inwardly and fought a fresh onslaught of tears. But despite her best efforts, they fell anyway, streaming down her face to plop onto the scarred tabletop. "Mama, I'm sorry," she blurted, darting one quick look into the woman's eyes before averting her own gaze. She couldn't bear to see Mama's rejection. Didn't have the heart to watch the light fade from her eyes to be replaced with disgust or anger. "I didn't mean to fall in love with him." She sucked in air like a drowning woman. She'd gotten most of it out. But there was more she had to say.

More she needed Mama to know. Carla was right. Love was too important. Too big.

"Mama, I didn't want to screw up the family. I love you all; you know that. And I didn't want to make you mad—but even if you are, there's something else you have to know." She sucked in another breath and stared at her hands as she shredded a paper napkin she'd plucked out of the holder in front of her. Swallowing hard, she said, "As much as I love you—and I do, Mama, so much—I will always love Paul." She exhaled

and felt a knot of tension in her chest dissolve at the simple truth. And now that it was said, the rest came easier. "Even if it means I lose you guys. Even if nothing works out between Paul and me. I'll love him anyway. I just—"

"Stevie," Mama said, and cupped her cheek in a palm, turning her face up.

When their eyes met, Stevie's breath shuddered from her lungs. Anger sparked in Mama's eyes and Stevie prepared for the worst. Though how could you prepare for losing the only *real* mother you'd ever known?

"This is what you think of me?" Shaking her head, Mama sighed. "You think I don't know about love? About how it comes?" She smiled softly. "I was seventeen when I met my Anthony." Her eyes went dreamy with sweet memory. "I saw him and I knew." Her smile widened. "He kissed me and I loved him. Will always love him, God rest his soul." She crossed herself quickly as the sparkle of tears glimmered in her eyes. "You think I would not understand?"

"But Nick and Paul are your sons, Mama."

"Yes, they are. And Carla is my daughter." She pulled Stevie in close and wrapped her arms around her for a comforting hug. "As are you."

Stevie melted into Mama's ample chest, overwhelmed by the relief crashing through her. Love, pure and simple, rushed through her, surrounded her, and Stevie knew. She wasn't an adopted member of the family. She *was* family. No matter what happened between her and Paul, *this* would always be hers.

"Mama—"

Mama clucked her tongue. "I'm ashamed you would think so little of me, Stevie."

"I just—" Her words came muffled as she fought past the tears to try to tell the woman holding her just how much this meant. "I was so afraid of losing you, Mama. I couldn't bear it."

"You don't lose family, Stevie. Family just . . . *is*. You are part of this family. No matter what my idiot sons do." Giving her an extra pat on the back, Mama asked, "So, do you want me to slap their heads?"

"No." Stevie laughed at the image of Mama clanking Paul's and Nick's heads together but knew it wouldn't solve anything. "It's all over now anyway."

The back door crashed open, slamming into the kitchen counter, and Nick stood in the doorway, flowers clutched in one tight fist.

blood and let her longer." You surprised you
avoid making fun of her. Stevie.

"That does it. Her words flung baffled at . so lonely
not one rejoinder. "Do you like goatish? Look at his lips.
how much his cream. If you won't get of doing you
think, I wouldn't bear it."

"You don't lose family. Stevie. Really, but
You are part of the family." No either told my little
sister that. Gloried in an urge on my back. Marie
at her. "Do you want me to do that to you?"

She . . . . the echoed in the image of Mama to his
. . . . , and . . . . . , in . . . judgement out. Even if
my mother . . . all still, . . . will be free for her.

The . . . . the . . .
. . . . and . . . . . the door. It the door. It drops It drops
. . . . . and in one night.

CHAPTER TWENTY

"Go home," Mama said.

"Not yet." Nick looked at Stevie, and all she felt was disappointment that he wasn't Paul. But she might as well get used to that right now, she thought. Paul wouldn't be coming back. He had his list to keep him from doing anything stupid like following after her.

Slipping out of Mama's comforting embrace, Stevie scooted out of the booth seat and stood on her own two feet to face her past. "What do you want, Nick?"

"First," he said, holding out the half-wilted bouquet of roses, "to give you these."

Red roses. Stevie took them and looked down at their curled petals. The heavy, cloying scent of them drifted to her and she wondered how she could have spent so much time with a man who didn't even know that she *hated* red roses. But it was the thought that counted, right? Too bad he'd never thought of bringing her flowers when they were actually together. "Thanks, but—"

He held one hand up and shook his head. Stevie stared at him and realized he looked . . . *different*. Maybe it was the wind-ruffled hair or the loosened tie hanging at a weird angle around his neck, or maybe the unbuttoned collar of his shirt. But for the first time since she'd known him—not counting the times lately when he'd been drinking—Nick didn't look picture-perfect.

"There's something I want to say to you and—"

"No more," Mama cut in, grunting as she shoved her way out of the breakfast booth. "No more talking, Nicky. Stevie's had enough."

He ignored his mother, keeping his gaze locked with Stevie's. And something she saw there in his eyes prompted her to say, "It's okay, Mama."

The older woman *hmmphed*, folded her arms across her chest, and took root in the kitchen. Clearly, she had no intention of leaving the room.

Nick's eyebrows lifted and a wry smile curved one corner of his mouth. "Look. I wanted you to know . . . I didn't get that CBS job."

So that was it, Stevie thought, vaguely disappointed in him. But true to himself, in his failure, he'd come running back to her, looking for comfort. Well, she was fresh out. Her heart ached, but she felt stronger than she had in weeks. She'd faced her biggest fear and survived it. Now she could take on the rest of her life and hold her own. Behind her she heard the swinging door to the living room open, and she guessed that now Carla had joined the crowd.

"I'm sorry it didn't work out for you, Nick," she said, "but—"

"No." He interrupted her and took a step closer,

never breaking eye contact. "That's not why I'm here, Stevie. I came to tell you *I'm* sorry."

"Ah, good boy," Mama murmured.

Stevie hardly heard her. She was just too stunned at Nick's declaration. "Sorry for what?"

He laughed shortly. "You want specifics? For screwing with your life, Stevie. For hurting you. For letting you down." Reaching up, he pushed one hand through his hair, then shrugged and sighed. "For a lot of things. See, it finally hit me this morning, when I got shuffled out of that meeting so fast I left skid marks on the guy's Berber carpet." That half-smile she knew so well drifted across his face again as he sighed.

"What hit you?" she asked quietly.

"That I'm not God's gift to the universe," Nick said. "That I had a pretty good thing going—my career, and *you*—and I screwed it up." He scraped one hand across his jaw as if trying to rub away the foul taste of the words he was saying. "I was an ass, Stevie. I didn't see it then, but I do now, believe it or not. And I needed you to know that I'm sorry—*really* sorry. For all of it."

Surprise hit her first. He actually meant it. And she couldn't remember a time when he'd been sincerely sorry for anything. A couple of years ago, she would have given a lot to hear him say these things. And even now, when it was too late for them, she could be glad he'd found himself.

"Nick," she said softly, "thank you." Smiling at him, she said, "That wasn't easy for you and I appreciate it. It's just, I don't know what to say."

"Say you forgive me?" he suggested.

Touched and amazed by his sincerity, Stevie set the

roses down onto the tabletop and crossed the room to him. Giving him a hug, she felt his arms go around her. A few years ago, this man's touch had fed her dreams—now, there was only the sensation of warmth shared between friends. So, just for a minute, she enjoyed the sensation of having something turn out right.

But just for a minute.

"What the *hell's* going on here?" Paul stopped dead in the open doorway and stared unbelievingly at his twin, wrapped around Stevie. Rage pumped through him and he finally understood that old saying about "seeing red." Blood in his eyes, the whole world looked bright red, with splashes of darkness at the edges.

"Paul?" Stevie stared at him over Nick's shoulder just before jumping back and out of his embrace.

Mama shouted something Paul couldn't hear over the roaring in his own ears.

Carla called out to him, but she looked like a mime to Paul. He couldn't hear anything but his own heartbeat, thundering out like a bass drum in a marching band. Seconds ticked past. He stared at Stevie—looking into her red-rimmed deep blue eyes, wide now with surprise. Then he shifted a glance at Nick, who looked too damned pleased with himself.

And that was it. Paul yanked off his glasses and tossed them to Carla, who caught them in one hand as he dashed past her.

"You son of a bitch!" Paul shouted, and crashed his fist into Nick's face.

Damn, it felt good.

But this time, Nick didn't just stand there and take

it. This time, he fought back. With a wild bellow, Nick caught Paul in the belly with his shoulder and drove him back out the door. They fell down the porch steps and rolled onto the lawn.

When Paul jumped to his feet, he was braced and waiting for Nick to make a move. Hell, he *wanted* Nick to rush him. He needed to pummel something. Needed to do something with the fierce fury pumping through his bloodstream—before he exploded.

Nick came in hard and Paul ducked under the blow, landing a solid right cross to his twin's eye. Nick howled but didn't pause before slamming a solid punch into Paul's belly. Pain ripped through him, but it only seemed to feed the rage within.

He stared at his twin, but all Paul could see was Nick wrapped around Stevie. Paul had come looking for Stevie, prepared to declare his love and take his chances. He'd never expected to find Stevie and Nick locked in a hug, being beamed at with fond approval by Mama and Carla. That mental image sent Paul's closed fist plowing into Nick's jaw again.

Pain shimmered up Paul's arm and tingled clean up to his shoulder. Muscles sang, blood pumped, and when Nick fought back, a primal, clamoring need to pound him into the dirt took over and the computer genius gave way to the Neanderthal. No way was Paul going to lose what he'd just found. He'd fight whoever he had to, to keep Stevie in his life.

Because the thought of living without her was just too unbearable. The yawning emptiness of his life would swallow him whole. Without her, there was darkness.

"Stop it!" Stevie yelled from somewhere far away.

"Are you guys nuts?" Carla's voice screeched into the war zone, but it didn't stop her brothers.

"Let 'em go!" Tony shouted, and Paul stopped, shook his head. When the hell did Tony get here?

Nick's fist got Paul's attention again quickly, though, and he countered, slamming an uppercut to Nick's chin that had the man's head snapping back.

Stevie grabbed Tony by the arm and shook him as soon as he walked up. Glancing back over her shoulder at the two men beating each other senseless, she shouted, "Stop them! They're gonna kill each other!"

"Nah, it's just a fight."

"Tony, you're a cop. You have to stop them! It's your job!"

Tony shook his head and laughed. "Not a chance in hell I'm gonna stop this. Today I'm not a cop. I'm just a brother. And I've been waiting *years* for this." He looked down at her briefly. "Nick's had it coming a long time. And Paul's just the one to give it to him."

"You're nuts, too." Stevie let him go and shook her head. She loved Paul desperately; she knew that. From the moment he'd walked into the kitchen with fire in his eyes, she'd wanted nothing more than to throw herself at him.

Then he'd turned into an idiot.

She watched from the sidelines, following Paul with her gaze, keeping an eye on him and wincing every time Nick landed a punch. Nick was getting in some good ones and she was worried. Yes, Paul was an idiot. But he was *her* idiot.

At least he *had* been.

Nick swung wildly; Paul dodged and brought his

fist up into his twin's belly. The blow knocked the air out of Nick and sent him sprawling to the grass, wheezing, trying to suck air into lungs shuddering with its lack. Paul stood above him, swaying, one eye already swelling, blood pouring from his split lip. He looked like an ancient warrior, and just for a second, Stevie's heartbeat quickened in response to his battered, bloodied victory.

Then she remembered reality.

"You're happy now?" Mama shouted, hands at her hips again, in her favorite battle stance.

"Ecstatic," Paul said, and winced as assorted aches and pains made themselves known. Damn, it had been a long time since he and Nick had gone a few rounds. It was pure hell getting older.

"And your brother? He's alive?"

"Yeah," Paul said, glancing down to where Nick was already stirring. And groaning, Paul noted with some satisfaction.

"You've got a good right," Tony said, "but your left hook needs work."

"I'll work on it," Paul answered his older brother, but his gaze was locked on Stevie as he left his twin lying in the grass and, stumbling, headed for her.

"I don't want to talk to you," she said, getting that stubborn glint in her eyes.

God, he loved her.

"Good. You listen, *I'll* talk." He didn't look at his family. He could only see Stevie. And in his mind, he saw her wrapped in Nick's embrace, and he blurted out, "No *way* am I gonna let you go back to Nick."

She blinked.

"No way is that gonna happen, Stevie." Paul kept right on talking, unaware of the sudden tension in her shoulders and the defiant tilt of her chin. "He only wants you because he can't have you. He's no good for you, Stevie."

"But you are?" she asked, and took a step closer to him.

"Hell, yes," he snapped, completely oblivious to the interested stares of his family. "*We're* good together. You know it. You felt it. And I'm through pretending that I don't care. I love you. I need you. And I'm not gonna let Nick have you. Not this time."

"You're not going to *let* Nick have me?" she countered, and finally Paul noticed the sparks flashing in her eyes. "Now that you've decided you love me, everything's okay and I should just fall into line? Who the hell do you think you are, anyway? You don't *let* me do anything."

"That's not what I meant. I just—"

The wind pushed her hair across her eyes and she reached up to pluck it free so she could glare at him clearly. "You come storming in here, uninvited, and punch Nick in the face while he's *apologizing* to me for hurting me."

Paul blinked and tried to clear his head and his vision at the same time. Sweat streamed into his eyes, stinging like fire, but his brain seemed to be even more blurry. Nick? Apologizing? Christ. Was it a sign of the Apocalypse?

"Something," Stevie added, taking another step closer to him until Paul wisely stepped back a pace or two, "I'd like to point out, that *you* didn't bother to do."

"I tried to apologize this morning, but you wouldn't listen." Crap, his mouth hurt like hell.

"I'd already read what you thought of me," she reminded him.

Paul cringed at the thought of that damn list. But there was nothing he could do about it now. "Stevie," he said, lowering his voice as he at last noticed the avid interest from their audience, "I love you. And I think you love me." Tears swam in her eyes and something inside Paul ached harder than the jaw he thought just might be broken. Damn, Nick's left was still a powerful thing.

Shaking her head, Stevie said, "It's not enough, Paul. It's just not. I won't be the juicy bone you and your brother fight over, for God's sake." She planted both hands on his chest and shoved. "Besides, who decided you two could pass me around to the winner of some dumb-ass contest?"

"It wasn't a contest," he started, but she cut him off.

"And I don't *want* to be with a man who makes up a spreadsheet to help him find ways to *not* love me." Her eyes flashed, but her bottom lip trembled, and Paul's heart dropped to his feet.

"What?" Carla whispered.

"A spreadsheet?" Tony said.

"What is spreadsheet?" Mama demanded.

"Don't you get it, Paul?" Stevie asked, keeping her voice at a pitch designed only for him. "All my life people have *not* loved me. And then, to see that you'd actually made a list of the reasons to join the crowd—" She shook her head. "No, Paul. I deserve better," Stevie told him flatly. Then, without another word, she walked past him to her car, parked around front.

As his sister, brother, and mother applauded, Paul stood stock-still in the rising chill wind and watched his world walk away.

Stevie had driven straight home, packed a bag, and picked up Scruffy. She had one thought in mind. To get the hell outta Dodge.

Somehow or other, news of her and Paul's relationship had taken off, and everywhere she went, people were staring. She heard the whispers about "naked driving" and "bathrobes on cars" and wondered how they'd gotten their information. But the bottom line was, she just couldn't bring herself to care.

How could she care what gossips had to say when every cell in her body was weeping for the loss of Paul?

Funny, she thought, the obstacles she'd thought would be standing between them and happiness were gone. Mama, the family, heck, even Nick—all of them were okay with the idea of Paul and Stevie.

Apparently, only Paul had a problem with it. He was the one making up lists. Sure, he'd *said* he loved her, but how could she believe that he loved her when he'd gone to such painstaking efforts to convince himself *not* to love her? What if she believed him and then next week or month or year he found another reason to add to the list? What then? Which one was the breaking point? Which one would mean that he'd walk away, as her mother had? As Nick had? Just how many reasons had to be on that list for Paul to leave?

No. She couldn't trust it. Couldn't take the risk.

She'd lain awake in her motel room last night, listening to the wind roar and the rain pound against the

shingled roof. Alone in her bed, she'd heard nature's fury, but her mind had been lost in memories more devastating than a little squall. Over and over again, she'd read that list in memory. She'd seen the neat columns. She'd seen Paul's face when she'd discovered it.

And her heart broke every damn time.

"But no more," she vowed as she walked along the beach with Debbie. Her sister, wearing jeans and an oversize sweatshirt, ran along the water's edge, Scruffy yapping at her heels, looking over her shoulder at the footprints she'd left in the wet sand. Her laughter and the little dog's excited barks rang out over the wind and Stevie told herself to count her blessings. Debbie loved her. The girl didn't *need* her; she just loved her big sister. Stevie had come to grips with the fact that Debbie would never live with her. The girl had a life of her own, and that was okay.

A big step for her, Stevie thought. Loving without trying to run everything. Debbie didn't need saving; she just needed loving. And Stevie owed Paul for teaching her that much, anyway.

She'd be fine, she thought, stepping over the driftwood tossed ashore by raging waves the night before. She had her sister. She had her shop. Her home. Scruffy.

That could be enough.

It would have to be enough.

"Hi, Paul!" Debbie shouted, and waved enthusiastically as she and the dog raced back up the beach.

Stevie stopped dead and held her breath. Her gaze focused on her younger sister, she could almost feel

Paul standing right behind her. She didn't trust herself to look at him, so she simply asked, "How did you find me?"

"Wasn't hard," he said, his words snatched by the wind and whirled around her in a deep, rumbling sound of comfort that she longed to cling to. "Where else would you go but to Debbie?"

She sucked in air and held it tight within to keep her lungs from collapsing. "I guess Margie told you where we were."

"Yep."

Stevie nodded, as Debbie came closer, and slowly turned around to face him. Dressed in a black sweatshirt over worn jeans, he looked indescribably handsome, and Stevie's blood thickened just looking at him. Sunlight glinted off his glasses and the wind ruffled his too-long hair. His left eye was swollen and a lovely shade of purple, and a grayish bruise splayed across his jaw. But his mouth was curved in a smile—despite the cut lip—that tugged at her heart.

Scruffy reached them first, plopped onto her butt in front of Stevie, and growled at Paul.

"Hi, Scruff," he murmured warily.

Debbie ran up to join them and, breath puffing, asked, "Whatcha doing here, Paul? What happened to your face? Does it hurt? Did you come to see me?"

Paul smiled at her and only winced a bit when his split lip tugged painfully. "My face hurts a little, and this time I came to see your sister," he said, his gaze locked with Stevie's.

"How come?"

"Because I want to ask her to marry me."

Stevie swayed as his words slammed home. She swallowed hard, and as if from a distance, she heard Debbie giggling.

"Are you gonna say yes?" Debbie asked, and without waiting for an answer, went right on talking. "'Cause if you do I could be in the wedding and everything 'cause Marybeth was in her cousin's wedding and she had a really pretty dress and—"

Stevie only half-heard her sister as the girl kept talking, building an imaginary wedding, starring *her* as the beautiful bridesmaid. Stevie was too busy staring into Paul's eyes to hear anything. Well, she stared into the one eye that wasn't swollen shut. And for the first time since she'd known him, he wasn't trying to hide his emotions. Everything he felt was there for her to see, and it stole her breath away.

Debbie picked up Scruffy and nuzzled her. "I think you should marry him," she said, and moved off, talking to the little dog and laughing at wet, sloppy doggy kisses.

"Smart girl," Paul said, smiling, then winced and touched a finger to his lip. "Glad she took Scruffy, though. Don't think the little thing was happy to see me."

"Smart dog," Stevie said, then added, "You look terrible."

"You should see the other guy."

"Paul—"

He stepped in close. Hell, he'd been practicing this speech since last night. It hadn't taken long to convince himself that he couldn't live without Stevie. About ten minutes in his silent house had done it for him. The thought of never being with her again was like staring into a black hole.

Nothingness.

"Stevie," he said, his voice low, hurried, "I deserved everything you said to me yesterday, I know that, but that doesn't change how I feel about you. How I will *always* feel about you."

She reached out to gingerly touch the bruise on his jaw, then let her hand drop to her side. "You hurt me, Paul. That list—" She shook her head, remembering the one most damning thing on it. "How could you believe that I could still love Nick and be with you?"

"I didn't," he said. "Not really. It was just that damned logical side of me." He choked out a laugh. "Okay, that didn't come out right."

"That damn spreadsheet, Paul."

"Stupid, I know," he said, and reached into his pocket. Pulling out a piece of folded paper, he handed it to her. "But I'm a spreadsheet kind of guy, Stevie. Helps me think when I write it all down. Helps me recognize what's important."

"I know that. I mean, I know you're a list person. But what was on that list—God, it was just so cold. So damn logical. It made me doubt you. Doubt what I felt. What we had. Doubt us. And—" She looked at the paper in her hand, then shifted her gaze to his. "What's this?"

"The new version."

Stevie sighed and shook her head. "Another one?"

"Just read it," he said, his gaze moving over her features like a dying man staring at heaven's gates and hoping for entry.

With shaking fingers, Stevie unfolded the paper and read the now-familiar header, "The Pros and Cons of

Loving Stevie." Then she read the list itself. It didn't take long. There were only two entries:

> *Pro: Loving Stevie, have a life.*
> *Con: Losing Stevie, have nothing.*

Tears clogged her throat and threatened to choke her. Her fingers crumpled the edges of the list, but she couldn't seem to tear her gaze from those few simple words. Paul tipped her chin up with his fingertips until she was staring into his eyes—*eye*—instead.

"Remember when I said I didn't need saving?" he asked.

"Yeah."

"Well, I was wrong." His fingers caressed her jaw-line, then smoothed her hair back from her face. "Without you, I'm lost, Stevie. Rescue me."

She smiled softly and shook her head. "A very wise man told me I should retire from the rescuing business."

"Not so wise," he said, one corner of his mouth lift-ing. "Not if he could risk losing you."

"Paul—" Again her fingers traced the outline of the bruise decorating the side of his face.

"Stevie, I've loved you my whole life. I want to be the man you turn to in the night. I want to listen to your dreams and help you make them come true. I want to make babies with you. I want us to get old and cranky together. I want to be there for you, with you." He leaned in and kissed her forehead, the tip of her nose, and, briefly, her mouth. "I want to build a family—a future—with you."

Her breath hitched in her chest as she listened to the

man she loved offer her everything she'd ever wanted. Just yesterday, she'd thought everything was over. Today, there was a whole new world opening up in front of her.

"I need you, Stevie," Paul said softly. "As a partner. A lover. A wife. A friend."

She swallowed hard, inhaled deeply, and said the words she'd wanted to say for so long. "I love you, Paul. More than I ever thought I could love anyone."

A brief smile flashed across his features, and relief shone in his one good eye. He caught her hand and turned his face to plant a kiss at the heart of her palm. "Marry me, Stevie. Put me out of my misery."

"I want to," she said softly, knowing there was one more thing she had to say. Another risk. But one she was willing to take, because Paul, she knew, was worth any risk. "But you have to know that Debbie will always be a part of my life. And I don't know what that might mean in the future."

"She's family," Paul said, summing it all up in two beautiful little words.

Family.

Her family. Paul. Debbie. The Candellanos.

"I really do love you," Stevie said through her tears, and felt laughter bubbling up inside her. How could you be so happy and so teary at the same time?

"So does that mean yes?"

She gave him a wide smile, then looked around at her sister and asked, "What do you think, Debbie?"

The girl thought about it for a minute, whispered to Scruffy, then tilted her head to one side, grinned, and said, "I think you should kiss him."

"I said it before," Paul said, smiling, "and I'll say it again. Smart girl."

Stevie looked up into his warm brown eyes—*eye*—and knew that finally she'd found what she'd always longed for.

And it had been right there in front of her the whole time.

Throwing her arms around his neck, she grinned up at him and said, "Yes, I'll marry you."

"Thank God," he said, holding her close enough that even if she'd tried to get away, she never would have managed it. Drawing his head back, he looked down at her and added, "The whole town's buzzing about us, you know. Gotta keep those gossips quiet."

She blinked and stared up at him. "But how did they find out? We were so careful."

He kissed her, winced at the accompanying pain in his lip, and shrugged. "I told Virginia."

"You did?"

"Hell, Stevie," he promised, "give me a couple days and I'll tell the world."

Dear Reader,

I hope you've enjoyed your introduction to the Candellano family. It's been a real treat, writing about a big, loving Italian family. A little something I have some experience with.

I married into a big Italian family and, as the only Irishman in a sea of Italians, learned a few things right away. Like the Candellanos, my new family was loud, loving, and loyal, and incurable buttinskies (I fit in perfectly in that department). Everyone has an opinion and no one has a problem sharing it. We all rant and rave on occasion (hey, I'm Irish, and we love a good argument, too!). But when there's trouble, the family bands together and no one can defeat them.

In the fictional town of Chandler, California, the Candellanos have been through plenty—but there's more to come. Mama has to get her last chick settled, and Nick Candellano hasn't exactly been in a cooperative mood lately.

The ex–NFL running back is resisting building a new life for himself. He liked his *old* one just fine! But the old life is gone for good. He's lost his career, his self-confidence, and even the woman he'd once thought was his. Resistance just might be futile after all. And to top it all off, Nick's got another surprise headed his way.

Look for *Loving You*, Nick Candellano's story, coming next month! I hope you'll come along for the ride!

Happy Reading,

Maureen Child

FOR THE FIRST TIME in his life, the cameras *weren't* focused on Nick Candellano.

He didn't like it.

Nick had spent years in the limelight. As an NFL all-pro running back, he'd had more cameras flashed in his face than a member of the Kennedy family. Hell, he'd even been featured in one of *People* magazine's "Sexiest Bachelor" articles. He'd done radio, tv, and print interviews and was glib enough to charm his way through any situation. Kids had been known to stand in line outside the stadium for hours, just to get his autograph.

And now?

"You're still in my shot," Bill, the cameraman, muttered.

"Right." Biting down hard on the quick flash of temper that jittered along his spine, Nick took a single long step to the right. Wouldn't want to mess up the camera angle. No telling when they might get another

chance to film an earthshaking athletic contest like this one.

Pushing one hand through his hair, he squinted into the afternoon sunlight and let his gaze slide across the playing field. The players were in position. The ball was in play. The crowd roared, half of them cheering, the other half heckling the officials.

It should have been familiar. Comforting, almost, to a man who'd spent most of his life suiting up for a game. The only problem here was, the players were high school girls and they were playing *soccer*, for God's sake.

And it was Nick's job to cover it for the local television station.

The taste of bitterness filled his mouth, but he choked it back down. *A new leaf*, he reminded himself. That's what he was doing here. Starting fresh. A new career. Something he could do even *with* a bum knee.

Christ, though.

Girls' soccer?

A man had to start somewhere, right? Nick shifted position, taking the weight off the bad right knee that had ended his career. While the pain shimmered along his nerve endings, he couldn't help thinking, as he often did, about that one play that had sidelined his career. If not for that one stinkin' tackle that had sent his body east and his knee west, he'd still be playing. Still be signing autographs. Still be doing what he loved doing.

Instead, he was standing on the sidelines, in a bone-chilling, early November wind, getting dust on his Gucci loafers, and trying to look interested in a play-

off game that meant nothing to anyone not attending either Santiago or Saint Anne High.

Local TV my ass, he thought. He should be working at ESPN. Probably would have been except for the one guy who'd voted "no" to Nick's application. Seemed the man still held a grudge about some comments Nick had once made about their coverage of a game. So instead of the big time, here he was, working at a station that included farm reports in the local news. But he had plans. He'd work his way up. Be at ESPN where he belonged. Doing commentary for football games—interviewing players—*something* that would allow him to stay a part of the game he loved. But until then, he got the shit jobs.

And they didn't come much shittier than this.

Out on the neatly trimmed grass, one of the girls from St. Anne's kicked a well-aimed ball at the net, and when the goalie missed it, the game was suddenly over. Screaming teenaged girls swarmed across the field, shrieking and laughing as they jumped at each other in celebration.

A momentary twinge jabbed at Nick's heart and he almost felt a kinship with the high schoolers. He'd done a lot of those victory dances himself. He'd been in the center of the locker room festivities after a big win. He'd popped a few champagne corks and showered in the foamy stuff, blinking back tears as the alcohol nearly blinded him.

Damn, he missed it.

He missed everything about it.

"Okay, that's it," Bill announced as he straightened up from behind the camera. Glancing at Nick, he said,

"You wanna get an interview with the coach first, or with the girls?"

It was like being asked if he'd rather be shot to death or stabbed.

But this was his life, now. And bitching about it wasn't going to move him up the ladder or get him to ESPN. So he'd choose the lesser of two evils. He just didn't think he was up to trying to interview some high school soccer player and listening to her "um" and "oh" and "uh" her way through a conversation.

"The coach," Nick said, and scooped one hand through his hair again. He checked his tie, smoothed one hand down the front of his camel-brown sport jacket, and fell into step behind Bill.

The stands emptied of people and they all seemed intent on getting in his way. Bill was a few yards ahead of him, and Nick was in no hurry to catch up.

"Hey, aren't you Nick Candellano?"

Nick stopped, caught by the awed tone in the voice coming from right behind him. Turning, he looked down at a short, balding man with a wide grin.

"You are," the guy said, nearly breathless with excitement. "Nick Candellano."

Fond memories reared up and Nick basked in the glow of them for a second or two.

The guy shook his head and blew out a breath. "Man. Imagine that. Seeing you here. I remember the time you took the ball and ran it back eighty-five yards for a TD." He sighed. "Never saw a run like it—before or since. Man, you cut through those other guys like they weren't even there."

Nick remembered, too. "Yeah," he said, enjoying

this quick trip down memory lane. "That was the Atlanta game. '98. Good game."

"Great game," the shorter man corrected. "You were awesome, man."

Pride swelled, along with the memories and puffed out Nick's chest. Hell, maybe this wouldn't be such a bad gig after all. He still had lots of fans out there. Running into one or two of them now and then would cheer him up and give the fans something to talk about when they went home to dinner.

"Thanks," he said, automatically offering his right hand. Giving the man the smile he used to reserve for close-up, post-game interviews, he said, "Appreciate it. Always good to meet a fan."

The little guy's grin went even wider as he slapped a manila envelope into Nick's waiting hand. "Good to meet you too, man. Oh. And you've been served."

"Served?"

"It was great meeting you, though." The short man was already turning to leave.

What the hell was going on? Served? As in served with a lawsuit? Who would be suing him? Nick stared down at the envelope as if waiting for it to open up and announce itself. When it didn't, he lifted his gaze to the retreating back of the little guy who'd sounded like a fan.

"Hey, Nick," Bill called from the sidelines, "you coming?"

The cameraman's voice suddenly sounded muffled—but that was probably because of the sudden roaring in Nick's ears. A cold trickle slipped through his bloodstream. He gave his head a shake, but the roaring

was still there. This couldn't be good. His hand fisted around the envelope as if he could squeeze the truth out of it. "What the hell's going on?" he demanded.

The bald guy chuckled as he kept walking. "Read all about it, Nick. Oh, by the way, congratulations. It's a boy."

Tasha Flynn finished the comb-out on Edna Garret's hair, then stood back and aimed a torrent of hair spray at the woman's head. Naturally, the stream of toxins didn't shut Edna up. But then at this point, why bother? At eighty, the old woman had probably inhaled enough hair spray over her lifetime to put a nice, glossy shine on her lungs already. What was another coat?

"So anyway," Edna was saying, "when I found out that Francine Chase was gambling away the rent money, I just knew her husband was going to leave her. What man in his right mind would put up with that?"

"Richard Chase should have," a woman under the dryer piped up. Tilting the old-fashioned space helmet dryer back so she could get in a little gossip herself, Alice Tucker stuck her head farther out, stared at Edna, and said, "Francine was the only woman who would have put up with Dick's meandering eye."

"It wasn't just his eye that meandered," Lorraine Tuttle said with a chuckle.

Tasha rolled her eyes at the gossip. The same women kicked around the same topics of conversation every Tuesday. You'd think they'd run out of things to

talk about. But no. Every week, they showed up to be washed, curled, and dried. And every week, they had more dirt to dish.

The FBI should know about these women.

But there was a comforting sameness to the routine. A familiarity that told Tasha everything in her world was as it should be. She glanced around the interior of the small shop and smiled to herself. Three hair dryers, only one of them occupied, sat against one wall. Opposite them were three comfortable chairs clustered around a low table littered with hairstyle magazines. Wooden shelves marched along one wall, stuffed to bursting with hair products and supplies. The pink-and-white linoleum was peeling up in one corner, but it was clean, scrubbed nightly by Tasha herself. The wide window overlooking the front yard was sparkling, and a thick slice of sunlight jutted through the glass beneath the half-opened blinds.

She supposed that to most people, the place wouldn't look like much. But to Tasha, it was everything. It was home. Stability. A future.

This was her place.

Where she belonged.

"What do you think, Tasha?" Edna asked.

"Hmm? What do I think?" She glanced into the mirror, ignoring the handful of postcards tucked into the edges of the glass, and met the older woman's direct stare. "I think you're finished, Edna."

The older woman sniffed and waved an impatient hand. "I don't mean my hair, girl. I mean what do you think about roving Dick."

Tasha's lips twitched as she met Edna's still sharp blue eyes. "I try not to think about roving dicks of any kind."

Heck, it'd been so long since she'd been on a date or come anywhere near a man who wasn't at the shop to pick up his wife, Tasha was pretty sure she could qualify for sainthood. Which, she thought wryly, in her case, was really saying something.

"Smart girl," Edna said as Tasha yanked the Velcro closure at her neck free and snapped the hair-littered plastic cape up and off of her. "You'll find men are usually more trouble than they're worth."

From under the dryer, Alice snorted. "This from a woman with four dead husbands."

One of Edna's steel gray eyebrows swept up. "And all four of them were—"

Whatever she'd been about to say was cut off when the door swung open so quickly, it slammed into the wall with a crash. Tasha whipped around in time to watch her framed print of Tahiti hit the floor. The boy standing in the open doorway hunched his shoulders as it fell, winced, and said, "Sorry."

"Like a bull in a china shop," Edna muttered, but her smile took the sting out of her words.

Jonas Baker, eleven years old and already he was taller than Tasha. Which, she kept reminding him, wasn't that difficult. Since she stood only five-foot-two, most good-sized kids could pass her height at a walk. His dark brown hair fell across his forehead in a sweep that dusted his eyelashes and had the boy continually squinting or swinging his head to one side to clear his vision.

Attempts at a haircut had so far failed.

Thin and gangly, his body seemed to be a collection of sharp angles. And if, like a puppy, he grew into the size of his feet, he'd end up at least seven feet tall. But at the moment, he was just a kid. And the center of Tasha's heart.

"How was school?" she asked as she took Edna's money without bothering to count it. Heck, Edna knew the prices at Castle's Salon better than Tasha did. But then, why wouldn't she? The old woman had been a customer here for forty years. Tasha'd only been here seven.

And before that, there'd been only—

Nope. No point in going down that road. The past didn't matter. Anything beyond her arrival on Mimi Castle's doorstep was ancient history and better forgotten than revisited.

Especially now.

"It was okay," Jonas said with a shrug that could mean anything from "school was boring" to "I won the Nobel Prize."

Though the Nobel Prize was a long shot, there were other things to be considered. Like homework, for instance. Or that math test she'd helped him prepare for.

"How about your test?" Tasha asked, stuffing Edna's money into her jeans pocket and giving it a satisfying pat. "How'd you do?"

"Okay," he said again, and Tasha wondered if they gave lessons in evasive maneuvers in junior high these days. Or maybe it was just genetic. Become a preteen, forget how to talk. A couple of years ago—heck, even *one* year ago—Jonas would have come into the shop

bursting to tell Tasha or Mimi what he'd done in school. He would have told all the ladies some dumb knock-knock jokes and then complained of starvation.

But times change, Tasha told herself.

People die.

Kids grow up.

And secrets were born.

She buried the ache in her heart that always leaped into life when she thought of Mimi Castle, and forced a smile that didn't quite reach her eyes. God, she missed Mimi.

Jonas grunted to the women clustered in the shop portion of the Victorian, then ducked through the connecting doorway that would take him into the main house.

Tasha was right behind him.

Just because he was closing up, trying to shut her out of his life, didn't mean Tasha was going to stand by and let it happen.

She hurried through the service porch, with barely a glance at the mound of laundry waiting to be washed. She didn't spare a glance at the dishes in the sink as she moved through the kitchen. As she quickened her steps, her sandals clicked noisily against the scarred wood floor of the dining room.

Tasha caught him at the base of the stairs. He might be younger, but she was quicker.

"Hey," she asked, reaching out for him to slow him down, "what's the big rush?"

"No rush," Jonas said, and slipped out from under the hand she'd laid on his shoulder.

Tasha ignored the tiny pang around her heart as she

let her hand fall to her side. There was something going on here. Something that kept him from meeting her eyes.

And a tiny tendril of fear rippled through her. Heck, she knew better than anyone what kinds of things were out there in the world, just waiting for a chance to snatch at a kid. Just the thought that he might have already stumbled into trouble tore at her.

"Jonas," she said, reaching for him again before he could scoot out of range, "what's going on?"

He flipped his hair back, then looked at her through those wide brown eyes of his. "Nothing, Tasha," he said with an "I'm so innocent, how could you not believe me?" expression on his face. "Everything's cool."

"Cool, huh?"

"Totally."

Tasha smoothed his hair back from his face and he didn't pull away, so she counted that as a plus. "You're not in trouble or anything, are you?"

"No way." He actually looked insulted.

"Would you tell me if you were?"

He grinned. "No way."

That smile of his jolted her heart. She hadn't seen it very often lately and she'd missed it. God, she loved this kid. She smiled back at him. "Okay then. Go on up and do your homework."

His whole body moped. "Aw, man. Come on, Tasha. How about a half hour of TV and *then* homework?"

"Let me guess," she said. "The Sports Channel."

He nodded.

"Fine," she said to his back as he raced up the stairs, making enough noise for six kids his size. As his bed-

room door slammed shut, she shouted, "A half hour. I'll be checking!"

Jonas tossed his backpack onto the floor, dropped onto his mattress, and propped a pillow under his chest as he lay on his stomach, grabbed the remote, and pushed the ON button. The TV flickered briefly, and for one short second Jonas was afraid the old set wasn't going to come on this time. Heck, it was older than him; it was bound to go out sooner or later. "Just not today, okay?" he said softly.

As if it had heard him, the picture rolled wildly, jittered like someone was shaking the set, and then suddenly straightened itself out.

He whistled out a relieved breath and punched in the right channel. The camera moved in for a close-up on the reporter's familiar face and Jonas studied the man carefully.

When the reporter smiled into the camera, Jonas smiled back. His stomach jumped like millions of butterflies were bumping into each other down there. He slapped one hand against his belly, trying to tame them, but it didn't work. There was just too much going on.

Too much about to happen.

He'd waited for this for so long, Jonas didn't know whether to be excited or scared. He knew Tasha would be mad when she found out. But sometimes a guy just had to do stuff that girls didn't understand.

Another guy would get it, though.

Jonas looked at the reporter again. "You'll understand, won't you?"